MURDER AT THE MANCHESTER MUSEUM

By Jim Eldridge

Murder at the Fitzwilliam
Murder at the British Museum
Murder at the Ashmolean
Murder at the Manchester Museum

MURDER AT THE MANCHESTER MUSEUM

JIM ELDRIDGE

Allison & Busby Limited
11 Wardour Mews
London W1F 8AN
allisonandbusby.com

First published in Great Britain by Allison & Busby in 2020.

A CIP catalogue record for this book is available from
the British Library.

First Edition

ISBN 978-0-7490-2449-9

Typeset in 11/16 pt Adobe Garamond Pro by
Allison & Busby Ltd.

The paper used for this Allison & Busby publication
has been produced from trees that have been legally sourced
from well-managed and credibly certified forests.

Printed and bound by
CPI Group (UK) Ltd, Croydon, CR0 4YY

To Lynne, for ever

CHAPTER ONE

1895

'Crewe next stop!' called the train conductor. He then began to list the various stops after Crewe the train still had to make before it reached Manchester, before adding in ringing tones, 'For all other destinations, change at Crewe!'

Daniel Wilson studied the telegram he and Abigail had received the day before.

'Murder at Manchester Museum. Please come urgently. Bernard Steggles, Director,' he read, then folded it and put it back in his pocket with a weary sigh. 'But who's been murdered? When? And how?' asked Daniel. 'There's been nothing about a recent murder at the Manchester Museum in the newspapers.'

'Because they're the London papers,' Abigail pointed out, turning a page in her magazine.

'But they carry news from further afield,' said Daniel. He

tapped the copy of *The Times* that lay on his lap. 'There are stories in here from Glasgow, Newcastle, Paris and Berlin. But nothing concerning Manchester.'

'Which suggests whoever was murdered was not seen as an important figure.'

'So why bring us all the way from London when they have a perfectly adequate police force capable of investigating a local crime?'

'Do you know much about the Manchester police force?'

'No,' admitted Daniel.

'It's a pity the telephone service hasn't yet been connected nationally, otherwise you'd have been able to talk to Mr Steggles and got the answers you wanted.'

'The telephone?' repeated Daniel with a frown.

'Yes,' said Abigail. She held the copy of the *Museum Digest* she'd been reading towards him. 'It says here—'

The scream of a woman in terror from the corridor cut through the rattling background chug-chug of the train. Immediately, Daniel was out of his seat, had pulled the door of their compartment open and was in the corridor, Abigail close behind him.

A middle-aged man was at the end of the corridor, holding a young woman viciously by her hair. In his other hand he held a knife, which he was pointing at the two uniformed railwaymen, a guard and the conductor, who stood watching the pair nervously.

'Leave us alone!' shouted the man. 'It's not your business.'

The man was drunk, realised Daniel. Not drunk enough to be easily overpowered, but drunk enough to do something dangerous. Like stab someone. And the young woman he was holding tightly on to looked the most likely victim. The man was short but stocky, his jacket barely able to contain his muscular upper body. The young woman was wearing a skirt and short-sleeved blouse. There

8

was no sign of a coat or a bag or other outer garments. Daniel guessed they must have been left behind by the woman when she fled the compartment.

'Sir . . .' began the guard uncomfortably.

'Go away!' yelled the man. 'This whore took my wallet. I want it back!'

'I never!' sobbed the woman. 'He must have dropped it!'

'Dropped it?' sneered the man, adding vengefully, 'I'll drop you, you whore!'

And he slashed at her, the blade opening a wound in her upper arm that sprayed blood towards the two railwaymen, who hurriedly pressed back as far as the corridor would allow them to as the woman screamed.

Daniel moved. He took his wallet from his pocket and threw it at the man's face. Instinctively, the man let go of the woman and threw his hand up to protect himself. As he did so, Daniel chopped down hard on the wrist of the hand that held the knife with the edge of his right hand, at the same time following it with a hard left hook that smashed into the man's face, sending him crashing backwards into the wall of the corridor. The man crumpled as he and the knife fell to the floor. Daniel put his foot on the knife and kicked it away to a safe position, but the fact the fallen man hadn't moved showed the danger was over.

Abigail went to the terrified and sobbing young woman, taking a large handkerchief from her pocket, and placed it against the knife wound, staunching the flow of blood.

'Here,' she said. 'If you come to our compartment I can clean and bandage that.'

The guard stepped forward, his face grim.

'I'm afraid that won't be possible, madam,' he said. 'This man accused her of stealing his wallet. This is now a police matter. We have to take her into custody and hand her to the police when we reach Crewe.'

'In that case you can have her once I've dealt with her wound, and not before,' snapped Abigail.

As Abigail led the young woman to their compartment, Daniel gestured at the fallen man and the knife.

'I'd advise you to secure his hands in case he tries anything else when he comes round,' he said to the two railway officials.

'Thank you, sir, I'd already thought of that,' said the guard curtly. 'Everything was under control before you intervened.'

Daniel nodded and headed back to their compartment, where he found Abigail cleaning the wound. Once she was sure there was no chance of infection, she took a small bandage from her bag and proceeded to bind it around the woman's upper arm.

'It might need stitches,' said Abigail. 'Unfortunately, the needle I carry in my sewing kit is only suitable for cloth.' She looked at the conductor, who had appeared in the doorway of the compartment and was studying the scene with a look of some discomfort on his face.

'I hope you have more compassion than your oaf of a colleague,' she said. 'When you hand this young lady to the police, inform them that she will require stitches in the wound.' She fixed him with a steely glare. 'I shall check with the railway company later to make sure my instructions were carried out. If I find they weren't, I shall report you to your superiors.'

'Yes, ma'am.' The conductor gulped nervously. 'They will be.' His tone changed to one of officialdom as he turned his attention to the young woman. 'I must ask you to come with me, miss.'

Daniel followed the young woman into the corridor as the conductor took her gently by the elbow and escorted her along the corridor to the guard's quarters. The man that Daniel had hit still lay on the floor, and although he was conscious, he was firmly secured by a rope at the wrist and ankles with the guard standing over him.

Daniel returned to the compartment and pulled the door shut.

'All's well that ends well,' he said. 'Well done for the swift way you acted on treating her knife wound.'

'It wasn't as vital as the way you acted in disarming him,' said Abigail. She gave an angry snort of derision. 'I heard what the guard said to you. "Everything's under control." Ha! Lunacy! And not a word of thanks!'

'You can't please everyone,' said Daniel wryly.

'He might have killed that woman. And the guard and conductor!'

'It's all sorted out now,' said Daniel. He looked at her inquisitively. 'You were talking about telephones before all that.'

Abigail stared at him in amazement. 'You've just saved a woman's life, overpowered a dangerous knife-wielding maniac, and you want to talk about telephones?'

'I'm interested,' he said. 'They say that the telephone is going to be the thing of the future. That there are already plans to put in telephone lines that will link Europe and America, and even Australia. Imagine, being able to talk to someone at the other side of the world without leaving your house!' He nodded towards the *Museum Digest* on the seat beside Abigail. 'You were about to read me something before the trouble began.'

'Yes,' said Abigail. She opened the magazine and began to flick through the pages. 'Last night, when you said we were going to Manchester, I decided to look through some of the recent editions to see if there was anything in any of them about the Manchester Museum, and I found this article. Ah yes, here it is.' She began to read. 'The museum in Manchester is among the latest to subscribe to the newly installed telephone exchange in that city. It is believed the number of subscribers has now passed seven hundred, many of them private customers. This means that people as far apart as Stockport, Oldham and Bolton can now communicate with one another through the telephone system, making Manchester the first city in England to have a fully operational telephone exchange, with plans to extend the lines to Liverpool, Leeds, Sheffield, and even as far as Birmingham.'

'But not to London,' observed Daniel.

'That day will come, if the rest of the report is to be believed,' said Abigail. She offered the magazine to Daniel. 'Would you like to read the rest of it?'

Daniel was about to take it, when they heard the conductor's shout of: 'Crewe station! Crewe station!'

'Later,' he said, passing the magazine back to Abigail. 'I've been told that Crewe is one of the busiest junctions on the whole network, and if that's so then I feel this compartment might suddenly become rather crowded and we'll be spending most of our time stopping our comfort being encroached on by hordes of travellers bound for Manchester.'

'Don't worry.' Abigail smiled. 'I'll protect you. If anyone tries to sit on you, I'll deal with them.'

CHAPTER TWO

As it turned out, although other travellers joined them in the compartment, it did not turn out to be the free-for-all that Daniel had envisaged, just three apparently respectable businessmen and a husband and wife. When Daniel had sometimes taken a train in central London, especially one travelling east towards Southend, he'd often found himself besieged by families with numerous children of all ages who seemed to only want to fight with one another and generally cause mayhem, while their parents sat seemingly oblivious to the distress their offspring were causing the other passengers. The quiet mood of their fellow passengers meant that Daniel was able to take time to read about the Manchester Museum in Abigail's magazine. As a result he learnt that, as well as the museum enjoying telephone access in the area of Manchester and surrounding cities, the museum was a relatively recent establishment. Although it incorporated material from the earlier collections of the Manchester Natural History and Geological Societies, the newly designed building that housed the Manchester Museum had only been opened to the public seven years before, in 1888. The article highlighted the large number of mounted animals on display, many of them from someone called Brian Houghton Hodgson, who seemed to have discovered many species during his travels in India and Nepal which had been previously unknown to the West. The museum also seemed to have one of the largest collections of beetles and other insects outside of London's Natural History Museum.

'Not much here about your particular area of expertise,' commented Daniel, referring to Abigail's reputation as one of Europe's leading Egyptologists, a reputation based on her archaeological work at the pyramids in Egypt, as well as her explorations of ancient temples in Greece and of Roman sites.

'It is expanding,' she said. She laid her finger on a paragraph. 'You'll see it mentions new finds being brought in from the excavations at Gurob and Kahun, as well as from Flinders Petrie.' She gave a smile of reminiscence as she added, 'I worked with him, you know.'

'Who?'

'Flinders Petrie.'

'In Egypt?'

'Yes, at Hawara in 1888. Then again in Palestine at Tell el-Hesi. 1890.'

'What was he like?' asked Daniel.

'Much the same as he still is today. A big bear of a man. It's astonishing to think that he's still so comparatively young for an archaeologist and he's achieved so much! He was in his late thirties then. In his early days the archaeological establishment considered him a bit of a maverick. He didn't always stick to the rules. For example, when he began the dig at Tanis in the New Kingdom site he took on the role of foreman in charge of the workers himself. He said it was one less level of bureaucracy which would otherwise slow things down.'

'Attractive?'

Abigail laughed. 'Very.' Then, with a glance at the other passengers, she whispered to him, 'But you have nothing to fear on that aspect. It was purely a meeting of two minds with one aim.'

On their arrival at the main London Road station they elected to walk to Oxford Road, where the museum was situated, rather than take a hansom. His years as a police officer had led Daniel to believe that the best way to see any new city was on foot, and he was fortunate that Abigail, with her many experiences exploring exotic towns and cities, was of the same opinion. The museum was a large, rather ornate building.

'It looks like a slightly smaller version of the Natural History Museum in London,' observed Daniel.

'It was designed by the same architect,' said Abigail. 'Alfred Waterhouse. But don't say anything to them about it being slightly smaller. Museums can be very sensitive about unfavourable comparisons.'

'I wasn't being unfavourable,' defended Daniel. 'I just said it looked slightly smaller.'

'But it may not be inside,' said Abigail. 'Sensitivity is all. We don't want to get off on the wrong foot with our new client.'

'Perhaps if I say it looks larger?' suggested Daniel.

'Better not to say anything,' advised Abigail.

Inside, they found a uniformed commissionaire on duty at the door and asked him for directions to the office of Mr Steggles, the museum's director.

'Would you be Mr Wilson and Miss Fenton?' asked the commissionaire.

'We are,' confirmed Daniel.

'Mr Steggles asked me to watch out for you. If you'll follow me I'll take you to his office.'

The commissionaire summoned a similarly uniformed man from inside the museum and indicated for him to take over on duty at the main entrance, then led the way to a narrow stone staircase to one side of the entrance doors. Daniel and Abigail followed him, carrying their overnight bags, and soon they were standing outside a dark oak door on the first floor. The commissionaire knocked at the door, then opened it and announced, 'Mr Wilson and Miss Fenton, Mr Steggles.'

'Thank heavens!' said a cultured voice from within. The door was thrown wider and Daniel and Abigail beheld a small, thin man in his fifties dressed in a close-fitting soberly dark suit. With his neatly trimmed hair and tiny moustache, he reminded Daniel of a senior bank clerk rather than the man in overall charge of a large and important museum.

'Do come in!' said Steggles. He led them across the plush, thickly piled carpet to two chairs waiting by his large desk. 'I'm so sorry,' he apologised as they put their luggage down. 'I should have thought and suggested you go to the hotel we've booked you into first before you came here, but I've been so worried over what happened that the distraction has played havoc with some of my thought processes.'

'What has happened?' asked Daniel, as he and Abigail seated themselves. 'Your telegram just said a murder had been committed here at the museum.'

'It's now two murders,' said Steggles grimly.

'Two?'

'The first we discovered on the day it happened. The

16

second only manifested itself this morning.' He looked at them apologetically. 'I'm forgetting my manners and common courtesy,' he said. 'Can I order tea for you? Or anything else?'

'Tea would be perfect, thank you,' said Abigail.

Steggles pressed a button on a large black machine on his desk, at the same time lifting what looked like a small metal speaker from it, which was connected to the machine by a length of wire. A woman's voice came from the black machine.

'Yes, Mr Steggles?'

'Tea for three, please, Mrs Wedburn. With biscuits.'

'Certainly, Mr Steggles.'

As Steggles replaced the metal speaker on the machine, Daniel commented, 'We were reading about the telephone system here in Manchester.'

'Ah, this isn't that system,' said Steggles. 'It's a variation. Internal only. It uses similar technology, but it doesn't have to go through an operator as it's only connected to my secretary in her office.' He smiled. 'It saves me having to walk along there if I have something to tell her about.'

'The murders?' prompted Daniel gently.

'Yes,' said Steggles. 'On Thursday last week, four days ago, a young woman was stabbed to death here in the museum. She'd been sitting at a table in the reading room, apparently doing some research work, and been stabbed in the back, the knife penetrating into her heart and the point of the knife coming out through her ribs at the front of her chest.'

'That would have taken a lot of strength,' said Daniel. 'There were no witnesses?'

Steggles shook his head. 'She was in an isolated corner of the reading room. She was found lying face down on the table, with blood by her.'

'You say she was doing some research,' said Abigail. 'Was she a student of some sort?'

'No,' said Steggles. 'In fact, she seemed to have been someone from a poor background, to judge by her clothes. Her clothes were clean, but very worn and repaired many times. Indeed, her shoes had holes in the soles and newspapers had been put inside to give protection against cobbles.'

'Do you know her name?'

Again, Steggles shook his head.

'No. She gave no name, and there was no form of identification on her. She did have a bag with her, but that had gone. I assume whoever stabbed her took it.'

'A robbery?' hazarded Abigail.

'Unlikely,' said Daniel thoughtfully. 'Whoever did it was obviously strong. If they simply wanted the bag all they had to do was take it from her. At worst, a punch to knock her out if she resisted. What do the police say?'

'To be honest, that's why we've asked you if you'd look into it. As far as the police are concerned, there is no case to investigate. A woman no one knows has died. There were no witnesses, so no sighting of a suspect. Her obvious poverty means to them she is of no importance. They say they haven't the resources to waste investigating something that can't be solved.'

'That's very harsh,' said Daniel.

'That's what we thought. The board of the museum, that is. Although there's been a museum in Manchester since 1821, this building was only opened seven years ago. It is our ambition to provide the resources for education not just for students and staff of the university, but for the wider public. Especially those from poor and deprived backgrounds. We are an establishment with a social conscience, as are many others in Manchester. We feel that the violent death of someone should not be ignored simply because they are poor or are not recognised as important to society. If the police won't agree to look into this poor woman's death, then we feel it is up to us to do something.'

A gentle knock at the door interrupted them.

'Ah, that will be the tea,' said Steggles.

He got up and walked briskly to the door, opening it to admit a kindly looking woman of middle age carrying a tray on which were cups and saucers and all the other accoutrements for tea, including a plate of mixed biscuits.

'On the desk, please, Mrs Wedburn.' Steggles smiled.

Once Mrs Wedburn had deposited the tray and departed, Steggles busied himself with pouring the tea to their specifications – milk for both, sugar for Daniel but not for Abigail – and served them, placing the biscuits within easy reach.

'You said there was a second murder,' said Abigail.

Steggles nodded. 'That was only discovered this morning. There'd been reports of a foul smell inside the cellar. This morning Walter Arkwright, one of our attendants who also acts as our storeman, traced it to behind some packing cases. The body of a woman was there.' He gave a shudder as he said, 'Someone had sliced her face off.'

Abigail and Daniel stared at him, shocked.

'How?' asked Daniel. 'What with?'

'The police just said it must have been with a large, sharp blade. Someone had sliced off the front of her face, right back to the bones of her skull.'

'Where is the body now?'

'At the hospital mortuary, along with the body of the young woman.'

Daniel and Abigail were silent for a moment as they took

all this in, then Daniel said, 'Surely there are private enquiry agents here in Manchester, Mr Steggles. I say this because Miss Fenton and I are unfamiliar with the city. A local enquiry agent would have easier access to sources of information and local contacts.'

'True,' said Steggles. 'But we have been following the successes the pair of you have had when murders have occurred at other museums. The Fitzwilliam in Cambridge, the British Museum, the Ashmolean in Oxford. On every occasion you succeeded when the local police force had failed.'

'I wouldn't say "failed",' said Daniel carefully. 'On those occasions we worked with the local police force and were able to bring a different eye to the investigation. I have a policeman's experience, but Miss Fenton is the one who is at home in a museum setting, and her instincts proved invaluable in those cases.'

'Yes, we are very aware of Miss Fenton's reputation,' said Steggles. 'I have read your articles concerning your excavations at Giza, and your recent work on Hadrian's Wall. And we have some artefacts here from your own work at Hawara. We are privileged to have you here with us. I would deem it an honour for you to spend some time exploring the museum and letting us have your comments and recommendations.'

'With the greatest respect, Mr Steggles, I feel that sometimes my reputation as an archaeologist has become somewhat inflated, possibly due to the rather purple prose of the popular newspapers.'

'I am basing my opinion on reports on you and your work from other archaeologists and curators, Miss Fenton. Your peers hold you in high esteem.'

Abigail coloured, and Daniel had to hide a smile at the idea of Abigail blushing.

'Thank you, Mr Steggles. But, as far as conducting investigations, Mr Wilson gives me too much credit. The truth is, we complement one another and so bring different observations to cases.'

'As we hope you will to this.'

'But those other cases were connected to the museums,' stressed Daniel. 'We're not sure if that's the case here. We have to look at the possibility that these women may have been killed for reasons that have nothing to do with the museum.'

'In which case, that will be a relief to us. The idea that in some way the museum may have been the cause of their deaths hangs heavy on us.' He gestured at the plate. 'Biscuit?' he offered. He selected one himself and looked at it in a guilty fashion. 'My wife says I eat too many of these and they're bad for my health, but with the stress we've been under lately over this murder, it's a relief to have some kind of solace.'

CHAPTER THREE

Replenished by tea and an occasional biscuit, Daniel suggested going to the reading room to examine the site of the murder, and then the cellar where the most recent body had been discovered.

'Yes, I was just going to suggest that,' said Steggles. 'It will give you a chance to meet Jonty Hawkins. He's the librarian in charge of the reading room, and it was he who discovered the first body.'

'In that case we definitely need to make his acquaintance,' said Daniel.

Steggles led the way to the reading room, this time their route taking them through the actual museum.

'Hawkins is a remarkable young man. Many young men would have been too disturbed by the awful discovery he made to have been able to continue to work, but he absolutely refused my suggestion he go home. A fine young man. He's also quite an accomplished poet. His work has appeared in magazines here in Manchester.'

They entered the reading room and Steggles led the way to the desk at which a young man was sitting, examining a book. He stood up as they approached, and Daniel and Abigail exchanged glances that meant they were both thinking the same: Jonty Hawkins was in his twenties, and his style of dress and manner was as far removed from the bank clerk appearance of Steggles as was possible. He was tall and thin and wore a long, green velvet jacket over a flowered waistcoat, but it was his long hair that caught their attention, curling luxuriantly over his ears and collar in the style of Oscar Wilde's most ardent followers. There was even a hint of rouge on his otherwise pale face.

'Mr Hawkins, these are Mr Daniel Wilson and Miss Abigail Fenton, the people from London I spoke about.'

Hawkins gave them a smile and held out his hand to shake theirs in greeting.

'Welcome,' he said. 'I know of your reputations, of course. Yours in particular, Miss Fenton. Your work at Giza is an inspiration to all.'

'You are interested in archaeology?' asked Abigail.

'Fervently,' said Hawkins earnestly. 'You must allow me to show you the pieces we have from Kahun and Hawara.'

'Flinders Petrie,' murmured Abigail.

'You were with Petrie at Hawara, I believe,' said Hawkins excitedly.

Abigail nodded. 'I was.'

'For the moment I've brought Mr Wilson and Miss Fenton here to talk to you about . . . what happened here last Thursday,' interrupted Steggles, lowering his voice almost to a whisper.

'Of course.' Hawkins nodded. 'My apologies.'

Steggles turned to Daniel and Abigail.

'I'll leave you with Mr Hawkins. When you've finished with him perhaps you'd return to my office and I can give you directions to your hotel and details of the booking. Or, if I'm not available for any reason, my secretary, Mrs Wedburn, will be able to supply the information.'

Daniel and Abigail thanked him, and then turned back to Jonty Hawkins.

'Perhaps it would be better if we moved outside,' suggested Hawkins. 'We can talk freely there.' He gestured at the room, where already some of the people sitting at the various tables were glaring at them disapprovingly. 'It is a reading room, after all, and people expect a quiet atmosphere.'

Daniel and Abigail nodded in acquiescence and followed the young man out of the reading room into the corridor outside.

'We can talk here, but it's still better if we keep our voices low.'

'Of course,' said Abigail. 'Mr Steggles said it was you who found the body.'

'Yes, and no,' said Hawkins. 'A man came to my desk and said there was a woman slumped over the table. To be honest, that's not unusual. We get many people coming in here to seek shelter, and some of them fall asleep. It's not something we encourage, but we don't like to throw them out. Times are hard. But this man said he thought he saw blood on the table.' He hesitated, then added, 'It would make more sense if I show you where she was found, and you can see the arrangements for readers.'

'Excellent idea,' said Daniel. 'But before we do that, as we can talk here, it would be useful to learn what you knew about her?'

'Knew?' said Hawkins. He gave a rueful sigh. 'Very little, I'm afraid. She appeared on Wednesday last week and asked me if we had anything about the Manchester army from a long time ago. I told her that the army records are kept at the barracks. Much of what we have are newspaper reports about different campaigns. She said she'd been to the barracks but they hadn't been able to help her. I said the barracks was still her best choice, but she said she couldn't go back there. I got the impression they'd turned her away quite harshly.'

'She asked about the Manchester army?' said Daniel. 'Not a particular regiment?'

'No,' said Hawkins. 'She said she was looking for information about the army from about eighty years ago.'

'Eighty years,' said Daniel thoughtfully. '1815. That would be during the Battle of Waterloo.'

'Yes, but there was no actual Manchester army at that time, just other regiments that later formed it. The Manchester Regiment was created in 1881 with the amalgamation of the 63rd West Suffolk, the 96th Regiment of Foot, the 6th Royal Lancashire Militia and some volunteer battalions.'

'You are a keen student of military history?' asked Daniel, impressed.

'Not really,' admitted Hawkins. 'I only found this information when I made enquiries about the Manchester Regiment, after the young lady asked me. And I've been helping Mr Steggles with some background work on the exhibition about the Manchester regiments he's planning.'

'Were these other regiments at Waterloo?' asked Daniel.

'No, but the 15th Hussars based at Hulme were, although I don't think they can be described as purely a Manchester regiment.'

'Did she find what she wanted in the documents you provided?'

'I assume not, because she came back the next day and asked if I had any different papers about the old regiments. I asked her what she was actually looking for, but she said she'd know it if she saw it.' His face looked troubled as he added, 'It was during that second visit, last Thursday, that she was killed.' He gestured towards the reading room. 'Perhaps now would be a good time to show you where she was.'

Daniel and Abigail followed Hawkins back into the reading room, past long rows of floor-to-ceiling bookshelves, before coming to four long tables. Each table was divided by wooden partitions into six small compartments.

'The official reason for putting the partitions on the tables in this way was so that each person has privacy for their research,' explained Hawkins as they approached the tables.

'And the unofficial reason?' asked Abigail.

Hawkins gave a rueful smile.

'Before we put the partitions in place, some people would spread their books and papers so far out they'd take up the whole table, which led unfortunately to strong arguments. This way, readers can only have what they can fit into their compartment.'

There were a handful of people at the tables, some with newspapers, some with books, some scribbling notes, others just reading. Hawkins led the way to the furthest of the tables. Two men were sitting in the compartments, both intent on their work. One, a bearded man, looked up as Hawkins, Daniel and Abigail arrived, then he turned back to the pile of books he'd assembled.

Hawkins stopped by an empty compartment at the end of the table.

'She was here,' he said. 'There was no one else at any of the tables. She was slumped across the table. I tapped her on the shoulder, then – when she didn't respond – very gently raised her to sit up so I could see how she was, and then I saw the blood staining the front of her blouse and that it had run down.'

'That must have been a dreadful experience for you,' said Daniel sympathetically.

'Awful,' said the young man. 'I've seen dead people before – you'd be surprised how many come in here for warmth and then die – but not like this. The police said she'd been stabbed in the back and the knife had gone deep into her heart and out through her ribs at the front.' He shook his head. 'It makes me sick just to think of it.'

'What else did the police say?' asked Daniel.

'Not much,' said Hawkins. 'In fact, they didn't seem unduly concerned. The inspector in charge said he didn't think it worth investigating as no one knew who she was. I think that was because she was dressed in shabby clothes and obviously poor. And when I told him she was Irish . . .'

'Irish?'

Hawkins nodded. 'There are a lot of Irish in Manchester. The inspector said he expected it was some boyfriend she'd upset. When I told him that the bag she'd brought with her had gone, he said that was the answer: it was a robbery.'

'Yes, Mr Steggles told us the police said they wouldn't be investigating. Did you get this inspector's name?'

'Inspector Grimley.'

'Where can we find him?'

'He's based at Newton Street police station. It's not far from London Road railway station.' He hesitated, then added warily, 'He didn't seem the most compassionate of people. But perhaps he'll be different with you, Mr Wilson, you being an ex-Scotland Yard detective.'

'What about where the most recent body was found? The one this morning.'

'The cellar,' said Hawkins. 'I wasn't involved in that. I only heard about it afterwards.'

'We understand the body was found by Mr Walter Arkwright. Is he still here?'

'He is. If you come this way, I'll take you to him.'

They followed Hawkins downstairs to the reception area, where an elderly man in the blue uniform of a museum attendant stood to attention, back ramrod straight, hands behind his back, as he surveyed the people coming and going.

'Mr Arkwright,' said Hawkins. 'These are Mr Daniel Wilson and Miss Abigail Fenton.'

Arkwright nodded. 'Yes. Welcome. Mr Steggles told me you'd be coming.'

'We understand you found the body in the cellar this morning.'

'I did, sir,' said Arkwright crisply. 'I assume you wish to see where I found it?'

'Yes, please.'

'I'll leave you in Mr Arkwright's care,' said Hawkins. 'If you wish to talk to me again, you'll find me in the reading room.'

Daniel and Abigail followed the elderly attendant through a door, then down some stone steps, a musty smell coming to them as they descended deeper.

'Damp,' observed Arkwright. 'You'll always get that in cellars. Luckily this place has been well-built so at least you don't have rats getting in.'

At the bottom they came to a large room with a floor of flagstones, other rooms going off it. Each room was stacked with wooden packing cases, some large, some small.

'Pieces awaiting exhibition,' Arkwright informed them. 'Every so often the displays are changed to keep people coming. Not every one, though. Some are always kept as they are because they're so popular that people keep coming back to see them. Like the remains of the dodo, for example. Now that's a rarity.'

He took them to where a stack of smaller wooden crates was piled one of top of the other in one of the inner rooms.

'This is where I found her,' he said. 'I came down as I always do when I come in, and I knew that smell straight away. The smell of death. An old soldier, see. At first I thought it might have been something like a cat had got in and died, but the nearer I got to these crates, the stronger the smell of blood. I pulled the crates out, and there she was. She'd just been stuffed behind them and the crates pushed back.' He shook his head. 'It were a mess. Someone had bashed her head in, then sliced her face clean off, right back to the bone. All the skin and flesh gone.'

'It must have been a dreadful experience for you,' said Abigail sympathetically.

'Like I said, I'm an old soldier, miss. I've seen a lot worse than that.'

'Was there any sign of the remains of her face?' asked Daniel.

Arkwright shook his head. 'He must've took it with him. Mebbe a trophy. I've known that happen in wars. Soldiers collecting the ears of their enemies. But never a whole face.'

Daniel knelt down and studied the area behind the wooden crates where the body had been lodged.

'The signs are that you've cleaned up the blood here,' he said.

'I have, sir. Couldn't have that sort of thing making a mess here.'

Daniel pointed to the floor a few feet away from the packing cases.

'This must be where he took her face off,' he said.

'Correct,' said Arkwright. 'That's where most of the blood was. It took a lot of scrubbing.'

'And you've done a very good job, Mr Arkwright,' complimented Daniel.

As Daniel and Abigail headed back up the stairs towards Steggles's office, Abigail said, 'I presume that Mr Arkwright's zealous cleaning has removed any possible clues that might have been there.'

'Indeed,' said Daniel. 'But one can't blame him. He was doing his job. And I assume he was told he could clean up by this police inspector, who must have come to look at the dead body and the scene of the crime.'

As they approached Steggles's office, Abigail asked, 'What did you make of Mr Hawkins?'

'I liked him,' replied Daniel. 'Despite the fact that he decides to dress in the style that emulates Oscar Wilde and the aesthetic movement. That alone I think would take some courage in an industrial town like Manchester, but he gave a very lucid and thoughtful report of his encounters with the young woman. Intelligent.'

'I'd be interested in looking at some of his poetry. That often gives the measure of someone. Whether they are genuinely gifted, or whether it's all just superficial appearance.'

'I'm sure he would be only too pleased to share his works with you,' Daniel said. 'I got the impression he was quite admiring of you.'

'Of my work and reputation, in reality, I expect,' said Abigail. 'I somehow feel I may not be the right object of affection for young Mr Hawkins.'

'You are for me.' Daniel smiled.

'And that's all that matters to me.' Abigail smiled back.

Steggles was still in his office, looking forward to hearing their initial report. They both made a point of complimenting Jonty Hawkins and Walter Arkwright to him.

'Two very good witnesses,' said Daniel.

'Yes,' said Steggles, but they could both tell he seemed uncomfortable at the mention of their names.

'Is there an issue with either of the men?' enquired Abigail.

Steggles gestured for them to sit, then said, 'It's not either of them personally, rather something that Mr Hawkins said about the young woman found in the reading room. He said that she was looking into old records of the Manchester units of the army, and she was doing that because she was turned away from the barracks when she made her initial enquiries there.'

Abigail nodded. 'Yes, he told us the same.'

'I'm concerned because I've been having discussions with Brigadier Wentworth, the Commanding Officer at Hulme Barracks, and a local military historian, Hector Bleasdale, about mounting an exhibition here highlighting the achievements of the Manchester regiments.'

'Yes, Mr Hawkins mentioned it,' said Daniel.

'We are very keen to involve as many sections of the local community as we can, to bring the public into the museum so they can see it as *their* museum. For their part, I believe the army is keen because it would counter some of the stories about Peterloo.'

'Peterloo?' asked Abigail.

Steggles looked at her in surprise. 'I thought what happened at Peterloo was common knowledge,' he said.

'Not to me,' said Abigail.

'Nor me,' added Daniel. 'What was it?'

'It was an unfortunate incident that happened here in Manchester in 1819. There was a . . . a riot at a public meeting. The army was called in and a number of civilians died.'

'Killed by the army?'

Steggles nodded. 'I'm sure there are any number of people in Manchester who will be able to furnish you with the details far better than I can. Although it is still a sensitive subject as far as the army are concerned.'

'Understandably,' said Abigail.

'That's one of the reasons we've been discussing the idea of an exhibition about the local regiments, to promote the positive side of the army and help to heal any divisions between them and the civilian populace that may still exist.'

'Divisions after eighty years?' asked Abigail.

'People have long memories, and sometimes the stories that get handed down from generation to generation can be distorted,' said Steggles. He gave an unhappy sigh. 'My concern is that if the army are implicated in any way in this young woman's death, however obliquely, they may decide not to collaborate with us. Which would be a pity; the army is a core part of Manchester society with a long and prestigious military tradition.' He hesitated, then added awkwardly, 'Apart from what happened at Peterloo, of course. But even then, it could be argued that wasn't the regular army at fault, but a local militia.'

'We will need to go to the barracks to ask questions,' said Daniel. 'About the young woman going there and being turned away.'

Steggles nodded. 'I understand. It's at Hulme. You'll be able to get a hansom cab, or buses go there. But I would ask you to be discreet.'

'We will be, I can assure you,' said Daniel. 'Perhaps if we spoke to this commanding officer you mentioned . . .'

'Brigadier Wentworth,' said Steggles. 'Yes. And by all means mention my name. He's a good chap.' He hesitated, then added, 'Although, a bit of a stickler for rules and regulations. Comes with being part of the army, I suppose. I hope this business of the young woman doesn't put a block on the exhibition we're planning. We like to be very active.'

'Yes, I saw a poster for an illustrated talk on tropical birds you have coming up,' said Abigail.

At this, Steggles brightened. 'Indeed! Given by none other than Henry Eeles Dresser, acknowledged across the world as the expert on exotic birds. As well as being a former secretary of the

British Ornithologists Union he's also an Honorary Fellow of the American Ornithologists Union. And his studies in Eastern Europe, especially in Finland . . .' He stopped and gave an apologetic smile. 'Forgive me. Sometimes I get overenthusiastic and go on alarmingly. My wife is always telling me off about it.'

'Not at all,' said Abigail. 'I'm a great admirer of enthusiasm, especially when it's accompanied by expertise. If we're still here when Mr Dresser gives his talk, Mr Wilson and I will be delighted to attend.'

And Abigail shot a look at Daniel, who said as politely as he could, 'Indeed. It would be a pleasure.'

'In the meantime, I would urge you to take a look at our ornithology section here at the museum,' said Steggles. 'We have an array of wonders among the exhibits, including the bones of a dodo, a male and female ivory-billed woodpecker, stuffed birds, eggs and bones from the Hawaiian islands, and many examples of rare exotic species. Not to mention some wonderful examples donated by Charles Darwin following his important journeys, including a very rare warbler finch.'

'We certainly will.' Daniel got up. 'But right now, we need to book in at our hotel, and then make ourselves known to the local police inspector in charge of the case.'

'Inspector Grimley at Newton Street police station,' answered Steggles. He rose, saying carefully, 'A . . . difficult man, from what little I saw of him. Rather abrasive. But I'm sure he is good at his job.'

Steggles handed them the address of the Mayflower Hotel.

'Your room reservations are in the name of the museum,' he said. Then he hesitated, before adding in an awkward tone, 'Initially I reserved two rooms, one for each of you, but I have since learnt that you are – ah – quite close. I therefore took the liberty of adding a rider to the reservation that you may decide to – ah – share a room.' As Abigail and Daniel stared at him, he added, 'Because the Mayflower is quite a conventionally managed hotel, I told them that it was my understanding that you were married but that you, Miss Fenton, elected to be known by your maiden name because of your international renowned reputation as an archaeologist. I hope you will not be offended by my temerity.'

As he said this, Steggles's face, and especially his ears, became suffused with colour, and they realised that he was blushing. It was Abigail who moved forward and took his hands in hers.

'Mr Steggles,' she said, her voice trembling with passion, 'that is one of the nicest things anyone has ever said to me, and we are both eternally grateful to you. I will not lie to you, we are married in all but name, and have every intention of marrying as soon the opportunity arises. But your generosity here . . .' Temporarily words failed her, and instead she squeezed his hands. 'You don't know what a weight off my mind your kind words have been.'

CHAPTER FOUR

'A talk about birds,' groaned Daniel as they left the museum.

'It will be instructional,' defended Abigail. 'And it will keep our client happy.'

'I can imagine nothing more boring,' said Daniel. 'The only birds I'm familiar with are the pigeons in Trafalgar Square, who seem to make me a target as soon as I venture there. The number of times I've had to get pigeon excrement removed from my hat . . .'

'Exotic birds are not the same as pigeons,' countered Abigail.

'I bet they'd still drop their deposits on me if I was in some tropical jungle. I expect Charles Darwin returned from his travels with his coat spotted with their droppings.'

'Unlikely,' said Abigail. 'I'm sure Mr Dresser's talk will enlighten you.'

Despite the authorisation that Steggles had given the Mayflower Hotel, as they were taking just the one room, the receptionist insisted they sign the register as Mr and Mrs Wilson.

'It's a small price to pay,' said Daniel as they made their way to their room.

'I have never given up my name before,' said Abigail.

'Perhaps we should have signed as Mr and Mrs Fenton?' suggested Daniel.

'Would that worry you?' asked Abigail.

'No,' said Daniel. 'However, as the hotel had already been told who I was before our arrival, I don't think we could have got away with it.'

'How thoughtful of Mr Steggles!' exclaimed Abigail as they unlocked the door of their room and entered. 'No rumpling the bed linen in one of two rooms to keep up a ludicrous pretence. I hope there's a Mr Steggles in every case we are hired to investigate. It's a relief to meet such enlightenment.'

'It's also time for us to meet Inspector Grimley,' said Daniel. 'However, based on what we heard from both Mr Steggles and Jonty Hawkins, I'm not expecting very much in the way of a welcome.'

Daniel's expectations were confirmed as soon as they were shown into the inspector's office at Newton Street police station. Inspector Grimley was sitting behind his desk as they entered, a uniformed sergeant standing beside him, and there was no mistaking the look of venom on the inspector's face as he looked at them. He did not get up from his chair to greet them, nor offer to shake hands.

'You wanted to see me?' he grunted.

'Yes, and thank you for making the time to see us, Inspector,' said Daniel. 'I'm Daniel Wilson and this is Miss Abigail Fenton. We've been asked by the Manchester Museum to look into the killing of the two women there, and we thought it only courtesy to let you know of our involvement, and that possibly we may be able to exchange information as and when we come up with any.'

Grimley glowered sullenly at them, then grunted, 'There is no case.'

'Yes, that's what the museum said you'd told them, but as a young woman has been stabbed to death and the other we've been told had her face sliced off . . .'

'People die violently all the time,' snapped Grimley. 'Sometimes through accident, sometimes they've been assaulted. We're dealing with hundreds of cases here in this city, which means we have to prioritise, so the first thing we have to find out is who the person is who's died, or if there were any witnesses. In this case both persons are unknown, and there were no witnesses. So there's no chance of us finding out who killed either woman. If we had the luxury of a large force with lots of men, and spare time, like they seem to have in places like London, it might be different. But that's the way it is.'

'So you're not going to investigate?'

'We investigated and decided there was no point in spending more time on it.'

'But two women are dead!' exclaimed Abigail.

'In the case of the young woman, I expect it was an angry boyfriend who did it, or possibly a petty thief as her bag was taken. The woman in the cellar . . . who knows. But we haven't got the men or the time to go chasing that sort of thing when we've got cases we *can* go after. Now, if you've finished, I've got work to do.'

'Inspector, we are not just amateurs poking our noses in,' said Abigail angrily. 'Before he became a private enquiry agent, Daniel Wilson was a vital member of Inspector Abberline's team at Scotland Yard . . .'

'I knew who he was as soon as he introduced himself,' snapped Grimley, 'and we don't need people from London coming up here to try and teach us how to do our job. *Especially* people who've failed at it themselves.'

'Failed?!' echoed Abigail.

'You never caught the Ripper, did you?' Grimley scowled at Daniel. 'For all your fancy London ways. We may be far away, but we know what goes on. You failed at the Met, so now you're making money out of misguided fools like the museum here. Well, you'll get no encouragement on that score from us. Just be thankful I'm not arresting you for taking money under false pretences.'

'At least they didn't throw us out,' said Daniel as they left the police station.

'He did throw us out!' burst out Abigail.

'Yes, but not physically.'

'I'd have liked to have seen him try!' growled Abigail.

'At least we know where we stand in relation to the local police,' said Daniel ruefully. 'So far we're not having a great deal of success.'

'We have only just arrived,' Abigail pointed out.

'True,' conceded Daniel. 'But you must agree we haven't got a lot to go on, and with the police being obstructive . . . If only we knew what she was looking for at the museum. Hawkins said she wanted to research army records from eighty years ago, but that covers an awfully large area of information. Was she looking for a particular soldier? Or a particular unit?'

'Hawkins said she'd been to the barracks first, and been turned away,' said Abigail.

'Yes, so that should be our next port of call. But with discretion.'

CHAPTER FIVE

At the city centre, Daniel and Abigail managed to find two seats together on the top deck of the crowded horse-drawn bus that would take them to the army barracks, giving them a good vantage point to see the district of Hulme as they travelled through it. The main thoroughfare on which the bus travelled was wide, even though the large volume of traffic meant their journey was conducted at a slow pace. Branching off from the main road they could see a network of narrow streets and alleyways with small houses crushed together. Every now and then a tall, narrow chimney rose up above the houses, belching out black smoke, signifying the presence of a cotton mill, the smoke from the tall chimneys merging with the smoke from the railway trains that chugged through this part of the city, heading to and from the major termini, the smoke descending in a thick cloud. The overriding scent of this part of the city was thick, burnt smoke.

'It reminds me of parts of London,' commented Abigail.

'But smokier,' added Daniel.

'London has thick fogs, too,' said Abigail. 'Thicker than this. I've been out in them.'

'Yes, but those pea-soupers only happen now and then, depending on the weather stopping the smoke from rising. Looking at the soot coating the roofs and walls of the buildings in those side streets, I'm guessing it's like this most of the time.'

The bus did a busy trade, people getting on and off throughout the journey, many laden with goods of all types, including one woman with live chickens in a crate, another with two baskets filled with laundry which she dragged along behind her down the bus passageway, and a man with a broken bicycle in two parts which he struggled to hold on to as the bus jolted along the road.

At last they reached their destination.

'There it is,' said Daniel, nodding towards a Georgian building with a Union Jack and a regimental flag flying above it.

They descended from the bus and crossed the road. A metal fence surrounded the building, and the land beyond it. A large board on the fence adjacent to the open gate bore the legend 'Hulme Barracks; Home of 15th The King's Hussars', with the regimental insignia – a lion atop a crown within a circle, with the motto *Merebimur* – below it. A corporal wearing a dark blue tunic stood rigidly to attention on duty beside the gate, holding his rifle firmly by the barrel, the wooden stock resting on the pavement.

'*Merebimur?*' asked Daniel.

'We are not worthy,' said Abigail. 'It's Latin.'

'One of the advantages of a classical degree at Cambridge.' Daniel smiled.

They reached the sentry and Daniel said, 'Good morning. We'd like to speak to your commanding officer, Brigadier Wentworth.'

'I'm sorry, sir. Civilians need an appointment in order to see the commanding officer,' replied the sentry crisply.

'Very well, we'll make one,' said Daniel. 'But in the meantime, were you on duty here last Tuesday?'

'What is the purpose of your question, sir?'

'We're trying to find out who saw a young woman who called here last Tuesday. She was in her twenties and was Irish.'

'No one of that description came here last Tuesday.'

'Really. We've been reliably informed that she did call here but was turned away. Perhaps she arrived when you weren't on duty.'

'What's going on here, Corporal?'

A tall, well-built man whose uniform was heavily decorated, both with brass and rows of medals, had appeared in the gateway and he stood and glowered challengingly at Daniel and Abigail.

'Civilians, sir. Asking to see Brigadier Wentworth.'

'Do they have an appointment?'

'No, sir.'

'Meeting with the commander can only be done with an appointment. And at the moment he's not available.'

'Yes, so the corporal explained,' said Daniel politely. Taking in the man's insignias of rank, he said, 'I presume you are the regimental sergeant major here.'

'I am, sir, RSM Bulstrode.'

'I'm sure you'll be able to answer our enquiries. I'm Daniel Wilson and this is Miss Abigail Fenton. We are private enquiry agents and have been tasked by Mr Bernard Steggles at the Manchester Museum to make enquiries concerning a young woman. It was Mr Steggles who suggested we make contact with Brigadier Wentworth as he and the brigadier have been engaged in some arrangements concerning the army and the museum.'

Daniel could see by the stone-faced and obviously hostile reaction from the RSM that if this information was supposed to impress him, it had failed.

'We're trying to find out this young woman's recent actions, and we've been informed that she called here to make some enquiries last Tuesday,' continued Daniel.

'Her name?' demanded Bulstrode.

'That is something we're still trying to ascertain. She was in her early twenties and with a strong Irish accent. She was here last Tuesday.'

Bulstrode looked at them defiantly.

'You've been misinformed,' he announced. 'There was no such visitor.'

'That's what I told them, sir,' put in the corporal.

'Perhaps she arrived when you were elsewhere on the barracks,' suggested Daniel.

'No, sir. I was here at the barracks all day. And if any visitors arrive I will always be summoned, or advised of their call. No women called here last Tuesday.'

'Perhaps the next day? Wednesday?' put in Abigail.

'No, ma'am,' responded the RSM crisply. 'Nor any day last week.'

'Thank you, Regimental Sergeant Major.' Daniel nodded. 'You've been very helpful.'

With that, he tipped his hat, tapped Abigail gently on the elbow and headed for the bus stop.

'Is that it?' hissed Abigail. 'You're not going to challenge them?'

'Waste of time,' whispered back Daniel. 'They're both lying. We'll get nothing more from them. Nor, I imagine, from their commanding officer, this Brigadier Wentworth. It's only to be expected, I suppose. Despite what Steggles told us about a friendly collaboration, they're suspicious. Barracks are often visited by young women claiming a soldier has made them pregnant and demanding money.'

'This was about something that happened eighty years ago.'

Daniel shrugged. 'Made her grandmother pregnant?'

'So, you're going to leave it at that?'

'No. We find a different way.'

'And that is?'

'I think we're going to need to call on the services of the local newspaper.'

The corporal and RSM Bulstrode watched Daniel and Abigail as they walked away.

'What do you think, sir?' asked the corporal.

'Too smooth,' grunted Bulstrode.

'You don't think they believed us, sir?'

'No,' growled Bulstrode.

He stomped into the barracks and entered the Georgian building that housed the Hussars' headquarters, then made his way down the long corridor to the door marked 'Brigadier Wentworth'. He rapped at the door, and at the command 'Enter!' opened the door, marched in and saluted smartly.

'Begging your pardon, sir.'

'Yes, Sergeant Major. What can I do for you?'

'We've just had two people – a man and a woman – enquiring after a young Irish woman they say called here last Tuesday.'

'A young Irish woman?'

'Yes, sir.'

'Who were these people?'

'The man said he was Daniel Wilson. The woman was an Abigail Fenton. They said Mr Steggles from the Manchester Museum had asked them to look into her recent actions.'

'Were they local?'

'No, sir. He's from London. I recognised him from a few years ago when he had his picture in the papers. He used to be a detective with the Metropolitan police. Part of Inspector Abberline's squad.'

'Abberline? The Jack the Ripper investigation.'

'Yes, sir. The woman was difficult to place. Educated, by her accent. A bit upper class, by her manner.'

'And did they say why they were looking for this Irish woman?'

'No, sir. But two people like that come all the way from London to ask questions about her, it's not just a casual enquiry.'

'No,' said Wentworth thoughtfully. 'What did you tell them?'

'I told them no such person had called here at the barracks, sir.'

'I see. Did they say why they were looking into the recent actions of this Irish woman?'

'No, sir. But I heard reports that such a young woman was found dead at the museum a few days ago.'

'Dead?'

'Stabbed, apparently.'

'I see.'

'It's my feeling that this Daniel Wilson and Miss Fenton will continue their enquiries. It's my opinion that, whatever befell this young woman, we need to keep a distance from being associated with it.'

'Wentworth fell silent, obviously thinking it over, then he said, 'This comes at an awkward time. I'm currently in discussions with Bernard Steggles about the museum mounting an exhibition about the Manchester regiments, and the 15th Hussars at Hulme Barracks will be central to it.'

'Yes, sir, I recall you informing me of it. With respect, sir, I believe it may be wise to keep a distance between the regiment and the museum while the death of the young woman is being investigated. In view of what this Wilson said about reports of her having come here, it wouldn't do for us to be connected with it in any way. For the good name of the regiment, sir.'

'Yes, you may be right,' said Wentworth reluctantly. 'Very unfortunate. Perhaps I'd better write a note to Steggles and let him know.'

'With respect, sir, I wouldn't do that. It might raise questions. Far better to let the matter hover, as one might say. Do nothing. Let it hang in the air. Then, when this is all over, the discussions can resume again.'

'Yes, I suppose that might be best,' said Wentworth. 'Just until this matter is finalised.'

'Yes, sir,' said Bulstrode. 'That would be best.'

Wentworth looked enquiringly at Bulstrode and asked, 'Did she call here? This young woman?'

'No, sir.'

The brigadier nodded. 'That's all I need to know. Thank you, Sergeant Major. If there are any further enquiries on this matter, you may refer them to me.'

CHAPTER SIX

Once again, Daniel and Abigail managed to find seats on the top deck of the bus for their journey back to the city centre.

'Our problem is we have absolutely no information about the dead women at all, except that one seemed poor, had an Irish accent and wanted to find out something to do with the Manchester regiments from eighty years ago,' summed up Daniel. 'The other one . . .' He shook his head. 'No face, so there's little chance of getting any identification. For the moment we'll have more chance if we concentrate on the woman who was stabbed in the reading room. So first we try and discover her identity.'

'To do that, I suggest we use the same method we did with the unknown dead man in Cambridge,' said Abigail. 'We put a photograph of her in the main local paper and ask if anyone recognises her. That would be the *Manchester Guardian*. But first, we need an image of the dead woman.'

'I'm hoping that Mr Steggles will be able to arrange that for us,' said Daniel. He checked his watch. 'We should be back in time to see him before the museum closes.'

Fortunately, Steggles was still in his office, although preparing to leave for the day.

'How have you got on?' he asked.

'Not well,' admitted Daniel. 'The police and the army have both been obstructive.'

'You didn't upset them at the barracks?' asked Steggles, alarmed.

'No, we were nothing but polite, and very discreet,' Daniel assured him. 'Brigadier Wentworth wasn't available, but we met with an RSM Bulstrode, who seemed very protective of the barracks. He suggested I write to the brigadier to make an appointment, which will be our next course of action.'

'Can I ask you wait on that for the moment?' asked Steggles. 'As I said, it's a delicate situation between the museum and the army at the moment . . .'

'Of course,' said Daniel. 'We feel the big problem is that we don't know who these women are. Or were. We need to find that out so we can hopefully get a lead on who might have wanted to kill them. Sadly, only one of them still has a face, so we'd like to put her photograph in the main local newspaper, which I believe is the *Manchester Guardian*.'

'Do you think that will produce anything of value?' asked Steggles doubtfully.

'It's possibly the only course open to us,' Daniel pressed. 'We need someone who can tell us who she was, where she lived, who her acquaintances were, and then maybe we can learn what information she was after. If we find out who she was, it might well lead us to finding out who the other woman was. The one in the cellar.'

'It will have to be done with care,' said Steggles, his tone showing his concern. 'We don't want any mention of the museum in relation to it, otherwise we'll be overrun with ghoulish people coming to gawk at the place where she died. Also, it won't help our reputation with respectable people who we want to come here.'

Daniel nodded. 'Our intention was to take out an advertisement with the photograph of the dead woman asking if anyone recognises her, along with our names, saying that we can be contacted through the newspaper. I assume they operate such a system?'

'Yes,' said Steggles. 'The *Guardian* is fortunately a very respectable newspaper, so I think there'll be no breaking of trust. I know the editor, C. P. Scott, and he is certainly a man of integrity. There's also a reporter there called William Bickerstaff. He came to see me after he learnt about the dead woman. The first one, that is, the one who was stabbed. I don't believe he yet knows about the one that was found this morning. But he seems to be a fair young man.' Then he looked at them uncertainly. 'Although some of his reports in the paper have tended to be of a rather radical nature. I have a feeling Mr Scott keeps a close editorial watch on him to make sure he doesn't overstep the mark. But so far he's honoured my request not to write about the young woman who was killed here, so if you should meet him, it appears he can also be trusted.'

'Thank you,' said Abigail.

Steggles frowned and added thoughtfully, 'On reflection, it might be better to put that you can be contacted at the

Mayflower Hotel, rather than use a box number. It might speed up any information coming forward. I would have suggested the museum as another point of contact, but as we're trying to avoid publicity of any sort . . .'

'Of course, and thank you,' repeated Abigail. 'As for arranging for the young woman to be photographed . . .'

'We have a very good photographer on our staff,' said Steggles. 'Charles Burbage. We keep photographic records of all our exhibits and displays.'

'Would he mind taking a photograph of a dead woman?' asked Abigail.

A small smile played around Steggles's mouth.

'He has taken photographs of corpses before, though they've usually been a few thousand years old. I think he'd be delighted with the challenge. Charles is always in search of new developments in the world of photography.'

'Perhaps we could accompany him?' suggested Daniel. 'I've found it useful to examine the body of a victim when conducting an investigation. Often clues can be found that tell us something about the murderer. And at the same time we can look at the body of the other woman who was found and see if that gives us any clues.'

'Of course,' said Steggles. 'The first body was taken to the infirmary for storage while we ascertained if she had any family who would take charge of the funeral. Otherwise, it will be a pauper's burial. In fact, I was advised by the infirmary that they would need the body to be removed in the next few days. They have a severe lack of space, I believe. The second body was also taken there.'

'In that case, if you can give us a letter of authority in order for us to examine the bodies, and introduce us to your Mr Burbage, we'll go the infirmary without delay.' He looked at the clock.

'Do you think we'll be able to get it done this afternoon, even though it's now late? We've found that the faster information can be gathered, the more chance there is of reaching a conclusion with a case.'

Steggles gave them a smile.

'I think you'll find that time is of little importance to Mr Burbage. He is very keen for any opportunity to practise his craft.'

'I was thinking of time restrictions at the infirmary. Most infirmaries can be very rigid about members of the public, such as visiting hours.'

'I believe that Mr Burbage has cultivated a good relationship with staff at the infirmary,' said Steggles. 'This would be a good time to put that to the test.'

Charles Burbage's eyes lit up with delight when he was told what was required of him. He was a large man in every way, tall and broad; with his enormous bushy beard and unruly mane of dark hair he resembled a wild animal, one whose energy was barely contained in a suit and collar and tie.

'A dead body!' he boomed with relish. 'Someone who doesn't move!'

'The body might slip if it's leaning against something,' cautioned Daniel.

'No leaning for me!' boomed Burbage. 'I'll mount the camera on a base above the dead woman's face and we'll have the luxury of time in exposing the glass plates as I shoot downwards. It's the way I've done it before at the infirmary.' He clapped his hands together gleefully. 'If you arrange a hansom outside, I'll gather together my equipment and meet you there.'

'Don't you want a hand to carry things?' offered Daniel. 'The camera, the glass plates?'

'No need.' Burbage beamed. 'I have designed my very own system of portable cases on wheels. Your assistance in lifting them into the cab would be appreciated, though. Hansom drivers seem reluctant to do anything other than sit on their driving seat and look sullen if you ask them to stir and lend a hand.'

Daniel and Abigail hailed a hansom, which parked outside the front doors of the museum, and soon the bulky figure of Burbage appeared, hauling what looked like a pram loaded with small wooden boxes. Daniel helped him to lift the pram inside the hansom, and then at the command of 'The infirmary, driver!' from Burbage, they were off, rattling over the cobbles.

'Do you know much about the art of photography?' enquired Burbage. Turning to Abigail he said, 'You must do, Miss Fenton. I have seen photographs of various archaeological explorations in Egypt, and I'm sure there was one at Giza in which you featured.'

'It's possible,' admitted Abigail. 'But I was there purely to study the archaeology. I had no proper understanding of how the camera worked, or the later process of developing the pictures that subsequently appeared.'

'You should!' boomed Burbage enthusiastically. 'Art as we have known it – paint on canvas – is dead. The camera can produce the same effect, far more realistically, and much quicker. I doubt if many of the old portraits are true representations of the subject, kings and queens, lords and ladies, military heroes, but a photograph would show that person as they truly were, rather than some sycophant of a painter beautifying some ugly creature. The photograph never lies!'

And with that, Burbage launched into a lecture on the art of photography as the true record of history. 'People as they are! Rich and poor! War as it is fought, not some idealised version of a battlefield. Have you seen any of the photographs from America of their recent tragic civil war? Immense, I tell you! Immense! The suffering is there! The carnage!'

Is there anything worse than being trapped in a hansom cab with someone who is fanatical about their hobby, or who treats their occupation as a cause to be spread? thought Daniel. He looked at Abigail and saw that she felt the same. Both made polite noises at the intervals when Burbage stopped long enough from his lecture to take a breath, though it wouldn't have mattered if they'd made no comments at all; Burbage was a man on a mission to spread the gospel of photography to all and sundry.

When the hansom pulled up outside the infirmary, Daniel helped Burbage unload his equipment.

'If you wait here with it, I'll go in and check that the people I need are on duty,' he said.

With that, he hurried into the hospital.

'If the people he wants aren't here, I assume we'll have to haul the whole lot back again and suffer another lecture on the wonders of photography,' said Daniel gloomily.

'I find it fascinating to hear about the new technologies,' observed Abigail. 'Especially from the people who practise them professionally.'

'I confess that I switched off halfway through the journey,' grunted Daniel. 'He could have been talking about potatoes as far as I was concerned.'

'Actually, he was,' chuckled Abigail. 'Or, rather, vegetables that were misshapen enough to resemble something different. A carrot that looked like a three-legged dog. A potato that looked like Oliver Cromwell.'

Burbage appeared from the infirmary and bounded down the steps.

'Yes, the attendant I'd hoped is on duty in the mortuary. Karl Marston. Wonderful man, and a great student of the art of photography.'

Two of them, groaned Daniel silently. *Still, providing we get a good image of the dead woman, it will have been worth it.*

CHAPTER SEVEN

The mortuary smelt as mortuaries always smelt to Daniel: of decaying flesh mixed with the odour of disinfectant. He noticed a small bowl of vinegar on a table by the entrance, and he dipped his fingers into it and wiped it just below his nostrils, then gestured for Abigail to do the same.

She recoiled as she inhaled the strong of the vinegar.

'It still helps to mask the smell,' murmured Daniel to her.

'I've experienced dead bodies before,' she reminded him primly. 'In Egypt . . .'

'In Egypt I expect it was in the open air. Here, it's enclosed, so there's no movement of air to help dissipate the odour.' He looked at the mortuary table, where the attendant, Karl, had laid a body covered by a white sheet. Neither Karl nor Burbage seemed bothered by the strong smell of decaying flesh. Burbage was already busy, unpacking his cases of photographic equipment.

'The body begins to decay between twenty-four and seventy-two hours after death,' continued Daniel. 'The internal organs start to decompose. Usually, by the end of five days, the body bloats because of the gases being created in the abdomen, and after a week the flesh turns from green to red as the blood decomposes.'

'You certainly know how to sweet-talk a woman,' said Abigail rather acidly.

'Just explaining,' said Daniel. He went to Karl and offered him the letter of authority from Steggles.

'Good afternoon, Mr Marston,' he said. 'My name's Daniel Wilson and this is Abigail Fenton. We're investigators hired by the museum to look into the deaths of the two women found there. We've come to get a photograph of the young lady, and while we're here to look at the other victim. The one without a face.'

'You are a doctor?' asked Karl, after reading the letter and handing it back to Daniel.

'No, but I'm a former detective with the Metropolitan police, so I'm very familiar with examining bodies in mortuaries.' When he saw the wary look the attendant gave to Abigail, Daniel added, 'Miss Fenton is a graduate from Cambridge University, who also has had a great deal of experience with dead bodies. Perhaps we could examine the cadaver while Mr Burbage sets up his equipment. It looks as if it could take him some time, and we really only wish to see the wound that killed her.'

Karl nodded and led the way to the table. Burbage had erected a kind of small chair on the mortuary table, directly above where the head was hidden beneath the sheet. The seat of the chair had a hole in it, and Burbage was putting his bulky camera into place on the chair, with the long lens aimed downwards through the hole.

Karl peeled the sheet away from the dead woman's head, down as far as her shoulders. Once the young woman had been attractive, high cheekbones, long auburn hair, but now her face was absolutely white, mottled green, red and black as her flesh decayed.

'We won't be able to keep her here much longer,' said Karl. 'If she had family who'd paid for an undertaker, she'd have been embalmed. As it is, it looks like she's set for a pauper's grave.'

'That's why we're hoping the photograph Mr Burbage takes of her may lead to us finding out who she is and getting any relatives she may have to come forward.'

'They'd better do it fast,' said Karl. 'Once she starts to fall apart, there won't be much left.'

'May we look at the wound that killed her?' asked Daniel. 'It was through the heart, I believe.'

'I can only show you the exit wound,' said Karl, peeling the sheet down further, exposing the young woman's breasts. 'If I try to turn her over she might start to erupt. All the blood's sunk.'

Her body was indeed death white, and her flesh – like that of her face – beginning to change colour to green and a purplish red, with black spots appearing. Beneath her left breast was the wound like a mouth, the skin puckered and wrinkled around the opening.

'The entry wound in her back was bigger,' said Karl. 'At the front was where the pointed tip came out.'

'It must have been a long-bladed weapon,' said Daniel.

'And about two inches wide, to judge by the entry wound.' Karl nodded.

'Not a usual knife, then,' said Daniel. 'A sword? A bayonet?'

'It would need to be something like that, with a firm and strong blade,' agreed Karl.

'Have you finished examining her?' asked Burbage. 'I'm ready to take the pictures.'

Daniel nodded, and Karl pulled the sheet back up to the woman's shoulders, leaving her face exposed.

Burbage climbed on to a small set of steps he'd brought to enable him to operate the camera poised above the dead woman's head.

'Perhaps while Mr Burbage is taking his photographs, we could view the other body?' asked Daniel.

Karl shot a wary look towards Abigail.

'She's not a pretty sight,' he said cautiously.

'I have seen dead bodies before,' Abigail assured him. 'Including bodies where the flesh has been removed.'

Karl nodded and led them towards another room.

'Those bodies you mention were thousands of years old,' Daniel murmured to Abigail as they followed the attendant. 'This one will be recent. And rotting.'

'I will steel myself,' said Abigail.

When Karl peeled back the sheet from the second body, they saw she was still clothed.

'She only came in this morning,' explained Karl. 'We've got to wait until the doctor arrives before we undress her.'

Daniel saw that, despite her air of confidence, Abigail's mouth tightened at the sight of the damage to the dead woman's head. It was as Arkwright had described; a blade had been used to slice off the skin and the flesh from the forehead down to the chin. With no eyelids or lips, the pair of eyes and the teeth gaped at them grotesquely.

'I've seen enough,' muttered Abigail. 'I'll leave you to take a longer look.'

She headed back to the other room, where Burbage was in the process of taking his photographs. A few moments later, Daniel joined her.

'Not much more to see,' he said. 'A slightly broad-bladed weapon, by the look of it. If it was the same weapon used to kill the other woman, and it seems the most likely, unless there were two killers, then I'd say a sword or a bayonet.'

'Bringing us back to the army,' said Abigail.

'It's just a guess,' said Daniel. 'Though the blade of a sword stick would be easier to conceal if used in a place like the museum.'

'A sword stick,' mused Abigail thoughtfully. 'To all intents and purposes, a simple walking stick, but concealing a long, sharp blade. I met a few men who carried such a weapon on some of the digs I was on in the Middle East. They were mostly ex-military types. And former officers, rather than ordinary soldiers.'

'Yes, that's my experience as well. But we need to be careful about getting fixated on the idea that it is to do with the army. This is just our first day on the case. We don't know it's a military-style blade that was used here. There are plenty of agricultural implements with long blades.'

'Which would be extremely noticeable in a museum surrounding,' pointed out Abigail.

Burbage joined them.

'All done,' he announced. 'We can pack up and go.' He turned to the attendant, and Daniel noticed a flash of silver as the photographer slipped a coin into the mortuary attendant's palm.

'Thank you, Karl,' he said. 'The museum is eternally grateful, as always.'

On their journey back to the museum, Burbage was unusually silent, his face thoughtful.

'A remarkably pretty girl,' he said after a lengthy silence.

'Yes, she was,' said Abigail.

'What makes people do such dreadful things?' asked the photographer, his voice angry.

'That's what we're hoping to find out,' said Daniel. 'Which

is why the photographs you've taken are so important.'

'I'll develop them this evening and get them to you first thing tomorrow morning. May I deliver them to you at your hotel? I assume it's the Mayflower, that's where the museum usually put their guests.'

'Yes, it is, and that would be fine. We'll be able to get an early start on delivering them to the *Manchester Guardian*.'

'Ah, a wonderful publication!' Burbage beamed. 'I do quite a bit of work for them, you know. And the wonderful thing is, they pay on time!'

CHAPTER EIGHT

Daniel and Abigail were at breakfast in the hotel restaurant the following morning when Charles Burbage arrived, beaming proudly and holding a bulky package.

'All done!' he announced, dropping onto a vacant chair at their table. 'And, though I say it myself, the images are excellent!'

He pushed the package across the table to them. Daniel opened it and took out the pictures, which he and Abigail studied.

'You've done a wonderful job,' said Daniel admiringly. 'You've almost made her look as if she's alive.'

'Almost?!' echoed Burbage indignantly.

'You did say the camera never lies,' Abigail reminded him. 'Would you care for some tea or coffee?'

'Indeed, I would!' Burbage beamed. 'And possibly some kippers? The kippers here at the Mayflower are superb!'

The woman at the reception desk of the offices of the *Manchester Guardian* greeted them with a friendly smile.

'Good morning,' she said. 'How can I help you?'

'We'd like to place an advertisement,' said Daniel. 'We're hoping it might be able to get into today's afternoon edition.'

He produced one of the photographs that Burbage had printed and passed it across the desk to the woman, along with the caption to accompany it: *Do you recognise this woman? If so, please contact Daniel Wilson at the Mayflower Hotel.*

The wording had been a major cause of discussion between them.

'If we say contact Daniel Wilson or Abigail Fenton at the Mayflower Hotel, it will raise questions at the hotel where we are registered as Mr and Mrs Wilson.'

'Which we only did to avoid being forced to take two separate rooms because the hotel is so stiff-necked about its so-called standards of morality,' said Abigail indignantly.

'Yes, but if as a result of this someone arrives at the Mayflower and asks to see Miss Abigail Fenton . . .'

'I have already lost my own name in the hotel register, but at least that is a private document and not for public consumption,' said Abigail. 'People at the museum, and in the world of archaeology, know me as Abigail Fenton, not as Abigail Wilson, or Mrs Daniel Wilson.'

'You told Mr Steggles that we are going to be married.'

'But we are not married *yet*,' said Abigail firmly.

In the end, a compromise was achieved. Only Daniel's name would be used for any enquiries at the Mayflower Hotel. 'Because if I'm not there but you are, the hotel staff will be sure to contact you,' said Daniel.

The receptionist studied the photograph thoughtfully, then she said, 'I recognise her.'

'You do?' said Abigail.

'She came in here at the start of last week. She said she wanted to talk to someone about the army here in Manchester. I suggested she talk to one of the reporters.' She frowned, thinking hard, then her face brightened as she said, 'It was Mr Bickerstaff! William Bickerstaff!'

Daniel and Abigail exchanged looks. Bickerstaff was the reporter that Steggles had mentioned to them, and given a clean bill of health to as far as reliability and trust were concerned.

'Did she talk to him?'

'She did indeed,' said the receptionist. 'I sent a message in to him, and he came out and talked to her here in reception.'

'Is it possible to speak to Mr Bickerstaff?' asked Daniel.

'I believe he's here,' said the receptionist. She wrote a brief note on a slip of paper, then called a messenger over. 'Would you take this to Mr Bickerstaff, please?'

The messenger took the slip of paper, nodded, then disappeared through a pair of double doors to one side of the reception desk.

The receptionist gestured at the photograph and the accompanying wording.

'Do you still want to put this in, or do you want to wait until you've seen Mr Bickerstaff?'

'If he's able to identify her for us, the advertisement may not be necessary. But we'll leave it with you, just in case, if that's all right.'

'Of course.'

A young man wearing a tweed jacket over a rumpled shirt appeared through the double doors and looked enquiringly at the receptionist.

'You wanted me, Mrs Parks?'

'You remember that young woman who came in last week?' She offered him the photograph, which he looked at thoughtfully. 'She wanted to find out something about the army.'

Bickerstaff studied the photograph, his brow creased in a thoughtful frown.

'I see so many people,' he said. 'I'm not sure . . .'

'Yes, you do,' said the receptionist. 'A young Irish woman. You remarked on her afterwards, said you wished you could help her.'

Bickerstaff frowned as he studied the photograph more intently, then his face cleared. 'Yes!' he said. 'I remember her now. She wanted to know about the army. I suggested she try the barracks. She said she'd been there and they'd sent her away. I asked her what she wanted to know, but she was evasive. In the end I suggested she try the museum. They have some information about the local army regiments there.'

'Was she local?'

'I don't think so, otherwise she'd have known about the museum. And – as Mrs Parks said – she had an Irish accent, but then so do many people in Manchester.'

'But she knew about the barracks?'

'Everyone knows the barracks. All she had to do was ask.' He looked again at the photograph. 'She's dead, isn't she?'

'Yes, I'm afraid she is.'

'How did she die?'

Daniel and Abigail exchanged hesitant looks, then Daniel said, 'I'm afraid we've been asked to keep that information out of the newspapers for the moment.'

Bickerstaff studied the photograph more intently, then said, 'I'm guessing this is the young woman who was stabbed to death at the museum last Thursday.'

'Stabbed!' came the horrified gasp from the receptionist. 'Murdered?'

'I'm afraid so,' said Abigail.

'Perhaps it might be better if we continue this in a less public area,' suggested Bickerstaff.

'Yes, I agree,' said Daniel. 'Before we do, did she tell you her name? Or anything about herself?'

'No, I'm afraid not,' said Bickerstaff.

'In that case, Mrs Parks,' said Daniel, turning back to the receptionist, 'perhaps you'd proceed with the advertisement.'

'Yes, of course,' said Mrs Parks, still shaken by the revelation but doing her best to regain her composure.

Abigail smiled her thanks at the receptionist, then she and Daniel followed Bickerstaff through the double doors into the depths of the newspaper building. Inside, a very large room was a hive of activity, people at desks – mostly men, Abigail observed – writing feverishly or studying papers and letters. There was a strong smell of ink in the air, and the room echoed with calls and shouts, barked questions and loud retorts for answers.

'What's your interest in this young woman?' asked Bickerstaff.

'We've been asked to look into the case,' explained Daniel. 'We're private enquiry agents . . .'

'Daniel Wilson!' burst out Bickerstaff, with a delighted shout of recognition. 'I knew your face looked familiar! Abberline and the Ripper investigation!' He turned to Abigail and said, 'So you must be Abigail Fenton. Egyptologist and archaeologist extraordinaire!' He chuckled and added, 'We may be at the far reaches of the country, but we do get the stories from the south. The murders at the Ashmolean in Oxford, the Fitzwilliam in Cambridge, and the British Museum. And now here! How wonderful!'

He cast a look around the room and looked at them apologetically.

'I'm afraid a newspaper office is not a place for quiet conversation,' he said ruefully. He gestured towards a nearby door. 'This is our library where we keep our back copies. If you can put up with finding somewhere to sit among the piles of paper in there, it will be quieter.'

They found themselves in a tiny room with the walls packed with shelves containing piles of old newspapers. There was one chair in the room.

'If you'd take the chair, Miss Fenton, Mr Wilson and I will make do with the crates that contain the oldest editions of the paper. The *Guardian* goes back to 1821, you know.' As they settled themselves down, he said, 'As I said, I'm afraid I didn't find out her name, or anything about her.'

'But you knew a young woman had been stabbed to death at the museum,' said Abigail.

'I'm a newspaper reporter,' said Bickerstaff. 'It's my job to keep in touch with what's happening in this city. I was at the police station checking on something else, when someone came in and said there'd been a dead body found at the museum. I tried to go with the police, but they put me off.' He grinned. 'The powers that be at the local police force think we're rabble-rousers stirring up the populace, so they're not exactly helpful to us.'

'We've met Inspector Grimley,' said Daniel. 'He wasn't very helpful to us, either.'

'No, he wouldn't be. He has one style of investigation: find a suspect and use brute force and ignorance on them until they confess.'

'You know that for certain?' asked Daniel.

'Sadly, yes,' said Bickerstaff. 'I've found three cases where an innocent person has been jailed for a crime they didn't commit, and each time Inspector Grimley has been in charge of the investigation.' Hastily, he added, 'Don't get me wrong, there are good police officers here, but the Grimleys of this world are popular with the important people in this city because they protect the status quo. As a result, the authorities turn a blind eye to his methods.'

'But you don't.'

'No. As a result, he doesn't like me or the *Manchester Guardian*.'

'But you found out about the killing, despite them putting you off.'

'Of course. I went to the museum and spoke to one of the attendants there I know. He told me a young woman had been found in the reading room, stabbed to death. I tried to talk to Steggles, he's usually available and very supportive of our stance on social justice, but on this occasion he wasn't available. I tried again the next day, and this time he saw me. I like Steggles. He told me an unknown young woman had been stabbed, but he asked me not to mention anything about it for the moment. I could tell he was worried about the reputation of the museum, so I agreed, on the understanding that when he knew more I could write about it.' He looked again at the photograph. 'So we still don't know who she is.'

'No. We're hoping that putting her photograph in the paper might get us that information.'

'Who's hired you to look into her death?' asked Bickerstaff.

'Not her family, because no one knows who she is. It can only be the museum.'

Daniel and Abigail exchanged uncomfortable looks. *So much for keeping the museum out of it*, he thought wryly.

'At the moment that has to be confidential,' he said.

Bickerstaff grinned. 'Of course,' he chuckled. 'That sounds just the sort of thing that old Steggles might say. Trust me, I'll keep that secret for the moment, even though it's the only obvious answer.' He looked at Daniel and Abigail and asked, 'Do you want me to run a story about her?'

'Thank you, but we'd prefer to put our own advertisement in the paper asking if anyone recognises her,' said Daniel.

'I'd be happy to write the story,' pressed Bickerstaff.

'I'm sure you would, but our client has been very firm about there being no publicity concerning their involvement with this situation. Once we have more information that may change.'

Bickerstaff nodded. 'I understand. So, what are you planning?'

'We're hoping that if anyone recognises her that they'll get in touch with us at our hotel.'

'And if you do find out anything, you'll let me know?' pressed Bickerstaff again.

'We will,' Daniel assured him. 'But after we've spoken first to our client.'

As they left the *Guardian* offices, Daniel said, 'I'm wondering what our next move should be until the paper appears. We have a few hours before we'll get responses, if any.'

'For my part, I'd quite like to go to the museum and look at the Egyptian displays,' said Abigail. 'I haven't had the opportunity before to see the things we brought back from Hawara in a museum setting.'

'Of course!' said Daniel. He took her hand in his and said, 'My love, forgive me for being so single-minded. I should have thought. We'll go and see them together.'

'You don't have to,' she said.

'I want to,' he assured her. 'These aren't just relics of an ancient civilisation, they are such a big part of who you are.'

Walter Arkwright was on duty at the reception entrance, and he saluted smartly when he saw them.

'Might I enquire if there's any progress?' he asked.

'It's that waiting time at the moment, Mr Arkwright,' replied Daniel.

Arkwright nodded. 'You don't need to tell an old soldier about waiting time,' he said wryly. 'That's what most soldiering is. Waiting for orders. Waiting for the attack. More waiting.'

'In the meantime, we're here to look at the Egyptian displays.'

'Of course. Follow me and I'll take you right there.'

As they entered the Egyptian room, Daniel saw Abigail's face light up.

'How wonderful!' she breathed.

Daniel had seen and admired other displays of ancient Egyptian artefacts at the other museums they'd been to, but he could see from Abigail's face as she moved from display case to case how much these exhibits meant to her, bringing back memories of her times in the hot sun of Egypt, uncovering objects that had lain hidden for many thousands of years. He looked at the descriptive labels: *Pyramid at Kahun, 1889*; *The town of Gurob, 1890*; *Pyramid and field at Meydum, 1890–91*; *Town and temples at Amarna, 1891–1892*; and the one that had drawn Abigail especially, *Pyramid, field and cemetery at Hawara, 1888–1889*. Her dig, as part of Flinders Petrie's team, though only Petrie's name appeared in the display, along with that of

Jesse Haworth and Henry Martyn Kennard as the expedition sponsors. Daniel noticed that these same two men had been the sponsors of most of the other expeditions which had brought these ancient artefacts to the museum. As well as a large display of ancient pots inside the glass cases, there was also a label made of wood covered in hieroglyphics in black ink.

'What's that?' asked Daniel, pointing at it.

'It's the label from a mummy,' said Abigail. 'When I found it, it was attached to the mummy by a cord.'

'*You* found it!' said Daniel, impressed.

Abigail nodded. 'The Petrie dig at Hawara was such an event. The pyramid was the tomb of Amenemhet III, a ruler during the Middle Kingdom.'

'When was that?'

'Roughly from 2000 BC to 1500 BC. Amenemhet died in about 1797 BC. Karl Lepsius did the first excavation at the pyramid in 1843, but he never found the way into the actual chamber. By the time I joined his team, Petrie had found the way into the interior of the pyramid. To do that he'd had to navigate two twenty-ton stone trapdoors which concealed entrances to what in effect was a labyrinth. Inside what he – and we – found was truly astonishing. As well as the burial sarcophagi, we discovered papyri from the first and second centuries BC. In addition, just north of the pyramid we uncovered a huge burial ground with 146 coffins, each with a painted portrait on it, all from the Roman era.'

She gestured at the artefacts on display. 'These are just a small part of what we uncovered. Many of the pieces went to the museum at Cairo, and a great number to University College in London.'

'It must have been an incredible time for you,' murmured Daniel.

'It was!' exclaimed Abigail.

'Don't you regret the fact that you're not doing it any more?' he asked.

She took his hand and squeezed it tightly.

'No,' she said. 'That was then, and I will always treasure my memories of my time there. But this is where I want to be now. Doing what we're doing, together.'

CHAPTER NINE

The first result from the appearance of their advertisement in the newspaper came that afternoon. Daniel and Abigail had decided to take up temporary residence in the Mayflower Hotel's tea room. It was there that a porter appeared accompanied by a tall, thin woman wearing a long green coat.

'Mr Wilson, Miss Fenton, this lady says she'd like to speak to you about your advertisement in the newspaper,' said the porter.

'I know who the young woman in the photograph is,' said the woman curtly.

'Please, sit down,' said Daniel, gesturing at an empty chair at their table as the porter left them. 'Mrs . . . ?'

'Eve Preston,' said the woman, her tone as sharp as her appearance. She brandished the copy of the newspaper at them. 'Is there a reward?' she demanded.

'There may be, if your information proves useful,' said Daniel. 'You say you know who she is?'

The woman nodded. She still hadn't smiled. There was a hardness to her that both Daniel and Abigail found uncomfortable. This was an angry woman.

'Her name's Deborah. She's a pickpocket.'

'A pickpocket?'

'That's what I said,' snapped the woman. 'She works with a bloke called Terry Brady.' She tapped the photograph of the young woman in the newspaper. 'She looks dead.'

'I'm afraid she is,' said Abigail. 'Was she a friend of yours?'

The woman glared as if Abigail had insulted her. 'A friend? Of mine? Her? No! She was a cow! She stole Terry from me.' She tapped the photograph again. 'If you ask me, it was Terry who did her in. Her with her nasty ways. He finally got wise to her.'

'Where can we find this Terry Brady?' asked Daniel.

'He's usually at a pub called the Iron Duke in Hulme. Although it wouldn't surprise me to find he's run off once he sees this. He won't want anyone asking questions about this cow once he sees the paper. You'll need to move fast if you want to catch him.'

'Where exactly is the Iron Duke?' asked Daniel.

'Not far from the barracks,' said the woman. 'So, now you know who she is, what about the reward?'

'We'll be able to discuss that once we've spoken to this Terry Brady,' said Daniel. 'But first we have to talk to the authorities here at the museum.'

'I won't be cheated of what's due to me,' snapped the woman.

'I promise you, you won't be,' said Daniel. 'Where can we get hold of you?' he asked as she rose to her feet.

The woman hesitated, then said, 'I'll come to you. Are you going after him today?'

'We'll certainly aim to,' said Daniel.

'Then I'll call here tomorrow morning,' said the woman. 'Terry Brady is who you want. A thin, short bloke with a face like a weasel. Scar down the left side of his face. Wears a brown tweed suit. Usually got a white scarf round his neck as well. Say the word "Deborah" to him and see how he reacts. The Iron Duke in Hulme.' She gave them a brisk nod. 'I'll see you tomorrow.'

Abigail and Daniel exchanged looks as the woman departed.

'What do you think?' asked Abigail.

'It's the only lead we've got,' commented Daniel.

Abigail suddenly spotted something behind Daniel and murmured, 'It looks like we may have another.'

Daniel turned, and saw a short, elderly man wearing a long black robe at the reception desk as he looked in their direction, following the pointing finger of the receptionist.

'It's a priest,' said Abigail, noticing the white clerical collar as the short man walked towards them.

'Hopefully he's divine intervention arriving with answers,' muttered Daniel.

Abigail and Daniel stood up as the priest arrived by them.

'Mr Daniel Wilson?' he asked in a soft Irish accent.

'I'm Daniel Wilson, and this is my detective partner, Miss Abigail Fenton.'

The priest took the hands they offered and shook them.

'Father Paul O'Brien,' he introduced himself. He took the newspaper with the photograph of the young woman from his pocket and held it out to them. 'She's dead, isn't she? From the photograph.'

'Sadly, she is.'

'How did she die?'

'She was stabbed.'

'Was she one of your parishioners?' asked Abigail.

'If it is her, she was, but only this last week.'

'Was her name Deborah?'

The priest shook his head. 'No. It was Kathleen Donlan. She'd not long arrived from Ireland, which was why I describe her as only a very recent parishioner. She was staying with a cousin of hers, Mrs Eileen O'Donnell.'

Daniel shot a look at Abigail to say: *So, we have two very different identifications. Which is it? Deborah or Kathleen?* He turned to the priest.

'How sure of this are you, Father? That she's Kathleen Donlan. The reason I ask is because just a few moments ago we had someone else arrive who identified her as a woman called Deborah.'

'I'm fairly sure, though I agree that sometimes photographs can be misleading. Where is the body at the moment?'

'In the infirmary.'

'As you have a photograph I assume you have permission to get access to her,' said O'Brien. 'Can I suggest you take me to the infirmary and I can give you a proper identification if it is Kathleen.' He gave a wry smile. 'I doubt if the infirmary will object to my presence. One of the blessings of being a priest.'

Karl was on duty when they arrived at the hospital mortuary, and when Daniel and Abigail saw the almost obsequious way he greeted Father O'Brien, they realised the elderly priest was right about being a priest giving him entry to many places where officialdom might otherwise be obstructive. *Especially when the officials are Catholic*, thought Daniel. Which he suspected to be the case with Karl.

O'Brien looked down at the face of the young woman and nodded, his voice sad.

'It's Kathleen Donlan, right enough,' he said.

'You're sure?' asked Daniel.

'I am. She came to morning Mass for three days, one after the other, along with her cousin, Eileen. The first on Tuesday, then the next day, and the last was Thursday.'

'The day she was killed,' said Daniel.

'Which part of Ireland was Kathleen from?' asked Abigail.

'From her accent, I'd say Cork. To be specific, north Cork.' He smiled. 'Being a priest here with such a big Irish congregation you get to know accents. Eileen O'Donnell was from Mallow, so north Cork is more than an educated guess. Do you know Ireland?'

'I've had friends who've visited, but I've never been there myself,' said Abigail. 'They say it's a beautiful country.'

'Beautiful, and empty. We lost millions during the famine, some to their graves, more to America and England.'

'Would it be possible for you to let us have Mrs O'Donnell's address?' asked Daniel. 'We'd like to talk to her about Kathleen, see if she can throw any light on what she was looking for at the museum.'

'It would be better if I took you there,' said O'Brien. 'Ancoats can be quite a . . . a rough area. People who know it tend to avoid it, unless they live there.'

'Strangers are at risk?' suggested Daniel.

'They can be. Especially if they look like they might have some money about them.'

'I wouldn't have thought we looked particularly wealthy,' mused Abigail.

'You have shoes,' said O'Brien. 'That makes you look like you have money.'

'We have areas like that in London as well,' Daniel said. 'We'd be grateful for your assistance.'

'It'll be my pleasure,' said O'Brien. 'Young Kathleen seemed like a nice young girl. No one deserves to die, but to have her young life cut short in that way . . .' He shook his head. 'If I can help find the villain who did it, it will help bring some peace to her poor family. Also, I was thinking of calling on Eileen anyway, for pastoral reasons. She hasn't been to church for a few days now, which isn't like her. Especially missing Sunday Mass. That's the first time I've ever known that happen. I was guessing there might be trouble at home.' He gestured at the body of Kathleen. 'This could be the reason, her going missing suddenly.' He looked at Daniel and Abigail. 'Where was she killed?'

Both Daniel and Abigail hesitated. Yes, they were dealing with a priest, but Steggles had stressed he wanted the museum kept out of the picture.

'In the museum, Father.'

It was Karl who spoke, and both Abigail and Daniel looked at him sharply, but he responded with a look of defiance. *To a Catholic, the priest always has dominance over anyone else*, thought Daniel.

Daniel nodded. 'Yes, she was killed in the reading room at the museum, but we've been asked to keep that out of public knowledge, for the moment.'

'I can understand their reluctance to be associated with such a terrible event,' said O'Brien sympathetically.

'Actually, Father, there may be something else you can help us with,' said Daniel, feeling that they might as well go for broke, and the priest seemed like someone who would respond positively to requests for keeping things to himself after all his years in the confessional. 'Another woman was killed in the museum, and we believe it was on the same day. We'd be most grateful if you'd take a look at her and see if you can give us any clues as to who she might be.'

77

'It's not a pretty sight,' interjected Karl suddenly.

'Death rarely is, my son,' said the priest. 'Of course I will. I assume she's here.'

'In the other room,' said Daniel. He looked at Karl. 'I trust that will be acceptable?'

'If the father wishes it,' said Karl, but his disapproving tone showed he didn't like it.

Karl led the way into the other room, and the body covered with a sheet.

'We must prepare you for something very, very unpleasant, Father,' said Abigail. 'Her face has been badly mutilated.'

'Thank you,' said O'Brien. He looked at Karl and nodded, and the mortuary attendant turned back the top of the sheet. As the horror that had once been the dead woman's face was revealed, the elderly priest visibly recoiled.

'Holy Mother of God! What monster would do such a thing?'

'That's what we're hoping to find out. We know it's impossible for anyone to identify her as she is, but is there anything about her that strikes you as familiar? I ask because she was also killed at the museum, so we're guessing there could be a connection between the two women.'

O'Brien studied the body and nodded.

'Indeed, I think you may well be right.' He turned to Karl. 'Is she clothed?'

'She is, Father.'

'Then let us see her. There may be something in her clothing that will give us a clue.'

Karl slowly removed the sheet and O'Brien studied the clothes of the dead woman, the wedding band on her finger, a decorative bracelet and a necklace that still hung around her neck.

'It's Eileen O'Donnell. The cousin Kathleen was staying

with.' He gave a heavy sigh. 'Poor Eileen. And poor Kathleen. I have to go to the O'Donnells' and give them the bad news.'

'Would it be inappropriate for us to accompany you?' asked Daniel. 'They may have information that could lead us to whoever's done this, and the sooner we can get hold of something, the sooner we can catch them.'

O'Brien looked down at the mutilated body of Eileen O'Donnell. 'Ordinarily I'd ask for them to be given some space, but in this case, I feel you're right,' he said. 'We need to bring this monster to justice.'

CHAPTER TEN

Their journey on foot through Ancoats was made slower by the amount of people who stopped to greet Father O'Brien, and although it was the cloth that people genuflected to, Abigail also sensed a real feeling of love and respect towards the elderly Irish priest among the people they met. O'Brien didn't try and hurry people along; he stopped and listened patiently to the worries and fears they expressed, and always ended by giving them a blessing. As she watched the women – and they were mostly women – move off after their conversations with the priest, smiles on their faces, she reflected that the encounter may not do much for their pockets, but it seemed to give them an emotional lift to their spirits. There was something else that Daniel had observed, which he commented on.

'I got the impression that this area was where the Irish immigrants came to, but most of the people you've talked to have been Italian; and many of the signs above the shops are in Italian.'

'That is true,' said O'Brien. 'In fact, Ancoats is known locally as Little Italy. Hulme, meanwhile, is known as Little Ireland. But poverty and the struggle to survive knows no national boundaries. In every district, and it's the poor districts I'm talking about, you will find people of all nationalities, mainly immigrants, because housing is cheap, and surviving is all about making the money last. So, here in Ancoats, yes, there is a very large Italian population. Most of them came from the rural areas of Italy, shortly after the immigrants from Ireland came here. And for similar reasons.'

'There was famine in Italy?' asked Abigail.

'If a harvest fails, there is famine,' said O'Brien. 'It may not have been on the same scale as the famine in Ireland, but it meant hunger and people being pushed off their land because they couldn't pay their rents. Stories about the money to be made here in Manchester at the cotton mills were heard as far away as Italy, and so they came. At the moment, Ancoats is roughly half and half: half-Irish, half-Italian.'

'And there's no trouble between the two communities?'

'Only now and then,' said O'Brien. He gave wry smile. 'And it's usually the result of too much drink being taken. It's the way of the world. But they all come to worship at St Michael's, and I like to think it gives them a mutual feeling of community.'

He gestured towards a large building made of grey brick they were approaching. Although it looked fairly modern, the doors and windows retained the traditional pointed surrounds seen in Norman churches.

'This is my church, St Michael's,' he told them. 'I've brought you this way so you can see where it is. If you need me for anything, this is the best place to find me. The church is always open. If I'm not there, leave a note in the box and I'll call on you.'

'I expected something older,' commented Daniel. 'Most churches seem old.'

'This one was built in 1858,' said O'Brien. 'Before the mills came, most of this area was fields.'

'I'm not sure we'd be able to find it easily on our own,' said Abigail. 'Ancoats is a bit of a warren.'

'We're in George Leigh Street,' said O'Brien. 'Or, even better, just tell anyone that you're looking for Father O'Brien at St Michael's.'

He set off again, heading through the narrow streets, and now Daniel noticed that the shop signs began to change, the names above the shops now showing Irish rather than Italian names, and also goods. There was also a sourer and stronger smell.

'The middens,' said O'Brien, noticing both Daniel and Abigail wrinkling their noses. 'The only form of sanitation there is, open cesspits, one at the end of each street. Those of us who live here have got used to the smell, but it's one of the first things visitors notice.'

'What sort of household is the O'Donnells'?' asked Abigail, as they walked.

'Eileen was the backbone, the one who held the family together,' replied O'Brien. 'Her husband, Patrick, is a good man, but inclined to take drink when he shouldn't. He works at the mill, as do most of the people around here, and a few times lately he's been sent home because he was the worse for wear. No work means no money. Fortunately, most of the children work, the older ones anyhow, so there's still some money coming in.'

'How many children are there?' asked Daniel.

'Ten. Five boys, five girls. The youngest is just seven months, baby Sean. The eldest is Breda, she's sixteen. Then there's John, fourteen. Peter, thirteen. The twins, Marie and Molly, eleven. Kieran is nine. Oona is eight, Thomas six and Margaret three.'

'You have an amazing memory if you remember all your parishioners like that,' said Daniel admiringly.

'Only some of them,' admitted O'Brien. 'In the O'Donnells' case it's because of Eileen. Until this happened, she's been a regular at Mass, and has such faith and the best heart you could ever find, despite all her troubles.'

'Troubles?' asked Daniel. 'What sort of troubles?'

'I would think ten children, a husband who drinks, and living squashed together in a tiny back-to-back in Ancoats is enough trouble for anyone, wouldn't you?' The priest slowed his pace and murmured, 'Here we are.'

An unkempt man was sitting slumped on a wooden chair outside a house. His face and clothes were grimy and he seemed to be in a kind of daze.

'Not at work today, Patrick?' asked Father O'Brien.

Patrick O'Donnell jerked his face towards them, tears filling the man's eyes.

'They sent me home, the bastards!' he burst out. 'Told me I was too drunk to work! Too drunk! All I'd had was a little sip to calm me nerves because I was worried about Eileen.' He began to sob. 'Where is she? That's all I need to know! Five days now, and no sign of her!'

'Are the children at home?' asked the priest.

'Some are. Some are at work,' said O'Donnell. Then he gave a moan and shouted in anguish, 'Where's Eileen?'

'I need to talk to you and the children.'

A small girl appeared from inside the house, a baby held in her arms.

'I heard your voice, Father,' she said, and Daniel and Abigail

83

could see the pain and misery on her face. 'Do you have news of Ma?'

'I do, Oona,' said O'Brien. 'Who else is at home today?'

'Molly, Marie and Kieran, and Thomas and Margaret,' said the small girl. 'The others are at work.'

Abigail whispered to Daniel, 'This is no place for us, Daniel. Not today. It's only the youngest who are here now, and their poor father, who doesn't look in a fit state to answer any questions. They'll need to cope with their grief. This isn't the place for us.'

Daniel nodded. 'You're right,' he said.

'Father!' called Abigail, moving towards the small priest. He turned towards her, and she said: 'Today is not the right time for us to be here. We thought it would be, but it isn't. With your permission, we'll come again another day. Will tomorrow be acceptable?'

'Tomorrow will be better,' said O'Brien. 'The older ones will be here, Breda, John and Peter. They'll be the best ones for answers. If you call for me at my church first, I'll come with you to introduce you. Otherwise they'll be wondering what an educated couple like yourselves is doing here, and wonder in Ancoats makes people suspicious.'

'So they won't talk to us?'

'They'll talk to you if I tell them it's all right.'

'Thank you,' said Abigail. 'And our apology for getting it wrong today.'

'The fact you say that shows you have good hearts,' said the priest. 'Bless you for that.' He turned to Oona. 'Come on, Oona, let's go inside.' He took hold of Patrick O'Donnell's arm and hoisted him up from the chair, showing surprising strength from the small and frail-looking man. 'And yourself, Patrick. I have something to tell you which is better said indoors.'

The priest led Patrick inside the house, with tiny Oona trailing after them, and closed the door.

'It's my fault,' said Daniel apologetically as he and Abigail turned and walked away. 'I was too eager to get some answers. You were right, this was totally the wrong time.'

CHAPTER ELEVEN

As they made their way through the winding narrow streets, Abigail said, 'I get the impression Ancoats is a rough area and we're strangers here. Are we safe?'

'We would have been seen on our way to the O'Donnells' walking through the area accompanied by Father O'Brien. That's our passage,' Daniel said.

'Because we walked along with a priest?'

'This is a very Catholic area,' said Daniel. 'Irish and Italians. An attack on us would bring down the wrath of the priest, which is greater than the wrath of God to these people. Not so much as far as the men are concerned, but it is to the women. And they're the ones who rule the families.'

'Not the drunken brutes of husbands who beat them up? I've heard stories about Irish and Italian men.'

'Take them with a pinch of salt. Trust me, it's the women who run things in these communities. That's why Patrick O'Donnell is so bereft. He doesn't know what to do. Father O'Brien was being astute when he said that the oldest girl, Breda, is a second mother. I bet you even young Oona, at eight years old, is more capable than her father.'

'They have a hard life,' said Abigail. 'Five in a bed.'

'I can show you communities in London not far from our own house in Camden Town where living standards are exactly the same,' said Daniel.

'What are we going to do about Eve Preston?' asked Abigail. 'And her claim that the dead woman was a pickpocket called Deborah.'

'She said she'd call on us at the hotel tomorrow morning,' said Daniel. 'If she does, we'll tell her we've had a different identification. And by the dead woman's parish priest. I doubt if she'll argue with that.'

'And if she doesn't turn up?'

'Then I suspect she either found out she was wrong, or she lied to us to try and get this Terry Brady character in trouble.'

'You don't think we ought to go and look for her to tell her what we've learnt?'

'We don't know where to find her,' Daniel pointed out.

'She mentioned the Iron Duke pub,' said Abigail.

'If we go there and say we're looking for an Eve Preston, it might cause trouble for her. I may be wrong, but I'm guessing it's not the most salubrious of drinking establishments.'

'So we do nothing?'

'We'll leave a message at the hotel reception that if she arrives and asks for us, and we're not there, for her to leave an address where we can get hold of her. Honestly, I think that's the best we can do. My gut feeling is that we won't see her again. I still feel she only came to get this Brady in bother.'

'Why would she do that?' asked Abigail.

'Because part of what she told us may well be true: that this Deborah had stolen Terry Brady from her. My guess is she wanted to have her own back on Mr Brady for leaving her.'

'By having him charged with murder? And of someone she didn't know?'

'And who no one else knew. She would have gleaned that much from the fact that our advertisement asked if anyone recognised her.'

'But he might have been hanged!'

'Not necessarily. He'd be able to produce the real Deborah, if she exists. And there'd have to be a trial first,' pointed out Daniel. 'At least we've moved forward. We now know who both women are. We also know Kathleen wanted to find out something to do with the army. And she was stabbed with what could have been a military-type blade, the same blade being used to mutilate Eileen O'Donnell.'

'But you said yourself, the blade that killed her may have nothing at all to do with the military,' said Abigail.

'The RSM we spoke to at the barracks lied about Kathleen going there,' said Daniel. 'And she was only here for a few days before she was murdered, and the only places she went to in that short time were the barracks and the museum. Everything so far suggests her death is connected with the army, in some way. And the fact that both women were killed shows this was no random attack. They were targeted. I think our next move is to return to the museum and report what we've found out to Mr Steggles.'

'Do you mind if we go to the hotel first?' asked Abigail. 'I could really do with a cup of tea.'

'There'll be tea at the museum,' said Daniel. 'And possibly biscuits.'

'The hotel first,' said Abigail firmly. 'After our experience at the O'Donnells', I just need to take a break from it for a moment.'

CHAPTER TWELVE

As they entered the lobby of their hotel, they were confronted by the excited figure of William Bickerstaff pacing around. When he saw them he hurried over. 'I've been waiting for you for ages!' he burst out. 'So the bodies have been identified!' When he saw the suspicious look Daniel and Abigail gave one another, he said, almost smugly, 'A good reporter cultivates important connections.'

'Like Karl, the mortuary attendant at the infirmary,' said Daniel.

'Amongst others,' said Bickerstaff. He gave a satisfied grin. 'Kathleen Donlan, who was staying with Mrs Eileen O'Donnell. The proof the two murders are connected. Now we know there's a link between the two women, I'm going to Newton Street and see what Inspector Grimley says about it. See if he still insists there's nothing to investigate. Would you like to come with me? You might be able to discern something useful from the way he responds.'

'It looks as if we'll have to postpone that cup of tea,' murmured Daniel to Abigail as they followed Bickerstaff out of the hotel.

As they walked to Newton Street police station, Bickerstaff plied them with questions, eager to find out what information they might have learnt, but Daniel and Abigail did their best to remain non-committal.

Apart from a uniformed sergeant on duty at the desk, the reception area was empty when they arrived at the police station.

'Is Inspector Grimley available?' demanded Bickerstaff.

'Who wants to see him?' enquired the sergeant.

'William Bickerstaff from the *Manchester Guardian*. And Mr Daniel Wilson and Miss Abigail Fenton.'

'Wait here,' grunted the sergeant.

He disappeared through a door at the back, reappearing a moment later.

'The inspector will be with you,' he said.

'In his office?' asked Bickerstaff.

'He said he'll see you here.'

'But we have important information,' said Bickerstaff. 'It would be better if we were to see him away from where the public can hear.'

The sergeant looked around the otherwise empty reception area.

'You're the only public here,' he pointed out. With that, he returned to leafing through some papers on his desk.

'Typical!' snorted Bickerstaff to Abigail and Daniel. 'He's doing this because he doesn't like me. If anyone else was in here they could pick up this latest information and go to one of the *Guardian*'s rivals with it! I'm aiming for an exclusive!'

They waited, watching the clock. In the time they waited, no one else came in from the street. After ten minutes Inspector Grimley appeared, accompanied by a uniformed sergeant.

'Sergeant Merton,' muttered Bickerstaff darkly to Daniel and Abigail.

'All right, Bickerstaff, what do you want?' demanded the inspector aggressively.

'We've got information regarding the double murder,' said Bickerstaff. 'The young Irish woman who was stabbed to death at the museum, and the woman whose body was found in the museum cellar. The young woman who was stabbed was called . . .' He stopped as he realised he'd forgotten her name, and turned to Daniel and Abigail.

'Kathleen Donlan,' said Abigail. 'She was staying with the woman whose face was sliced off: Mrs Eileen O'Donnell.'

'See, Inspector!' said Bickerstaff triumphantly. 'Two women from the same address murdered at the same place and possibly on the same day! Now you've got their names, surely you have to investigate.'

Grimley glared at them, an unfriendly scowl on his face. 'All right, you've brought me this new information. It's noted, and we'll look into it.'

'And that's all?' asked Bickerstaff.

'I'll tell you what I told these two before: with a case like this there's little or no chance at getting to the bottom of it, not with the resources we've got. If either of them was someone important, there might be time to dig into it. But they were both nobodies, by all accounts.'

'Can I quote you on that, Inspector?' snapped Bickerstaff angrily. '"We're not going to bother investigating her murder because neither was of any importance. We only investigate crimes against important people."'

'Ah, now we have it!' growled Grimley. 'That's what all this is about. You stirring things up against the police and the people who run this city, trying to get the rabble to rise up. That's what you want, isn't it! Bricks thrown through our windows. Agitating the mob against the mill owners.' Then a sarcastic leer crossed his face as he added, 'But then, maybe you're doing that to divert attention from what really happened.'

'What do you mean?' demanded Bickerstaff.

'You know what I mean,' sneered Grimley. 'We know about you and lower-class women. Hanging around them, trying to get off with 'em. Was that what happened here? Did one of 'em finally get sick of you pestering her and tell you off for the sick worm you are? Was that it? So you taught her a lesson, showed her she couldn't do that to you and stuck a knife in her back. And then you bumped off the other one because she happened to see you do it.'

'How dare you!' snarled Bickerstaff, moving menacingly forward towards the inspector.

Grimley smiled. 'Come on,' he invited the reporter. 'Lay a finger on me and I'll have you inside for assaulting a police officer.' He gestured towards Daniel and Abigail. 'And I've got witnesses. Independent witnesses, so you can try and twist things as much as you like, but you'll be inside.' He gave a menacing leer at Bickerstaff as he added threateningly, 'In my jail.' And he smacked his right fist pointedly into the palm of his hand.

Bickerstaff hesitated, then thrust a finger towards Grimley's face.

'You haven't heard the last of this, Inspector,' he promised.

With that, he turned on his heel and left.

Grimley turned and gave Daniel and Abigail a broad smile.

'Reckon I touched a nerve there, wouldn't you say?' he chuckled. He shook his head, still smiling. 'My constables know what goes on with him. If you're such a good detective, Wilson, ask around about your friend Bickerstaff. It might put a different dimension on things.' He turned to his sergeant. 'Come on, Merton. Back to the office so we can get on with some real work.'

CHAPTER THIRTEEN

Bickerstaff was waiting for Daniel and Abigail outside the station. By the way he paced agitatedly around he was obviously angry.

'What else did Grimley say?' he demanded.

'Nothing much,' said Daniel.

'It's all nonsense!' said Bickerstaff. 'Just because I do my best to offer my help to those poor, unfortunate women, as I do with everyone in that dreadful situation, the police spread gossip and slander about me.' He scowled. 'Well, this time Inspector Grimley has gone too far. He needs to be shamed into investigating these murders properly. In fact, he needs to be shamed, full stop.' He hesitated, then said, 'I didn't tell you this before because we've been keeping a lid on it, and I didn't know you well enough.'

'We?'

'My editor at the *Guardian* and me. As I said before, there are good officers on the Manchester police, but there are also rotten apples.'

'Inspector Grimley?'

'He's one, along with a coterie of some uniformed officers. Anyway, at the *Guardian* we're planning an exposé of the rotten apples in the hope it gets rid of them. To be honest, I wasn't sure where you'd stand on that, as an ex-police inspector yourself.'

Daniel regarded the reporter coldly. 'In my view, there's no room for those sort of people in the police force.'

'But you had them in the Met,' said Bickerstaff. 'I remember the reports in the London papers about four years ago.'

'I can assure you we had no such people in Abberline's crowd,' said Daniel firmly. 'Admittedly, there were some dubious officers in the Met. There always will be in any organisation. You scratch my back and I'll scratch yours. Money speaks. All the clichés come from somewhere. But it's usually just a small proportion.'

'Which can be tolerated?' suggested Bickerstaff.

'Providing they don't draw attention to themselves,' said Daniel. 'But, as I say, even *one* such person would have been too many for my old guv'nor. Fred Abberline ran the cleanest ship ever.'

'And I believe that's true of most of the Manchester force,' said Bickerstaff. 'The trouble is the rotten apples here lean on the poorest people, the most vulnerable, while the real crooks get off scot free.'

'Who do you mean by the real crooks?'

'The ones who run prostitution. Extortion. Large-scale robberies. But many of them are untouchable because they're paying off the local police officer.'

'And you're suggesting that Grimley . . .'

'I can't pin it down that high,' admitted Bickerstaff. 'The stories

I've got involve constables, sergeants, all uniforms, all operating in the poorer areas of the city. But one sergeant who's been mentioned has a link with Grimley. Sergeant Merton, the one you saw with him today.'

'What about the senior officers?' asked Daniel. 'Surely they're aware of what's going on?'

'I'm sure they are,' said Bickerstaff. 'Superintendent Mossop, for one, seems honest. The trouble is the watch committee and the board that run the police are dominated by some very rich people, including some of the mill owners, and they find it useful to have certain police officers in their pocket to stop what they term "sedition and industrial sabotage".'

'Is there much of that going on in the mills here?'

Bickerstaff looked at them thoughtfully. 'How much do you know about Manchester as a cotton town?' he asked.

'Not a great deal, to be honest,' admitted Daniel.

He looked at Abigail, who gave a rueful look. 'It's not something I've ever thought about,' she said.

'Most people in the south don't,' said Bickerstaff. 'They wear the clothing made here, but they don't think about how it's made, or the people who make it.

'Cotton rules Manchester. Not just Manchester, the surrounding towns as well. This area was known as Cottonopolis. The world's first ever steam-driven textile mill was here, in Miller Street. And that opened the floodgates. Now there are hundreds of such mills.'

'The main employer,' observed Abigail.

'But on the mill owners' terms. They use the smallest children to crawl under the machines, while they're still working, to gather up the loose cotton.'

'It sounds dangerous work.'

'Is it. Many die when they get caught up in the machines. Those that don't end up with their bodies wrecked from having to keep crouched so low. Their lungs get ruined.'

'I'm not sure how this relates to the murders of two women,' said Daniel carefully.

'Because they came from Ancoats, which is the death black spot of Manchester. It's got the highest death rate in the city, much of it connected to the mills, and that makes people angry.'

'You're suggesting that they were killed because they were seen as a threat to the mill owners?' asked Abigail, bewildered.

Bickerstaff let out an unhappy groan, then shook his head. 'No,' he admitted. Then added, 'I don't know.'

'Is there a great deal of radical politics in Manchester?' asked Daniel.

Bickerstaff gave a derisive snort. 'Considering the conditions the mill workers live under, I'm surprised there hasn't been a revolution here. People rising up and attacking the machines and the mills and demanding fair pay and better conditions.' Abruptly he stopped and forced a false smile. 'I think we're getting off the subject of the murders. As I said before, Superintendent Mossop's hands are tied. Although he does what he can.'

'Which doesn't sound much,' commented Daniel sourly.

'I'm sure if he had some solid ammunition he'd be able to start to weed the rotten apples out. The problem I've got is that no one is willing to talk, or name names, for fear of reprisals. And without concrete evidence I can't go into print. It wouldn't surprise me to find that Grimley takes his cut from the pay-offs Merton and the constables pick up. At the moment all I can do is lean on Grimley when I can, put pressure on him. Which is where the idea of shaming him in the pages of the *Guardian* over these murders comes in. It lets him know he's being watched.'

'I think, from what he said, he's already got that idea,' said Abigail.

'What I'd like to do is go and see Mr Steggles at the museum and tell him I'm going to run a piece about the murder of Kathleen Donlan and Eileen O'Donnell and demand why the police refuse to investigate. I'd like to mention that you two are involved. There's a chance it may help your enquiries.'

Daniel looked doubtful. 'I don't know if he'd agree to that. Yes, the museum is our client, that much is obvious. But Mr Steggles has stressed to us how important it is that the museum doesn't get attached to any sort of scandal.'

'There wouldn't be any scandal the way I'd write it,' persisted Bickerstaff. 'And you're not getting very far. Yes, you now know who the dead women are, and that was the result of the piece appearing in the paper. The more information that we can put out – done with discretion, I promise you – the bigger the chance you have of getting some crucial evidence coming to you.'

Daniel looked at Abigail, who gave a slight nod of approval. *Yes*, thought Daniel, *it makes sense*. But first they'd have to persuade Steggles it could be done without harming the museum's reputation.

'We'll talk to Mr Steggles and see what he says.' He looked at his watch. 'It's possible he may still be at the museum. If he is, we'll talk to him now, and then come and find you at the *Guardian* offices.'

They watched as the reporter nodded in agreement and hurried off, then they set off towards the museum.

'What did you think of what Bickerstaff said about the possibility of a radical connection?'

'I think it highly unlikely,' said Abigail. 'Eileen O'Donnell had enough to deal with looking after her family. And Kathleen had only been in Manchester a few days, so there was no time for her to become involved in anything. I think far more interesting are the allegations Inspector Grimley made about Mr Bickerstaff and women.'

'What's your opinion?' asked Daniel. 'Do you get any feeling from him about his attitude towards women?'

'He's been perfectly courteous to me,' said Abigail.

'The inspector specified lower-class women,' Daniel pointed out. 'If that's the case, then I doubt if you qualify.'

Abigail let this register, then said thoughtfully, 'I suppose it's a possibility.'

'If so, could he have killed Kathleen because she refused him?' asked Daniel.

'It depends on how she refused him,' said Abigail. 'I've known of many men, educated men, who feel inadequate around women of their own class and so they prey on women lower down the social scale.'

'It sounds similar to where our investigations into Jack the Ripper were leading us,' said Daniel. 'Upper-class men who took revenge on the whole female sex for some imagined slight.' He frowned. 'But if he's the guilty one, why would he press Inspector Grimley to go on with the investigation rather than disregard it?'

'Pride,' said Abigail. 'He wants to prove he's more intelligent than the police. He's frustrated because they're ignoring him.'

'That's quite complex,' said Daniel.

'Too complex?' asked Abigail.

'No,' said Daniel. 'In its way, it makes perfect sense. We might need to look into Mr Bickerstaff a bit more closely.'

CHAPTER FOURTEEN

Steggles studied them from across his desk.

'You believe that the deaths of these two women are connected?' he asked.

'We do,' said Daniel. 'Kathleen was staying with Eileen O'Donnell in Ancoats. We believe both women were killed here on the Thursday.'

'But you feel that Inspector Grimley is not going to investigate.'

'Which is why Mr Bickerstaff has suggested an article about the murders in the newspaper might bring forward information which would lead to uncovering the motive for their murders and the reveal of their murderer,' said Abigail.

'We've found in the past that reports in a newspaper can be of enormous assistance,' added Daniel. 'Providing the reporter works with us, that is.'

Steggles weighed this up, his expression showing his concern.

'We want this mystery solved, that's why we brought you in. But I'm concerned about the tone of the story Mr Bickerstaff will write. He tends to produce rather purple prose in support of the radical cause. I don't want his report to suggest that the museum is in any way advocating a particular political stance. Our aim is for the widest possible social groupings to use this museum, for it to benefit society as a whole, not just be favoured by narrow sections.'

'We will certainly stress that to Mr Bickerstaff,' said Abigail.

'In fact, I'd suggest that he lets you see the article he writes for approval before it goes into print,' added Daniel.

Steggles looked thoughtful, then he asked, 'You believe making this story public in this way will lead to a successful conclusion?'

'There's no guarantee,' admitted Daniel, 'but it could very well be read by someone who's unaware that the information they may have could be vital in us finding out *why* the women were killed. Once we know that, finding out *who* becomes much easier.'

'Very well,' said Steggles. 'You may tell Mr Bickerstaff to write his article.'

'And for him to bring it to you for approval?' asked Abigail.

Steggles looked uncomfortable. 'To be honest, although I believe Mr Bickerstaff to be sincere, I also find him to be an overwhelming young man. I feel he is about to lecture me at length whenever we meet. I'd prefer it if he gave the article to you for you to bring it to me.'

'That's no problem,' said Daniel. He smiled. 'We have also been at the end of Mr Bickerstaff's views. There is one other thing.'

'Oh?'

'On the Thursday when the women were killed, do you know if anyone reported seeing anyone military in the museum?'

'Military?' Steggles frowned. 'A soldier?'

'A soldier or perhaps an officer,' said Daniel.

Steggles shook his head. 'Not to my knowledge. Though I'm in my office most of the time. Mr Hawkins or Mr Arkwright or one of the attendants would be more likely to tell you if anyone in uniform was here.' Then he gave a frown and said, 'Actually, one high-ranking officer was supposed to be here that day. I had an appointment with Brigadier Wentworth for that morning to discuss the army exhibition we're planning, but on the day he sent a note offering his apologies. He'd been called elsewhere at short notice.'

'Who delivered the note?' asked Daniel.

'I don't know,' admitted Steggles. 'It was left at the desk at main reception. Might it be important?'

'At the moment we're just gathering information,' said Daniel. 'Sifting through everything. But if anything comes of it, rest assured, we'll keep you informed.'

As they left the museum, Abigail asked, 'What was that about did anyone see an army officer on the day they were killed? You really believe the army are involved?'

'They're certainly involved,' said Daniel. 'The question is, to what degree?'

'So what are we going to do about it?'

'Once we've seen Bickerstaff, we're going to do what Steggles suggested: have a word with the museum staff and see if anyone did notice any army people there on that day.'

Bickerstaff was waiting impatiently for them by the reception desk at the *Guardian* offices.

'What did Steggles say?' he demanded. 'Did he agree?'

'Yes, but with the proviso that you give your copy to us to take to him first for his approval.'

Bickerstaff looked unhappy at this. 'That's hardly supporting the freedom of the press,' he complained.

'Mr Steggles just wants to make sure there's nothing in your article that smacks of political bias. He's concerned about the museum's reputation.'

Bickerstaff hesitated, then he gave them a smile. 'Very well,' he said. 'If that's what he wants, that's what he'll have. I'll leave it at your hotel shortly for you to pass on to him.'

Bickerstaff was about to leave, when Daniel stopped him. 'There's one more thing you may be able to help us with, Mr Bickerstaff. Do you have any contacts with the soldiers at the barracks?'

'In what way?'

'Where do the soldiers go when they are off-duty? Which pubs or drinking dens? We're trying to find out what Kathleen was after that provoked such a defensive response at the barracks. All we know is it's something that happened about eighty years ago.'

'In that case I doubt if a loose-mouthed drunken soldier will be much help to you,' said Bickerstaff. 'You'd be better off with a local historian interested in military affairs.'

'Yes,' said Daniel thoughtfully. 'Mr Steggles mentioned to us he was having discussions with one. A Hector Bleasdale. Do you know him?'

Bickerstaff looked at him in disapproval. 'To be honest, Bleasdale and I are poles apart in political terms. We don't really have anything to do with one another. I've read articles he's written about the local military in magazines, and they're well-written, if a bit dry. But they're very much supporting the status quo.'

'Still, he sounds like he might be our man. I'll ask Steggles to arrange an introduction.'

Bickerstaff scowled, then added, in an angry tone, 'While you're with Bleasdale, ask him about Peterloo.'

'Mr Steggles mentioned Peterloo to us,' said Abigail. 'He described it as a tragic incident.'

'Tragic?' Bickerstaff gave a sarcastic laugh. 'I suppose that's one way to describe the deliberate massacre of peaceful civilians by the military in a major city in England.'

'What exactly happened?' asked Abigail.

'You don't know?' demanded Bickerstaff.

'Only what Mr Steggles told us.'

'One of the most infamous things to ever happen in this country, and you don't know about it!' There was no mistaking Bickerstaff's anger now. 'I thought you were supposed to be enlightened people.'

'As I understand it, it was a long time ago,' said Daniel.

'So was Waterloo, but I bet you remember that,' said Bickerstaff bitterly.

'Look, all we're asking—'

'Ask Hector Bleasdale,' snapped Bickerstaff. 'And after he's told you his version, I'll tell you the other side. The *real* story.'

With that, Bickerstaff disappeared through the door into the inner offices of the newspaper.

As they entered the museum, Abigail asked, 'While we're here, are we going to talk to Mr Steggles about getting in touch with this Hector Bleasdale?'

'I thought I'd leave that until we bring him Bickerstaff's article,' replied Daniel. 'He's a very busy man, and I feel we don't want to interrupt his work too often or he might get fed up with us.'

Instead, they made their way to the reading room where they sought out Jonty Hawkins.

'Mr Hawkins, on the day the young woman was killed, did you notice any army types in the reading room?'

'Army types?'

'You know, military men.'

Hawkins shook his head. 'No, there was nobody in an army uniform here that day.'

'What about out of uniform?'

Hawkins looked at Daniel, then at Abigail, bewildered.

'How would anyone know?' he asked. 'Out of uniform, military people look the same as anyone else.'

'That's true,' said Daniel. 'Thank you, Mr Hawkins.'

As they left the reading room, Abigail said, 'That's a very good point. How would anyone know? Out of uniform, military people look the same as anyone else.'

'To ordinary people, I agree,' said Daniel. 'But not to another soldier. There's a bearing about a professional soldier that marks them out. I agree there was no way someone like Hawkins should spot it, but there is someone at the museum who might.'

They made their way down to the cellar where they found Walter Arkwright sorting through small wooden crates.

'Hello again, Mr Arkwright,' said Daniel.

'Sir, madam.' Arkwright saluted. He gestured at the small wooden cases. 'Just getting some more exhibits out of store in readiness for this talk Mr Dresser's doing on birds. We've got some special pieces we've kept in store for just this occasion and I want to make sure they're ready for the talk before I go on my annual holiday.'

'When is that?' asked Abigail.

'Tomorrow,' said Arkwright. 'Me and Mrs Arkwright go to Blackpool every year at this time. It's a pity because I'd have liked to be here to have things ready on the night for Mr Dresser's talk, but Mr Steggles arranged it with Mr Dresser just a month ago and our holiday at Blackpool has been booked for almost a year. Me and the missus stay in the same boarding house, you see, Mrs Bailey's, and she's very popular so you have to book well in advance. But everything'll be all right for the talk, I'll make sure of that. Everything's in place and I've got one of the young attendants, Edward Page, standing by to double-check things on the day. He's young but he's a good and reliable worker.'

'I'm sure he is,' said Daniel. 'Mr Arkwright, you said you used to be a soldier.'

'I did, sir, and I was.'

'On the Thursday when the young woman was killed in the reading room, did you notice any military types in the museum? They most likely would have been wearing civilian clothes.'

Arkwright frowned. 'Civilian?' He thought, then said, 'Out of uniform, most soldiers look the same as everyone else, honestly, sir. Except for officers. They look different.'

Yes, that's it, thought Daniel. *An officer, not an ordinary foot soldier.*

'Did you notice any such in the museum on that Thursday?' he asked.

Arkwright fell silent, thinking hard. Then he said, 'Now you come to mention it, there might have been. As I was coming down to the cellar I noticed a man near the entrance, and I thought I saw the shape of a scabbard under his long coat.'

'A scabbard? For a sword?'

Arkwright shook his head. 'No, not a sword. A regimental sword is long, and even a short sword would have poked out. No, it was more like a scabbard for a bayonet. You wear 'em attached to your belt.'

'Can you describe this man? His facial features?'

Arkwright shook his head.

'I only saw him from the back, and just a glance, really.'

* * *

107

'So, an officer in civilian clothes with a bayonet in a scabbard,' said Daniel as they headed back to their hotel. 'And a bayonet is a weapon that fits the injuries. Steggles was supposed to meet Brigadier Wentworth at the museum that day, then the brigadier cancelled at the last moment. But say he didn't? Say he cancelled his meeting with Steggles, but he came to the museum anyway, and killed the two women.'

'But why cancel his meeting with Steggles?' asked Abigail. 'If he was spotted at the museum by anyone, that was his reason for being there. His alibi.'

'Unless his note of cancellation was to back up his lie about not being at the museum. And, if he was spotted by anyone, he could say things had changed and he was able to come after all.'

'In which case, why didn't he go to see Steggles?'

Daniel frowned. 'Because he didn't think he'd be spotted so he went with his original plan – to pretend he wasn't at the museum, with his note as evidence. But an officer was there on that day, armed with a bayonet. If it wasn't Brigadier Wentworth, who was it?'

True to his word, Bickerstaff's article was waiting for them at their hotel.

Abigail studied it first.

'How does it read?' Daniel asked.

'Surprisingly moderate,' said Abigail. 'It states the facts, with the names of the two women, and where they were found. It also mentions the museum bringing us in to investigate.'

'Does he castigate the police?'

'No,' said Abigail. 'To be honest, after what Mr Bickerstaff threatened to publish about Inspector Grimley and the local force, I expected a far more angry piece.' She handed the pages to Daniel. 'I believe Mr Steggles will find nothing there to worry him.'

'In that case, we'll take it straight to him. And at the same time we'll talk to Mr Steggles about arranging a meeting with this Mr Bleasdale.'

They delivered Bickerstaff's article to Steggles, who expressed his pleasant surprise at the tone, commenting, 'I'm relieved to see that Mr Bickerstaff has respected my wishes. I feared he might be too extreme in his condemnation of the police, and in particular name Inspector Grimley, which could lead to a rift between the police and the museum. In a burgeoning city like Manchester, it is vital that the different arms of the social structure work together, judicial and artistic, if we are to avoid creating anarchy.'

'There's one other thing,' said Daniel. 'We're trying to find out what Kathleen Donlan may have been asking about at the barracks that resulted in her being turned away. It was something that happened about eighty years ago, which means it could be connected with Waterloo, or even this Peterloo incident. Or possibly something else that happened about that time. What we'd like to do is talk to a local military historian to see if he can throw any light on what her interest may have been. I recall you mentioned someone called Hector Bleasdale.'

'Hector Bleasdale indeed!' Steggles beamed. 'The perfect person! Would you like me to write a letter of introduction to him on your behalf?'

Daniel smiled. 'Actually, that was what I was about to ask. You're sure you don't mind?'

'Not at all!' Then he gave a rueful smile. 'I must admit it wouldn't be completely altruistic on my part. Since this dreadful incident happened there's been a lack of response when I've asked the army for further meetings about the exhibition we're planning. I wrote to Brigadier Wentworth last Friday asking when we could meet to move things forward, but he hasn't replied. Of course, he may be very busy, but it's unlike him not to respond. Writing to Hector Bleasdale as an introduction to you will give me an opportunity to mention to him that we are keen to start making preparations for the exhibition.'

'And I'll be very happy to add a prompting of my own when I meet him,' said Daniel. 'If you think it might help.'

'I believe it might. Mr Bleasdale is a very sociable man, very friendly, whereas the brigadier can be slightly stand-offish.'

'In that case, I'll write a brief note to Mr Bleasdale of my own, if you wouldn't mind enclosing it with yours,' said Daniel.

Daniel was unusually quiet during their meal, causing Abigail to remark on it. 'You seem very thoughtful this evening,' she commented.

'I'm always thoughtful,' said Daniel.

'But this evening you seem particularly deep in thought. Something about the case puzzles you?'

'Everything about this case puzzles me,' admitted Daniel ruefully. 'But no, I was thinking about this city. Manchester.'

'Oh?'

'I'm having difficulty reconciling the opinion of it expressed in your magazine as "the most modern city in Britain" and "the city of the future". The two areas we've visited, Hulme and Ancoats, are just the same as many of the slum areas of London, places like Whitechapel and Shoreditch and the area around the back of King's Cross station. Hardly "the city of the future".'

'That's because those are the only two areas we've been to outside of the city centre, and those are where the workers live. It's always been this way, throughout history. Ancient Rome was viewed as a marvel, a wonder to behold. Another "city of the future". And parts of it were, the areas where the rich lived with hypocaust systems that gave the houses central heating, the sewage systems, the coliseum, the places of government. But it all needed a large labour force to keep it working, and they didn't live in these luxurious houses. They lived in hovels crammed together in the poorer areas, without proper sanitation, and living on what scraps they could gather.'

'So the Romans invented the slum, along with all their other innovations.'

'Oh no. Slum conditions like that had been around as long as cities had existed. In ancient Egypt, for example. And until the day comes when the rich find a way to be able to live in luxury without the physical labour of the poor, it will always be that way.'

Daniel smiled. 'Now it's you who sounds like one of these radicals.'

'Absolutely not,' said Abigail. 'I'm not arguing for a change to the system, I'm simply describing the way things are, how they've always been, and will continue to be. But if I were to argue for change, this city would be the place to do it.'

'Why? As I've already remarked, the social inequality doesn't seem any more unfair here than in London, or many other cities.'

'But it's here in Manchester there have been the biggest calls for social change,' said Abigail.

Daniel frowned. 'There was nothing about that in the magazine article.'

'That article was mainly about technological revolutions. The cotton machines. The telephone system. The canals. But Manchester has been at the forefront of modern political thought for decades. Do you know the writings of Friedrich Engels?'

'No,' said Daniel. 'But my guess is that I wouldn't enjoy them. I'm averse to heavy tomes on political thought.'

'You don't know they're heavy tomes,' said Abigail.

'Yes, I do,' retorted Daniel. 'From the way you mentioned them. Modern political thought. I have yet to hear of any of these modern political thinkers using few words.'

'Yes, all right, his works do tend to be lengthy, and quite heavy in content,' admitted Abigail.

'You've read him?'

'I started to,' said Abigail.

'Ha!' Daniel exclaimed in triumph.

'But other things interceded,' said Abigail firmly. 'My point is that Engels spent much of his life in Manchester, and his experiences here led to the development of his social philosophy. In fact, along with Karl Marx, it could be said that he developed Marxism.'

'Ah, now Karl Marx I've heard of,' said Daniel. 'When I was in the Met we often used to get radicals attacking banks and such places, claiming it was in the cause of fairness and quoting Karl Marx.' He looked at Abigail quizzically. 'But I can't recall him being associated with Manchester. For one thing, he's buried in north London at Highgate Cemetery. There was a lot of fuss about it in the London papers at the time because he was buried in what's known as Agnostics Corner, where George Eliot is buried.'

'Mary Anne Evans,' said Abigail.

'Yes, if you want to be particular about it. I'm not getting into this,' said Daniel, shaking his head. 'I'm still curious about what Karl Marx has to do with Manchester.'

'He came here to meet Engels,' said Abigail.

'I bet that was a cheerful conversation,' said Daniel sourly. 'Not many jokes and singing comic songs.'

'They met at Chetham's Library,' continued Abigail. 'Which has the distinction of being the oldest public reference library in Britain.'

'And free to use?' said Daniel, surprised.

Abigail nodded, then said, 'It's one of the places I intended to visit when I knew we were coming to Manchester.' She gave a sigh. 'So many things to see here.'

'Mr Wilson?'

Daniel looked and saw that a hall porter had appeared by their table. He held out an envelope.

'This has just been delivered for you.'

'Thank you,' said Daniel.

He opened the envelope and took out the neatly written letter it contained.

'It's from Hector Bleasdale,' he said. 'He says he'll be delighted to meet us. He suggests eleven tomorrow morning at his house.'

Abigail looked unhappy at this. 'We told Father O'Brien we'd go to see the O'Donnells with him tomorrow morning. That's important.'

'They're both important,' said Daniel. 'I'm hoping that Mr Bleasdale will be able to throw some light on just what poor Kathleen Donlan was looking for.'

'Then I suggest you go and see Mr Bleasdale, while I go and see the O'Donnells.'

'On your own?'

'With Father O'Brien.'

'You know what I mean, a woman of means walking through that area on her own.'

'Daniel, I am perfectly capable of looking after myself. And it might be better for it to be just me going. The eldest girl, Breda, seems to be the mainstay of the family, according to Father O'Brien. She might talk easier if it is to a woman. We've taken this case on; we owe it to the family.'

Daniel hesitated, then nodded. 'You're right, as you often are. I'll see this Hector Bleasdale, you go and see the O'Donnells.'

'And if Eve Preston arrives here at the same time looking for us?' asked Abigail.

'As I said, we'll leave a note for her at reception asking her for a contact address. But I somehow think she won't turn up.'

CHAPTER FIFTEEN

The next morning, at Daniel's insistence, Abigail agreed to take a hansom to St Michael's Church to meet Father O'Brien, but only under protest.

'I am only doing this for your sake to make you feel at ease,' Abigail told Daniel sternly. 'I can't have you meeting this man, Bleasdale, while you're worried about me. It will affect the efficiency of the way you question him.'

'Good,' said Daniel.

'However, I do intend to walk back to the hotel. And I insist I will be perfectly safe. Just because an area is poor it does not mean that everyone in it is of criminal intent.'

'I can't win against you,' groaned Daniel.

'I'm glad you've realised that.' Abigail smiled. 'It will make our life together much easier in the future.'

With that last riposte, Abigail hailed a hansom, gave the driver the address of St Michael's Church in Ancoats, and set off.

A service was just finishing as Abigail arrived, with Father O'Brien standing outside saying goodbye to his parishioners. His face lit up with pleasure when he saw Abigail.

'Miss Fenton, I wondered if you would come.'

'I gave my word,' said Abigail. 'Mr Wilson will not be with us because he has another avenue to pursue. How did the family take the news?'

'Sadly, Patrick's gone to pieces,' said O'Brien. 'But he was never the strongest of people. It was Eileen who held that family together. The children were devastated, as you can imagine. While I was there Breda, John and Peter came home from work, so I was able to tell them the dreadful news. Those three, the oldest, are more stoical. I'm afraid their hard life has made them that way. Of them all, Breda's the strongest one. She's like her mother. She was the only one who didn't cry yesterday, but that will come later. Right now she's putting all her strength into making sure the family holds up, giving orders to the older ones while at the same time taking care of the young ones.' He gave a sigh. 'The middle ones are a bit left to their own devices, but that's good in a way, because the three of them will support one another.'

'Will my calling on them cause an upset?' asked Abigail. 'I don't want to make things worse for them than they already are.'

'No,' O'Brien assured her. 'In fact, it will do them good to see someone different, rather than just neighbours calling to offer sympathy. Actually, I was hoping you'd come today because I've been hearing words on the street from some of my parishioners that may have ideas for why Kathleen was murdered. Then again, it may have nothing to do with it, but I thought I'd share it with you.

'You remember I said that Kathleen was likely from north Cork, the Mallow area? Well, it seems that two weeks before Kathleen arrived in England, a woman was killed in the town of Kanturk in north Cork. Kanturk's about ten miles from Mallow. The man who did it was Con Gully, and it seems he stabbed his wife to death with a kitchen knife while he was out of his head on drink. By all accounts, he was a dangerous man, especially when he'd drink taken.

'He was arrested and put in the local jail while awaiting transfer to the main jail in Cork city, where he was to stand trial for murder.'

'From the way you're telling this, I'm guessing that something happened to change that.'

O'Brien nodded. 'Gully escaped from Kanturk Jail. How is unclear, but there is a suggestion that he may have had help. Anyway, he disappeared, and there's been no sign of him in the area since. Which is strange, because in that area everyone knows everyone. And very few would be on Con Gully's side. His wife's family, for sure, want to lay their hands on him. Plus, there's a reward for his recapture.'

'You think he might have fled to England?'

'It's possible. And the O'Donnells aren't the only people in Manchester from that part of north Cork.'

'So it's possible that Con Gully fled and sought refuge with friends here, and spotted Kathleen when she arrived.'

'Although it may just be conjecture.' He sighed. 'I may be totally wrong and Con Gully could have fled west to Connemara, or somewhere else in England. London's full of Irish, as is Liverpool.'

'But if he did come to Manchester and recognised Kathleen as someone from his home area, he'd feel the need to silence her. And, if Eileen was with her at the time, he'd need to silence her as well.' Abigail mused over this, then asked, 'If there's a reward for

117

Gully's arrest, wouldn't it be of benefit to the people who told you about this to take it to the police?'

O'Brien shook his head. 'It doesn't work that way. The person who told me about this heard about it in a letter from a brother of his back in Kanturk. Neither he nor his brother are fond of the police, and the police aren't fond of them. There's no way on God's earth they'd talk to the police.'

'How about you?' asked Abigail. 'You could pass it on.'

Again, O'Brien shook his head. 'The people in my parish trust me to keep their secrets. Not just the things they tell me in confession. Yes, they expect me to gossip and chatter, but if it was discovered that I'd gone to the police with something I'd been told by a member of my parish . . .' He gave a sigh. 'I might as well give it up here and now.'

'But you're telling me.'

'Mr Wilson's an ex-policeman, and I believe a good man. He's not got the taint of the local force. He could take it to the local constabulary.' He hesitated, then added, 'I'm doing this because I hate what happened to Kathleen. And, if it is Con Gully who did this, I'd like him brought to justice. For this, and for what he did to his poor late wife in Kanturk.'

'We'll do what we can, Father,' said Abigail. 'But the police inspector has made it pretty clear he has no time for Mr Wilson. I doubt if he'll listen to us. But I promise we'll do all we can to get him to. But just in case it isn't this man Gully, I'd still like to talk to the O'Donnell girls.'

Daniel also decided to take a hansom to Hector Bleasdale's house as it was in Gorton, a part of Manchester he was as yet unfamiliar with. In his letter, Bleasdale had added: *You will find my house not far from the Belle Vue Zoological Gardens.*

Another place for Abigail and I to visit, when we have time to spare, Daniel reflected.

The borough of Gorton was very different from either Ancoats or Hulme, the houses more spacious and not crammed together as the back-to-backs had been, with floral displays in tubs lining the pavements, along with stone troughs filled with water for the horses that pulled the buses and the wagons. Despite the presence of the blooms with their various scents, it was the smell of horse dung that prevailed. But not as badly as that of the middens in Ancoats, Daniel reflected.

Hector Bleasdale's home was a neat terraced house in a long and immaculately kept road. Once more, Daniel compared Gorton with Ancoats and Hulme, and was just feeling relieved that Abigail had been persuaded to take a cab to see Father O'Brien, when he remembered that appearances were often deceptive. As a detective in London he'd seen just as many violent murders in the wealthy areas of Chelsea and Kensington and Maida Vale as he had in the poorer districts.

So Abigail is right, after all, he thought ruefully.

Hector Bleasdale was a short and very round man, wearing a waistcoat that strained at its buttons over his large stomach. He was in his late fifties, almost bald, with just a few thin strands of hair stretched across his scalp. He smiled in welcome as he opened the door to Daniel.

'Mr Wilson!' He beamed. 'This is a pleasure. Of course I am aware of who you are; your fame has spread this far north.'

'I fear you flatter me, Mr Bleasdale.' Daniel smiled back. 'I was just an ordinary policeman, but I was fortunate to be working with Inspector Abberline and at Scotland Yard during a time of some notoriety.'

'Would you care for tea or coffee?' asked Bleasdale. 'My housekeeper is a grand provider.'

'A coffee would be greatly appreciated, thank you,' said Daniel.

Bleasdale picked up a small bell which he rang to summon his housekeeper in order to request a pot of coffee – 'and some tasty biscuits, please, Mrs Barden' – then he gestured for Daniel to sit in one of the comfortable leather armchairs, while he took the other.

'Before we begin, I promised Mr Steggles I'd ask how the exhibition about the army planned for the museum is going.'

'Ah,' said Bleasdale, 'I was just wondering about that myself. I haven't heard from Brigadier Wentworth lately about what the next move is. I was planning to call on him and see if he's made any progress on what sort of things he'd like to see. I think it would be a great opportunity to promote the local regiments, with features on heroes of the past, focusing on their great engagements, which I'm sure would help to bring in more recruits. It is people who are the lifeblood of the army, after all.'

'Very true,' said Daniel. 'And if you receive any news from the brigadier . . .'

'I shall be in touch with Mr Steggles at once,' Bleasdale assured him.

The door opened and his housekeeper appeared bearing a tray with coffee and biscuits, which she placed on the low table between them.

Bleasdale smiled. 'Thank you, Mrs Barden.' He picked up a cup and settled back in his chair. 'You mentioned in your note you were interested in military affairs in Manchester some eighty years ago. That covers quite a large canvas. Which particular aspects are you researching?'

'To be honest, I'm not sure,' admitted Daniel. 'But I'm guessing it must have been something quite impactful.'

He hesitated, wondering how much to tell Bleasdale, having promised Steggles that he and Abigail would be doing their best to keep the museum's involvement with the murders in confidence. Then he realised that would be irrelevant as soon as Bickerstaff's article appeared in the *Guardian*. Bleasdale's next words resolved any dilemma he might have had, when the historian asked, 'Is this anything to do with the dead woman found at the museum?'

'You know about that?'

Bleasdale nodded. 'I went to the museum on Saturday to talk to Steggles about the army exhibition he's been planning, but he wasn't there. So I fell into conversation with Jonty Hawkins and he told me about the poor young woman being found. Stabbed! How dreadful!'

'Yes, and the coincidence is that her death happened after she began to make her own enquiries about the history of the army in Manchester all those years ago. In fact, William Bickerstaff of the *Manchester Guardian* suggested I ask you about Peterloo.'

'Ah, yes.' Bleasdale nodded.

'He described it as the massacre of working people.'

'I think "massacre" is too strong a word. At Peterloo, or St Peter's Field to give it its proper name, fifteen people died. Tragic, but by no means a massacre.'

'What actually happened?'

Bleasdale looked thoughtful for a moment, then he said, 'There was a public meeting at St Peter's Field in Manchester on 16th August 1819 at which a radical politician was to speak. I can't give you chapter and verse on the politics behind the meeting, my interest is in military history, but I'm sure you can find out the details. There are plenty of people who are very vocal about radical politics in Manchester.' He hesitated, then added, 'William Bickerstaff, who you mentioned, I would count as one of them.'

Daniel nodded. 'Yes, I gathered that. He said he would give me his side of the story after I'd heard yours.'

Bleasdale gave a wry smile. 'I am a practical man. Mr Bickerstaff is more – shall one say – emotional. But to the facts, as I know them. A large crowd had gathered for the meeting. Estimates put the number at between 50,000 people and 150,000.'

Daniel stared at him, stunned. 'That many!'

'Yes. There was a great interest in social conditions, and a lot of ill feeling about social deprivation in the area. As I said, I'm sure Mr Bickerstaff can let you know about social conditions and the radical movement of the time. The meeting was to be addressed by Henry Hunt, a radical orator. Truth to tell, I don't believe the authorities had expected such a large crowd, so the task of controlling them had initially been given to special constables.'

'How many?' asked Daniel.

'According to the records, by noon there were several hundred.'

'To arrange for several hundred special constables would have taken advance planning,' pointed out Daniel. 'Which suggests the authorities had been expecting a very large crowd.'

'Or a small crowd with the constables outnumbering them,' countered Bleasdale.

'True,' admitted Daniel. 'So how did troops become involved? I assume they did.'

'Yes,' said Bleasdale. 'Henry Hunt's carriage arrived about one o'clock and he took to the platform, along with some others.'

'Who were the others?'

'I'm not sure of all of them. I do know they included a man called Joseph Johnson, who'd organised the meeting, and a reformer and cotton manufacturer, John Knight.'

'I'd be interested to know why their names stick in the memory?'

'Because their names were on the arrest warrant.'

'The arrest warrant?'

Bleasdale nodded. 'William Hulton, the chairman of the magistrates, was in a house on the edge of St Peter's Field along with other members of the committee, and it was from there he watched the events unfold. He decided, from the very warm welcome that enormous crowd gave Hunt when he took to the platform, that there was a risk of rioting. So he issued an arrest warrant for Hunt, Johnson and Knight. When he gave the warrant to the constable, a man called Jonathan Andrews, Andrews said he wouldn't be able to make his way through the crowd to serve it without the help of the military. So Hulton sent letters to Major Trafford, the commanding officer of the Manchester and Salford Yeomanry, and Lieutenant Colonel L'Estrange, the overall military commander for Manchester, asking them to attend urgently at St Peter's Field in order to preserve the peace.

'The Manchester and Salford Yeomanry were nearest, in Portland Street, and they immediately set off for St Peter's Field.' He hesitated, then added sadly, 'Because of the phrase about them being needed urgently to preserve the peace, they drew their sabres and proceeded to the field at a gallop. In their haste, one trooper knocked down a woman in Cooper Street. Unfortunately, she dropped her two-year-old son she was carrying at the time. He died.'

'Soldiers on horseback galloping and brandishing their sabres, it was lucky more weren't killed in that charge,' said Daniel gravely.

'Actually, they were,' said Bleasdale in sombre tones. 'But only on their arrival at the field. The Yeomanry made a cavalry charge towards the platform where the speakers stood, but their horses became stuck in the crowds. Some of the troopers panicked and began to lay about them with their sabres. Panic spread throughout the crowd and some began throwing objects at the soldiers.

'It was then that William Hulton ordered L'Estrange to send

in his troops. He said afterwards it was done to protect the Yeomanry who were bring attacked by the crowd.

'L'Estrange sent in the 15th Hussars, who charged the crowd with sabres drawn. The crowd rushed to get away from them, but the 88th Regiment of Foot, with bayonets fixed to their rifles, blocked the main exit from St Peter's Field into Peter Street, stopping them escaping that way.'

'So the soldiers trapped them and continued cutting them down,' said Daniel.

'The soldiers were just following orders,' said Bleasdale defensively. 'The responsibility stands not with the army or the soldiers but with William Hulton, who ordered them into action.'

Daniel nodded thoughtfully. 'I would imagine certain people in the military here wouldn't be keen on someone digging up what happened at Peterloo, after all this time,' he said.

'If you're suggesting that someone in the military killed this poor woman to stop her asking awkward questions, I think that highly unlikely,' said Bleasdale. 'Everyone here knows about Peterloo and what happened. It was tragic, but it's now part of history from long ago, just as the Peninsular War or the Anglo-American War could be seen. There is nothing hidden to reveal about what happened at St Peter's Field. It's all been documented. There are no secrets about it for anyone to feel the need to kill to protect them.'

'Indeed. I have one last question, if you don't mind?'

'Of a military nature?' asked Bleasdale.

'Regarding conventions of dress. Do you know which officers might carry a bladed weapon about them when they are in civilian clothes. In a scabbard. For example, a bayonet.'

'Very few, I would think,' said Bleasdale. 'If an officer or a gentleman wished to carry a blade for his own protection as a civilian, I believe most prefer a sword stick. I'm sure you're familiar with them. Ostensibly it looks like a walking stick . . .'

'Yes, I've seen them,' said Daniel. 'But if an officer chose to carry a bayonet in a scabbard about them while in civilian dress, which ranks might that be?'

'Only the higher ranks,' said Bleasdale. 'General, lieutenant general, major general, brigadier, colonel, lieutenant colonel. Possibly a major.'

'What about a regimental sergeant major?'

Bleasdale frowned. 'An RSM is defined as a warrant officer class 1, but comes under the heading of other ranks,' he said. 'An RSM is not of officer class.'

'But he may carry a bayonet about his person?'

'When in uniform,' said Bleasdale.

'And out of uniform?'

'It would be most irregular.'

'But not impossible.'

'No,' said Bleasdale. 'But, as I say, it would be irregular.'

CHAPTER SIXTEEN

The wooden chair that Patrick O'Donnell had occupied the previous day was still outside the house, but there was no sign of Patrick himself. Instead a small boy was sitting on the chair and he stood up as he saw the priest and Abigail approach.

'Is your da in, Thomas?' asked O'Brien.

'He's not well,' said the small boy.

O'Brien nodded and gave Abigail a meaningful glance, which said: *He's taken to seeking solace in the bottle again.*

'So who's at home today?' he asked.

'Breda's upstairs with the baby,' said Thomas. 'Peter, Marie and Molly have gone to the infirmary. It's Ma's funeral tomorrow.'

'A pauper's funeral, I'm afraid,' whispered the priest to Abigail. Aloud he said, 'We'll go up and see Breda. This lady is here to talk to her.' Abigail followed the priest up the narrow stairs and entered a bedroom. Abigail stood, adjusting her eyes to the gloom in the small bedroom, caused in part by the layer of soot that covered the outside of the single window. A smell of earthy damp and urine pervaded the room. A girl of sixteen was sitting on the bed, sewing a torn pair of trousers. Other items of clothing with rips and tears in them were on the bed beside her, as was a sleeping baby wrapped in a woollen shawl. Next to them sat a young girl of about three, sucking her thumb and looking with blank eyes at the priest.

'That's young Margaret, baby Sean and Breda,' introduced O'Brien. 'I see you're hard at work, Breda.'

'We want the boys to look right for the funeral,' said Breda.

'Breda, this is Miss Fenton,' O'Brien introduced Abigail. 'She's a detective.'

Breda stared at Abigail. 'A woman detective?'

Abigail gave a wry smile. 'I know it's unusual, but the fact is I work with someone else who was a police detective, and we both investigate things. Right now we've been asked to look into what happened to your mother and Kathleen.'

'Do you think the same person killed them both?' asked Breda.

'We don't know,' admitted Abigail. 'At this stage we're trying to gather as much information as we can to try and find out what happened, and why. Were you here when Kathleen arrived from Ireland?'

Breda nodded.

'Did you speak much to Kathleen?'

'Only to say hello,' said Breda. 'I'm usually busy doing things around the house.'

'Now I've done the introduction, I'll leave you two together and go downstairs and have a word with Thomas,' said O'Brien. 'Is that all right with you, Breda?'

'Yes, Father,' said Breda.

'If you need me for anything, just call,' O'Brien said to Abigail.

'He's a good man,' said Abigail, sitting down on the bed after the priest had left them.

'Better than some,' said Breda. 'He's honest and decent and he doesn't put his hands on you.'

'He seems to care,' said Abigail.

'Yes, he does,' Breda agreed. 'He said you'd be coming round to ask questions about Kathleen today. You and a man.'

'It's only me, I'm afraid. Mr Wilson has another appointment. Are you sure you can cope with answering questions?'

'If it helps find the bastard who killed Ma and Cousin Kathleen,' said Breda grimly.

'Did you know about Kathleen going to the barracks?'

Breda nodded. 'Ma took her on Tuesday.'

'Your mother went with her?'

'Yes. Kathleen had only arrived the day before and Ma said she'd get herself lost if she tried to find it on her own. So Ma left me to look after Sean and Margaret while she took Kathleen to the barracks.'

'Did they say anything when they got back?'

'No, but Kathleen looked upset, so I guess things didn't go like she'd wanted.'

'Did she say why she wanted to go to the barracks?'

'No.'

'You didn't ask her?'

'It wasn't my business,' said Breda. 'I guessed it was something to do with a soldier.'

'*What* to do with a soldier?'

Breda looked at her and winced. 'You know what soldiers are like with women.'

128

'You thought a soldier might have got Kathleen into trouble?'

'It's happened to others,' said Breda.

'But Kathleen had only just arrived in Manchester,' pointed out Abigail. 'There wouldn't have been time for a soldier from the barracks here to get her in trouble.'

Breda shrugged. 'Maybe the soldier who'd got her in trouble had been in Ireland and then moved to England. Or maybe she said she'd just come from Ireland, but she hadn't. Maybe she'd been somewhere near, like Bolton or Stockport.'

'But why would she lie?' asked Abigail.

'I don't know,' said Breda. 'People do. Anyway, she was upset.' She gave a sly smile. 'That's why she hit Dapper Dan.'

'Dapper Dan?'

'Dan Daly's his name, but they call him Dapper Dan because of the fancy waistcoats he wears. It was that evening and she was sitting out on the street with me – I was trying to find out more about where she'd come from, and why; she said she was from Mallow in the old country – when Dapper Dan comes along and starts chatting to her. Fair play to her, she knew what he was up to. I left them to it and went indoors, because I knew what Dapper Dan was after from her and I didn't want to listen to that kind of talk. Ma always said if Dapper Dan tried to talk to me, to walk away from him. Suddenly I hear this smack, and a yell from Dapper Dan. I went out, and there he was, bending over and holding his face, as Kathleen hit him again, a real hard one that almost knocked him over.' She chuckled. 'It was wonderful to see. Well, Dan was all raging at her, telling her he'd sort her out, but she just pulled back her arm to let him have another one and he went off fast.' She gave a smile of admiration as she added, 'Kathleen may have looked like a quiet one, but she had a fire in her and she wasn't afraid.'

'She sounds like she'd be a good person to have on your side.'

Breda nodded. 'That's what I thought. I'd really have liked to have got to know her. But there wasn't much chance for that. I had to go to work at the mill, and by the time I come home the house is always full, so there wasn't much chance to talk.'

'You shared a bed, I understand,' said Abigail.

'Yes, but along with Marie and Molly, and with Oona and Margaret on a mattress next to the bed. So there's no place for talk that means anything. The girls need their sleep.' She gave a thoughtful frown, then said, 'There was another man who called looking for her. A stranger. A toff. It was the next day, the Wednesday.'

'What did this man want?'

'He asked if the young woman who'd come to the newspaper office was in. I said I didn't know who he meant. He said she'd come to ask about the army, so I knew he must mean Kathleen. I didn't know she'd gone to the newspaper office, but later I heard from Peter that she'd asked him which was the best local newspaper. Peter's the one who reads, see.'

'He didn't ask for her by name?'

'The toff said he'd forgotten it. But that he'd met her at the newspaper office. The *Manchester Guardian*.'

'Did you tell him her name?'

Breda gave a smirk of a smile and shook her head. 'I'm too wise for that. I told him again I didn't know who he was talking about.'

'But he knew the address she was staying at.'

'He said she'd given it to him, but I didn't believe him. Then he gave me a card with his name on and asked me to give it to her. I was going to give it back to him, but he went before I could. Anyway, I kept it just in case he might have been telling the truth and gave it to Kathleen that night.'

'What did she say?'

'She looked at it and said it must be the man she'd met at the newspaper who'd told her about the museum. She asked me what he wanted with her. I said I didn't know, he didn't say.'

'What did she do with the card?'

'It looked like she was going to throw it away, but then she stopped and put it in her bag.'

'Do you remember the name on the card?'

She gave Abigail a smile. 'I remember it because he told me. William Bickerstaff.'

CHAPTER SEVENTEEN

As Abigail and O'Brien walked back towards St Michael's, Abigail told him what she'd learnt from Breda.

'It seems that Kathleen lost her temper with a man called Dapper Dan. Dan Daly, I believe.'

'Him!' snorted the priest with heavy disdain and disapproval.

'Another of your parishioners?' asked Abigail.

'Thankfully, no,' said O'Brien. 'I'm not sure what religion he is, if any at all. He's a loathsome man who preys on young women, and he seems to target those who are single who arrive on their own from Ireland. I'm told he watches the boat train and makes a note of any obviously poor young women arriving carrying a large bag.'

'Prostitution?' guessed Abigail.

O'Brien nodded. 'At first he charms them, then he tells them he can give them the chance to make more money than they can working in the mills, and easier.'

'From what Breda said, he obviously made that offer to Kathleen, and she hit him,' said Abigail. 'I like this young woman. She had spirit. It makes me more than ever determined to find out who killed her and bring them to justice. Do you think it's possible this Dan Daly was the one?'

'It's possible, although I've never heard of him killing anyone. I know he beats the women when they won't do what he says, but there's been no mention of knives.'

'But it is possible?' pressed Abigail. 'Especially if none of the women have hit him before. And publicly, for all to see. That won't have done his reputation any good. Some of his women might start to think they could react the same way.'

'And so he kills her as an example to them?' said O'Brien. He looked doubtful. 'It seems unlikely. For one thing, if he was going to do it he'd select somewhere other than the museum to do so. Daly is a coward. There'd be too big a risk of him being caught there. If he was going to do something like that, he'd choose a spot where he wouldn't be likely to be seen. And somewhere in the slums, not in a place like the museum.'

'Actually, Father, on that same topic, I wonder if you'd heard any rumours about other men preying on the young women in your parish. The poorer young women.'

O'Brien gave a snort of derision. 'Endlessly!' he said. 'When they've taken drink it seems to be worse.'

'I don't just mean the men in your parish, I was wondering about educated men.' She hesitated, then said, 'Like a reporter on the *Manchester Guardian*, William Bickerstaff, for example. Breda said he called last Wednesday asking for Kathleen. Although not by name. We know he met her at the newspaper office the day before.'

O'Brien frowned thoughtfully. 'Bickerstaff. The name isn't familiar to me. But that's not to say it may not have happened. Some men from what could be called the upper strata are attracted to women who appear poor and vulnerable.' He scowled. 'It's not much different to what Dapper Dan does, except those sort of men don't do it for the money. But it's still taking advantage of women who are vulnerable and at a disadvantage.'

Daniel was already back at the hotel when Abigail arrived.

'How did it go?' he asked.

'Most interesting. We have three new suspects. One is an escaped murderer called Con Gully, and another a pimp called Dan Daly. Dapper Dan Daly, the locals call him, because he wears fancy waistcoats.' She filled in him on what she had learnt about both men from the priest and from Breda. 'Of the two, this Con Gully sounds the sort who'd kill without compunction. Father O'Brien thinks it unlikely the other one, the pimp, would have had the nerve to stab Kathleen in such a public place as the museum. He says he would have chosen somewhere more private, like a quiet back lane.'

'Yes, that makes sense but he's still worth bearing in mind. You said three new suspects.'

'The third is one we're familiar with. William Bickerstaff. Apparently he turned up at the house in Ancoats looking for the young woman he'd met at the newspaper office. This was the day before she died. He told Breda he'd forgotten her name, but I don't believe that.'

'Kathleen never told him it,' said Daniel.

'And if she didn't tell him her name, I don't believe she told him where she was staying. So how did he find out?'

'He must have followed her,' said Daniel.

'Why would he do that?' asked Abigail.

'Remember what Inspector Grimley said about him. Maybe there's something in it. I think I need to have a word with Mr Bickerstaff.'

'I wonder if we oughtn't to take this information to the police,' said Abigail thoughtfully.

'Inspector Grimley hasn't been very receptive so far. And we know he's biased against Bickerstaff.'

'Perhaps there's another inspector we can take it to. This Superintendent Mossop that Bickerstaff told us about.'

'Grimley was the investigating officer in Kathleen's killing. Protocol says that any information has to go to him.'

'But he's declared the case closed!'

'I think we need to look into it and get some stronger evidence before we take it to the police to avoid the risk of them just ignoring it.'

'How did it go with your military historian?' asked Abigail.

'Interesting,' said Daniel. 'Peterloo was definitely a military disaster, and a social tragedy. Civilians died, cut down by the soldiers, however much Bleasdale would prefer to excuse it.'

He gave her the facts as Bleasdale had given them to him.

'That's dreadful!' said Abigail, horrified.

'It is,' agreed Daniel. 'And now I think it's time for us to hear what Bickerstaff calls "the other side of the Peterloo story".'

'What other side can there be? The soldiers cut down innocent civilians.'

'Acting under orders, according to Bleasdale, and therefore innocent. I feel sure that Mr Bickerstaff will have a less tolerant opinion. And after we've heard what he's got to say, when I give you a signal, perhaps you'd find an excuse to slip away so I can talk to Bickerstaff about why he was stalking Kathleen.'

'What's the signal going to be?' asked Abigail.

'A cough?' suggested Daniel.

'Too open to error,' said Abigail. 'You might get a bout of coughing halfway through a question, and I hurry out of the door. No, a look will be sufficient, then leave it to me to make my departure.' She frowned. 'I must say, the more we find out about Mr Bickerstaff, the less I like him.'

'Suspicious, certainly,' agreed Daniel. 'But let's hide our feelings about him for the moment; we don't want to put him on alert when I start probing about him and Kathleen.'

They found Bickerstaff still at the offices of the *Manchester Guardian*.

'Just putting the copy of my story to bed,' he said. 'It'll be in tomorrow morning's paper. How did you get on with Hector Bleasdale?'

'Most interesting,' said Daniel. 'As you indicated might be the case, he gave the official version that favours the army, although admitting that there were tactical errors on their part.'

'Tactical errors!' snorted Bickerstaff, outraged. 'It was bloodthirsty carnage!'

Daniel noticed the few other people in the reception area reacting to Bickerstaff's anger, concerned looks on their faces.

'Perhaps it might be better to talk somewhere less public,' he suggested.

'Yes, that might be a good idea,' admitted Bickerstaff. 'Sometimes I get a bit too excited when things make me angry. But where can we go? There aren't many places around here where we can talk without people eavesdropping on us.'

'How about our hotel?' proposed Abigail. 'I notice they have rooms available for meetings. We can see if one is free. It'll certainly be more comfortable than in your office's little box-room, or the museum, both with the risk of interruptions.'

'I'll get my coat,' said Bickerstaff, and disappeared into the bowels of the building.

'Good thinking,' complimented Daniel. 'The perfect setting for getting him to unburden himself.'

With Bickerstaff in tow, they left the newspaper offices, and a short while later were sitting relaxing in one of the hotel's small private meeting rooms, this one decorated comfortably as a sitting room. Or, rather, Daniel and Abigail were relaxed; Bickerstaff became agitated once Daniel asked him to tell them about Peterloo, 'the real story'.

'The men of the Manchester and Salford Yeomanry were drunk when they attacked the crowd,' said Bickerstaff. 'Completely out of control.'

'So you believe they are the ones at fault, rather than William Hulton.'

'No,' said Bickerstaff firmly. 'Hulton bears responsibility for sending the troops in. As did the government of the time for actually sending troops to Manchester in order to attack the meeting.'

'You're sure they did that?'

Bickerstaff nodded. 'The meeting was organised by The Manchester Patriotic Union. They were connected to the *Manchester Observer*, which was the radical newspaper of the time, by a man named Joseph Johnson. Johnson wrote a letter to Henry Hunt in London asking him to chair the meeting and speak. Johnson's letter was intercepted by spies of the government and read before it reached him. The government interpreted the letter as a planned insurrection and ordered hundreds of troops to be deployed, but I've seen the letter and it was no such thing. Yet the government sent six hundred men of the 15th Hussars to Manchester, along with several hundred infantrymen, four hundred men of the Cheshire Yeomanry, and a

Royal Horse Artillery Unit with two six-pounder guns.'

'Hector Bleasdale mentioned the Manchester and Salford Yeomanry,' said Daniel.

'Ha!' snorted Bickerstaff derisively. 'Shopkeepers playing at soldiers. A militia made up of tradesmen who hated everyone who subscribed to radical politics, or who had a social conscience.'

'And they were drunk?'

'Most of them,' scoffed Bickerstaff. 'They were nearest to the event by choice because they were spoiling for a fight. As they weren't regular army they weren't under the control of the commander, and all they wanted to do was attack the crowd. There was no reason for them to do that, and with such savagery. The crowd at the meeting was orderly, well-behaved. The journalists who reported on the meeting for the *Manchester Observer* and for *The Times* in London both said so in print.'

'With a crowd of that size, I find that difficult to believe,' said Daniel. 'We used to have meetings of radicals when I was in the Metropolitan police, and even a crowd of as few as fifty could turn very nasty if inflamed by a charismatic speaker.'

'Which is why the organisers of the meeting worked hard to ensure that didn't happen,' said Bickerstaff. 'Strict instructions were given to each contingent to make sure their conduct was orderly. Whole communities came, many marching en masse from their hometowns, such as Stockport and Rochdale. It was a happy occasion, full of expectation. There was no trouble. Many of those who attended were women bringing their children, and the menfolk were determined that no harm should come to them.

'The trouble came about because, as I said, the idiots from the Manchester and Salford Yeomanry were eager to attack the crowd and cut them down to teach a lesson to these so-called radicals, and the instruction from William Hulton to intervene and arrest Henry Hunt and the others was all the excuse they needed. That was the trigger. They charged, cutting women, children and men down left, right and centre with their swords. It was a bloodbath, made worse when Hulton sent the Hussars in as well. There were dead bodies everywhere.'

'Fifteen dead, I understand,' said Daniel.

'Fifteen *known* dead,' insisted Bickerstaff. 'Another five hundred were injured, and it's not known how many of those died from their injuries afterwards because the injured were afraid to come forward and admit they'd been wounded at the meeting for fear of losing their livelihood. I know of one wounded man whose children lost their jobs at the mill just because he had been at the meeting. The particular mill was owned by one of the Manchester Yeomanry.' He shook his head and added bitterly, 'The soldiers and their commanders should have been charged with murder. And the mill owners should have been dragged up before the courts for the part they played!'

'I understand that one of the speakers alongside Mr Hunt that day was a mill owner, John Knight,' said Daniel. 'That his name was on the arrest warrant.'

'Yes, well, there are always exceptions,' muttered Bickerstaff grudgingly. 'Knight was one of the rare mill owners with a social conscience. And that was then, not *now*,' he finished firmly.

'But *now* in Manchester you have Mr Jesse Haworth,' said Abigail. 'A mill owner who I would suggest has a strong social conscience. It was he who put up most of the money to sponsor Flinders Petrie's recent excavations in Egypt, with the result that the artefacts that were uncovered by Petrie are in the Manchester Museum for everyone to see, not just the privileged.'

'Or so that Haworth could get his name known,' retorted Bickerstaff. 'On profits made on the backs of the poor.'

'Hardly,' responded Abigail coolly. 'Outside of the archaeological world, although the name Flinders Petrie may appear in the pages of the national newspapers, very few know of the role people like Mr Haworth, or his financial partner Henry Martyn Kennard, play in subsidising Petrie's expeditions.' Daniel took the opportunity to shoot their pre-planned meaningful look at Abigail, and she rose to her feet. 'My apologies, Mr Bickerstaff, but I've suddenly remembered that I'd promised to see Mr Hawkins at the museum today.' She smiled at Daniel. 'I'll see you later.'

With that, she left.

Bickerstaff sat glowering at the door. 'She's wrong, you know,' he grumbled. 'Yes, there may be some mill owners who aren't as bad as the others, but they make their money through the misery of the masses.' He got to his feet. 'I suppose I'd better be off as well,' he said. 'I hope what I've given you may be of use.'

'It certainly adds to our store of information,' said Daniel. 'Actually, if you have a moment . . .'

'Of course,' said Bickerstaff, and he sat down again. 'Anything I can do.'

'The thing is, something's come up that puzzles me, and I hope you might be able to enlighten me.'

'If I can, it will be my pleasure.'

'The day before Kathleen was killed, you went to see her at the house in Ancoats where she was staying.'

Bickerstaff frowned, puzzled, then shook his head. 'No. Not me.'

'According to one of the daughters of the family she was staying with, you asked her about Kathleen, told her you'd met Kathleen at the offices of the *Guardian* the day before. She said you gave her your card with your name on it, William Bickerstaff.

140

She said you also told her your name and asked her to give the card to Kathleen.'

'No,' said Bickerstaff, more firmly this time. 'If she told you that, she's lying.'

'How would she know your name?' asked Daniel.

'I have no idea,' said Bickerstaff. 'Unless someone was impersonating me.'

'Why would they do that?'

'Again, I have no idea,' said Bickerstaff. 'Except that some of my articles have upset certain powerful people. Possibly they're trying to blacken my character, in the same way that Inspector Grimley tried to do at the police station.' He stood up. 'I can assure you, Mr Wilson, that I made no call of any sort to any house in Ancoats to enquire about Kathleen Donlan. I met her at the office of the newspaper on the Tuesday before she was killed, exactly as I told you before, but that's all.' He stood up. 'Now, if there's nothing more, I need to get back to the office.'

Brigadier Wentworth sat at his desk checking through the duty rota sheets and regretting as he had so often of late that his days on active duty were long behind him. What was he now but a pen-pusher, an office clerk. A glorified one, admittedly, with the power to order men into battle, to be able to tell them to do this or do that. But the truth was that it was the lower-ranked officers who ran things. He could give a command to someone like RSM Bulstrode, and Bulstrode would carry it out because he was a loyal soldier whose first duty was to his commanding officer. No, amended Wentworth, Bulstrode's first duty would always be to the reputation of the regiment; the officer in command came second to that. And if Bulstrode, or another officer of the same ilk, felt that the officer in command was acting against the reputation of the regiment, then any order given to him would be ignored, although at the same time creating the illusion that it had been carried out.

He wondered if it had been him thinking about the RSM that had suddenly conjured his appearance up, because there was a brisk rap at his door, which he recognised as Bulstrode's.

'Enter!' he called.

The door opened and the RSM marched in.

'Sorry to disturb you, sir, but Mr Bleasdale's here and he asks if you've got a moment to spare for him.'

Wentworth gave a silent prayer for the arrival of one of his oldest friends. Anything as an excuse for putting aside the paperwork, and a visit from Hector Bleasdale was always a pleasure.

'Of course! Show him in, Sergeant Major!'

Bulstrode stepped back out into the corridor and stood smartly to attention as Hector Bleasdale walked past him into the brigadier's office.

'Hector!' Wentworth beamed. 'Take a seat!'

As Bleasdale settled himself down on the chair, Wentworth pulled open the top drawer of his desk.

'Fancy a small one?' he enquired. Then he chuckled. 'Not too small, of course.'

'Thank you, Cedric. Yes, please,' said Bleasdale.

Wentworth took out a bottle of brandy and two glasses, filled them and passed one to the military historian.

'So, business or social?' the brigadier asked, noticing the rather worried expression on his friend's face. 'Anything happening that I ought to know about?'

'Yes, I believe there is,' said Bleasdale. 'I had a visit this morning from a Daniel Wilson. He's a detective from London, and he came to ask me about Peterloo.'

'Peterloo? Specifically?'

'In his letter asking to meet me he said he wanted to find out about the Manchester units from eighty years ago. I assumed he would be asking about Waterloo. But when he arrived he asked me for details of what happened at Peterloo. I don't know what he's stirring up, but I thought I'd better let you know about his visit.'

'Did he say why he was interested in Peterloo?'

'He said it was to do with the murder of some young woman at the Manchester Museum.' He looked at Wentworth. 'Apparently she was stabbed to death there last week.'

'And what has that got to do with Peterloo?'

'I don't know,' admitted Bleasdale. 'I really can't see a connection between the two. Peterloo was almost eighty years ago. This woman wouldn't have even been born. I doubt if her parents were even born when it happened. And apparently she was Irish. We've had Irish troopers in the Manchester units, just as we've had Scots and Welsh.' He shook his head. 'I really don't know what this chap Wilson's after. But the fact is, he used to be a very high-powered detective with the Metropolitan police. I don't know if you remember the Jack the Ripper case in London some seven years or so ago.'

Wentworth nodded. He decided not to tell his old friend that he'd already heard about Wilson from RSM Bulstrode; by not interrupting him he might be able to glean what Wilson was really after.

'Wilson was part of Inspector Abberline's team, and highly respected. He said he was looking into this girl's murder, but why bring Peterloo into it? I thought you ought to know. Do you think he knows anything?'

Wentworth hesitated, then he said, 'Highly unlikely. But I'll certainly take steps.'

'Yes,' said Bleasdale, adding quickly, 'Not that I need to know, of course. He also asked a question that struck me as odd. He wanted to know which officers might carry a bayonet in a scabbard as a matter of routine when dressed in civilian clothes.'

'Why on earth would he want to know that?' asked Wentworth.

Bleasdale gave a shrug. 'I can only guess he must have heard something. Some sort of gossip.' He shook his head. 'It struck me as an odd thing to say.'

'It was indeed. But I do thank you, Hector. Your coming here with this is very much appreciated.'

'There's one other thing this Wilson chap mentioned,' said Bleasdale. 'The exhibition you're planning at the museum.'

'Oh?' said Wentworth guardedly.

'Yes, he said that Bernard Steggles asked him if he'd mention it to me for when I saw you, because he says he hasn't heard any more from you.'

'No,' said Wentworth. 'I'm holding off on it for the moment.'

'Why?' asked Bleasdale. 'It's a wonderful opportunity to promote the regiment and the barracks.'

'Is it?' asked Wentworth. 'Think about it, Hector. The museum, and Steggles in particular, have hired this chap Wilson to look into the unfortunate death of the young woman who was killed there. But he seems to be fixed on what happened at Peterloo, which wasn't exactly the army's best hour. So I'm asking myself, what's this Wilson's motive? Does he have an axe to grind about the army, and if so, how will that affect the museum's portrayal of us?'

'I thought he came across as very reasonable,' said Bleasdale.

'But he was still nosing around about Peterloo,' pressed Wentworth. 'Something which is best forgotten about. Who's to say he won't influence Steggles in some way. Prejudice.' He shook his head. 'My feeling is that we want the exhibition to go ahead, obviously, and it will. But let's wait until this Wilson chap is out of the way, so that we can determine the style and tone of it.'

'Well, if you think that's best, Cedric,' said Bleasdale, although Wentworth could tell he wasn't happy about the decision. 'So, will you write and tell Steggles that, or shall I, as he's written to me?'

'Neither, I think,' said the brigadier. 'No sense in putting something in writing that this chap Wilson could use against us. Let it lie in abeyance for the moment.'

Bleasdale sighed. 'I suppose you're right. But it seems a pity.'

'It's about protecting the regiment's good name,' said Wentworth. 'That's always the most important thing.'

The two old friends then turned to cosier topics: old friends, army stories and reminiscences, and by the time Bleasdale left Wentworth's office, half the bottle of brandy was gone.

There was a short pause after Bleasdale's departure before RSM Bulstrode's familiar *rat-tat* sounded on the door.

'Enter!' called the brigadier.

Bulstrode marched in. 'I just saw Mr Bleasdale leave, sir,' he said. 'It might not be my place to say it, sir, but he did seem to be very concerned when he arrived and asked to see you. If it was of a personal nature, sir, then of course I do not wish to know. But if it concerned the regiment . . .'

'In a way, it does,' said Wentworth. 'But I'm not sure how. It appears that London detective you talked about paid a visit to Hector Bleasdale.'

'Daniel Wilson, sir?'

'That's the man. He was after details of what happened at Peterloo.'

Bulstrode frowned. 'Did he say why, sir?'

'No. I remember you said he was here before.'

'That's right, sir. I informed you at the time. He was asking after a young woman who he claimed had called here.'

'But she hadn't?'

'No, sir.'

The brigadier frowned. 'This chap Wilson seems to be very persistent.'

'Yes, sir.'

'We just have to hope whatever he's doing won't impinge on the regiment.'

RSM Bulstrode looked suddenly very grim, and very determined. 'I'm sure it won't, sir. In fact, I'll make sure it doesn't.'

'Thank you, Sergeant Major,' said the brigadier.

CHAPTER EIGHTEEN

Abigail had waited in the hotel lobby until she saw Bickerstaff appear from the private sitting room and leave the hotel, before looking for Daniel.

'Well?' she asked. 'Was he angry with you?'

'He was angry at the accusation,' replied Daniel. 'He denied that he went to the house, or spoke to Breda about Kathleen. He also denied leaving his card with her. He claims that someone must have impersonated him in an attempt to smear his character.'

'But who would want to do that?' asked Abigail.

'According to Bickerstaff, lots of people. Prominent and powerful citizens who've been upset by the tone of his newspaper articles.'

'Breda was very definite in her story,' said Abigail firmly. 'A toff called William Bickerstaff.'

'There's only one way to find out the truth, and that's to ask Breda to take a look at Bickerstaff and tell us if that was the man she met,' said Daniel.

'Yes,' agreed Abigail. 'Tomorrow I'll go to Ancoats and ask Breda to come with me to the offices of the *Guardian*. I feel she trusts me. Once there, I'll ask to see Bickerstaff in the reception area. I'll make up some question to get him talking. Possibly compliment him on his article, which should have appeared by the morning. I'm sure he'll be happy to talk about that. I'll place Breda somewhere she can see him and hear him.'

'A good plan.' He looked at her with a puzzled frown. 'The big question it raises, if it turns out it wasn't Bickerstaff who called, is: who was it? And why?'

'You don't agree that it may have been done to smear Bickerstaff's reputation?'

'I can't see that a visit like that would damage him, except for the fact that shortly afterwards the young woman was stabbed to death.'

'So someone was doing it prior to killing her, to implicate him in her murder?'

'That's what it seems like to me,' said Daniel. 'But we'll soon find out once Breda's said if it was him who called at the house, or not.'

The following morning they picked up a copy of the *Manchester Guardian* at reception and took it in to breakfast. Abigail scanned it for Bickerstaff's story, while Daniel studied the menu.

'I fancy boiled eggs this morning,' he announced.

'I rather fancy you'll also want to give Mr Bickerstaff a telling-off,' said Abigail.

She handed him the newspaper, folded so that he could read the article. As Daniel read it, his face showed his anger.

'He lied!' he said.

'He did,' agreed Abigail.

The article had changed from the copy Bickerstaff had handed to Daniel and Abigail, and which Daniel had passed to Bernard Steggles. That copy had simply given the bare facts, but in this version Bickerstaff had added more about Daniel and Abigail, referring to their previous successes as investigators at the Fitzwilliam and Ashmolean Museums, along with the British Museum, for which Bickerstaff had dubbed them the 'Museum Mystery Detectives'. He also spent two paragraphs highlighting Daniel's career with Inspector Abberline at Scotland Yard, and Abigail's continuing career as 'an internationally renowned archaeologist and Egyptologist'. It was the paragraphs at the end that aroused Daniel's anger. Despite his promise to Steggles to keep the tone non-political, the final section was a rant at the police and at the mill owners, describing them as cogs in a wheel of mutual corruption aimed at suppressing the poor and getting rich on their misery.

'He lied!' repeated Daniel. 'He promised there'd be nothing in any way political! He betrayed our trust and that of Mr Steggles.'

'We now know that he's duplicitous, underhanded and a brazen liar, who will say one thing while planning another, and who plays games with people,' said Abigail. 'Still think he's not the one who called on Breda in Ancoats?'

'This calls for a change of plan,' snapped Daniel. 'I'm going to confront him about this article. So we'll both go to Ancoats and bring Breda back to the city centre, and you and she can place yourselves somewhere in the reception area of the *Guardian* while I call him out and demand he write a letter of apology to Mr Steggles. Two birds with one stone. I vent our anger on Mr Bickerstaff, and we also find out if it was he who went looking for Kathleen.'

* * *

A copy of the *Guardian* was open on Bernard Steggles's desk when Daniel and Abigail entered his office. The museum manager's face was ashen and he stared at the newspaper as if he couldn't believe what he was reading.

'Have you seen this?' he demanded.

'Yes,' said Abigail, 'and we've come to reassure you that nothing in that article came from us, Mr Steggles. In fact, Mr Bickerstaff gave us his assurance that the article would contain nothing of a political nature.'

'Indeed, the piece he submitted through Mr Wilson kept to that.' He looked at the newspaper in disgust. 'But this!'

'I can assure you that after we've seen you we are going to call on Mr Bickerstaff and demand an explanation and an apology from him.'

'It's not enough,' said Steggles, and they could see that he could barely control his anger. 'I was betrayed. Lied to. And now the museum has been implicated in a political diatribe which could be very injurious to our reputation.'

'We can only apologise again—' began Abigail.

'No, I know neither of you are at fault. Like me, you trusted this man and took his assurances that the piece he gave you was what would be published. It seems to me that he was already planning to put this out instead.'

'We should not have allowed ourselves to be duped,' said Daniel. 'We feel we are culpable for that and will completely understand if you decide that you no longer require our services.'

'No, no, absolutely not!' Steggles said, his tone firm. 'You have already shown your expertise in establishing the identities of the two women found here. We want you to continue with your work and find out what the motive was, and who carried out these dreadful acts and have them brought to justice. Have your investigations established any possible motives?'

'Miss Fenton has identified two possible suspects, a man called Dan Daly and one called Con Gully,' said Daniel. He looked towards Abigail, and she proceeded to tell Steggles what she'd learnt from Father O'Brien and Breda the previous day. 'Fortunately, that information came to us after Mr Bickerstaff had written his piece, otherwise I'm sure he would have included it to sensationalise his story. The pimp and the killer.'

Steggles shuddered. 'My hope would have been that the editor would have frowned upon such gutter press images and stopped them before they got to print.'

'He didn't prevent Bickerstaff's article appearing,' observed Daniel. 'Even though he must have realised it would be inflammatory.' Then he added, 'Unless Mr Bickerstaff told his editor it had been approved by you.'

Steggles nodded, and again a look of anger crossed his face. 'Yes. I think I'll write to Mr Scott, the editor of the *Guardian*, expressing my feeling of betrayal over this matter. I thank you for coming to see me, and assure you that we do not hold you responsible for this . . . this outrage! I look forward to receiving more information from you as you discover it.'

'Thank you, Mr Steggles.'

It was with a feeling of relief that they left Steggles's office and walked down the stairs that led to the reading room.

'We shouldn't have trusted Bickerstaff,' she muttered.

'We needed to get the story out to the public in the hope that it would produce results, more information, and so we took the risk,' countered Daniel.

'We were still too trusting,' retorted Abigail.

'Which is why I want to double-check something with Mr Hawkins,' said Daniel.

Jonty Hawkins's face lit up when he saw them. 'Miss Fenton,

Mr Wilson. It is a pleasure to see you again!' Then his face clouded as he added, 'Although this story by William Bickerstaff in today's *Guardian* . . .'

'Yes, I know. We've just been to see Mr Steggles to apologise and explain that we had no part in it.'

'I'm sure he never thought you did,' said Hawkins. 'How can I help you today?'

'We're just wondering about Mr Bickerstaff's movements on the day that Kathleen was killed. Nothing suspicious, but as it relates to his reporting, he told us he came here to try and find out what had happened because he'd heard a rumour of a stabbing.'

'Yes,' said Hawkins. 'He often pops in to check on something for a story he's writing.'

'And what time was that?' asked Daniel.

Hawkins frowned thoughtfully, then he said, 'Actually, he was here twice that day.'

'Twice?'

'Yes. I noticed because it was the second day in succession he'd called, so he was obviously preparing something.'

'He called here on the Wednesday as well?'

Hawkins nodded. 'But he didn't stay long that time. On the Thursday, the first time he came in was shortly after we opened. About half past nine. He said he wanted to check on something.'

'Did he say what?'

'No.'

'How long was he here?'

'I'm not sure,' admitted Hawkins. 'I got very busy. I do know he'd gone by the time the unfortunate young woman was found.'

'Oh?'

'Yes. It was about eleven o'clock when a man came to me and told me he thought something was wrong. I recall that there was no sign of Mr Bickerstaff, so he must have gone. He came back in the afternoon, after the police had been.'

'Did he come back because you'd sent him a message about what had happened?' asked Daniel.

'No,' said Hawkins, looking shocked at the suggestion. 'Mr Steggles is very clear on that. The staff are not to contact the press about anything that happens here. That is his decision to make.'

'Was the young woman in the museum when Mr Bickerstaff came in the day before, the Wednesday morning?'

'No. She didn't come in until mid-morning that day.' He looked enquiringly at them. 'Was any of what I've told you helpful?'

'Very,' said Daniel. 'Although in what context, I'm not sure yet. But it helps to build a picture of what happened.'

As they left the desk, Daniel whispered, 'That's very interesting. So Bickerstaff was here before the young woman was stabbed.'

'He's already proved himself untrustworthy, a liar, and quite likely a man who preys on women,' Abigail muttered quietly. 'Is he also capable of murder?'

Daniel and Abigail made their way to the O'Donnells' house in Ancoats, expecting to find at least one person home, but the place appeared empty, with no reply to their knocking. Daniel knocked again, louder this time. The door of the neighbouring house opened and a woman looked out at them.

'They've all gone to the funerals,' she told them.

'Of course. Kathleen and Mrs O'Donnell,' said Abigail. 'With everything that's happened, I'd quite forgotten.'

'We have to leave it for today,' said Daniel. 'We can't break into their grieving at their mother's funeral.'

He started to turn back the way they'd come, but Abigail stopped him.

'No, we must,' she said. 'Say Bickerstaff is our man? If he is, we need to act fast.'

'But the family . . .' repeated Daniel.

'I saw Breda's face yesterday,' said Abigail. 'Heard her voice. She's angry, very angry. She wants the person who killed her mother caught. And quickly. I know she'd want to work with us to catch him, even today.'

Daniel studied her face, looking into her eyes, then nodded.

'If that's what you feel,' he said.

'I do,' Abigail replied firmly.

Daniel walked to the neighbour's house and knocked on the door. When the same woman opened it and looked out, he asked, 'Where are they being buried?'

'Potter's Field,' she said. 'They used to be at Granby Row, St Augustine's burial ground, but that got full, so it's Potter's Field now.'

She gave them directions, and after half an hour of walking they came to a brick wall around a large field with a sign announcing Catholic burial ground. They could see the O'Donnell family on the other side of the field, gathered around an open grave, with the small figure of Father O'Brien. As they walked towards the group, Abigail commented, puzzled, 'No headstones.'

Instead of the usual headstones and statues found in cemeteries, the field was dotted with wooden posts stuck into the ground. Each post had a list of numbers painted on them.

'Pauper's funerals,' explained Daniel. 'For people whose families are too poor to bury them. The local corporation have to foot the bill, and they do it as cheaply as they legally can. Every slum, every poor area has a place like this. Wooden posts banged into the ground marking where perhaps as many as twenty coffins have been laid, one on top of the other, in pits twenty feet deep. If the O'Donnells are lucky, this will be a recently dug grave, so the smell won't be bad. When it's a funeral where they're the last to go in, the corpses at the bottom have started to ooze out of the coffins and the smell can be overpowering.'

'You have such a charming way with descriptions,' said Abigail cuttingly. 'Have you ever thought of taking up poetry?'

'I would think even our sweetest-tongued poets would have difficulty with a pauper's funeral,' said Daniel.

As they arrived, Father O'Brien was just giving the oration over the grave, his final words the signal for the family to leave the graveside and shake the small priest's hand. Daniel and Abigail noticed that Patrick seemed to be held up by his two eldest sons, who guided him away on his unsteady legs, the other children following.

Father O'Brien came up to Abigail and Daniel, a quizzical look on his face.

'A sad occasion,' he said. 'I'd hoped more of the neighbours might come, but going to work and getting money in their pockets is a priority. I didn't expect either of you to be here.'

'Actually, Father, there's an ulterior motive in our presence,' said Abigail. 'Some information has turned up, and we hoped that Breda might be able to come with us to check on something.'

'What sort of information?' asked O'Brien.

'When I saw Breda she told me that a man called William Bickerstaff had called at their house looking for Kathleen. He denies it and claims it must have been someone else impersonating him.'

'And you'd like her to take a look at this man,' said the priest.

'If it's appropriate,' said Daniel. 'But in view of the fact they've just buried their mother . . .'

'To be frank, I think Breda would be glad of the chance to take a break from it,' said O'Brien. 'She's been doing everything for days now, working, looking after the family. She could do with a rest for a brief while.'

'Perhaps, after she's taken a look at this man, we could take her to tea at our hotel,' suggested Abigail.

'That'll be nice,' said O'Brien. 'She doesn't get many treats, or chances to go to nice places. Tell her she has my blessing.'

They turned and saw that Breda, her baby brother in her arms, was still standing in the burial ground along with her younger sisters, watching them, as if she suspected they'd come for a purpose that might involve her. Meanwhile, Patrick O'Donnell was making his unsteady way out of the ground, still supported by his sons. Father O'Brien gestured for Breda to join him and Daniel and Abigail.

'Breda, these people would like you to go with them to check on something,' he said. 'They're decent people and I've told them you have my blessing to go with them this afternoon. I shall take charge of the others and get them back to your house.' He turned to eleven-year-old Molly and said, 'Molly, can you be a big girl and look after Sean while Breda goes with them?'

'Yes, Father,' said Molly, and she took the baby from her eldest sister.

'Thank you.' Abigail smiled. 'I promise you, Breda, there'll be no trouble for you. We just want you to look at someone from a distance and tell us if you know them.'

'Is it the man who killed Ma?' she asked.

'We don't yet know,' said Abigail. 'We want to know if he's the man who called asking for Kathleen.'

'William Bickerstaff,' said Breda grimly. 'I'll do it.'

'Thank you,' said Abigail. She leant forward and whispered, 'And afterwards, there'll be tea and cake. And we'll pay you for your time, just like wages.'

'How much?' asked Breda.

'A shilling,' said Daniel.

Breda nodded. 'Where are we going?'

'To the offices of the *Manchester Guardian*,' said Abigail.

Daniel stood in the reception area of the *Guardian*'s offices, waiting. He had been waiting for twenty minutes, ever since the receptionist sent a message to William Bickerstaff that Daniel Wilson was here and would like to see him. Abigail and Breda were standing patiently, half hidden behind a pillar near the entrance.

Daniel approached the desk, smiled politely at the receptionist and said, 'Excuse me for bothering you, but you sent a message through to Mr Bickerstaff about twenty minutes ago telling him that I was here and wishing to see him. My name's—'

'Daniel Wilson.' The receptionist smiled back. 'Yes, I remember.' She looked apologetic. 'I can only assume he's got held up on something. I know he's in today.'

'Would you mind very much sending him another message?' asked Daniel. 'Perhaps, with everyone being so busy, he might have forgotten.'

The receptionist stood up. 'Better than that, I'll go and remind him myself,' she said.

Daniel thanked her, and as he watched her disappear through the door into the main office where the journalists worked, he reflected again on the old adage that a friendly and polite word often worked where bluster failed. He knew that had been the way it was for him when he was at Scotland Yard. Usually, when someone had called and insisted on seeing him, adding, 'Tell him I'm a very important person indeed and there'll be serious repercussions if he doesn't attend to me at once', the result had been that Daniel had left the 'very important person' to kick their heels in the reception area for an annoyingly long time. And if that was how Daniel felt about being treated that way, then he reasoned others would usually feel exactly the same.

He wondered if Bickerstaff was deliberately avoiding him because of the article. If that was the case and the man refused to appear, Daniel had decided he would march into the inner offices and confront Bickerstaff that way, and drag him into the reception area in order for Breda to get a look at him.

As it turned out, that course of action wasn't necessary. The receptionist reappeared, and behind her came Bickerstaff. But Daniel could see at once that Bickerstaff appeared very defensive; it was clear from the expression on his face and the posture of his body.

'Ah, Mr Wilson,' he said. 'I'm sorry for the delay.' He forced an awkward smile. 'Have you seen the article?'

'I have,' Daniel answered politely. 'Which is why I'm here. You sent me to Mr Steggles at the museum with one article, and then completely rewrote it with an altogether different tone.'

'I decided that the first version was too bland.'

'Then you should have let Mr Steggles see the version you intended to publish.'

'There was no time. We were going to press.'

Daniel shook his head. 'I don't believe that, I'm afraid. I have journalist friends in London who write for papers like *The Times* and *The Telegraph*, and who've worked with me on cases, so I do have some understanding of how newspapers operate.'

'That's London!' burst out Bickerstaff defensively. 'Things are different here in Manchester.'

'I doubt that,' said Daniel. 'But, whatever the reason, the outcome is that you have betrayed the word you gave to Mr Steggles, and to us. So I will need a letter from you to Mr Steggles explaining that the decision to change the text that had been agreed was yours and yours alone, and that Miss Fenton and I were not a party to it. As the situation stands at the moment, Mr Steggles, as our employer, would be entitled to think that we were part of your deception.'

'It was not a deception!' Bickerstaff snapped.

'I believe it was,' said Daniel, remaining calm. 'And so might he. Please deliver your letter to our hotel and I will pass it on to Mr Steggles personally.'

'There's no need for your involvement in this,' said Bickerstaff curtly. 'I am perfectly capable of sending a letter direct to Mr Steggles at the museum.'

'Based on what happened with the article, I would prefer to check the letter myself to verify that it says what you say it says,' said Daniel.

'And if I refuse?' demanded Bickerstaff.

Daniel fixed him with a hard look. 'Then I would have to come to look for you again to repeat my request,' he said, his tone letting just enough of his anger show. 'And that would not please me. I look forward to receiving your letter by tomorrow lunchtime. Otherwise, as I say, I shall return.'

Bickerstaff glared at him, then turned on his heel and disappeared back into the offices. Abigail and Breda joined him.

'Well?' asked Daniel.

Breda shook her head. 'That wasn't the toff who called. That wasn't the bloke who said he was William Bickerstaff.'

Daniel and Abigail exchanged concerned looks. If that was the case, who had been the mysterious caller? And why the deception?

Daniel, Abigail and Breda were about to mount the steps of their hotel, when a small, wiry man approached them.

'Excuse me, sir. Would you be Mr Daniel Wilson?' he asked politely.

'Yes,' said Daniel.

'I wonder if I could have a brief word,' asked the man genially.

Daniel turned to Abigail and Breda.

'I'll join you in just a moment,' he said. 'You can order tea and cakes.'

As the two disappeared into the hotel, Daniel turned back to the man. 'Yes?' he asked.

The sudden punch the man threw struck Daniel in the side of his face, sending him staggering backwards. Before he could recover, two other men had appeared, one on either side of him, each grabbing him by an arm, while at the same time planting one booted foot on Daniel's feet, preventing him from defending himself.

'Stop asking questions about Peterloo,' said the small, wiry man. 'And stay away from the barracks.'

With that, he sank a fist hard into Daniel's stomach. The other men let go of Daniel's arms and he sank to the pavement, winded, his head throbbing.

CHAPTER NINETEEN

Daniel pushed himself to his feet, politely refusing the offers of help from passers-by who'd witnessed the attack.

'I'm fine,' he assured them.

'Do you want us to call the police?' asked one man.

'No, thank you. Everything will be fine. A case of mistaken identity, I believe.'

With that he walked into the hotel and made his way to the lounge, where Abigail and Breda were sitting waiting. Pots of tea and plates of cakes were already on their table. Abigail rose from her chair as he approached, shocked at the sight of the vibrant red and black bruise around his left eye.

'My God!' she exclaimed. 'What happened?'

'A trio of military types just attacked me.'

'Military?'

'I'm judging by the very efficient way they worked, quite unlike traditional street thugs.'

'That man who stopped you?'

'And two of his friends.' He settled into the waiting chair, aware that Breda was looking at him with a mixture of concern, but also suspicion. 'I'm afraid this sort of thing happens now and then,' he said to her apologetically. 'It's one of the occupational hazards of asking difficult questions. But I can assure you I'm fine. My pride is hurt more than my head.'

'Did they say why they did it?' asked Abigail.

'They told me to stop asking questions about Peterloo, and to stay away from the barracks. With that they gave me a last blow to the body, that winded me badly enough for me to fall to the pavement, and they left.'

'You're sure they were military?'

'It wasn't just their warning about not asking questions about Peterloo; I could tell by their stance and the way they worked together. Also, if they'd just been thugs for hire they'd have kicked me when I was lying on the ground. As it was, they simply disappeared. I almost expected them to salute me before they vanished.'

'Will they come after us?' asked Breda anxiously. 'I mean, if it's the army, and they're doing this because of Kathleen going to their barracks . . .'

'No, no,' Daniel assured her. 'They made no mention of Kathleen. They were only concerned with the questions we've been asking about Peterloo, and turning up at the barracks. You're not in any danger.'

'But they saw me with you . . .' said Breda, still worried.

'If it was you they were after, they'd have done something there and then,' said Daniel. 'It was me they were after, and it was only about Peterloo. I assure you, you and your family are quite safe.' He reached for a teapot and poured himself some tea, then topped up Abigail's and Breda's cups as he asked, 'This man who called at your house and said he was William Bickerstaff; what did he look like?'

'Well-dressed. Smart. A toff.'

'Any distinguishing features? Scars, that sort of thing? Beard? Moustache?'

She shook her head.

'What about his build? Thin? Fat? Muscular? Tall? Short?'

Breda sat and thought about the man's visit.

'Tall,' she said. 'Thin-ish. In fact, he looked a bit like the real Bickerstaff, the bloke you showed me at the newspaper office. Same sort of height. Same posh voice. Only his voice was nicer. Gentler.'

After more tea and cake, Breda said she'd better be going. 'Pa will be all in a mess. He won't know what to do,' she said.

Daniel offered to walk her home, but she shook her head. 'I'll be fine,' she said. Daniel gave her the shilling he'd promised her, while Abigail wrapped the cakes that were left in a napkin and gave them to her 'for your brothers and sisters', and Breda left.

As Daniel and Abigail walked up the stairs to their room, she looked at him, concerned, and asked, 'Are you sure you're all right? That's quite a black eye he gave you.'

'I've had worse,' said Daniel. 'Although it does add a new dimension to the case. If I'm going to be beaten up with every new line of questioning, I need to make sure I'm better prepared.'

'Armed, you mean?' asked Abigail. 'With a gun?'

'No, absolutely not,' said Daniel. 'Bring guns into the equation and innocent people get hurt. No, I was just thinking that if we were in London I'd bring in some boxer friends of mine to watch out for me.'

'But we're not in London,' said Abigail.

'No, so I was considering asking around for possible protectors.'

'There's always the army,' said Abigail dryly. 'I'm sure they'd do it very efficiently.'

'Oh, very amusing,' said Daniel. 'What gets me is that I expected this sort of thing when we were walking through Ancoats or Hulme, Instead, I got caught right outside our hotel.'

They entered their room, then Abigail said, 'I didn't want to ask while Breda was with us, but were you telling the truth when you said they didn't mention Kathleen, or tell you to stop asking questions about the young Irish woman? I know you didn't want to frighten her at the thought they might.'

'No, it was exactly as I said. They didn't mention her at all,' said Daniel. 'Which I thought was interesting, because I'd assume it was our visit to ask about her that led to the attack. This would indicate their concern is about Peterloo. But I'm sure there's a connection.'

'I am, too,' agreed Abigail. 'But what?'

'Say someone that Kathleen knew of – say, a family member – was killed at Peterloo. She goes to the barracks to ask about them. They deny all knowledge and send her on her way. Then try to cover up the fact she'd been asking questions.' He frowned and shook his head. 'But why kill her? Peterloo is a dreadful episode in the army's history here, but there are no secrets about it. Everyone knows what happened. So what is someone trying to conceal?'

'I think we need to share what we've discovered with the police,' said Abigail.

'About Bickerstaff being at the museum on the day Kathleen died, and the business of someone pretending to be him and calling at the O'Donnells'?' queried Daniel.

'I suggest we keep those aspects to ourselves,' advised Abigail. 'If Bickerstaff is innocent, and what we've heard about the inspector is true, that could lead to him taking a terrible beating because of us. No, I meant about Con Gully and Dan Daly.'

There was a knock at the door. Abigail opened it to find a pageboy standing there.

'Excuse me,' he said, 'but there's a man downstairs says he wants to see you.'

'Did he give a name?' asked Abigail.

'Yes,' said the boy. 'Detective Constable Simms. He says he'd like you to accompany him to see Inspector Grimley.'

Inspector Grimley was sitting at his desk studying the story in the *Guardian*, a scowl on his face, as Daniel and Abigail were shown into his office. He got to his feet and brandished the paper at them.

'What's the meaning of this?' he demanded angrily. 'I told you the case was closed!'

'As far as the museum is concerned the case isn't closed,' retorted Abigail. 'And we work for them, not for you.'

'No, but you take sideswipes at us!' And angrily he read aloud, 'The local police and the mill owners are cogs in the wheel of corruption, working together to suppress the poor for the sake of the rich.'

'The tone of the story is nothing to do with us,' said Abigail. 'In fact, we've already been to see Mr Steggles at the museum to make that point.'

'And demanded a letter of apology for that article from Bickerstaff,' added Daniel.

'Oh yes?' sneered Grimley. 'You expect me to believe that when it depicts you two as some kind of detecting geniuses brought in to correct the stupidity of the local police! And in case anyone's in any doubt, it makes a point of mentioning my name!'

'As Miss Fenton has just said, we had nothing to do with the tone of the story. In fact, we expressly told Mr Bickerstaff when we talked to him that we only agreed to the story appearing if he avoided anything political, or any criticism of the police.'

Suddenly, Grimley seemed to become aware of the bruising around Daniel's eye, because he asked, 'Who punched you?'

'I'm guessing they were military types,' said Daniel. 'Which confirms something we'd already suspected: that the murder is connected with the army. Or, at least, the local barracks.' As Grimley stared at him in obvious disbelief, Daniel continued, 'You remember that Kathleen Donlan was stabbed just a couple of days after she'd been to the barracks to ask some questions, and been turned away. Well, I decided to look into that line of enquiry, and we also went to the barracks, where they told us the young woman hadn't been there at all. Which was a lie. She was there, and she went there with Eileen O'Donnell. I wondered what the barracks might be covering up, and someone mentioned Peterloo to us.'

'Peterloo!' snorted Grimley dismissively. 'That was nearly eighty years ago!'

'I must admit I couldn't see the relevance either,' agreed Daniel. 'But after I made enquiries about Peterloo, three men, who I'm sure were soldiers out of uniform, grabbed me and told me to stop asking questions about Peterloo, and gave me this to make sure I understood the message.'

'How does this relate to the women who were killed?'

'I'm not sure,' admitted Daniel. 'But the attack on me only happened after I went to ask questions about her, and about Peterloo. The person I saw, who I'm sure was the one who put the attackers on me, is Regimental Sergeant Major Bulstrode.'

'Did these men who attacked you mention the young woman? Like, "Stop asking questions about her"?'

'No,' admitted Daniel.

'Well there you are, then,' said Grimley. 'It's not connected. They just didn't like you asking questions about Peterloo. And that's because it's a sensitive subject for some in the army, even though it was a very long time ago.' He paused, then asked, 'Are you going to press charges against the men who attacked you?'

'Not at the moment,' said Daniel. 'For one thing, they were in civilian clothes, so I've got no proof they were connected to the army, except for the way they went about things. Also, there are about a thousand men in the barracks. RSM Bulstrode would make sure those men won't be around if I try to insist on checking everyone to pick them out. And in addition, Miss Fenton has picked up some new information that we believe may be pertinent, and points in a different direction.' He caught the warning look from Abigail to remind him they'd decided not to reveal what they'd learnt about Bickerstaff, and nodded as he continued, 'It concerns two men, once called Con Gully, a murderer from the same area the young woman came from, north Cork in Ireland, who has escaped and may be in Manchester. And a pimp called Dan Daly, known as Dapper Dan.'

'And where did you get this information?' demanded Grimley.

Before they could respond, there was a knock at the door, which opened to admit a tall, distinguished-looking man.

'Sir!' barked Grimley, springing to attention.

'At ease, Inspector,' said the new arrival. 'Mr Wilson and Miss Fenton. I'm Superintendent Mossop,' he introduced himself, extending a hand first towards Daniel, and then to Abigail. 'I heard that you were in the building, so I had to come to welcome you and say it is an honour to meet you. Mr Steggles informed me that he's engaged you both over the tragic deaths of the two women at the museum. I assume you have come to consult with Inspector Grimley over it.' And he looked enquiringly at Grimley, who forced a smile and said through gritted teeth, 'Indeed, sir.'

'Excellent.' Mossop nodded. 'The more minds, the better. Initially I was informed that the inspector felt there was insufficient evidence to continue with the investigation, but the fact he has invited you here suggests the contrary. Is there new evidence, Inspector?'

Grimley hesitated, then said, 'There may be, sir. I have received certain information from Mr Wilson and Miss Fenton, which I am looking into.'

'Excellent,' said Mossop. He turned to Daniel and Abigail. 'What is the nature of this information?'

'We've been reliably informed that the young lady who was killed was in an altercation in the street with a known pimp called Dan Daly, also known as Dapper Dan. It seems he was trying to importune her into becoming a prostitute for him. She got angry and struck him, and quite a few times, we've been told.'

'In public?'

'Yes, sir.'

'I see what you mean. A criminal like that can't afford to lose face. You think he may have killed her to warn any other women thinking of reacting the same way?'

'It's possible. We thought it an avenue worth exploring.'

'I agree.' Turning to Grimley, he asked, 'What do you think, Inspector?'

Grimley swallowed, then forced a nod. 'It's certainly worth investigating, sir. I shall have Daly brought in for questioning.'

'Very good,' said Mossop.

'There's also another possibility,' said Daniel.

He told the superintendent about Con Gully.

'And he may be here? In Manchester?'

'It's possible. On the other hand, it may be a false errand.'

'True, but it's worth exploring, don't you think, Inspector?'

'Indeed, sir,' said Grimley. 'I shall get in touch with the Irish police and get the man's description and have it circulated.'

'Excellent,' said Mossop. 'We cannot let the deaths of these poor women go unavenged. So, I'll leave you to your deliberations.' He smiled at Daniel and Abigail. 'It is an especial pleasure to meet you, Miss Fenton. Mr Steggles will tell you that I have long been interested in archaeology, as an amateur, obviously, and I have followed your work through the pages of the archaeology magazines which he has passed to me. Your work at Giza, in particular, makes the chance for me to shake you by the hand a very special occasion indeed.'

With that, he left. Daniel shot a look at Abigail and was again amused to see her face colouring at the compliment. Then he turned to Grimley. 'We are not your enemy, Inspector,' he said.

Grimley didn't answer, but they could see from the look of deep resentment in his eyes that he didn't agree.

They both nodded at Grimley and left.

The inspector stood staring vengefully at the closed door after them, then he wrenched it open and strode to the reception desk.

'Where's Sergeant Merton?' he demanded.

'I believe he's in the canteen, sir,' said the duty sergeant.

'Send someone to tell him I want to see him in my office,' barked Grimley. 'Now.'

He marched back to his office and reseated himself behind his desk. He picked up the newspaper with its offending article, scowled, then thrust it into the wastepaper basket. A short while later there was a knock at his door, which opened to reveal Sergeant Merton.

'You wanted to see me, Inspector?'

'Yes. Come in and shut the door,' snapped Grimley.

When Merton had done so, Grimley fixed him with a glare and said, 'Dan Daly. Dapper Dan.'

'What about him?' asked Merton.

'I've just had a pair of nosey parkers in telling Mossop that he may be the one who stabbed that young woman in the museum.'

'No, boss!' burst out Merton, shocked. 'Dan would never do nothing like that!'

'Are you sure of that?' asked Grimley. 'It seems she gave him a smacking in front of people.'

Merton shook his head. 'Even if she did, he'd never do that.'

'I know he's one of your narks, but I can't ignore this. Bring him in.'

Merton looked worried. 'He's very important to us, sir. He keeps us supplied with the inside track on most of the villains.'

'I don't care. He's been named.'

'I could ask him questions, sir. I know where he hangs out.'

'*I'm* going to question him,' growled Grimley. 'Which means it's done here, at the station. So bring him in.'

CHAPTER TWENTY

'Thank heavens for your work at Giza, and the fact that you're a famous celebrity,' said Daniel as they headed back towards their hotel. 'Otherwise I doubt if Superintendent Mossop would have come to our aid the way he did.'

'I am not a famous celebrity,' Abigail rebuked him.

'To those who are devotees of the archaeology of ancient Egypt, and there seem to be many of them, you are,' said Daniel. 'And it's something we should be grateful for. It gives us – or, more specifically, you – entrée to people and places we would find it difficult to penetrate.'

'It didn't help us at the barracks.'

'I doubt if RSM Bulstrode can be included in the list of your admirers,' said Daniel.

'I do not have a list of admirers!' burst out Abigail, annoyed.

'Honestly, Daniel, you make me sound so . . . shallow!'

'No. You would only be shallow if you cultivated it, and I know you don't.'

'To be honest, I find it embarrassing,' said Abigail crossly.

As they entered the hotel and walked towards the reception desk to collect their room key, they recognised the burly figure of Charles Burbage there. He smiled as he saw them.

'Miss Fenton! Mr Wilson! I was just about to leave a message for you. My contact at the mortuary told me that another woman has been brought in, stabbed to death. I thought I'd let you know in case it might be connected to the young woman I photographed.'

'It might be, or it could just be an unfortunate happening,' said Daniel. 'Is anything known about her?'

'Just her name,' said Burbage. 'Eve Preston.'

Daniel and Abigail exchanged startled looks.

'You know her?' asked Burbage.

Daniel nodded. 'If it's the same person. After your photograph appeared in the paper, a woman approached us and said she recognised her. As it turned out, the information she gave us was a lie.'

'Or mistaken,' put in Abigail. 'The dead woman in the photograph may simply have resembled this woman she mentioned. Deborah. Anyway, she told us her name was Eve Preston.'

'There's one way to find out,' said Burbage.

'Yes,' agreed Daniel. 'Is your friend Karl still at the mortuary now?'

'Even if he isn't, I know the other attendants,' said Burbage.

Daniel, Abigail and Burbage watched as Karl, the mortuary attendant, rolled down the top of the sheet to reveal the head of the woman on the table.

'That's her,' said Abigail. 'That's the woman who came to see us.'

'How was she stabbed?' asked Daniel. 'In the back?'

'No,' said Karl. 'In the front. The blade went into her heart.'

'Where was she killed?'

'Her body was found in an alley in Hulme.'

'That's where she said we'd find the man she accused,' murmured Abigail. 'At a pub called the Iron Duke.'

'Oh, that place is a hellhole!' said Burbage.

'You've been there?'

'Just once, when I heard the police were mounting a raid on it, looking for stolen goods.' He gave a shudder. 'If you're thinking of going there, it's not somewhere I'd go without some kind of protection.' He looked enquiringly at Abigail and Daniel. 'Is this connected with the other two deaths, do you think?' he asked.

'It's possible,' replied Daniel. He looked at Abigail. 'I think we have to take this to Inspector Grimley. And I've got a feeling he isn't going to be happy with us.'

William Bickerstaff arrived outside the door marked C P SCOTT. He wondered why the editor of the *Guardian* had summoned him. Was it his latest piece? Possibly he'd gone a bit far in his attack on the police, but it was about time someone did. In his opinion, there was a vicious circle of corruption at work involving the mill owners and the police that he was determined to expose. One day the masses of Manchester, the poor and the underprivileged, would realise how much they owed William Bickerstaff, but for that day to come there would need to be proper social justice.

He tapped at the door, and at the command 'Come in!', entered.

Charles Prestwich Scott, more commonly known as CP, sat stiffly behind his desk, a serious look on his face. But then, that was not unusual; CP took many things seriously – his Liberal Party politics, social conditions, and especially the reputation of the *Manchester Guardian* as a forward-looking newspaper. He was in his late forties and cut a well-known figure in Manchester with his formal dress, his high starched collars, his bushy beard.

'Mr Bickerstaff,' he said.

'You wanted to see me, CP?' asked Bickerstaff, taking the chair that Scott gestured towards.

'Yes,' said Scott. 'I've received a letter from Bernard Steggles at the museum accusing you of dishonesty. He says he asked you to submit the article you intended to write to him for his approval as a prerequisite of him agreeing for the article to appear. He says he had agreed to the article being written, mentioning the museum, providing it avoided political bias. You sent him the article, which he approved, but the one you put into print was very different. *Very* different. He says in his letter it attacks the police as corrupt and calls for social insurrection against the ruling establishment. I have read your article and, indeed, that is the message you convey in it.'

'That's true,' said Bickerstaff. 'I made certain changes after Mr Steggles had approved the story because I felt the existing tone was too bland.'

'Without referring those changes back to him?'

'Surely our job is to report the news with comment as and where we see fit,' snapped Bickerstaff. 'I didn't realise that we were in the pocket of the ruling class and were here to act as a mouthpiece for the establishment. I thought this was supposed to be a radical newspaper!'

'It is also a newspaper that prides itself on its honesty!' thundered Scott, and there was no mistaking the anger in his voice or on his face. 'You have lied and deliberately deceived one of the most honourable and respected people in Manchester. According to Mr Steggles, you also did the same to Mr Wilson and Miss

Fenton. You have brought shame and disrepute to this newspaper.'

'I did what I thought was best.'

'You betrayed the confidence that was entrusted to you.'

'For the common good.'

'No, for your own agenda. I have warned you about this before, Bickerstaff. Yes, the *Manchester Guardian* is proud of its crusading liberal style, but we do not cheat and lie. You have broken a special trust. You cannot be trusted. You are dismissed with immediate effect.'

'You can't do that!' exclaimed Bickerstaff, leaping to his feet.

'I have just done it,' snapped the editor. 'Clear your personal items from your desk and leave. You will not be allowed back into the building.'

CHAPTER TWENTY-ONE

Sergeant Merton spent most of the day trawling pubs and drinking dens that he knew Dapper Dan frequented, finally tracking him down in a den with no name on the fringes of Ancoats.

'Well, well!' Daly smiled. 'Pete Merton, as I live and breathe. Is this a social visit?'

Merton shook his head. 'It's not social or official,' he said.

Daly caught the worried tone to the sergeant's voice and frowned, apprehensive. 'What's that supposed to mean?' he asked.

'I've been told to bring you in for questioning.'

'Who by?'

'Grimley.'

Daly shook his head. 'No way,' he said firmly. 'We all know how he questions people. Well, I'm not going to sit there and let him beat me to a pulp. What's this all about, anyway?'

'You know that young Irish woman who got stabbed in the museum?'

'What about her?'

'Well, someone told Grimley that you and her had had an argument, and she belted you.'

'Rubbish!'

'There were witnesses.'

'I never touched the girl!'

'No, but she touched you, that's what the word is.'

'And Grimley thinks I did her in because of that?' He stared at Merton, incredulousness on his face. 'Do you know how many times I've been hit by a woman? And I've never done anything back about it!'

'Oh, come on, Dan! I've seen 'em.'

'Yeah, all right, maybe the odd slap, just to keep 'em in order. But nothing else! Nothing worse! And certainly nothing like this! I don't even carry a knife!' He glared at Merton. 'Anyway, what do I pay you for? The agreement is you keep me out of trouble.'

'And I would, but in this case Mossop's on Grimley's back, so he's on mine.'

'So square Grimley. Bung him a few quid, like you have before.'

Merton shook his head. 'That won't work in this case, Dan.'

'Well . . . square the super!'

'You're talking mad, now, Dan. The super's on the straight and narrow.' He hesitated. 'I was going to suggest you did a runner. Just for a day or so, until this all blows over.'

'Leave?'

'Think of it as a holiday. A week away. Blackpool, say. Then I tell Grimley that I couldn't find you. Trust me, it'll all soon die down.'

'Yeah, I suppose so,' said Daly. 'Better than being on the end of Grimley's flying fists. But you find who did it, Pete! Killed the girl, that is. So I can come back. I've got a lot invested in this area.'

As Daniel had forecast, their return to Newton Street police station was not welcomed with open arms. A message from the sergeant at the desk brought a scowling Inspector Grimley from his office.

'You two again!' he growled. 'Don't you think I've got work to do?'

'Something's happened that may have a bearing on the case,' said Daniel. 'A woman called Eve Preston was stabbed. Her body's in the mortuary.'

'Yes, I'm aware of that,' said Grimley. 'I suppose you're going to tell me she's another victim of our mystery killer.'

'There's one thing that connects them,' said Daniel. 'After the photograph of the dead woman appeared in the newspaper, Eve Preston called on us at our hotel and told us the young woman was called Deborah, that she was a pickpocket, and the person who she thought had killed her was a man called Terry Brady. She said he could be found at the Iron Duke pub in Hulme.'

Grimley stared angrily at them. 'You didn't think it was worth telling me this before, but you bothered to let me know about this mystery escaped Irish murderer and Dan Daly?'

'We believe she was either lying or mistaken,' defended Abigail. 'We've just told you, Eve Preston said the dead woman was called Deborah and was a pickpocket who worked with this Terry Brady. Immediately afterwards we discovered that she was actually called Kathleen Donlan and had just arrived in England from Ireland, so it was wrong information.'

'Except perhaps the bit about Terry Brady murdering her,' snapped Grimley. 'Maybe she knew what he'd done and was telling the truth about that bit, but decided to colour the rest of it.'

'Why would she do that?' demanded Abigail.

'Who knows,' barked Grimley angrily. 'Eve Preston could have told us if I'd known about it and had a word with her, but it's a bit late for that now.'

'Once we knew her information was false there was no sense in spending more time on it,' said Daniel.

'No? If you had, she might still be alive now instead of being dead on a table in the morgue!'

'There was obviously something about this Terry Brady that had upset her, which is why she came to us,' said Daniel. 'So the obvious thing is to pull in this Terry Brady and talk to him.'

'Don't try to tell me my job,' snapped Grimley. 'That was my first thought as soon as you told me about her and what she told you. So if you'll excuse me and get out of my hair, I'm going to get some proper police work done and send some men to the Iron Duke.'

He muttered darkly under his breath as he watched them leave. 'Damn interfering amateurs playing at detectives.'

He was still standing in reception when Sergeant Merton arrived, an unhappy expression on his face.

'What are you looking so miserable about?' demanded Grimley.

'Dapper Dan,' said Merton, and he gave a rueful sigh. 'He's vanished.'

'What do you mean, vanished?' barked Grimley.

'Like I said, he's done a runner. I've been to every place he hangs out, and everyone says there's no sign of him. One of my narks reckoned he's gone to Newcastle.'

Grimley stared at his sergeant. 'Why would he go to Newcastle?' he said, incredulous.

'Maybe he's got business there,' suggested Merton. 'D'you want me to go to Newcastle and see if I can find him?'

'Absolutely not!' snorted Grimley. 'I reckon it's a wild goose chase anyway. No, I've got another job for you. Go to the Iron Duke in Hulme and bring in a bloke called Terry Brady.'

'The Iron Duke?' said Merton doubtfully. 'That's a rough pub, guv.'

'Well, take some men with you,' snapped Grimley. 'Men who know how to fight and aren't afraid to crack a few heads if needed. But bring him in.'

CHAPTER TWENTY-TWO

Sergeant Merton made his way towards the Iron Duke pub with a feeling of apprehension. Not because of the threat of violence that waited there; if that had been the case he would have done as Grimley ordered and brought reinforcements along with him. No, his worried state of mind concerned the lucrative business he'd built up over his time in the police and which now looked to be under threat. He knew the Iron Duke well, as he did most of the pubs and drinking dens in the poorer parts of Manchester. He'd built up good relationships with the owners and landlords of most of the pubs and dens, like Billy Scargell at the Iron Duke. Billy knew which of his clients was up to a bit of criminality. Nothing as bad as murder, usually robbery or burglary, pimping or running small gangs of pickpockets, often kids. In exchange for regular payment, shared with Billy, Merton would turn a blind eye to such activities, and if an arrest was made by someone else, Merton would find a way to square the situation. Where poor people were involved, money always had an impact.

Merton had found a good trick was to hint that any money that was paid to him was shared higher up the scale, including Inspector Grimley. Most small-time criminals knew about Grimley's reputation as a hard man with his fists and boots, and so were more than happy to pay up to keep out of his clutches. The truth was that none of the money that Merton received went to the inspector. In fact, as far as Merton knew, Grimley was unaware of his sergeant's sideline. Grimley knew that Merton had his informers, his narks, as most coppers did, and it was generally accepted that those narks could be allowed a bit of leeway so long as they passed information about other criminals back. In Merton's case, there was always some up-and-coming youngster trying to make a name for himself as a crook, who wasn't yet part of Merton's source of additional income, who could be arrested and brought in to fit a particular crime. And always from the poor. The poor knew there was no point in protesting their innocence. They had no rights. Every arrest made Merton look good in his boss's eyes. All in all, it was a good system that had seen Merton prosper. But now it was under threat, and all because of those two busybodies, Wilson and the Fenton woman. If they hadn't talked to Superintendent Mossop, the super wouldn't have leant on Grimley, and the inspector wouldn't have sent him after two of his clients, Dapper Dan Daly and now Terry Brady. The inspector seemed to have accepted the idea that Dapper Dan had done a runner, but would he swallow the same excuse twice if Merton told him that Brady, too, had vanished? It was unlikely, knowing the inspector.

In which case, Grimley might well go to the Iron Duke himself and start shaking people up to find out where Terry Brady had gone. And if that happened, there was a good chance that someone like Billy Scargell might start protesting that this went against the payments that had been made to the inspector through the sergeant for them to be looked after.

Merton shuddered at the thought of what Grimley's reaction would be if he found out how Merton had been taking money in his name. The sergeant had seen the inspector at work on a suspect, giving out beatings that had made him feel sick to watch them. It was because of that, people found it easy to believe that someone that vicious and violent could also be corrupt. The truth was, Grimley was honest, damn him. Anyone offering him a bribe could expect a kick in the balls and a beating.

There was only one way round this situation and that was to tell Terry Brady to vanish, just as he'd done with Dan Daly, and then report back to Grimley that Brady was dead. If Grimley asked to see Brady's body, he'd say that Brady had got run over by a train and his body was so badly mangled it had gone straight for burial. Grimley might even believe it; lots of people got killed by trains.

Yes, he decided, that was the answer. Brady would be dead, and when this was all over and Brady reappeared on the scene, if he was asked, Merton would say it was a case of mistaken identity. Everyone thought the bloke run over by the train was Brady because he looked like him. What was left of him, that was.

Feeling more confident than he had done earlier, Merton arrived at the Iron Duke and made his way in. At this time of day there were just a few people in the pub, and Merton was surprised how subdued everyone appeared to be. Usually, whatever the hour, there was lively chatter going on, boisterous banter and the occasional song belted out in drunken tones, but today an air of sombre silence had descended.

Merton walked to the bar, where Billy Scargell was wiping glasses, although the cloth he was using looked so filthy that Merton was sure it was adding dirt to the glass rather than cleaning it.

'Afternoon, Billy,' said Merton.

'Sergeant.' Scargell nodded, his expression unsmiling, which was unusual for the pub landlord.

Something's happened, thought Merton. *Something bad.*

'Usual?' asked Scargell.

'Pint,' said Merton, adding, 'in an unwiped glass.'

As Scargell poured his pint, Merton said, 'I'm looking for Terry Brady.'

At his words, there was a wailing sound from one of the women in the pub, followed by sobbing, and a hubbub as other patrons gathered round the woman to comfort her.

'What's going on?' asked Merton.

'Terry Brady was found a couple of hours ago,' said Scargell. 'It looks like someone had taken an axe to him.'

Merton stared at Scargell, stunned. 'Dead?' he asked.

'What do you think?' hissed Scargell, his voice low as he shot a glance at the sobbing woman. 'His head was cut almost in half.'

Well, ain't I the lucky one! thought Merton, relieved. *The guv'nor will have to believe this!*

William Bickerstaff lifted the cloth package from the chest of drawers in his rented room and unwrapped the hessian to reveal the revolver inside. He held it, feeling the butt hard and snug in his grip. He'd bought the gun from a criminal he'd met while reporting a story. It had seemed an exciting thing to do at the time, though he had no intention of actually using it. Until now.

A sense of anger filled him as he thought about what had happened. His attempts to bring social reform about through his writing had come to naught. Political pamphlets and tracts offered an opportunity, but the pages of the *Manchester Guardian* had meant his words reached thousands. And now that voice had been silenced. Now he was unemployed, and – even worse – unemployable because C. P. Scott wouldn't give him a reference. He didn't blame the editor for that; he did it from his own sense of strong belief in right and wrong. But in Bickerstaff's mind there were a whole bevy of people who could be blamed for his situation. Starting with his father, Lord Trevelyan Norton-Wallace-Bickerstaff. Rich, privileged, and – to Bickerstaff's shame – a major shareholder in many of the cotton mills, getting fat off the misery of the poor. Things had always been difficult between his father and himself. And, also, between William and his two older brothers. When William had first shown signs of support for radical politics – or social justice, as Bickerstaff preferred to think of it – he had been derided at home, then verbally abused, and finally ordered to end his involvement in such politics, or leave his father's house. He had chosen to leave and had taken this room in one of the poorer areas of the city, believing it would make him one of the people he aspired to help. It hadn't. They heard his voice, the upper-class accent, even though he tried to disguise it, and were wary of him.

The truth was, he didn't fit. His upbringing had been intended to make him feel superior, part of the elite of society, but he hadn't felt at ease in his family's social class. But nor did he feel comfortable among the lower classes with their sweated labour and their drinking.

And then he'd gone to that lecture at the university about social justice, and about Karl Marx, and suddenly he realised that there was something he could do. He could write about it, encouraging others, which meant exposing the corruption that lay behind the whole rotten system, showing them the human cost of this social disorder. The inhumanity. Yes, he had to admit, occasionally he'd skated a bit close to dangerous territory in some of his articles, but by keeping it general and not naming specific people, he'd been able to get away with it. Until now. Now, he was out in the cold.

His grip on the revolver tightened and a sense of determination filled him.

He would have his revenge, and at the same time he would bring about the change that was so very much needed. For that to happen he needed a high-profile victim. And he knew just the person. The one whose complaint had landed him in this position.

CHAPTER TWENTY-THREE

Bernard Steggles sat at his desk on Friday and reread the letter he'd received from Henry Eeles Dresser with a sense of shock.

Dear Mr Steggles,

It is with great regret that I have to write to you at such short notice to advise you that I have recently contracted an infection of the throat that has resulted in my losing my voice. Because of this I will be unable to give my talk at the museum. I am deeply sorry about this and hope that we can reorganise it for a later date.

With apologies again.

Yours sincerely,

Henry E. Dresser

This was a disaster! This talk was going to be one of the jewels in the crown of the museum. As he'd proudly told Abigail Fenton and Daniel Wilson, Dresser was not just famous as an ornithologist in Britain but across the world! Honorary Fellow of the American Ornithologists Union! Secretary of the British Ornithologists Union! Devotees of birdwatching would have flocked to the museum in their hundreds to hear Dresser talk. The evening would have been reported in the most prestigious ornithology magazines. And now . . . nothing!

As soon as Steggles had received Dresser's letter he'd sent a telegram to Thomas Coward asking if he could take Dresser's place. Coward was perhaps not as famous as Dresser, but he was still a noted and highly respected figure in British ornithology. He was also a local man, a former student at Owens College, living in Hale.

Alas, the reply from Coward's family had dashed Steggles's hopes: Thomas Coward was in Cornwall, so not available. Who else could he get, and at such short notice? The truth was, there was no one to match Dresser.

The telephone on his desk rang, and he picked it up to hear Mrs Wedburn say, 'Mr Steggles. Mr Jesse Haworth is here to see you, if you've got a moment.'

Jesse Haworth. One of the museum's prime benefactors!

'Of course. Please send him in.'

Jesse Haworth, sixty years old and still in fine fettle, as he kept assuring everyone. A partner in James Dilworth and Son, one of Manchester's main textile merchants, but most importantly one of the major sponsors of archaeological expeditions to Egypt, which had led to the Manchester Museum having one of the best collections of ancient Egyptian artefacts in the country.

The door opened and Haworth entered, stopping when he saw the look of anguish plain on Steggles's face.

'You're looking a mite frazzled, Bernard,' he commented.

'We have a disaster on our hands!' groaned Steggles.

'Aye, the two dead women,' said Haworth.

'No, worse than that!' Then Steggles corrected himself. 'No, obviously not as bad as that. But it's a more immediate problem. Henry Eeles Dresser has lost his voice! He can't talk!' He thrust the letter at Haworth. 'See, he's written in urgency to tell me.'

Haworth scanned the letter then handed it back. 'So he won't be able to give his talk.'

'No!' Steggles groaned. 'A disaster! At this short notice! I tried Thomas Coward . . .'

'A good man,' said Haworth. 'None better when it comes to birds.' Though he added cautiously, 'But British birds are Thomas's speciality. I'm not sure if he's the man to give a talk on exotic birds.'

'He can't do it anyway, he's in Cornwall,' groaned Steggles. 'What am I going to do? We have to cancel the evening! It will be a major blow against the museum's reputation!'

'Not necessarily,' said Haworth.

'You have someone else in mind?' asked Steggles, a light of hope dawning in his eyes.

'I do,' said Haworth. 'The reason I was coming to see you was because I saw in the paper . . .'

'About the two murdered women!' groaned Steggles.

'Well, yes and no. It said you had Abigail Fenton here.'

'Yes, she's here with Daniel Wilson investigating the murders.'

'You know who she is,' asked Haworth. 'When she's not detecting.'

'Yes, of course I do.'

'One of the most respected Egyptologists in Europe. If not the world,' continued Haworth.

'We are very privileged to have her here,' said Steggles.

'So I was going to suggest you see if she can't do a talk about her experiences as an archaeologist in Egypt while she's here. With Henry Dresser having to cancel, it seems to me you've got a space to fill. Why not ask her if she can do a session that evening instead? As many people would come to hear her talk about ancient Egypt as would hear Henry Dresser talk about birds.'

'You think she might?'

'The only way to find that out is to ask her. Personally, I've always found her to be very professional. Not that I've actually met her, but I funded the dig she and others did at Hawara, so I know what a hard and excellent worker she is. And it will be my pleasure to meet her face-to-face.'

Abigail and Daniel were comparing notes on what they'd discovered so far about the case, and trying to make sense of the different strands, when there was a knock at the door of their hotel room. Daniel opened it, and a pageboy handed him an envelope addressed to him.

Abigail looked at Daniel enquiringly as he opened the envelope and took out the single sheet of paper.

'News?' she asked.

'It's from Inspector Grimley,' said Daniel.

'Oh?' said Abigail. 'What's he say?'

'Terry Brady's been found.'

'And?'

'That's all,' said Daniel, passing her the note.

'A man of few words,' observed Abigail, reading it and passing it back to him.

'I suppose we have to go and see him to find out anything further,' said Daniel.

'If he'll share it with us,' said Abigail doubtfully.

'Oh, he will,' said Daniel. 'This is to put us in our place. He's done his job. If we want to know more we have to go and ask him.'

This time Grimley seemed almost pleased to see them when they arrived at Newton Street police station. At least, he wasn't as aggressively hostile as he'd been on Daniel's last visit.

'We got your note, Inspector,' said Daniel. 'So, Terry Brady has been found.'

Grimley nodded. 'He has.'

'Where is he? Can we talk to him?'

Grimley gave a chuckle. 'You can talk to him, but don't expect much in the way of an answer. What's left of him is in the mortuary. It looks like someone hit him over the head with an axe. So if it's our killer who did it, it looks like he's graduated on from knives.'

Abigail expressed her seething anger as they walked to the mortuary.

'He was playing with us,' she said angrily. 'He took delight in telling us that Brady was dead.'

'He did,' agreed Daniel.

'The man is a moron,' continued Abigail. 'How could he be pleased that a man has been viciously murdered? One who might have been able to give us a clue as to what all this is about!'

'I'm not sure that the inspector is very bothered about finding out who killed Kathleen or Eileen,' said Daniel. 'Or Eve Preston, for that matter. As far as he's concerned they're people of no importance. He'd rather their cases were just forgotten, and they would have been if it hadn't been for us being in the picture. As it is, he's going through the motions because Superintendent Mossop showed interest, but he's hoping that will wane.'

'How can he call himself a policeman!' burst out Abigail in disgust.

191

'He sees the job of policeman differently,' said Daniel. 'I believe he sees it as being one who keeps the peace, stops disorder.'

'But allows murder and violence to flourish!'

'On a small scale, rather than large-scale social disorder.'

'Which is what William Bickerstaff was suggesting in his article,' said Abigail.

By now they had arrived at the infirmary. They made their way down to the basement and the mortuary.

'Our third visit,' observed Daniel. 'We're becoming part of the fabric of the place.' He stopped suddenly as they neared the door of the mortuary. 'But this may be different. Grimley said he'd been attacked with an axe. This may be one body you may choose not to view.'

'I am perfectly capable of controlling my emotions,' retorted Abigail tartly.

'It's not your emotions I'm thinking of,' replied Daniel. 'I've seen victims of axe attacks, and the way the body responds to such a sight . . .'

'My body is under the same control as my emotions,' responded Abigail curtly. 'We'll go in.'

She pushed the door open and they walked in, their noses receiving the same smell of disinfectant and decaying flesh as before. Karl the attendant was on duty, as he had been before during their visits, and he gave them a smile of welcome.

'Inspector Grimley said you might be along,' he told them. 'But I have to tell you that this one is rather unpleasant, if you're not familiar with murder by axe.'

'Thank you for your concern, but I assure you I will be fine,' said Abigail. 'When I was in Egypt I saw many people who'd been maimed by sharp implements.'

'This is rather more than being maimed,' said Karl.

'I will be fine,' Abigail repeated.

'Very well,' said Karl. 'He's over here.'

Karl led the way to a cloth-covered shape on a table at the far side of the room. As the attendant peeled back the sheet and revealed the remains beneath, Abigail let out a gasp of horror.

'My God!'

'Are you sure you want to be here?' asked Daniel, concerned. Abigail had gone deathly white and was swaying slightly, and he was afraid she was going to fall.

'I'm fine,' said Abigail in a faint voice, though Daniel could tell she wasn't. He wasn't surprised. For all her insistence that she'd seen dead people before in Egypt and elsewhere, he doubted if anyone could be prepared for the butchery that was on display here. The head had certainly been split in half from top to bottom, the two sides of the skull, left and right, having been tied around the temples to hold the head together. In addition, the killer had attacked the rest of the body with the axe: the left arm was smashed and almost severed just below the shoulder, the broken right collarbone was poking through the skin, and there were gaping open wounds in the skin on the chest. Daniel had thought he was immune to being affected by violence inflicted on the human body after the Jack the Ripper investigations and the eviscerated corpses he'd had to examine, but this attack was monstrous.

'I think I will wait outside,' said Abigail suddenly, and she left the room and the horror that was on the table.

'Thank you, we've seen enough,' Daniel thanked the attendant, and he followed her.

Abigail was on a chair just outside the mortuary, her head down and almost in her lap, and Daniel wondered if she'd fainted. He laid his hand gently on her shoulder, and immediately she jerked upright.

'I'm all right,' she managed to say.

'If you want to be sick, there's a toilet just along the corridor,' said Daniel.

She shook her head.

'There's no shame in it,' said Daniel. 'I was sick when I was a constable and saw my first body.'

'Was it as bad as this?' she asked.

Daniel hesitated, then said, 'Yes, I'm afraid it was.'

'Who could do such a thing?' burst out Abigail. 'That's not murder, that's . . . that's . . .'

'Slaughterhouse butchery,' said Daniel.

He sat down on the chair beside her and took her hand in his.

'I'm sorry,' she said in a faint voice.

'Don't be silly,' said Daniel. 'I've just said, it happens to everyone the first time we see something as terrible as this.' He paused, then said quietly, 'One thing it tells us, this was done by a different person to the one who killed Kathleen. The way that Kathleen was killed was controlled, methodical. The killer did it in the museum and slipped away without anyone noticing. That's about being in control. The way that Terry Brady was killed is someone filled with rage, bringing the axe down hard enough to split his head almost in two and then continuing to batter the body . . .' He stopped as he saw her close her eyes and shiver. 'I'm sorry. I won't talk about it any more.'

'We have to,' she said. 'It's what we do.'

'It's what *I* do,' Daniel corrected her.

She turned to him, and although her face was still white, there was anger in her eyes. 'We're partners,' she snapped. 'Equal partners.' Then she dropped her gaze. 'I'm sorry, I didn't mean to be angry with you. I'm not. I'm just . . .'

'Shocked?' said Daniel.

She nodded. 'Talk to me,' she said. 'If this isn't the same killer, who is it?'

'I'm guessing it was someone who wanted revenge for something. Someone driven mad by fury. Why? What had Brady done to merit that much anger and violence?'

'Killed Eve Preston,' said Abigail.

'That's right,' said Daniel. 'It has to be. The person who killed Brady did it because he was in love with Eve Preston. Passionately in love with her. And when he found out it was Brady who'd killed her, he went after him with an axe.'

'But why would Brady kill Eve Preston?'

'Because in some way he'd found out that she'd come to us and named him as the one who'd killed the woman in the paper.'

'So he killed her in revenge?'

'Or anger.'

Abigail fell silent, thinking this over. Finally, she said, 'If you're thinking of going to Inspector Grimley with this, he'll say it's all speculation.'

'And he'd be right, but it's a feasible explanation,' said Daniel. 'I believe that if we find the person who was in love with Eve Preston, we'll find the person who killed Terry Brady.'

'And we take this to the inspector?'

'No,' said Daniel. 'I take it to him. With the negative attitude he's got towards us, it's highly likely he'll become abusive and throw us out. And you've had enough nastiness today. There's no need for us both to suffer the inspector's anger.'

Abigail still felt queasy as she entered the Mayflower Hotel. Despite her best efforts to control her emotions, she couldn't put the image of Terry Brady's shattered body out of her mind.

I need to do something to take my mind off it, she thought. *Sitting alone in our hotel room won't help me.*

Suddenly reaching a decision, she turned and left the hotel

and made her way to the museum. As she walked through its main entrance, she almost bumped into Jonty Hawkins, who was wearing his outdoor coat and heading somewhere in a hurry.

'My apologies,' she said.

'Not at all,' said Hawkins.

'Please, don't let your sense of politeness towards me detain you.' Abigail smiled at him. 'You're obviously off somewhere important.'

'Yes, to see you,' said Hawkins. He pulled an envelope from his pocket and held it out to her. 'This was delivered here for your attention. I was just about to bring it to the hotel and leave it for you.'

'Why thank you,' said Abigail.

She examined the envelope. It was addressed in very neat handwriting to Miss Abigail Fenton, care of the Manchester Museum. She didn't recognise the handwriting.

'I thought it might be important,' said Hawkins.

'It might be,' said Abigail. 'Thank you, Mr Hawkins.'

'Actually it's opportune that you've come in,' added Hawkins. 'Mr Steggles said if you did, he'd be grateful if you'd call on him. He's in his office.'

'Thank you,' said Abigail. 'I'll go and see him now.'

She put the envelope in her pocket and made her way to Bernard Steggles's office, wondering what possible new turn of events had made him want to see her. Would it be good news, or bad? Despite his obvious support for them, he must be aware that the reality was they were no further forward in their investigations. They had suppositions, but no firm evidence pointing the finger at any individual. Her tap on the door received the response 'Enter!'

Steggles's face lit up with a welcoming smile as Abigail entered the room, allaying her fears that this might turn out to be an awkward interview.

'Miss Fenton. Please, sit down.'

As Abigail took her seat opposite him, he lifted a sheet of paper from his desk and held it out to her. 'I received today this from Mr C. P. Scott, the editor of the *Manchester Guardian*.'

Abigail took the letter and read it. It was polite and apologetic in tone.

'You'll see that he accepts full responsibility for the article that appeared and makes it quite clear that Mr Bickerstaff rewrote it after I'd seen and approved it, without Mr Scott's knowledge or consent. As a result, he has dismissed Mr Bickerstaff from the staff of the *Guardian*.'

'Harsh, but understandable,' she commented, handing the letter back.

'Absolutely,' said Steggles. 'Unfortunate, but Mr Bickerstaff brought it on himself by his actions.' He looked inquisitively at Abigail. 'Are there any new developments on the case?' he asked.

Abigail filled him in on the murders of Eve Preston, and of Terry Brady, and noted the look of shock and disgust when she told him that Brady had been killed with what appeared to have been an axe.

'How dreadful!' he gasped. He shook his head. 'It seems the case is getting out of hand. We now have four people dead, and the manner in which they've been murdered seems to be escalating into extreme violence.'

'We don't know that the murders of Eve Preston and Terry Brady are connected with those of Kathleen Donlan and Eileen O'Donnell,' said Abigail. 'Mr Wilson is convinced they are separate to the other two.'

'Are you and Mr Wilson still of the opinion the murders of these poor unfortunate women are connected in some way to the army?'

'We are,' said Abigail. 'The problem is that the army appears to be a law unto itself, its own military judicial procedures apparently having precedence over civilian law.' As she saw a look of concern cloud Steggles's face, she added with a confidence she didn't really feel, 'However, we believe we may be able to circumvent that, and we'll be putting a plan of action into operation to effect that very shortly.'

'Excellent!' Steggles smiled. 'And if there's anything I can do to facilitate your efforts, don't hesitate to ask.'

'Thank you,' said Abigail.

She began to rise, but Steggles waved for her to remain in her seat, as he said, 'Actually, there's another topic on which I'd like to talk to you. One close to your heart. Ancient Egyptian archaeology.'

'Oh?' said Abigail, her interested piqued.

'I've been approached by Mr Jesse Haworth – I'm assuming you might be familiar with his name . . .'

'Of course!' exclaimed Abigail. 'He and Mr Henry Martyn Kennard were the ones who sponsored Flinders Petrie's excavations at Hawara, as well as at Kahun and Gurob. I was delighted to note that in the museum's guide you give them the credit for your superb display of ancient Egyptian artefacts.'

'Although most of Mr Kennard's share went to the Ashmolean in Oxford,' said Steggles. 'It was Mr Haworth who donated his share of the finds to us here. He is doing his best to make the world aware of Manchester. He's a partner in James Dilworth and Sons, the cotton manufacturers.'

'Yes, I've already had a conversation on that point with Mr Bickerstaff,' said Abigail bitterly. 'It rather gives the lie to Mr Bickerstaff's comments about the mill owners sucking the lifeblood of the poor so they can amass riches.'

'This museum would not have the Egyptian display without his financial generosity,' agreed Steggles. 'Anyway, Mr Haworth contacted me after he read in the newspaper that you were here in the city, and he . . . er . . .' He hesitated, before adding awkwardly, 'You remember I told you about the forthcoming talk by Mr Henry Eeles Dresser.'

'On exotic birds,' said Abigail.

'Yes. Well it appears that Mr Dresser has unfortunately contracted a throat infection and lost his voice, so he will not be able to give his talk. And Mr Haworth suggested that you might agree to give a talk in his place on your archaeological experiences in Egypt. This is not just as a substitute; Mr Haworth suggested it even before he knew that Mr Dresser would be unable to be here . . .'

'Of course I will,' said Abigail.

'You will?' Steggles beamed delightedly. 'This is superb!'

'It will be a pleasure to finally meet him, and thank him,' said Abigail. 'I was at one of the sites Mr Haworth sponsored. At Hawara.'

'With Petrie,' observed Steggles. 'That must have been a wonderful experience.'

'I must tell you, Mr Steggles, when I saw the artefacts from Hawara on display here, they transported me back to my time at the pyramid.'

'Perhaps you could make Hawara the subject of your talk?' suggested Steggles. 'It would bring in Petrie, and the fact that Mr Haworth funded the expedition, and the fact that you were there as part of it, with your personal reminiscences . . .'

'That is an excellent suggestion. Would it be possible to have some of the artefacts out of their cases and on display? That way I can talk about them, and – with your agreement – allow the people there to touch them. Because there is nothing that brings that time alive better than being able to touch something that is thousands of years old.'

'I'm not sure about that,' murmured Steggles doubtfully. 'They are fragile, and the risk of them being broken . . .'

'Perhaps we could select just one or two of the pieces?' suggested Abigail. 'I could select the more robust.'

'Yes, that would be acceptable,' said Steggles. He smiled happily. 'This is wonderful, Miss Fenton! Mr Haworth will be delighted when I tell him.'

CHAPTER TWENTY-FOUR

Grimley sat behind his desk and glared at Daniel.

'So let's make sure I've got this right,' he grunted. 'You say that Terry Brady killed Eve Preston, and some person we don't know about chops Terry Brady up in revenge because he's in love with her?'

'Yes,' answered Daniel.

'Poppycock!' snorted Grimley.

'Who else would want to kill her?' insisted Daniel. 'She'd shopped this Terry Brady to us, put him in the frame for murder.'

'For a murder that she made up,' retorted Grimley. 'There've been no reports about anyone called Deborah turning up dead.'

'She mistook the woman in the photograph, or she made it up to have her own back on him,' said Daniel.

'This is nonsense!' spat Grimley. 'Pure speculation! Is this how you did things at Scotland Yard?'

'Yes,' said Daniel.

'Then it was no wonder you never caught the Ripper!' snorted Grimley. He pointed at the door. 'Out. And don't come back here bothering me again.'

'But . . .'

'Out! And leave police work to proper working coppers.'

Abigail waited until she was back in their hotel room before she opened the envelope Jonty Hawkins had handed to her. The signature at the end of the letter inside brought a smile to her lips. Septimus Creighton had been a student at Cambridge at the same time as she'd studied there, and now – according to the letterhead – he was a professor at Manchester's Victoria University. The letter said that he'd read in the *Manchester Guardian* that she was in town, investigating a murder at the museum, and he wondered if it might be possible to meet up.

It would be wonderful to catch up and reminisce about old times, he wrote. *Do you remember when we went punting on the Cam and my pole got stuck and I was left high and temporarily dry clinging to the pole as you drifted away in the punt, before gravity won over and I was immersed, ruining the outfit I'd worn especially for the occasion.*

Yes, she did remember, and also other occasions when his best-laid plans had gone awry. Perhaps that was the reason she'd resisted taking their possible relationship further. Septimus had been keen, but Abigail had been rather more serious about things in those days. For a woman to be able to study for a degree had been a privilege, one not to be taken lightly, or treated frivolously. And if there had been a word to describe Septimus in his Cambridge days, 'frivolous' would have fitted the bill. But her time spent with him had been fun. Harmless fun. And there had been something about him, a puppy-like naivety, that had stopped her from putting an end to their meetings. In the end, they'd sort of fizzled out, once Septimus accepted that Abigail was never going to view him as a suitable romantic prospect.

She wondered what sort of man he'd turned out to be. Academically, he'd always been bright, so his becoming a professor came as no surprise, but she wondered why he was a professor at Victoria University rather than at Cambridge. Possibly that had been a side effect of his rather light-hearted approach to life. The college authorities had not approved; they preferred their professors to be of a serious demeanour.

I shall write back and invite him to meet us at the hotel, she decided. She wondered if Septimus had ever married. She debated with herself suggesting that when he called he bring his wife, if he had one – but then reflected that might be sending a wrong signal, that she was asking if he was married or single, and she didn't want him to think she had ambitions towards him in that direction. Polite and friendly, but not intimate, she decided, would be the right tone.

She was just taking a sheet of the headed notepaper the hotel supplied for the use of guests in order to begin her reply, when Daniel returned. The rueful smile he gave her told her his visit to the police station had not been successful.

'The inspector threw you out again?' she asked.

'Not physically,' said Daniel. 'I left of my own accord, but Grimley made his feelings towards us very clear.' He caught sight of the letterheaded notepaper and the inkwell and pen in front of her, and asked, 'Catching up on correspondence? To your sister, Bella, perhaps, to try and offer a truce? She still seems to resent the fact that we are – in her words – living in sin.'

Abigail smiled and shook her head, and offered him Septimus Creighton's letter. He read it, and then looked at her quizzically.

'Punting on the Cam?' he said. 'This sounds like a romance.'

'Hardly,' said Abigail. 'Everyone punts on the Cam.'

'Unchaperoned?'

'It was not like that at all,' said Abigail crisply. 'Septimus read Classics at Trinity at the same time as I was studying in Cambridge, and we'd meet up occasionally as fellow students. Now he's a professor at Victoria University here in Manchester, so I think your prayers may be answered.'

'What prayers?' asked Daniel.

'For physical protection, in case anyone tries to attack you again.'

Daniel looked at her, puzzled. 'What use would a university professor be against a bunch of soldiers, or thugs?'

'The second most important university competition in the English sporting calendar, after the sporting rivalry between Oxford and Cambridge, is the Christie Cup,' explained Abigail. 'It's an annual varsity match between the universities of Manchester, Leeds and Liverpool, and includes sports such as rugby. Septimus was a Cambridge blue at rugby, very keen on the sport, so I'm pretty sure he has access to the rugby squad at Victoria, and if so it's possible that some of them might want to take on the role of our physical protectors. If they're anything like their Cambridge counterparts, they'll be ideal for the job.'

'Why would they want to protect me?'

'Because Septimus will ask them. And, if they're the sort of people I think they will be, they love a physical scrap. I was just about to reply and suggest he meet us at our hotel.' Then she turned to him, her face very thoughtful. 'Another possibility has just occurred to me. Could it be that Kathleen's death might have its roots in Ireland? After all, she was only here for a few days. That's not much time for her to make a mortal enemy.'

'She was asking questions,' said Daniel.

'Her asking questions may well have provoked someone to kill her to stop her finding answers, but about what?' pressed Abigail. 'I think we need to look to Ireland and find out why she'd come to England.'

'Yes,' Daniel agreed, 'that's an excellent suggestion.' Almost angrily, he added, 'I should have thought of it before. If I hadn't got so obsessed with the army aspect . . .'

'No, I think you're right about that,' said Abigail. 'But I hope we might get the missing piece of the puzzle from Ireland. And luckily we have a very good connection there.'

'Father O'Brien.'

Abigail nodded.

As they walked to St Michael's Church, Abigail told Daniel about Steggles asking her to give a talk on her archaeological work in Egypt.

'I think that's a wonderful idea,' he said.

St Michael's Church was empty, except for two women arranging flowers and the elderly priest himself, whose face lit up when he saw them.

'It's good to see you,' he said. He gestured them to a pew, and the three of them sat down. 'Have there been any developments?'

'Nothing we can say for certain,' said Abigail. 'Which is why we thought we'd see if there's any information in Ireland that could help us, particularly if we can discover the reason Kathleen came to Manchester. We're hoping we might be able to make contact with someone who knew her, who was close to her, who we can talk to. To that end, we thought we'd try putting something in a local paper over there, asking for information. You said she came from north Cork. Do you happen to know anyone at the newspaper that serves that area?'

'As it happens, I do,' said O'Brien. 'The Irish community is quite tight-knit. You could say that everyone knows everyone, regardless of wherever they may have travelled to. I know a man at the *North Cork Reporter* called Sean Fitzpatrick quite well. If you let me have details of what you want to know, I'd be happy to send it to him.'

'We thought a word about what had happened to her and the fact that we're private enquiry agents, so there's no hint of the police,' said Abigail. 'After what you said about people being suspicious of the police. Also, we'll send the photograph of Kathleen, and say we're trying to find out why she came to Manchester, and that people can get in touch with us at the Mayflower Hotel.'

'That seems to cover everything,' said O'Brien. 'If you can let me have that today, I'll send it off to Sean at once.'

'Thank you, Father,' said Abigail. 'We'll be back later.'

As they left the church, Daniel said, 'Now to hopefully get approval from Mr Steggles for us to travel to Ireland, if anything comes of an article in the Cork local paper. As you're in his good books with this talk, I suggest you do most of the talking when we see him.'

'Am I in danger of becoming the senior partner in this team?' asked Abigail, amused.

'A temporary matter,' said Daniel. 'Think of this as part of your training.'

Bernard Steggles received them in his office with a look of apprehension.

'I hope you aren't here with news of more deaths?' he asked.

'Not as far as we are aware of,' said Abigail.

'Thank heavens for that!' said Steggles, sinking back into his chair.

'We've decided to make enquiries in Ireland,' continued Abigail. 'The young woman had only been in England for three days before she was killed, not much time to have made enemies, so we're thinking we may be able to discover the reason for her murder if we can find out why she came to Manchester.'

'So you might have to travel to Ireland?' said Steggles, weighing this latest information up.

'It's possible,' said Abigail. 'We're going to put an announcement in the local newspaper in Ireland, the *North Cork Reporter*, so it will depend on what sort of replies we get.'

Steggles nodded. 'Very well. If you feel it's necessary. The sooner we can get to the bottom of this and return to normal, the better.'

CHAPTER TWENTY-FIVE

Daniel looked at the ornate clock on the wall of the Mayflower Hotel's lounge, and then gave Abigail an enquiring look.

'He was never late when we knew one another in Cambridge,' she said. 'Always punctual.'

'People change,' said Daniel.

'Septimus came across as the kind of person who'd never change,' said Abigail. 'People knew where they were with him, which was a rarity.' Then she spotted a movement by the entrance and her face lit up into a smile. 'Here he is,' she said, getting up.

Daniel rose, too, and turned to see a very tall, muscular-looking man in his late thirties, a huge smile on his face, and a mop of thick red hair sticking up from the top of his head, approaching them.

'Septimus!' she said, and Creighton lumbered towards her, hand outstretched, but just as he was about to take her hand to shake, he tripped, stumbled and then fell to the floor with a crash.

Abigail and Daniel stared down at him in alarm, then Daniel hurried forward and bent down and offered the fallen man a hand.

'Are you all right?' he asked, concerned.

'Only my pride is injured,' said Creighton with a rueful sigh. He pushed himself up off the floor and dusted himself down, then looked at them both apologetically.

'Sorry about that, Abi,' he said. 'Still falling over my own feet.'

'It was because your shoelace has become undone,' said Daniel, pointing at the offending item.

'Drat!' said Creighton. 'New shoes as well.' Again, he gave his apologetic grin. 'I was so hoping I'd make a good impression after all this time.'

'You made a good impression on the carpet,' said Abigail. She smiled. 'The main thing is, you're here now. And uninjured.'

She gestured to the three chairs around the small table, which had been set out with three cups and saucers ready for their guest's arrival. Creighton settled himself down on the chair, but as he swung round to face them his elbow knocked against the cup nearest to him and it fell from its saucer and rolled off the edge of the table. With lightning reflexes, Daniel managed to catch it before it hit the carpet and placed it neatly back on its saucer.

'Oh my gosh!' groaned Creighton, shamefaced. 'What must you think of me!'

'To be honest, Septimus, it's a relief to find you haven't changed,' said Abigail. 'I recall in your Cambridge days it was said you could destroy a table just by looking at it.'

'Unfair, and wrong,' said Creighton. Then he added awkwardly, 'At least, an exaggeration.' He looked at Daniel and said, 'But I must apologise. This is our first meeting, and I did so want to impress you, Mr Wilson. After all, you're famous for what you do.' His attention went back to Abigail. 'As you are, Abi. The famous Egyptologist. Two celebrities. And here am I, tumbling around like a clown in a circus.' He shook his head. 'All my plans to show you how sophisticated I've become, gone up in smoke.'

'It doesn't matter,' Abigail assured him. 'The main thing is that you're here.'

'And late,' continued Creighton with his self-berating. 'I was determined to be on time, but I got caught up in the crowd coming out of a football match. So many people, it took ages to get away!'

'Who was playing?' asked Daniel.

'Newton Heath against Bolton Wanderers. Incredible game!'

'I thought you were a rugby man,' said Abigail, surprised.

'I am, but Association Football has a quality all its own. I must admit, I've discovered it more since I've been here in Manchester. And there's a few problems in rugby up here with the players over money, which has led to a talk of a breakaway league. And not just that, there's talk of a different way of playing the game.'

'I'm afraid I don't understand the world of rugby,' said Daniel.

'You never played yourself?' asked Creighton.

'No.'

'Pity. You have the build, and the slightly bent nose.'

'That came from being a policeman,' said Daniel.

'How can there be a breakaway league?' asked Abigail. 'I thought the rules for rugby were set by the Rugby Football Union?'

'Well yes, they are, and that includes charging entrance money to watch games.'

Abigail frowned, puzzled. 'I only ever saw a few matches when I was at Cambridge, and there was no mention of paying to see it,' she said.

'No, there wasn't,' said Creighton. 'And that's still the way it is in the south of the country, where most of the players do it for pleasure, and most have – shall we say – private income.'

'Gentlemen players?' pondered Daniel.

'I think they prefer to be called amateurs. Whereas here in the north, most of the players have jobs. They work in the mines, or the mills. So when they take time off to play rugby they get compensated for the money they lose from work.'

'That sounds fair,' said Daniel.

'Not to the Rugby Football Union, which is dominated by affluent southerners, the older members who run it still believing in the purity of the game. That no money should be involved.'

'Having seen some of the poorer areas of Manchester, I'd say that may be all very well for people from privileged backgrounds in places like Oxford or Cambridge, but bears little relation to the reality of life up here,' said Abigail.

'I don't see how people being paid to play rugby up here in the north would have any effect on those in the south who play for free,' observed Daniel.

'Because the money to pay players has to come from somewhere,' explained Creighton. 'At the moment it comes from entrance money paid at the gate. But the RFU has just issued a proclamation that rugby is banned from being played at clubs where an entry fee is charged.'

'But that would mean the end of rugby in the north,' said Daniel. 'At least, as an official game.'

Creighton nodded. 'Exactly. That's why a large number of northern clubs are intending to start their own league, called something like the Northern Rugby Football Union.' He sighed. 'It'll be a sad day.' Then he brightened into a smile, the issue of rugby dismissed. 'Anyway, what's new with you, Abi? Still travelling all over the world digging up things? I thought you'd have been married by now.'

'I am,' replied Abigail.

Creighton's mouth dropped open, then he beamed and said, 'My gosh! Who's the lucky man?'

'He is,' said Abigail, gesturing at Daniel.

Creighton turned to Daniel, who stared at Abigail, stunned.

'Well I never! So you're Mrs Wilson now?'

'No, we decided to keep our own names,' said Abigail.

'Ah, suffragist stuff, eh!' Creighton grinned. He got up and walked over to Daniel, hand outstretched. 'Allow me to congratulate you, sir, and most heartily! You've got a winner there!'

'Yes, I've become ever more aware of that.' Daniel smiled, shaking Creighton's hand.

He signalled for the waiter to bring them a pot of tea and biscuits, and was relieved that this time Creighton took his seat without knocking anything over.

'What about you?' asked Abigail. 'Are you married?'

'Me? No,' said Creighton. 'I got engaged a couple of times, but both were scratched before the day.'

'Cold feet?' asked Abigail.

'Not on my account,' said Creighton. 'Both times the bride's parents called off the match. Seems they wanted better for their daughters.'

'Surely a university professor would be quite a catch,' commented Daniel.

'Well, possibly. But I got the impression they wanted someone with more interest in the business world. Someone with better financial prospects. Or someone with a title. Preferably both, to be honest. I didn't fit either bill, alas.'

As Daniel listened to the red-headed man and watched him, he realised why Abigail had felt fond of him. Septimus Creighton was, as Abigail had described him, a rarity – someone honest and without duplicity, and also caring about others. His clumsiness was part of his appeal. He reminded Daniel of a friendly dog that was too big for its surroundings, often causing unintentional havoc, but one that would be faithful and loyal. Even on this very short acquaintance, Daniel knew this was a man that could be trusted, and he liked him.

'So, back to you two: the *Guardian* calls you the Museum Mystery Detectives,' said Creighton with a smile.

'Literary hyperbole from the reporter,' responded Abigail.

'Yes, I saw the by-line. Our friend William the radical.'

'The radical?' queried Daniel.

Creighton nodded. 'Like most universities, ours has got many societies, and one of them is the Socialism Society. They put on talks, and about four months ago they had this guest speaker talking about Karl Marx. I don't know if you've heard of him.'

'We were discussing him not long ago,' said Abigail. 'He and Friedrich Engels.'

'Politics, eh!' Creighton grinned. 'To be honest, it's not my thing, but I went along out of curiosity. Frankly I found it boring and long-winded, but some of the students lapped it up. It was all very radical. You know, common ownership of property, that sort of stuff. Well, William Bickerstaff was there reporting on the meeting for the *Guardian*, and he got quite carried away, applauding like mad when this chap said something about freeing the workers from their chains. Anyway, he came back again, to other events the Socialist Society put on, and pretty soon he started spouting off himself, all about the evils of the mill owners and so on.'

'Interesting,' said Daniel thoughtfully.

'It struck me that he only took the job at the *Guardian* because it gives him space to air his views,' said Creighton. 'There's no doubt he's a serious radical, overthrow the capitalist system, all that sort of thing. What did you think of him when you met him?'

'At first he seemed reasonable,' said Daniel cautiously.

'But then he betrayed us,' said Abigail, her tone showing her anger. 'He promised that in the article he would write for the *Guardian* about the case he would avoid bringing in radical politics.'

'That's not the way I read it,' said Creighton. 'It was the same old Bickerstaff but even more so.' He frowned thoughtfully. 'It struck me when I met him that there's a lot of anger burning deep inside William B. No, more than just anger. Rage. There's violence lurking under that educated surface, just waiting to blow up if things get out of control. Like a lot of these aristos.'

'Aristos?' asked Abigail.

'Like many of these radical chaps, he actually comes from quite an elite family. The Norton-Wallace-Bickerstaffs.'

'Two hyphens?' said Daniel, amused.

'I believe his father's a baronet, or something, but he prefers to keep that quiet.' He gave them an amused look. 'Anyway, the Museum Mystery Detectives, eh! Like Sherlock Holmes and Dr Watson.' He chuckled. 'But which one is which? I presume as Mr Wilson was a famous detective in his own right, you, Abi, are Dr Watson.'

Before Abigail could respond, Daniel put in, 'Absolutely not. Abigail is my equal, if not my superior, in many aspects of working out the criminal, so we prefer to think of ourselves as equal partners.'

'Well said.' He shook his head in wonder. 'I must admit, Abi, a detective was one thing I never thought you'd become. Wonders will never cease. And, if there's anything I can do to help while you're here . . .'

'There is actually,' said Abigail. 'Are you involved with the sporting fraternity at the university?'

'Absolutely!' said Creighton. 'And a finer pack of lads you're unlikely to meet. At the moment we're preparing for the Christie Cup. I'm helping to put the rugby team through their paces.'

'Do you think they might be interested in a little discreet bodyguarding?'

Creighton regarded them, puzzled. 'How discreet? And whose body?'

'Daniel's,' said Abigail.

'Ah, the black eye!' Creighton grinned. 'I wasn't going to mention it in case it was something of a personal nature.' He chuckled. 'I once saw Abi here lay out some lout who insulted her. An absolute corker of a right-hander!'

'Yes, I have some experience of her abilities in that regard,' said Daniel. Then, as Abigail and Creighton shot him surprised looks, he hastily added, 'Not personally, you understand, but as an interested observer.'

'Daniel was assaulted after asking some questions at the barracks.'

'About this case?'

'Yes. It seems the woman who was murdered had been asking questions there just a day or so before, and had been sent away. We went along to ask why, and what she'd gone there for, but they refused our request. So I was put in touch with a local historian with knowledge of local military matters.'

'You think her death had something to do with the barracks?'

'We don't know,' admitted Daniel. 'What we do know is that after I'd met this military historian, I was set upon and warned to keep my nose out of it.'

'Out of the local military's business?'

'That was the inference.'

'The thing, is, Septimus, we're not going to be warned off. But when we persist in asking questions . . .'

215

'It's likely you'll get another pasting.' He looked at Abigail, concerned. 'They haven't threatened you?'

'No,' Abigail reassured him.

'And we want to make sure they don't,' said Daniel. 'And the best way to stop that is to find out who's behind it.'

'The barracks, you say. So it's the army.'

'Or *someone* in the army. So what I'm thinking of doing is going back to the barracks and making a bit of a nuisance of myself, and get turned away again.'

'And then, when they come to have another go at Daniel . . .'

'My chaps will be waiting ready to pounce on them!' exulted Creighton. 'Brilliant!'

'Are you sure they'll be agreeable?' asked Daniel.

'Absolutely! You should see my lads when they play rugby against the army. No love lost there, I can assure you!' He looked inquisitively at Daniel. 'What's your plan?'

'I thought I'd return to the barracks and ask one or two questions that would upset them, and say that I insist on a meeting with their commanding officer. There's a regimental sergeant major there, Bulstrode, who seems to be the main obstacle to our investigation. I'm fairly sure it was he who set the men on me before. I suspect he'll insist that any request to meet his commanding officer has to be made in writing, so I'll tell him that I'll return with my letter at such-and-such a time. That will give him time to round up some men to give me a going-over when I return, and also for your men to be in place to come to my aid when it happens.'

'Say he invites you into the barracks to beat you up?' asked Creighton, worried. 'My boys won't be able to follow you in.'

'He won't,' said Daniel. 'He won't want to expose the army to the questions that would raise. My guess is that once I've handed in my letter and walked away from the barracks, he'll get his men to follow me, all in civilian clothes, and they'll pounce on me at some convenient spot. So we get your rugby players stationed in a side street not far from the barracks, one which I'll walk past.'

'They might attack you before you get to that street,' pointed out Creighton. 'Or they might let you get some distance after it before they attack.'

'Which is why I thought I'd take my old police whistle with me. That way, if your boys are out of sight and can't see me, a blast on that will bring them running.'

'Along with local constables.'

'So much the better,' said Daniel. 'The object of the exercise is to catch one or two of them and find out who's behind it.'

'You already suspect who's behind it,' pointed out Creighton. 'This regimental sergeant major.'

'I think he's just an intermediary,' said Daniel. 'I could be wrong, but I feel he's protecting someone else. I'm hoping that this might lead us to who that is.'

'We're also going to Ireland,' said Abigail. 'We feel the reason for everything that's happened may lie there. The young woman who was killed arrived from there just a few days before she died.'

'Ideally, we'd like to carry out our ruse at the barracks before we go, in case we get more information we can take with us,' said Daniel. 'Would that be possible for you and your rugby players?'

'When were you thinking of?' asked Creighton.

'Would tomorrow be too soon?'

'Not at all,' said Creighton. 'I'm due to meet the boys this afternoon at three o'clock. Come along to the university and I'll introduce you and we can make arrangements.'

After, when Creighton had left and Daniel and Abigail were back in their room, she asked him, 'What did you think of Septimus?'

'I liked him,' said Daniel. 'In fact, I liked him a lot, and I can see why you liked him. He's decent and honest and without duplicity.'

'He's still clumsy,' said Abigail.

'With someone as nice as he is, that's easily forgiven,' said Daniel. He smiled as he added, 'Talking of duplicity, you lied. You told him we were married.'

'As far as I'm concerned, we are. Don't you agree?'

'Well . . . yes. But in legal terms . . .'

'Oh, fiddlesticks to legal terms!'

'But look at the fuss you made earlier about being forced to use my surname for the register at the hotel. You haven't said that to anyone else. Not even to your sister, Bella.'

'Because Bella would be deeply upset that she wasn't invited to our wedding. As you said yourself, she considers me a fallen woman, living in sin with a man who is not my husband.' She hesitated, then added, 'And also I wanted Septimus to know where we stood in regard to one another.'

'He was a previous . . . ah . . . ?' asked Daniel.

'No, he wasn't,' said Abigail quickly. Then she added, 'But he would have liked to be. I just wanted to clear that up, so he wasn't under any illusions about the reason I responded to his letter.'

'So, Mrs Daniel Wilson,' chuckled Daniel, amused.

'Or Mr Abigail Fenton,' countered Abigail.

'Perhaps we could go for a hyphenated name,' suggested Daniel. 'Like William Norton-Wallace-Bickerstaff.'

'Wilson-Fenton?'

'Or Fenton-Wilson?'

Abigail went to him and put her arms around him and kissed him, her lips gentle at first.

'I love you, my husband, whatever your name is,' she said. And she kissed him harder.

Daniel picked her up and carried her to the bed.

'I am the luckiest man there's ever been,' he said, as he laid her down and began to unbutton her blouse.

CHAPTER TWENTY-SIX

'Have you noticed that all the important places in Manchester are very near to one another?' commented Daniel as they approached the John Owens Building in Oxford Road which housed the Victoria University. 'The museum. The infirmary. Our hotel.' He studied the Gothic building and added, 'And so many of them in the same style. This university building and the museum for example.'

'Designed by the same architect,' said Abigail. 'Alfred Waterhouse.'

'The same man who designed the Natural History Museum in London?' asked Daniel. 'I recall you mentioning that.'

'You have a good memory,' said Abigail. 'Yes, that's the man. Very prolific. He also designed the town hall here.'

'How do you know so much about him?' asked Daniel. 'I didn't realise that architecture was one of your special interests.'

'He also built Girton College in Cambridge, where I did my degree,' said Abigail. 'The college authorities made great play to we students about his reputation as a master architect.'

They entered the building and told the porter on duty that they'd an arrangement to meet Professor Creighton that day.

'Ah yes. Miss Fenton and Mr Wilson. Professor Creighton told me to take you to him when you arrived. If you'll follow me.'

They followed the porter through a maze of corridors, finally stopping at a door on which were the words 'Lecture Theatre B'. The porter knocked at the door, then opened it and gestured for Daniel and Abigail to enter.

Septimus Creighton stood in front of a large blackboard, facing rows of seats which rose upwards in a bank, like an old-fashioned theatre. Fifteen young men were sitting on these seats, and they rose to their feet as Abigail and Daniel entered.

'Mr Wilson! Miss Fenton! Welcome! These are the sturdy souls from the university rugby squad who've volunteered to give assistance. I'll do the proper introductions, names and all that, later, if that's all right. I've given them a rough idea of what's planned, without going into details, but I thought if we got straight to the nub of what this is all about it would expedite things. Is that all right with you?'

'Perfect,' said Daniel.

Creighton looked at the young men. 'Therefore, without further ado, I'll hand over to Mr Daniel Wilson, former detective with Scotland Yard and a key figure in the notorious Jack the Ripper investigations.'

With that, Creighton moved to take his seat on the front row among the students, inviting Abigail to join him there.

Daniel took Creighton's place in front of the students. 'Thank you very much for allowing me to address you, gentlemen,' he said. 'The reason I'm here is because Miss Fenton and I have been engaged by Manchester Museum to look into two tragic deaths that occurred there recently. They wish us to find out who may have been responsible. Our enquiries have led us to believe that some members of the army barracks at Hulme may have had some involvement, but we have met difficulty when we have tried to pursue our investigations there. In fact, the determination by some at the barracks to prevent us asking questions led to my recently being . . .' Here, Daniel stopped, then he grinned as he finished, '. . . punched in the eye and warned there would be worse for me if I kept poking my nose in.'

Some of the students joined Daniel in grinning at this, amused.

'However, it is not in my nature to be warned off, nor is it in Miss Fenton's. So we intend to pursue that line of enquiry. Having been warned off once, and at that time by three men, I fully expect that the next time there may be more of them.

'Now I'm not looking for a brawl. Ideally, we'll be able to settle this without the need for physical violence and get them to tell us who they're protecting. The situation is complicated by the fact that the local law enforcement appears to have no jurisdiction over the army.

'To that end the plan is that I return to the barracks and say that I insist on seeing the commanding officer. I've already been told that to do this I have to submit a request in writing. So I'll inform them that I intend to return at such-and-such a time with that request in writing. It's my guess that when I make that visit with my letter, they'll send some men to follow me as I leave the barracks and attack me. And that is where you come in.

'When they grab me I'll blow my old faithful police whistle. That will be the signal for you to appear. My hope is that at the sight of you, they'll surrender. But they might not.

'Our aim is to get hold of as many as we can and take them to the local police station where I'll make a citizen's arrest and insist they are charged with assault. I'm hoping that at least one or two will be eager to avoid that, so they'll tell us who is behind their actions. At this stage, that's all we need – the identity of the person pulling the strings.

'Now there may be violence, if they resist. I'm telling you this in advance and I won't think less of you if some of you, having heard this, decide not to be involved. I will absolutely understand.'

A hand went up from a young man at the front. 'How many of them do you think there will be, sir?' he asked.

'I have no way of knowing,' admitted Daniel. 'But my guess is there won't be too many; they won't want to draw attention to themselves by having a platoon walking along, none of them in uniform. They'll look too much like a gang and someone might raise an alarm. And, as far as they're concerned, there'll be just me to deal with.'

Another hand went up.

'When do you intend to do it?' asked the student.

'I was thinking of tomorrow morning, if you're available,' replied Daniel.

'We're available!' offered a chorus of voices, and most of their faces broke into broad smiles and they rubbed their fists together in gleeful anticipation.

'Thank you, gentlemen,' said Daniel gratefully.

Creighton rose from his seat and joined Daniel at the front. 'Well, there we are, chaps,' he said. 'I will be with you, of course.

As Mr Wilson says, hopefully they'll capitulate at the sight of us, but if they don't . . .' And he began to chuckle. 'There'll be a scrum to remember!'

Creighton made arrangements for them all to meet up again at the university the next morning, and then waved the students off to their various classes. One student, however, stayed behind, a shy-looking, short, young man, and slim for a rugby player, thought Daniel. Creighton gestured for the young man to join him with Abigail and Daniel.

'Abi, I'd like to introduce Simon Cardew, our fly half, who's very keen to meet you. He's studying archaeology here.'

'It's my pleasure to meet another student of archaeology.' Abigail smiled at the young man.

'I'm not on your level, I'm afraid,' said Cardew. 'But I hope to be one day. When Professor Creighton told us you were here and that you'd be coming in today, I was almost lost for words. I've been an admirer of your work ever since my father told me about working with you at Giza.'

'Cardew?' said Abigail. 'Not Hereward Cardew?'

'Yes, that's him.' He gave an apologetic smile and said, 'Actually, he's Sir Hereward now, which he tends to be a bit dismissive of when it's mentioned, but it's bucked up my mother no end.'

'Lady Cardew.' Abigail nodded. 'I can understand that.'

'The thing is that Pa told us about you when he came back from Giza, said you were the most brilliant archaeologist he'd ever worked with. Even better than Petrie.'

'Oh really!' scoffed Abigail, but Daniel was amused to see that she was blushing, even though she was trying to appear nonchalant about this praise. 'Your father was always a very nice man. I'm sure he was just being kind.' Then she added, 'And he's an archaeologist of the highest stature himself, otherwise he wouldn't have received the knighthood.'

'Pa says it's certainly helped when they're trying to raise funds for an expedition. Anyway, Miss Fenton, I know this is terribly forward of me, but when I heard you would actually be coming here today with Mr Wilson, I asked Professor Creighton if he wouldn't mind introducing us so I could shake your hand.'

'It will be my pleasure to shake the hand of the son of Hereward Cardew,' said Abigail, and held out her hand for the young man to shake. 'And do please pass on my regards to your father when you're next in touch with him. And to your mother, of course.'

As they walked away from the university, Daniel grinned as he said to Abigail, 'I'm beginning to understand how Prince Albert must have felt when he and the queen appeared somewhere. Like "Who's that man standing beside that famous woman?"'

'Jealous?' Abigail smiled. 'It's the same for me when people talk about the famous Inspector Wilson from Scotland Yard, hunter of Jack the Ripper, and treat me as if I'm not there.'

'That's not been the case here, or elsewhere when we've been investigating a case,' said Daniel. 'Everyone seems to have heard of the internationally renowned Egyptologist Abigail Fenton.'

'That's because the cases we've investigated have been centred on museums that are known for their archaeological displays,' pointed out Abigail. 'So of course my name is familiar to them. Just as yours is to the policemen we meet.'

'But often with a different attitude,' said Daniel. 'You are treated with veneration. For me, here, with Inspector Grimley, as with Superintendent Armstrong at Scotland Yard, the reaction is to treat me with open contempt.'

'Perhaps archaeologists are more polite than policemen,' mused Abigail. 'Although I can recall one or two who refused to work with me purely because I'm a woman.' Suddenly she stopped and looked at Daniel with a thoughtful expression. 'We keep talking about a mysterious someone in the army who RSM Bulstrode is working hard to protect. What if it's Bulstrode himself who's the murderer? He's a soldier; he'd know how to use a bayonet effectively. And if it's about protecting the good name of the regiment from some dreadful secret coming out, he's shown he'd certainly do that.' She looked at Daniel as he stared at her. 'Or is that too simple?' she asked.

'No,' said Daniel. 'I'm only staring at you because it's brilliant! I've been thinking that Bulstrode is trying to protect a senior officer, but say the secret is somewhere in his family? Many soldiers follow their fathers into the army. Say his father, or grandfather, were at Peterloo?' He frowned, frustrated. 'But how do we find out if he was in the museum on the Thursday morning? He'll deny it even if he was.'

'Jonty Hawkins,' said Abigail. 'He's got a good eye and a good memory. He spotted Bickerstaff. If Bulstrode was there that morning, he might have seen him.'

'Excellent!' said Daniel. 'I'll ask Mr Hawkins if he will agree to accompany me when I go to the barracks with Creighton and his rugby squad tomorrow.'

'You're surely not going to involve him!' said Abigail.

'No,' Daniel assured her. 'I can't see Jonty engaging in a brawl with some soldiers. I'll ask him to stand across the road from the barracks while I engage Bulstrode in conversation when I first arrive. After, he'll be able to say whether Bulstrode was at the museum that morning.'

'He might not; he told me the museum got very busy,' cautioned Abigail.

'It's worth a try,' said Daniel. He smiled at her. 'If it is him, he's been under our nose all this time, and I missed it. Thank heavens for a partner with a brain!'

CHAPTER TWENTY-SEVEN

Next morning they decided they'd go to the museum first and ask Hawkins if he would accompany Daniel to the barracks for discreet observation and hopefully recognition of RSM Bulstrode. Then, if Hawkins agreed, Daniel would take him to the university to meet up with Creighton and the rugby squad, while Abigail stayed at the museum looking at the artefacts from Hawara so that she could refer to them during her talk.

It was as Daniel saw the look of doubt on Jonty Hawkins's face as he outlined what they were planning that morning that he had misgivings about asking the young man.

'I can see you have reservations,' he admitted.

'Not really,' said Hawkins. 'I was just wondering how much you wanted me to be involved. You said you expected to be attacked.'

'You will absolutely not be involved in that,' Daniel assured him quickly. 'The extent to which we'd appreciate your assistance is for you to stand on the other side of the road when I meet with RSM Bulstrode at the main gate, and afterwards tell me whether you think he might have been at the museum on the morning when the young woman was killed. And then afterwards for you to take a bus back to the museum.'

'And shortly after that you expect to be attacked,' said Hawkins.

'If I'm right, I will be,' said Daniel. 'At which point the rugby squad from the university will come to my defence. You will have no part to play in that. Your role will be purely observational. But if that gives you pause, I will absolutely understand if you decide—'

'No, no,' said Hawkins quickly. 'I'm happy to join you. But first we need permission from Mr Steggles for me to leave my post temporarily.'

'Of course,' said Daniel. 'I'll come with you and explain the situation to him.'

Steggles was intrigued, and then supportive, after Daniel had explained to him their plan.

'Of course, the reputation of the museum is our top priority,' he said.

'Absolutely,' said Daniel. 'And Mr Hawkins will not in any way be involved in any action; his role will be purely to say whether he believes that RSM Bulstrode may have been here at the museum on that Thursday morning. After that, he will return here.'

Steggles looked enquiringly at Hawkins. 'Is that acceptable to you, Mr Hawkins?'

'Very much so, sir. I will do anything I can to help find out why this poor woman met such a terrible end.'

With approval granted, Daniel and Hawkins set off for the university. As they walked, Daniel glanced at Hawkins's attire of the long velvet frockcoat and his long hair curling over his collar, and the hint of rouge on his cheeks, and wondered how the rugby-playing students would react at his arrival. It therefore came as a complete surprise to Daniel when they entered the same lecture theatre where Creighton and the students were waiting, and Creighton let out a warm cry of 'Jonty! Look, lads! It's the Killer!' and the students rose from their seats and crowded around Hawkins, shaking his hand in obviously warm greeting.

'You know Mr Hawkins?' Daniel whispered to Creighton.

'One of the finest rugby players Manchester ever produced,' said Creighton. 'Used to play for the Old Athenians. A super flanker, before, sadly, he found his muse in poetry and abandoned the game.'

'Why did you call him the Killer?' asked Daniel.

'Because we played the Athenians twice, and both times Hawkins absolutely killed us with his pace and the way he ran the game. Gosh, I wish he'd been at this university; we could have built the team around him.' He looked towards where Hawkins was enjoying animated conversation and asked Daniel, 'Is he taking part in the action?'

'No. He's just coming with me to hopefully identify someone, then he'll be returning to the museum.'

'Pity,' said Creighton. 'You won't find a better man in a ruck.'

With that, he called the crowd to order and ran through the plan of action. They would make for a side road not far from the barracks, where Creighton knew they would be able to hide themselves. 'It's an alley by the railway arches where there are mainly small businesses. They're used to groups of young men hanging about there, so we won't look out of place. And it's near enough to the main road for us to be able to hear your whistle, Daniel. Providing you manage to get it to your mouth if they jump you.'

'I'll have it ready to hand,' Daniel assured him. 'We shouldn't have long to wait. Once Mr Hawkins and I have carried out our observations, I'll join you all for twenty minutes or so to give them time to assemble their men, then I'll return to the barracks and deliver my letter. That should be the trigger for them to make their move as I walk away.'

'And then, into battle!' exclaimed Creighton.

The party set off, and Daniel was surprised to observe how little notice the rugby players seemed to be taking of Jonty Hawkins's attire, or his hints of rouge. As far as they were concerned all they saw was an old rugby opponent who'd run rings round them, and they engaged in conversation with him on their walk, leaving Daniel and Creighton free to converse.

'You feel sure this will reveal the murderer?' asked Creighton.

'If the murderer and the person the army are covering up are one and the same,' said Daniel. 'Of course, there may be two different things happening here and they may not be connected, but my nose tells me they are.'

'Your nose?'

'A copper's nose,' said Daniel. 'It sniffs out the truth and what's really going on in a case. Coppers develop one after years on the force.'

They arrived at the alley leading to the railway arches, and Creighton and the rugby squad slipped down it. Daniel and Hawkins carried on, Hawkins deliberately falling back and then crossing the road. Daniel walked on, past two more side streets, until he reached the barracks, where he asked one of the two sentries on duty at the main gate if RSM Bulstrode was available. One of the sentries marched into the main building, reappearing a short while later accompanied by RSM Bulstrode. Out of the corner of his eye, Daniel saw Jonty

Hawkins materialise on the other side of the road and loiter, apparently studying the nearby houses.

'Good morning, Regimental Sergeant Major,' said Daniel. 'Do you remember me?'

'I do, sir.'

'You told me when I came before that if I wished to meet your commanding officer I would need to make an appointment.'

'That's correct, sir. That's the procedure.'

'Then I would like to make an appointment with him. Tell him I wish to talk to him about Peterloo.'

The RSM's face darkened and he glowered at Daniel. 'For what purpose, sir?'

'I'll tell him when I see him.'

The RSM hesitated. Daniel could see from the tic and contortions in his face he was doing his best to control the anger inside him.

'All applications for appointments need to be made in writing,' he said finally in a voice strangled with emotion.

Daniel nodded politely. 'Thank you. I'll do that. I'll return in a half an hour's time and bring my letter with me.' He tipped his hat. 'Good day.'

He walked away.

The RSM glowered after him. 'Oh no you won't, you bastard!' he muttered vengefully under his breath.

Daniel strode away, to be joined by Hawkins.

'Well?' asked Daniel. 'Was the man I was talking to at the museum on that Thursday?'

'I don't think so,' said Hawkins. 'But it's difficult to be absolutely sure. I tried to imagine him without the uniform and wearing civilian clothes. The problem is there were quite a few people around that day.' He fell silent, mulling it over, then announced, 'I don't believe so, sir. He had a very fixed glare about

232

him, an aggressive stance in the way he stood. I don't think I saw anyone with that face or that posture on that day. I'm sorry.'

'No need to apologise,' said Daniel. 'Your coming here today has been invaluable.'

Hawkins sighed. 'But not very helpful.'

'On the contrary,' said Daniel. 'It's eliminated someone from the investigation. At least, as far as him being a suspect is concerned.'

RSM Bulstrode strode into the barracks, a look of fury on his face, and found his way obstructed by a corporal standing in the doorway staring out into the street.

'What do you think you're up to, Corporal Watkins?' he barked.

'Sorry, sir,' said the corporal, springing to attention and saluting smartly. 'I was just spotting that bloke you was talking to.'

'Bloke!' snorted Bulstrode angrily. 'A snake in the grass, Corporal! A viper!'

'He's that all right, sir,' said Watkins with vehemence.

'You know him?' asked Bulstrode, intrigued.

'I met him,' said Watkins. 'That's the bloke got me nicked on the train back from Birmingham.'

'Oh?'

'I hooked up with this doxy on the train and she nicked me wallet. When I remonstrated with her this bloke poked his nose in, and next minute he's punched me out and got me arrested and I spent a night in the cells. Luckily, I played the old soldier bit and they let me go, but that's me good name gone! Bastard!'

Bulstrode smiled. 'In that case, you're just the man for what I've got in mind for him. I need you and a few others to carry out a special operation.'

Watkins frowned. 'What sort of operation, sir?'

'An unofficial one. But one that has the backing of the powers that be.'

Watkins was still frowning. 'I don't understand, Sergeant Major.'

'That same man is a pest that's been hanging around making trouble for the regiment. And, in particular, for the Old Man.'

'Oh?'

'He's trying to spread rumours and lies.'

'About the Old Man?'

Bulstrode nodded.

'Well, we can't have that,' said Watkins determinedly. 'Someone ought to have a word with him.' And he punched a meaty fist into his other palm. 'A serious word.'

'We've tried that, but he didn't take the hint. A couple of chaps took him aside in town and gave him a friendly warning.'

'They should have done more than that.'

'They gave him a black eye, but it didn't seem to have any effect.'

'Sounds like he needs more than just a black eye, sir.'

'I agree. He's coming back here in half an hour, he has the nerve to tell me, to give me a letter demanding a meeting with our commanding officer.'

'Demanding?' echoed Watkins indignantly. 'That sounds like bare-faced nerve and cheek to me.'

'It is, Corporal. And unless we stamp on it now, it will get worse. I know this kind of man. A troublemaker. Someone who hates the army.'

'When's he coming back? Half an hour, did you say?'

'That's what he said, and I don't doubt he'll turn up. He's that kind of man. Obstinate. Pig-headed.'

'I think he needs a serious talking-to.'

'There'll need to be a few of you,' said Bulstrode. 'He's not easily put off.'

Watkins smiled. 'Half a dozen of us should be about right.'

'I don't want him killed,' said Bulstrode.

'But damaged?'

Bulstrode nodded. 'Enough to make sure he gets the message.'

'Break his arm?' asked Watkins.

Bulstrode nodded again. 'Possibly both arms. Time in hospital might make him see sense,' he said.

Watkins suddenly looked worried. 'What happens if the law turn up?' he asked. 'The police station's not far away, and if they get told of a ruckus . . .'

'Leave that to me,' said Bulstrode. 'I've got a brother-in-law in the police who works out of Hulme station. I'll have a word with him, make sure there's no interference until it's over.' He smiled. 'In fact, Sam might be keen to throw his weight in as well. He's as much an admirer of the Old Man as the rest of us. And I know where he usually hangs out at this time of day.'

CHAPTER TWENTY-EIGHT

Daniel counted his paces as he walked away from the rugby squad, gathered in a bunch outside a second-hand furniture store, and walked along the alley to the main road. Two minutes for them to reach the main road, he assessed. Then, however long it took them to locate him, depending on how far the soldiers let him walk from the barracks before they launched their attack. It would be about him gaining time before the reinforcements arrived.

He arrived back at the main gate and addressed the sentries.

'I'm here to see RSM Bulstrode. My name's Daniel Wilson. He is expecting me.'

'Yes, sir. If you'll just wait here,' replied one, and marched smartly into the barracks.

* * *

RSM Bulstrode was waiting just inside the door of the building, along with seven men in civilian clothes, including Corporal Watkins and off-duty Police Constable Sam Adams. Watkins and Adams carried batons, as did two of the others.

'That bloke you said about is here, Sergeant Major,' said the sergeant. 'Wilson.'

Bulstrode looked at the clock. 'He's punctual, I'll give him that,' he grunted.

He accompanied the sentry back to the main gate, where Daniel stood waiting.

'RSM Bulstrode.' Daniel nodded.

'Sir,' said Bulstrode crisply.

Daniel produced an envelope from his pocket. 'My request in writing for your commanding officer, as promised,' he said.

Bulstrode took it from him. 'Thank you, sir,' he said. 'I shall pass it on.'

With that he turned and marched back to the main building. The eyes of the seven men in civilian clothes were on Daniel as he walked away along the street.

'All right, lads,' said Bulstrode. 'Get him.'

Watkins nodded and led the men out. Bulstrode opened the envelope Daniel had given him. It was, indeed, a written request for an appointment with the commanding officer. With a grim smile of satisfaction, Bulstrode tore the letter in two. 'There'll be no need for that now,' he grunted.

Daniel headed away from the barracks at a slow pace. He'd decided for his safety he'd stay as close as he could to the alleyway where the rugby squad were waiting; the less distance they had to travel, the better. As he neared the alley, he heard the sound of heavy boots behind him, and couldn't resist an ironic smile. Even off-duty, they marched in step.

He walked a few paces more, taking him just beyond the alley, then stopped and turned. Seven men in civilian clothes also stopped and stood, scowling at him. Some of them swung wooden clubs menacingly.

'You were warned but you wouldn't be told,' snarled one. 'Well, this is where you get told proper.'

It's the man from the train! realised Daniel with a shock.

As the men moved in on him, Daniel pulled his police whistle from his pocket and gave a long shrill blast on it. The men stopped at this sound and gave anxious looks at the man who'd spoken, but it was another man who spoke now.

'No need to worry about that, lads,' he said with a confident grin. 'I've tipped 'em the wink at the station. They won't be coming.'

'Maybe not,' said Daniel. 'But someone is.'

It was the shout of 'Hulloooo!' that made the men turn, and their mouths dropped at the sight of fifteen burly young men racing towards them. Immediately, three of the men ran off, leaving the remaining four to square up and stand ready. Daniel strode to the man who'd told the others with such confidence that the police wouldn't be coming, and who was now looking about him fearfully. Daniel grabbed him by the arm as he was about to run off. The man flung a punch at Daniel which struck him in the shoulder. In reply, Daniel sank a punch into the man's stomach and, as he doubled over, forced him to the pavement.

The remaining three were no match for the rugby squad, and after having their faces banged against nearby brick walls and their arms twisted, they were quick to surrender.

'Keep a tight hold on them,' said Daniel. 'Now, let's get them to the police station.'

* * *

The uniformed sergeant on duty at the reception desk looked with great suspicion as Daniel entered the police station, accompanied by a tall, red-headed man and fifteen burly students who were holding four men in their firm grasps, these four showing signs of a recent battering. The fact that this sudden influx completely filled the reception area obviously caused the sergeant even greater concern.

'What's going on?' he demanded.

'Good day, Sergeant,' said Daniel. 'My name is Daniel Wilson, I'm a former detective inspector with the Metropolitan police at Scotland Yard. May I have your name?'

At the mention of Scotland Yard, the sergeant suddenly stood straighter, almost to attention. 'Sergeant Bottomley, sir.'

'Well, Sergeant, my friends and I have placed these four men under citizen's arrest for common assault, with a possible further charge of attempted murder.'

'We didn't try to murder him!' shouted Watkins.

'Quiet!' barked the student holding Watkins. 'You'll have your turn in good time.'

Suddenly the sergeant's jaw dropped open in startled amazement as he caught sight of Constable Adams among those arrested.

'Sam?' he burst out.

Adams tried to hide himself behind the mass of bodies crammed into the small space, but this attempt to avoid identification failed miserably as the sergeant turned to Daniel and said, pointing towards Adams, 'That's one of our men there! Constable Adams!'

'Yes, I thought he might be part of the local force,' said Daniel. 'Just before he and his colleagues launched their attack on me he informed his friends that the police would not be coming because he'd fixed things at the station, so that the police wouldn't be coming to intervene. Would you care to comment on that, Sergeant? Or would you prefer to wait until the official investigation into Constable Adams's actions in this crime?'

Sergeant Bottomley stared at Daniel, then at Adams, then back at Daniel again, his mouth opening and closing helplessly, but no words came. Then his expression changed, hardened, and his eyes glittered with deep suspicion.

'How do I know you're who you say you are?' he demanded.

Daniel produced the letter from Bernard Steggles and handed it to the sergeant.

'This is a letter from Mr Steggles, the director of the Manchester Museum, authorising me to investigate a murder on their behalf.'

'Murder?' repeated Bottomley, horrified.

'My placing these men under citizen's arrest is part of that investigation. I shall be reporting this event to Superintendent Mossop, and the police officer in charge of the murder investigation, Inspector Grimley. You can always check with them as to my identity.'

Hastily, Bottomley thrust the letter back at Daniel, who put it back in his pocket.

'I'm sure you're familiar with the concept of citizen's arrest, Sergeant,' Daniel continued. 'It has been part of the English judicial system since medieval times and is enshrined in common law . . .'

'Yes!' snapped Bottomley, trying to regain his dignity. He looked at the assembled crowd, swallowed as if unsure of what to do, then said in prim tones, 'I'll need the names of the witnesses.'

'That will be no problem,' said Daniel. He turned to the students. 'Gentlemen, when the sergeant calls you, please come forward one at a time and give your statement about what you saw happening when these men launched their attack on me. Please make sure you give your full name. You can give your address as the Victoria University.'

'The university?' asked Bottomley.

Daniel nodded. 'They are the university's rugby squad. Fortunately for me they happened to be out on a training run in the area when the attack on me occurred.'

'A training run in Hulme?' said the sergeant, bewildered.

'Is there a rule against the university rugby squad going for a training run in Hulme?' asked Daniel.

'No,' said the sergeant. 'But . . .' He stopped and looked again at the students and the four bruised men, and then sighed. 'Very well,' he said. He took a pile of forms from the drawer in his desk. 'Let's get the names.'

RSM Bulstrode stared at the three men who stood before him, his mouth opening and closing in astonishment and anger, before he was able to speak. 'You ran away!' he bellowed.

'We got set on! It was a trap!' appealed one. 'This army of big blokes came at us as we moved in on him. We were lucky, we got away. But the others got caught.'

'What happened to them?'

'I think they took 'em to the police station.'

'Which one?'

'We didn't hang about to find out.'

Bulstrode fixed the soldier with a steely glare. 'You deserted your comrades and just abandoned them?' he roared angrily.

'If we hadn't, you'd never have known what happened to them,' protested the soldier.

Bulstrode stood glaring at him, then grudgingly nodded. 'All right, soldier. Leave it with me.'

'What are you going to do, sir?'

'Sort it out,' growled Bulstrode.

CHAPTER TWENTY-NINE

Abigail was in the reading room at the museum, writing notes for her talk, when Daniel returned.

'Was everything all right?' she asked, scanning his face for signs of bruising.

'Everything went exactly to plan.' Daniel smiled. 'Except that our friend Jonty didn't recognise Bulstrode.'

'Yes, he told me,' said Abigail. She nodded to the reception desk, where another young man was sitting. 'He's very kindly gone to look into some old files for me, hence someone else is taking his position.'

'Did you know that he played rugby?' asked Daniel.

'Who?' asked Abigail. She looked at the young man temporarily at the reception desk. 'Him?'

'No, Jonty Hawkins,' said Daniel. 'Your friend Septimus Creighton described him as the best flanker Manchester had ever produced.'

Abigail stared back at Daniel. 'Are we talking about the same Jonty Hawkins?' she asked.

'We are,' confirmed Daniel. 'When we arrived at the university the rugby squad were so delighted to see him it became difficult to separate them from him. Apparently, they used to call him the Killer because his brilliant play destroyed the other teams.'

'Good heavens!' said Abigail. 'This is a revelation!'

'It was to me, too,' said Daniel. 'It's a bit like discovering that Aubrey Beardsley used to box.'

'Did he?' asked Abigail, again stunned.

'No, I don't believe he did,' said Daniel. 'I was just using that as an example about not judging people by their appearance.'

'What exactly happened?' demanded Abigail.

Daniel related the events, the delivery of the letter to RSM Bulstrode and the abortive attack on him foiled by Creighton and the rugby squad.

'We duly handed them in to the police station at Hulme and insisted they be charged with assault. I don't have the authority to question the men myself now they're in police custody, so I'll tell Inspector Grimley what's happened and we'll see what he can get out of them.'

'Do you think he will?' asked Abigail. 'He hasn't been very supportive so far.'

'That was before Superintendent Mossop entered the case,' said Daniel. 'Incidentally, one of my attackers was the man we encountered on the train coming here. The man with the knife.'

'Good heavens!'

'Another of them was a police constable. I wonder what his tie-up with Bulstrode is?'

'You think whatever's going on might include the police as well as the army?' asked Abigail.

'I don't know,' admitted Daniel. 'I didn't get the impression that the desk sergeant was part of any conspiracy, but it may be above his pay grade. Remember that Bickerstaff mentioned Inspector Grimley's second-in-command, Sergeant Merton, as suspicious. I suppose we have to wait and see what names the men we arrested cough up, besides RSM Bulstrode.'

'How will you know?'

'I thought I'd call on Inspector Grimley. I dropped his name with the sergeant at Hulme police station, so I'm pretty sure he'd have got in touch with him. Even if he didn't, the bush telegraph works among police officers, especially when one of their own's been put in a cell.'

'I don't think Inspector Grimley will be very grateful to you,' said Abigail. 'The fact a policeman's been arrested will have created a bit of a nightmare for him.'

'It's yet another reason why I think it's best if I see the inspector on my own,' said Daniel. He smiled at her as he added, 'As I said before, it wouldn't be right for a woman to see her husband thrown bodily out of a police station.'

Sergeant Bottomley looked up from his desk as RSM Bulstrode stomped into the police station.

'Afternoon, Sergeant Major,' he said warily. He gave Bulstrode a rueful and apologetic look. 'I thought you'd be along sooner or later.'

'You're holding some of my men,' snapped Bulstrode. 'I've come to collect them.'

'I can't do that,' said Bottomley. 'There's a charge been laid against them.'

'This is a military matter,' said Bulstrode. 'Military rules apply. If there's a charge against them, they'll be court-martialled.'

'The bloke who handed 'em in seemed to know the law,' said Bottomley. 'Former detective from the Met in London.'

'He's got no power here,' said Bulstrode. 'No official authority.'

'Assault is a serious charge,' said Bottomley awkwardly.

'By all accounts, it was my men who got assaulted. Along with one of your own. Sam Adams. Not the other way round. A gang of ruffians, I was told.'

'University students,' said Bottomley.

Bulstrode stared at the sergeant, uncomprehending. 'University students? And they beat my men?'

Bottomley nodded. 'There were quite a few of them. I've got their names and addresses from when they gave their witness statements. All care of the university.'

'How come they got involved?'

'They said they were out for a training run and they heard this police whistle being blown.'

'A training run?' questioned Bulstrode.

'They're part of the university rugby team,' explained Bottomley. 'Anyway, they went to see what was happening, and saw this bloke from London being attacked by seven men, so they stepped in to help him.'

'Bastard!' spat Bulstrode.

'These students are from good families. Moneyed.'

'Yes, I bet they are!' snorted Bulstrode angrily. 'The bastard set this up. He set up an ambush.'

'They'll have to go to trial,' said Bottomley apologetically. 'This London bloke, Wilson, said he insisted on it, and so did the students.'

Bulstrode shook his head. 'It won't happen,' he said firmly. 'It

245

can't happen. This was just high spirits on my men's part. They'd heard that this Wilson bloke was smearing the good name of the regiment and decided to teach him a lesson. Nothing criminal.'

'That's not how the judge will see it,' said Bottomley.

Bulstrode leant across the desk so that his angry face was almost pressed against the sergeant's. 'Now listen here, Bottomley. I've got a barracks full of men who are feeling very angry with what's happened here, their comrades being put in jail for what was just high jinks. If I don't come back with 'em, those men are likely to come here themselves to insist on their release. That'll be a thousand angry soldiers coming in through that door to see you. Now if you feel it'll be safe for you to tell them what you've just told me, that's fine, but you know what soldiers can be like when they lose their tempers. And especially if they've had some drink taken. And it'll be no use you locking the door of the station, because those doors won't be able to withstand men who are determined to come in. These men have fought in wars; they're afraid of no one. And they won't be afraid of you and your lot. But you'll be afraid. Because I know where you live.' He fell silent and looked pointedly at Sergeant Bottomley, who gulped nervously. 'So think over what I said. Serving soldiers misbehaving is a military matter and is always dealt with by the military, no matter what this former detective from London says. So I'm ordering you to hand them over to me for them to be taken to the barracks where they can be investigated.'

Bottomley looked back at Bulstrode and swallowed nervously again. 'I'll need something in writing,' he said. 'Because there'll be questions asked.'

Bulstrode nodded. 'I'll be back with a letter of authority on official headed notepaper,' he said. 'And I'll have a lot of men at my back. So that letter had better work.'

'There's no need for you to bring any men back with you,' said Bottomley urgently.

'They'll be my insurance,' said Bulstrode. 'Just in case you change your mind.'

'I won't,' Bottomley assured him hastily.

'One more thing,' said Bulstrode. 'Sam Adams.'

'He's not in the military,' said Bottomley.

'He used to be,' said Bulstrode.

'But now he's a police constable,' said Bottomley.

'And in my book you should be ashamed of yourself for locking up one of your own,' said Bulstrode curtly. 'He ought to be let go on bail at least.'

'Bail hasn't been fixed,' said Bottomley.

'Then fix it,' snapped Bulstrode. 'The regiment will pay. I'll collect him at the same time I collect my men.'

CHAPTER THIRTY

Daniel waited for some hours before heading for Newton Street. He wanted to give Grimley time to question the men who'd been arrested. He guessed the army would try and interfere with proceedings, so the arrest of the police constable, Sam Adams, had been a bonus.

No one was at the police station reception desk when he arrived, so he walked along the corridor to Grimley's office and rapped on the door.

'Come!' barked the inspector.

Daniel walked in and saw Grimley scowl when he saw who his visitor was.

'Good afternoon, Inspector,' said Daniel.

Grimley groaned. 'Not you again!'

'I thought I'd come and see what information you got out of the men who were arrested after attacking me in Hulme.'

'We didn't get any information,' said Grimley.

Daniel stared at him. 'Did you see them?' he asked. 'Question them? Ask them who'd put them up to it?'

'No,' said Grimley. 'I had a report to say these men had been arrested on the say-so of one Daniel Wilson, a former detective inspector at Scotland Yard.' And here he glared at Daniel. 'And a short while later I had a second note to tell me the men had been released.'

'Who by?' exploded Daniel. 'On whose orders? Yours?'

Grimley shook his head. 'Nothing to do with me,' he said. 'The army stepped in. A letter of authority from the barracks saying the soldiers are the responsibility of the military and the army will be conducting their own investigation.'

'This letter signed by RSM Bulstrode, I assume.'

'I've no idea who it was signed by,' said Grimley. 'Anyway, the fact remains the army have got first call on any action against them.'

'What about the other man? Police Constable Sam Adams. He's not under the jurisdiction of the army.'

'He was bailed,' said Grimley. 'He was released while his case is being looked into.'

'Looked into!' repeated Daniel incredulously. 'And why was he bailed? Bail has to be set by a magistrate . . .'

'I don't know the ins and outs of it,' snapped Grimley. 'All I know is what I got in the reports from Hulme, and as far as I'm concerned that's the end of it.'

'But the case . . . the murder of the two women . . .' said Daniel, almost beside himself with anger.

'The case has been solved,' continued Grimley, interrupting Daniel. 'Which means you and that so-called woman detective friend of yours can leave Manchester. And good riddance.'

'So-called . . . !' exploded Daniel angrily.

'We know who killed them. A young thug called Davis Peach. He's part of a local gang called the Scuttlers. They carry all sorts of weapons, including knives. Well, yesterday this Davis Peach stabbed a man to death in exactly the same way the first woman was killed: in the back, right through the heart and out the front.'

'Who was the man who died?'

'Peter Perks, a young thug from a rival gang. They were always at war with one another.'

'But why would he want to kill Kathleen Donlan and Eileen O'Donnell?'

'We'll find that out when we catch him. Right now, he's gone on the run. But the fact remains one of the killings was exactly the same. Knife in the back and right through the body.'

'This is nonsense!' raged Daniel.

'No, this is police work! Proper police work!' snarled Grimley.

The sound of a loud disturbance outside in the corridor, shouts of alarm and people banging into walls, made both men swing round. The next second the door burst open and the figure of Bickerstaff crashed into the room. In his hand was a pistol, which he aimed at Grimley, then at Daniel, then back to Grimley. He kicked the door shut with his heel and turned the key in the lock.

Outside, the shouting continued, cries of 'He's got a gun!' and 'He's locked it!' as someone tried to open the door.

'What's the meaning of this?' demanded Grimley angrily, stepping towards Bickerstaff. He stopped as the former reporter jerked the barrel of the gun at him.

'Stay where you are!' ordered Bickerstaff.

'This isn't the way, William . . .' urged Daniel quietly.

'Oh, it's William now, is it?' snarled Bickerstaff. 'Now you've had me sacked.'

'I never had you sacked,' said Daniel.

'No? Your name was in the letter that Steggles wrote to the editor, complaining about me.'

'What you did was wrong,' said Daniel. 'It was unfair and dishonest, but shooting me . . .'

'Shoot *you*?' said Bickerstaff and gave a snort of disbelief. 'I'm not here to shoot you. I'm here to shoot him.'

'Me?' said Grimley, bewildered. 'Why?'

'Because of everything you stand for,' said Bickerstaff. 'The whole corrupt way you let the system destroy ordinary people.'

'Corrupt?' snapped Grimley angrily. 'I've never taken a penny . . .!'

'No?' sneered Bickerstaff.

'No!' barked Grimley. 'You may not like what we do, but someone has to stop this city turning into an anarchic battleground, where it's not safe for respectable people to walk the street.'

'You're in the pocket of the mill owners and all those others who grow fat on other people's misery!' said Bickerstaff.

'Then why not shoot them?' ventured Daniel.

'Because most ordinary people in the streets don't know who they are, but they know who the police are, and who they work for.'

'And you're prepared to hang for that?' asked Daniel, who now had both hands on the back of a wooden chair as he leant forward to emphasise his words. 'Because you won't get out of here. As soon as that gun goes off, that door will be broken down.'

'And I'll stand trial!' Bickerstaff smirked. 'And it will be glorious! I'll use it to make sure that everyone knows what goes on. People being worked to death in the mills, including children, for a pittance. The way the police and the army protect the moneyed people. It'll all come out, and there'll be changes!'

'You don't have to kill someone to get the changes,' said Daniel quietly.

'Yes, we do! People have tried public meetings and petitions, appeals to parliament, but they're as bad.' He levelled the pistol at Grimley. 'This will be the bullet that changes the world!'

Suddenly, in one swift movement, Daniel swung the chair up and hurled it at Bickerstaff, just as the gun went off. The bullet tore into the top of the wall. Before Bickerstaff could recover and bring the gun to bear on Grimley again, Daniel was on him, crashing him back against the door, one hand gripping the wrist of the arm that held the gun, the other digging into Bickerstaff's throat. Daniel brought his knee up into Bickerstaff's groin, and then smashed his forehead hard in a headbutt to the man's face.

Daniel snatched the pistol from Bickerstaff's fingers as the former reporter fell to the floor, clutching himself, his eyes blinded by tears of pain.

Daniel stepped back and unloaded the bullets from the gun and put them, along with the empty pistol, on the inspector's desk.

Roughly, Grimley hauled Bickerstaff's body away from the door and turned the key. The corridor was filled with uniformed police officers with anxious looks on their faces.

'Take him to the cells,' snapped Grimley, pointing at the fallen Bickerstaff. 'And take away his tie and shoelaces. I don't want him pulling any suicide stunt.'

As Bickerstaff was bundled out of the office, Grimley shut the door, then turned to Daniel, his face showing a mixture of conflicting emotions: relief, but also anger and guilt.

'I was wrong about you. I thought you were some southern softie,' he muttered.

'A failed police detective,' Daniel reminded him.

Grimley looked uncomfortable. 'Yes. I said I was wrong.' He fell silent, then said, 'Maybe he wasn't really going to shoot. It was all just bluff to get his day in court, so he could make his speeches.'

'He was going to shoot,' said Daniel. 'I recognised the signs. The eyes. The grip on the gun.'

'You've seen it before?'

Daniel nodded.

'Have you ever been shot?' asked Grimley.

Again, Daniel nodded. 'And stabbed. And beaten badly.' He smiled. 'It's what happens to we coppers in the soft south.'

'We don't usually get guns up here,' said Grimley. 'Knives. Coshes. Chains. Where did he get it?'

'From someone in the army, I expect. It wouldn't surprise me to find it's a service revolver.'

'Why would a soldier let him have a gun?'

Daniel shrugged. 'For money; that's the usual reason. Someone in the quartermaster's stores who's responsible for disposing of faulty weapons. Only they may not all be faulty.'

'You seem to know a lot about it,' said Grimley.

'We have barracks and arsenals in London as well,' said Daniel.

'Like I said, we don't get many guns on the streets up here,' muttered Grimley. He gave Daniel a challenging look. 'It's true what I said to Bickerstaff. I've never taken a penny off anyone. I keep the law, regardless of who it is.'

'Except for those soldiers and constable who attacked me,' said Daniel accusingly.

Grimley hesitated, then he mumbled awkwardly, 'The soldiers were the way I said; the military stepped in. They have first call on them.'

'And the constable?'

Grimley lowered his head. 'All right, I'm guessing it was his station sergeant looking after him.'

'Or someone else. All right, we can't question the soldiers, but I need to know who put Constable Adams up to it, because it's quite likely that whoever was behind it was behind the killing of the two women.' As Grimley was about to reply, Daniel interrupted, 'And don't tell me again this knife-wielding thug, this Scuttler, did it. That's hogwash.'

Grimley looked shamefaced. 'I'll have a word with him,' he muttered. 'With Constable Adams.'

'Thank you,' said Daniel.

As he made for the door, Grimley suddenly called out, 'Wait!'

Something in Grimley's voice, an awkwardness, struck Daniel as he turned and looked inquisitively at the inspector.

'You were right about why Terry Brady was killed,' muttered Grimley, unable to make eye contact with Daniel.

'Oh?' said Daniel.

'My men picked up this blacksmith in Hulme, name of Pigeon. Lying in the street, drunk as a lord and crying his eyes out. "I did it!" he said. They asked him what it was he'd done, and he told them he'd killed Terry Brady. Or, to be exact, he'd killed "that murdering bastard Terry Brady". It seems this blacksmith had been in love with Eve Preston for years, but never told her. The big, strong, silent, bashful type. When he learnt that she'd been stabbed he went mad. He found out it was Brady who'd done it because Brady boasted about sticking her for trying to drop him into trouble with the law over the dead girl. So the blacksmith went after Brady with an axe.' He gave an apologetic shrug. 'It was exactly as you said. Eve Preston came to you with that tale about him killing the Irish girl because he'd dumped her for someone else. Then the stupid woman went and told him what she'd done. She was proud of it, she told him, and she hoped he'd hang for being wicked and cruel to her.

'Next thing Brady loses his temper and pulls out his knife. Whether he meant to kill her or not, we'll never know, but he stabbed her, just the once, but it was in her heart. So now he starts bragging about it, how he'd shut her up, and he'd do the same to anyone else who tried to mess with him.'

'And the blacksmith hears about it, and kills Brady,' reasoned Daniel.

'Exactly as you said,' said Grimley. 'My men found his axe covered with blood in his smithy.' He looked quizzically at Daniel. 'How did you know?'

'I worked it out,' said Daniel. 'That's what Abberline taught me. Look at what you've got and try and make it make sense.'

CHAPTER THIRTY-ONE

Abigail stared at Daniel, horrified, as he related what had happened at the police station.

'He was going to kill Inspector Grimley!' said Abigail, horrified.

'He was,' confirmed Daniel.

They were back in their room at the Mayflower, and this latest news from Daniel had left Abigail stunned.

'I think we need to tell the inspector what we know about Bickerstaff with relation to Kathleen,' said Daniel.

'You think it was Bickerstaff who killed her?' asked Abigail, surprised. 'You said before . . .'

'I know,' said Daniel, 'and I still feel that the murder is in some way connected with the army, through RSM Bulstrode, and that Bickerstaff had nothing to do with it. But what happened today with Bickerstaff trying to kill Grimley has changed things between us. The inspector has become more . . . amenable to us.'

'Only because you saved his life.'

'It doesn't matter what the reason is, the fact is that we have the chance to get the local police on our side, and we're going to need that cooperation if we're going to get to the bottom of this. So far we've hit obstacle after obstacle, and one of the biggest has been Inspector Grimley.'

'The biggest obstacle has been this RSM Bulstrode,' pointed out Abigail.

'Which is why we need Grimley. He has the law on his side, and we're going to need that if we're going to break down the resistance from Bulstrode and whoever he's protecting.'

'You're sure he's protecting someone?'

'I am, and I'm sure it's linked to what happened at Peterloo, which means it's someone who was involved in the killings there.'

'Eighty years ago!'

'It's connected,' insisted Daniel. 'We need to find out who the senior officers are at the barracks, and if any of them have links back to Peterloo. The army won't give us that information, but Grimley can get it. And while the inspector's feeling friendly towards me for saving his life, I suggest we call on him and tell him about William Bickerstaff and Kathleen.'

'There's no connection between them except that someone impersonating him called looking for Kathleen,' said Abigail.

'But there may be something there, although we don't know what yet,' insisted Daniel. 'Who was the man who pretended to be Bickerstaff? And why?'

Grimley sat behind his desk, stony-faced, as Abigail related what she'd been told about Bickerstaff and Kathleen. When she finished, Grimley shot a tight-lipped glare towards Daniel, who just nodded in confirmation.

'Let me make sure I've got this right,' he said. 'Some bloke pretending to be Bickerstaff followed Kathleen Donlan back to where she was lodging. On the day she's murdered, Bickerstaff was in the reading room at the museum *before* she was stabbed.'

'Yes,' said Abigail.

'Like I said to you before, he's got a reputation for stalking women from poor backgrounds and getting obsessed with them. And we also now know he's got a tendency to violence.'

'Yes,' said Abigail again.

Grimley scowled hard, anger burning from his eyes as he hissed between clenched teeth. 'And you knew all this and you never came to me with it before! It was the same with this Eve Preston business! Hiding things that were relevant to the case!'

'You weren't very receptive to us before, Inspector,' said Daniel.

'In fact, you were dismissive of anything we came to you with,' added Abigail, her tone curt.

'But this was still vital information!' shouted the inspector. He looked accusingly at Daniel, then demanded, 'And despite all this, you still don't think that Bickerstaff was the one who killed her?'

'No,' said Daniel. 'I think he's a very disturbed and confused man with a lot of anger and potential violence inside him, but in this case, I don't think he did it. I still believe it's to do with the army, and Miss Fenton believes the crime may have its roots in Ireland. Which is why we intend to look into the Irish angle next.' Quickly, he added, 'And we promise to keep you fully informed with anything we find.'

Grimley nodded, his outburst of anger over. 'Very well,' he said.

'One more thing, Inspector,' said Daniel. 'I've said before, it's my belief that in some way the murders are connected with what happened at Peterloo, and RSM Bulstrode at the barracks is trying to protect someone who may have been involved.'

'It was eighty years ago!' burst out Grimley. 'Everyone who was at Peterloo is long dead.'

'But their descendants aren't,' pointed out Daniel. 'And a whole range of people who might have been connected with them. Can you get me a list of the senior officers at the barracks? It might be worth checking into them, see if any had links to Peterloo, either family or by association.'

Grimley looked thoughtful. 'It might be more than that,' he said. 'Soldiers look after one another. It needn't have been a senior officer. Say it was an ordinary soldier who killed people on that day, and it's his name Bulstrode is trying to protect.'

'Yes, that's a good thought. But would Bulstrode be able to do what he's been doing, having me attacked, without the support of a senior officer?'

Grimley smiled. 'I can see you don't know the power an RSM has, Mr Wilson. To a great extent, they're a law unto themselves. The senior officers appear to be the ones who run things, but in truth it's the middle rankers, the RSMs, the quartermasters and the like, who keep things stable and running smoothly, and the senior officers are happy to turn a blind eye if the odd corner may be cut to keep everything on an even keel. The last thing they want is trouble.'

CHAPTER THIRTY-TWO

As they walked away from the police station, Daniel mulled over the observation that Grimley had made.

'What the inspector said about Bulstrode maybe protecting the memory of an ordinary soldier makes sense,' said Daniel.

'But it gives us a much bigger list of suspects,' said Abigail. 'Thousands, in fact.'

'And only Bulstrode knows who,' said Daniel. 'And at the moment, we can't touch him. Not without proof.'

'Let's hope we get something from Ireland that will lead us to that proof,' said Abigail.

They returned to their hotel to see whether any post had arrived for them, hoping there might be something from Ireland. There was nothing for them except an envelope addressed to 'Daniel Wilson' in untidy block capitals. Daniel opened the envelope, and Abigail saw anger cross his face.

'What is it?' she asked.

His face grim, he handed her the note it contained. Like the writing on the envelope, the message was in block capitals. It was brief and to the point. STOP YOUR INVESTIGATIONS OR YOUR LADY FRIEND WILL DIE AT HER TALK.

'This is outrageous!' she said.

Daniel returned to the reception desk and held out the envelope towards the receptionist.

'There's no stamp on this, so I assume it was handed in,' he said. 'Can you recall who gave it in?'

The receptionist shook his head. 'No, Mr Wilson. I just found it on the desk. Someone must have just put it there.'

'Thank you,' said Daniel.

He went back to where Abigail was now sitting on one of the chairs, studying the anonymous threat, a frown on her face.

'The receptionist didn't see who left it,' he told her. He sat down and said, 'You have to cancel the talk.'

'Absolutely not,' said Abigail. 'The reason I agreed to do it was because I felt it was a way of paying Mr Steggles back for the way his trust had been abused.'

'By Bickerstaff, not by us!'

'I still feel responsible. Don't you? We're supposed to be detectives, and you – particularly – are supposed to be able to determine when people are lying. But we allowed ourselves to be duped by Bickerstaff.'

'It's too dangerous,' said Daniel.

'I will be in a public place, surrounded by dignitaries, with the resultant protection one expects on these occasions. I refuse to allow myself to be frightened off. I have given my word to Mr Steggles that I'll give the talk. I won't let him down.'

Daniel took the note from her and read it through again before putting it back into his pocket. 'We have to tell Inspector Grimley about it,' he said. 'And Mr Steggles.'

'No,' said Abigail. 'There's no need to alarm them.'

'There's every reason to alarm them,' said Daniel. 'It may be just to try and frighten us off, but we've seen that these people act. If it is the army who are behind this, they tried with me and failed, so now they're targeting you. And this doesn't just threaten to harm you, it threatens to *kill* you. For me, if it is the army behind it – or, at the very least, RSM Bulstrode – that suggests a sniper.'

'Ridiculous!' snorted Abigail. 'No one's going to shoot me!'

'We don't know that,' said Daniel firmly. 'So, if you intend to go through with this talk—'

'I do,' said Abigail equally firmly.

'Then we need to let them know so they can put protective measures in place.'

Abigail looked bewildered. 'I really can't believe the army would sanction something like this.'

'Not the army,' said Daniel. 'Rogue elements, with RSM Bulstrode behind it.'

'Perhaps if we had him arrested . . .'

'On what charge?' asked Daniel. 'We don't have proof this is from him. So, until we have solid enough proof and can have him arrested, we take this seriously and make sure you're protected when you give your talk.'

Dan Daly stepped off the train and followed the crowd out of the exit into London Road. Back in Manchester.

It had been all very well for Pete Merton to tell him to disappear, vanish, go to Blackpool or wherever, but what about money? After a few days in Bolton he'd found his money running low, and in a town where he wasn't known there was no chance of him laying his hands on some cash. Someone in Bolton had told him there was money to be made in the mills, good money, but Daly had just stared at them as if they were talking in a foreign language. Dan Daly work in a mill? With his hands?

No, there was only one way and that was for him to return to Manchester and seek out some of his old pals, people who owed him. And, of course, his women. They must have been earning while he was away; well, he was back for his cut. He reckoned it would take him just a couple of hours, and then he'd be able to get a train out again. Somewhere different from Bolton this time. Maybe Crewe. Somewhere he wasn't known.

He wondered if he ought to go in search of Merton and find out what the score was. The heat must have died down a bit by now. The danger was, if he went anywhere near Newton Street there was a chance of running into Inspector Grimley, which was definitely something to be avoided. No, his best and safest course was to head for Ancoats and find some of his women and get them to cough up some money, enough to keep him going for a week or so. Then he'd find a way of getting in touch with Merton to see if it was safe for him to return. Hopefully the fuss over the dead girl would have died down by then.

As he headed in the direction of Ancoats he felt a sense of deep injustice. The killing of the girl had been nothing to do with him, so how come his name had been put in the frame?

Yes, he thought grimly, 'frame' was the right word for what was happening. Grimley was set on framing him for the murder, despite all the money Daly had paid him over the years. Bastard! Well, he'd have something to say about that when all this was over. In the future he'd want some sort of guarantee he wouldn't be turned over.

The hand dropping on his shoulder made him jump, and the familiar voice chuckling and saying 'Well, well, well. Look who it is' made him sick to his stomach.

He turned and found himself staring into the grinning face of Inspector Grimley.

'Fancy running into you, Dapper,' said Grimley.

Daly gulped. 'I ain't got time to stop and talk, Inspector,' he said. 'I've got to be somewhere urgent.'

'Yes, you have,' said Grimley, and now the grin and the chuckle were gone, replaced by a venomous look. Suddenly Daly found his right wrist gripped tightly and twisted hard so that he was forced to double over in pain, and the inspector's knee thudded hard into the side of his thigh, giving him a dead leg, and he almost collapsed. 'You and I need to have a talk.'

Grimley pushed Daly into the cell and then pulled the door shut behind them. Daly turned towards the inspector, his hands held out in appeal.

'Please, Inspector, I don't know what this is about, but I've done nothing!'

'The young Irish woman in Ancoats who was stabbed to death in the museum,' said Grimley. 'You had words with her the day before, and she hit you.'

'That was nothing!' said Daly. 'I never saw her again after that! I didn't do anything to her! I told Pete Merton that, and I swear on my mother's life it's the truth!'

'You told Sergeant Merton?' asked Grimley suspiciously.

'Yes!' said Daly. 'That was nothing to do with me!'

'Well, that's unfortunate,' said Grimley. 'You see, the top

brass is on my back for someone to nab for it, and at the moment you're the only one in the picture. See, she'd only been in the country a couple of days and hadn't met many people. Except you.'

'Honest, Inspector! On my life!'

Grimley nodded. 'Yes, it is. If that's what it takes.'

And he took off his jacket and began to roll up his shirtsleeves.

'Now, now, Inspector!' said Daly, backing away, fear on his face. 'You don't want to do this! After all, we've got history, you and me.'

'And what history's that?' asked Grimley.

'You know. Through Sergeant Merton.'

Grimley stopped and studied Daly, puzzled. 'What do you mean?'

'Well . . . the favours.'

'Favours?'

'You know.'

Grimley didn't answer; instead he moved closer to Daly. 'What favours?' he demanded menacingly.

Daly gulped. 'Well, your share.'

Grimley reached out and grabbed hold of Daly by his throat, bringing the pimp's face close to his.

'Tell me about my share,' he growled.

'From what I give Pete Merton,' bleated Daly. 'To look after me. He told me people have to get their share, which is why he's put up what I had to pay him.'

'Pay him? For protection?'

Daly tried to nod, but his face was so close to the inspector's that he could only manage a wobble of his head.

'Sergeant Merton told you he was paying me to look after you?'

'Just a share,' said Daly. 'So I wouldn't be interfered with.'

'Well, I've got news for you, Daly,' snarled Grimley. 'I've never taken a penny off Pete Merton, or anyone else. And as far as you being interfered with . . .' He suddenly released Daly and, before the man could dodge, had swung a his first hard into Daly's face, sending him crashing to the floor.

CHAPTER THIRTY-THREE

Inspector Grimley stomped into the reception area and up to the desk.

'Where's Sergeant Merton?' he demanded of the desk sergeant.

'He said he'd be out and about today, seeing his narks,' replied the desk sergeant.

'When he comes in, tell him I want to see him,' said Grimley.

He marched down the corridor to his office, amazing himself that he was keeping his temper under control, not punching a wall or shouting at people. *That bastard Merton!* he raged silently as he entered his office and sat down at his desk, picking up a pencil and toying with it between his fingers. 'Out seeing his narks,' he muttered to himself bitterly. Yes, and tapping them up for bribes which he'd been telling everyone he was paying to the inspector to make sure they stayed out of jail.

Suddenly the pencil snapped in two under the pressure of his fingers.

I'll kill him, he vowed, throwing the broken pencil into his wastepaper basket. *As soon as he puts his head round that door, I'll smash his face in.*

The knock at his door startled him. So soon? He forced himself to stay in his chair rather than getting up and throwing his door open and grabbing Merton by his no-good throat. 'Come in!' he barked.

The door opened and Daniel Wilson entered.

'What do you want?' Grimley snapped curtly.

Daniel looked at the inspector in surprise. He'd thought they were on good terms after the Bickerstaff business, but now here Grimley was, obviously seething with anger and glowering. But not at him, Daniel noted. Which suggested something else had upset the inspector.

'We've had a threatening letter,' said Daniel. 'Anonymous, obviously.'

He gave the piece of paper to Grimley, who studied it, and then looked at Daniel, still angry but with a frown on his face that could have been concern.

'It might be a bluff, but it might not,' he said. 'She has to cancel this talk of hers tomorrow night.'

'She won't.'

'After someone's threatened to kill her if she does it?'

'You don't know Abigail. She is possibly the bravest person I've ever known.'

'This isn't bravery, it's stupidity! She doesn't know what she's doing!'

'She's faced death before, Inspector. Not so long ago she was held at knifepoint in a darkened tunnel by someone who'd already stabbed to death two fully grown men, and who threatened to do the same to her. Yet she never flinched. She never pleaded for her life.'

'Why on earth not?'

Daniel thought it over, then said, 'Because she knew I would come to her aid.'

'And you did?'

Daniel nodded.

Grimley studied him, then said quietly, 'You two must care for one another a great deal.'

Daniel gave a rueful smile and said, 'Is it that obvious?'

'I was married myself once,' said Grimley. 'I haven't always been this angry bastard.' He paused, then added, 'My wife died. She was crossing the road when she was knocked down by a runaway horse. It was as if my life ended there and then.'

'You never married again?'

Grimley shook his head. 'There was only ever my Maisie for me.' He fell silent, then said quietly, 'I found out whose horse it was and went to its stable, and killed it.'

Daniel nodded. 'I understand that feeling.'

Suddenly his usual pugnaciousness returned to Grimley and he said tersely, 'But that's between you and me! If it ever gets out, I'll deny it.'

'I promise, no one will hear it from me,' Daniel assured him. 'Any news about Constable Adams?'

'No,' admitted Grimley sourly. 'He's gone. Done a runner.'

'And with him goes our chance of getting proof that Bulstrode was behind the attack on me,' Daniel grunted.

'How do you think the attack on her will come?'

'My guess, if there's an army connection, which I think there is, it'll be a sniper,' said Daniel. 'And it doesn't have to be at the museum, at the talk itself. It could happen as she goes to the museum, or on the way back from it.'

'I'll have my men there on the night to search the interior of the museum and keep watch,' said Grimley. 'And we'll give her an escort to and from the museum.'

'She won't like that,' mused Daniel.

'We'll say it's a Guard of Honour, and if she doesn't like it she can lump it. She's not being killed on my watch.'

Leaving the inspector to arrange the police protection for the following evening, Daniel returned to the hotel where he collected Abigail, and the pair of them proceeded to the museum to talk to Bernard Steggles.

'You think we have to tell him?' asked Abigail.

'Of course we do,' said Daniel. 'For one thing, he needs to know why there will be so many policemen in the museum tomorrow. I doubt if we can convince him they're all there to hear about ancient Egypt. And say there is an attempt and someone else gets injured. One of his staff.'

'Yes, but I'm concerned he might want to cancel the talk.'

'It might be a good thing if he does. And at least he will have cancelled it, not you. So your conscience can be clear.'

'I will not let myself be frightened off,' said Abigail. 'The talk is advertised. Jesse Haworth will be there, and so will many other influential people. It will help the museum. And now we'll have a whole platoon of men inside watching over me, I will be perfectly safe.'

If only that were true, thought Daniel ruefully.

Bernard Steggles was full of happy anticipation as they entered his office. 'I was just thinking about you!' he said brightly. 'Do you have everything you need for tomorrow, Miss Fenton? I've arranged for one of the pots you mentioned to be on display on the podium. And we have a large and detailed map of Egypt that we are erecting immediately behind the

270

lectern, so that you can show the audience where the various digs you've been on were.'

'Thank you, Mr Steggles.' Abigail smiled. 'That is so very much appreciated. However, a small issue has arisen, which Mr Wilson felt you ought to know about.'

'Oh?' said Steggles, concerned.

Daniel produced the threatening letter and passed it to Steggles. 'We received this yesterday,' he said.

Steggles read it, and went pale. 'My God!' he exclaimed. 'This is terrible! We have to cancel!'

'Absolutely not,' said Abigail firmly. 'We've already been to see Inspector Grimley and he has assured protection here tomorrow evening.'

'He will have a large force of his men inside the museum, keeping guard,' said Daniel, adding quickly as a look of concern crossed Steggles's face, 'They'll be very discreet, of course, so their presence won't detract from the event.'

'Are you sure about this?' asked Steggles, directing his question to Abigail.

'Absolutely!' responded Abigail. 'We just thought we'd let you know, to explain the presence of the police. But there's no reason to alert anyone else.' She took the letter back from him and gave it to Daniel. 'There is another thing that's happened that you should know about,' she said. 'Mr Bickerstaff has been arrested.'

'Arrested?' Steggles gulped. 'For what?'

'I'll let Mr Wilson tell the story,' said Abigail. 'He was there when it happened.'

'When what happened?' asked Steggles, stunned.

'I'm afraid Mr Bickerstaff went to the police station to shoot Inspector Grimley,' said Daniel. 'Fortunately, he didn't succeed, and the inspector and I were able to overpower and disarm him.'

Steggles sank back in his chair, his mouth open in shock. The expression on his face showed he was having great difficulty in taking this in.

'He tried to shoot Inspector Grimley?!' he finally managed to croak.

'He did,' said Daniel. 'Luckily, he failed. But he will definitely be tried for attempted murder.'

'This is appalling!' said Steggles. Then, worriedly, he asked, 'Do you think my letter to Mr Scott at the *Guardian* had anything to do with it? That it may have caused it? That I am to blame?'

'No,' said Abigail firmly. 'If that were the case, he'd have tried to shoot you instead of the inspector.'

At this, Steggles's face paled. 'My God!' he whispered hoarsely. 'What in God's name is happening in this city?'

The knock at his door made Grimley look up from the list he'd been compiling of Merton's known narks. Once he'd dealt with Merton, he intended to pay them each a visit and let them know they'd been fooled by the sergeant. He smiled vengefully to himself at the knowledge that most of them would be extremely unhappy when they found out they'd been cheated, and would quite likely take their revenge on the sergeant. *But they'll have to get in line behind me*, he thought.

The knock came again at his door, and this time he called out 'Come in!', at the same time secreting the list of narks beneath some other papers.

It was Merton.

'You wanted to see me, guv'nor?'

Grimley gestured at the chair opposite his and said genially, 'Sit down, Pete. Take the load off.'

Merton looked at the inspector, puzzled. This wasn't his usual tone. Usually he was sour and angry. What had happened to make him act so . . . friendly? Whatever it was, it was a good thing, but the strangeness of it worried Merton. He sat down on the chair.

'Comfortable?' asked Grimley, getting up and strolling towards his seated sergeant.

'Yes, thanks, sir,' said Merton, still feeling that something wasn't right.

'Good.' Grimley smiled.

The next second his huge fist had slammed into Merton's face, breaking his nose with the force of the blow and sending him over backwards out of the chair to crash to the ground. Before he could recover, Grimley's boot smashed into his ribs and he screamed with the pain.

Grimley kicked him again, and then stamped on him, putting all his weight on to keep Merton imprisoned beneath his boot.

'You bastard!' snarled Grimley. 'You lying, thieving, crooked bastard!'

'Boss . . . !' begged Merton, spitting blood as he spoke.

'I've just been having a chat with your old friend, Dapper Dan,' said Grimley. 'And guess what he told me? How he's been paying me off through you to keep him from being arrested.'

'No, guv'nor! I swear on my kids' lives . . .'

'I wouldn't,' growled Grimley. 'Or I'll have to kill them as well.'

He took his boot off the sergeant, but stayed within kicking distance of the fallen man.

'I'm going to beat you to within an inch of your life, Merton,' he said, his voice edged with anger. 'And then I'm going to make sure what's left of you goes to jail for a long time. Not that it will be very long, because you know what happens to coppers who end up in jail.'

'Please, boss . . .' pleaded Merton. 'It was only once . . .'

CRUNCH! The inspector's boot struck home again, and once more the sergeant screamed. Grimley knelt down so that his face was close to Merton's.

'Don't lie to me again. If you do, I'll kill you.'

He stood up and looked coldly down at the bleeding, damaged body of his sergeant.

'There's one way to make this stop.'

'Anything!' begged Merton.

'Find Sam Adams.'

'He's disappeared,' said Merton. Then he coughed and spat up a clot of blood.

'I know he has,' said Grimley. 'And you're going to find him and bring him in to me.'

'I don't know where—' began Merton, then stopped as the inspector crouched down and glowered at him.

'I don't want excuses, or reasons why you can't find him,' he said menacingly. 'It's very simple. You bring him to me. You've got forty-eight hours. That should be plenty of time for a corrupt, dirty copper like you to track down another corrupt, dirty copper. If you don't, I shall take it out on you instead. I'll have you in a cell tied to the bars so you can't escape, and I shall kill you . . . almost. And don't think of running away, because I know where you live and I'll have your family brought in. And you won't like what I'll do to them.' He glared down at the groaning Merton. 'Forty-eight hours, Sergeant.'

CHAPTER THIRTY-FOUR

Daniel and Abigail sat at their table, tucking into their breakfast.

'Are you ready for this evening?' asked Daniel.

'Yes, and I'm looking forward to it, despite the threat contained in that anonymous letter.'

'We'll protect you,' said Daniel. 'Myself, and Inspector Grimley and his men.'

'It's such a turnaround by the inspector,' mused Abigail. 'One moment he's doing everything he can to run us out of town, and now he can't be more helpful.' She smiled at Daniel. 'You'll have to save people's lives more often.'

The hotel receptionist arrived at their table and held out an envelope to them.

'I'm sorry to disturb your breakfast,' he said, 'but this has just arrived in the post. I thought I'd bring it at once in case it was urgent.'

Daniel took the envelope from him. 'Thank you,' he said. He examined it. 'It's not from our anonymous friend. The handwriting's different, and it's got a stamp.' He opened the envelope and took out the letter, and as he read it he smiled. 'It's from Mallow in Ireland!' he told Abigail. 'It's from someone called Niamh O'Keeffe. She says she's writing on behalf of her great-uncle, Sean Donlan. He saw the piece in the newspaper and he recognised the photograph. Kathleen Donlan was his niece.'

'The poor man,' said Abigail. 'It must have been horrible for him to find out she was dead that way.'

'She says Mr Donlan has something to tell us. He invites us to visit him.' He handed the letter to Abigail for her to read, as he added, 'This could be the answer we've been looking for.'

'We'll go tomorrow,' said Abigail. 'I suggest we send a telegram to let them know we're coming, and that we hope to be with them some time tomorrow evening.'

'In that case, we say tomorrow evening or the following morning,' proposed Daniel. 'We don't know how long it will take us to get to Mallow, but as it will involve at least two trains, possibly more, and a ferry journey . . .'

'I'm sure Father O'Brien will be able to give us some guidance on how long it will take,' said Abigail. 'We'll send the telegram after we've seen him.'

Mass was just ending as they arrived at St Michael's Church, and they waited while Father O'Brien took his leave of his congregation, which seemed to consist mostly of Irish and Italian women with young children.

'Your church is popular,' commented Daniel.

'It's somewhere for people to escape to without it costing them money,' said O'Brien. 'For many it's their only outing of the day, especially the older ones.' He looked enquiringly at them. 'Is there any news? Has the culprit who killed Kathleen and Eileen been found?'

'Not yet, but we've had some news that we hope might throw some light on things,' said Abigail.

Daniel produced the letter they'd received and passed it to the priest.

'So, the little gamble using the *North Cork Reporter* paid off,' said O'Brien, reading the letter.

'We're intending to go to Mallow tomorrow and meet this Mr Donlan,' said Daniel.

'Very good,' said O'Brien. 'Do either of you speak Irish?'

'*Dia dhuit.*' Daniel gave a wry smile. When Abigail looked at him in surprise, he shrugged and said, 'It just means hello.'

'That's more than most English can say,' commented O'Brien.

'I grew up in Camden Town in London,' said Daniel. 'The area was half-Irish.'

'I don't even have that much,' said Abigail.

'I ask because the fact that this letter is written by Sean Donlan's great-niece, and the address is a townland outside of Mallow, suggests he may speak some English, but I expect mostly Irish. Country people in Cork and Kerry mainly speak Irish Gaelic. So I suggest when you contact her it might be courteous to say you understand she'll be there to help her great-uncle understand you, and tell them what day you'll be arriving. It'll avoid any embarrassment.'

'Thank you, that's a good thought,' said Abigail.

'As you've never been to the old country before, I hope you won't think I'm poking my nose in if I offer you some more practical advice.'

'Not at all,' said Abigail. 'We'd welcome it.'

'It might help if I give you a letter of introduction to the priest in Mallow, Father Patrick Brennan. You'll be strangers, and in country areas strangers are treated kindly, but there's always some reserve. Especially when it comes to questions being asked. A letter from me to Father Brennan might help to open some doors for you if there are any problems.'

'That will be very helpful,' said Daniel.

'I'm guessing you'll be taking the ferry from Liverpool to Dublin,' continued O'Brien. 'That's what most people do.'

'Yes, that was what we intended.'

'When you get to Dublin you'll want to catch the Cork train from Kingsbridge Station. It's a long journey to Mallow, so make sure you take refreshments. There are stops on the way, but there's no guarantee there'll be food left for you.'

'Do you think we'll be arriving in time to see Mr Donlan tomorrow evening?' asked Abigail. 'We ask because we're going to send a telegram letting them know when we'll be arriving.'

'It's possible,' said O'Brien. 'But finding your way around the townlands late can be difficult. You'd be safer booking into a hotel for the night and seeing Mr Donlan the next morning.' He handed the letter back to Daniel. 'I'd suggest the Mallow Hotel would be the best place to stay. It's a big building in the middle of the Main Street. Language won't be a problem for you in Mallow, you'll always find someone who can speak English.' He smiled. 'It's a pity you won't have a chance to stay longer. Mallow has a wonderful racecourse which always offers great racing. Perhaps you could treat it like a holiday?'

'Thank you, Father,' said Daniel, 'but we're honour-bound to return as soon as we can. It wouldn't be fair to Mr Steggles and the museum to take advantage of the occasion. We have a job to do, and the sooner we can bring it to a conclusion, the better.'

* * *

278

Sam Adams sat on a wooden box in the storeroom at the barracks and bitterly regretted ever getting involved in his brother-in-law's scheme. 'For the Old Man,' George Bulstrode had said. But he hadn't said why, just that the Old Man needed people to look after him. 'It'll be easy,' George had said. 'Just knock him about a bit. There'll be seven of you against one. All you have to do is tip off your mates at the police station there might be a bit of a ruckus and not bother looking into it and it's all taken care of.' But it hadn't been. And ever since he'd been stuck here, because George said it was too dangerous for him to be seen walking about outside. 'The police might be looking for you. We can't afford to have you picked up and questioned.'

'But I don't know anything,' Adams had insisted.

'You know who the Old Man is,' said Bulstrode.

'But I'd never say!' Adams said.

'You say that now, but I hear that Inspector Grimley's digging into what happened, and if you got into his clutches we all know what he'd do.'

'I'm a copper!' stressed Adams. 'He wouldn't touch me!'

But George had insisted Adams stayed inside, even when he'd protested that he needed to see Peg, his wife, and the kids to reassure them he was all right.

'I've seen Peg and told her,' Bulstrode told him. 'Not where you are. She might blab.'

'She wouldn't!' said Adams. 'Not if it puts her husband in it. You know her better than that, she's your sister.'

'And because I know her and what she's capable of, that's why I'm not telling her anything. I love Peg dearly, but she does like to talk.'

Which was true, Adams thought ruefully. But how long would he have to stay here, cooped up like this? It was worse than being in prison!

The door of the storeroom opened, and RSM George Bulstrode entered.

'Everything all right, Sam?' he asked.

'No, it ain't!' snapped Adams. 'How long have I got to be here?'

'That's why I came,' said Bulstrode. 'You're gonna have to leave. People are asking questions about what's going on with you in this storeroom.'

'Good!' said Adams, getting to his feet. 'At last I can go home!'

'No,' said Bulstrode.

Adams stared at him. 'What do you mean "no"?'

'You can't go back home until the heat dies down,' said Bulstrode. 'In fact, you can't stay in Manchester in case anyone spots you and turns you in.'

'But . . . but . . .' stammered Adams, aghast.

'I've made arrangements for you to stay at a boarding house in Carlisle. It's run by the widow of an old mate of mine who was in the Border Regiment. She'll look after you.' He pulled a piece of paper from his pocket and offered it to Adams. 'I've written down her name and address. Once things quieten down I'll write to you there and say you can come back.'

'No,' said Adams firmly. 'I ain't gonna throw good money away on a boarding house when I've got my own house here. And what will Peg and the kids say?'

'I'll square it with Peg,' said Bulstrode.

'And the money for the rent, and food and everything?' demanded Adams. 'I won't be getting paid if I'm not at work. What are they gonna live on?'

'I'll see to that,' said Bulstrode. 'We've got a hardship fund that I'm in charge of. The money will come from there.'

'No,' said Adams, even firmer this time. 'I'm not being run out of Manchester, away from my family. What will happen to them without me? Without my wages?'

'I've told you—'

'It ain't right,' said Adams. 'You got me into this!'

'And I'm getting you out of it,' said Bulstrode. He took some money from his pocket. 'This is for your train fare to Carlisle. Plus some extra for day-to-day costs when you get there. If things go right, it should only be for a few days, and, like I say, I'll see Peg and the kids don't go short.'

'What do you mean "if things go right"?' asked Adams.

'We've got plans,' said Bulstrode.

'Who's we?' Adams demanded.

'That's not for you to know,' said Bulstrode. 'But in a day or so this'll all be sorted out and everyone can go about their normal business again. And you can come back home.'

Adams hesitated, then took the paper with the address and the money from Bulstrode.

'I want to see Peg and the kids before I go,' he said.

'No,' said Bulstrode, shaking his head. 'It's too risky. Someone might see you going into your house.'

'Then we won't meet in our house. Somewhere else, somewhere she can bring the kids with her. I want to see them before I go.'

'No,' repeated Bulstrode, even firmer this time. 'You've got to trust me on this, Sam. We can't take the chance on you being spotted, or Peg or the kids saying something after they've seen you. Better for all if you just go and get the train to Carlisle.'

Sergeant Merton entered the gloom of the Royal Oak pub in Deansgate. It was the fifteenth pub he'd visited in his search. At each he'd sought out the landlord and said he'd pay good money if they got news of Sam Adams, because he needed to talk to him urgently. He'd also tried shops, local police stations, as well as seeking out his usual narks. With each one the reaction had been the same: a shocked expression as they took in his broken nose and the savage bruising all over his face. For Merton, the damage to his face was noticeable, but his real agony came from his ribs. He was sure Grimley had broken one or two, and he was determined that wouldn't happen again to him. He needed to find Adams.

'My God, Pete, what happened to you?' asked Bert Peet, staring at the sergeant's battered face.

'I fell,' said Merton.

'What on?' asked Peet.

'Never mind that,' said Merton. 'Have you seen Sam Adams?'

Peet shook his head. 'No, he doesn't come in here much. Mostly he hangs around Hulme. That's where his station is.'

'I've tried Hulme, and no one's seen him,' said Merton. 'It's very important I get hold of him. Spread the word, Bert. There's a good reward for anyone who tells me where I can find him.'

'I'll pass it on,' said Peet. He reached for a bottle. 'Beer?'

Merton shook his head. 'No, I've got to get on. Duty calls. But if you find out where Sam is . . .'

'I promise I'll get word to you.'

'But don't let him know I'm looking for him,' said Merton.

'Oh?' said Peet, curious. 'Why, what's he done?'

'Nothing,' said Merton. 'It's just I don't want him to know he's being looked for.'

'So he's in trouble?'

'No,' said Merton. 'It's just . . . something that's confidential. I'm not allowed to say, except to Sam. But it'll be worth his while if I can find him. He'll benefit.'

Merton left the pub to continue his search, feeling Peet's suspicious gaze on his back. He'd had to tell Bert Peet that, because he knew Bert would pass on the information to Adams. It was important that if Adams was found, he didn't do a runner. If he hadn't done one already. It was worrying that there'd been no sign

282

of him, which suggested he was either being hidden by someone, or he'd run off somewhere.

Merton's first port of call had been the small terraced house in Hulme where Adams lived with his wife, Peg, and their two kids, but he'd had no joy there. Peg Adams said her husband was out at work, but Merton knew that wasn't true because he'd gone looking for him at Hulme police station, where Sergeant Bottomley had told him they hadn't seen Adams since he'd been released after the business with the soldiers and those university students getting involved in a punch-up.

'Try the barracks,' Bottomley had suggested. 'It was Sam's brother-in-law, George Bulstrode, the RSM at the barracks, who sprung him. He might know where he is.'

Merton had tried to barracks, but received short shrift from Bulstrode.

'No, I don't know where he is,' the RSM had snapped at him. 'I got him out and he went home and I haven't seen him since. He should never have been locked up in the first place. Locking up one of your own? That's a disgrace! That's the difference between us in the army and you in the police: we take care of our own.'

Merton considered going back to see Peg Adams and talking to her again, but decided it would be a waste of time, and his time was valuable right now. Peg Adams had been lying, Merton had no doubt about that. But why? Adams had been freed from custody. He was safe to walk the streets and to return to work. What would make him vanish like this? Could he be dead? Merton hoped not. His only chance of surviving this was in finding Sam Adams alive.

Sam Adams trudged slowly and unwillingly towards the railway station. He didn't want to go to Carlisle. He wanted to go home. He couldn't understand why George was insisting he couldn't. 'We're protecting the Old Man,' Bulstrode had said. But against what? When he'd been in the cell with the soldiers at Hulme police station, one of the others had muttered it was to do with what had happened at Peterloo. But Peterloo was over eighty years ago. The Old Man hadn't even been born when that happened, so there was no way he could have been caught up in it.

It would have helped if George had told him what it was all about, but he'd insisted on maintaining secrecy. 'The less you know, the less you can say,' he'd said.

'But I don't know anything!' Adams had burst out.

'And that's a good thing,' his brother-in-law had retorted.

No, Adams decided. *I'm not going to Carlisle. Not until I've seen Peg and the kids*. But how could he manage that? George had told him he couldn't go home and see them.

In that case, I'll have to make arrangements, he decided. *I'll get hold of someone I can trust and get them to go and see Peg and tell her Sam wants to meet her*. But it had to be somewhere no one might think of, because he couldn't risk being seen. The trouble was: who could he trust? He couldn't trust George, for example.

He also couldn't be seen wandering around Manchester.

The Iron Duke, he decided. Billy Scargell had a backroom there, and Billy owed him favours. He'd get Billy to let him hide out in the backroom. George would assume he'd caught the train and gone to Carlisle, but he'd play it safe, he'd keep hidden overnight, just to make sure. Then, first thing in the morning, he'd get Billy to go and see Peg and bring her and the kids to the Iron Duke. They'd be safe there.

CHAPTER THIRTY-FIVE

Abigail and Daniel were sitting in the hotel lounge, drinking coffee, when they spotted Breda coming towards them, and the excited expression on her face and the speed with which she moved suggested something had happened. But was it good or bad? They both got to their feet as she reached them.

'What's happened?' asked Abigail.

'I saw him!' said Breda.

'Saw who?' asked Abigail.

'The toff. The bloke who said he was William Bickerstaff, but he wasn't. I was in town just now and I spotted him walking, so I followed him to see where he went.'

'That was very brave of you,' said Abigail.

'And dangerous,' added Daniel.

'I kept back from him,' said Breda. 'He went into the

museum. He's still there. So I came here to tell you.'

'He might not be there any longer,' said Daniel.

'Yes, he is,' said Breda. 'I think he works there, because he's behind a desk answering questions.'

The three of them hurried to the museum, and Daniel and Abigail followed Breda up the stairs, and then into the reading room. Breda pointed to the figure of Jonty Hawkins sitting at his usual desk.

'That's him,' she said. 'But he didn't have that make-up on before.'

Hawkins looked up and smiled as he saw Abigail and Daniel, but his smile faded as he caught sight of Breda standing with them, and they saw he'd turned pale, even beneath his rouge.

The miserable-looking Hawkins had accompanied Daniel and Abigail to Steggles's office, where they asked the museum director if they could use his room to talk to Hawkins.

'In your presence, obviously,' said Daniel. 'It concerns the museum and the young woman who was murdered.'

At this, Steggles shot a look of astonishment mixed with nervousness at his reading-room receptionist, but Hawkins kept his head down, his eyes lowered.

'Of course,' said Steggles.

Daniel gestured for Hawkins to sit in a chair, then Abigail sat while Daniel led the questioning, Steggles leant forward in his chair, his gaze resolutely fixed on Hawkins.

'You went to Ancoats and told the girl you met at the house where she was staying you were William Bickerstaff,' said Daniel. 'You gave her a card with his name on it.'

'Yes,' said Hawkins.

'How did you get it?'

'Bickerstaff gave it to me. He asked me to get in touch with him if I ever had anything he could use in the newspaper. I put it in my desk drawer and forgot about it.'

'How did you know where Kathleen was staying?'

'I followed her when she left the museum that first day.'

'Why? Were you planning to kill her already?'

At this, Steggles let out a gasp and looked towards Daniel in horror.

'I didn't kill her,' said Hawkins.

'You go in pursuit of her, pretending to be someone else, and the next day she's murdered in the reading room,' said Daniel. 'A young woman who's only been in the city for a couple of days. That seems too much of a coincidence.'

'I did not kill her!' repeated Hawkins.

'Then why did you go in search of her? And why pretend to be William Bickerstaff?'

'I wanted to have my own back.'

'On a girl who'd done nothing to you!' said Daniel angrily.

Hawkins looked at him, pained. 'Not on her! On Bickerstaff.'

Daniel and Abigail exchanged puzzled looks, then Daniel sat down, watching Hawkins intensely the whole time.

'You'd better explain,' he said.

Hawkins fell silent, as if gathering his thoughts, then he gave a heavy sigh. 'It all began about four months ago,' he said. 'A young woman started to come to the reading room. Her name was Etta Harkness. She was similar to the young woman who was killed, obviously poor, attractive, but what made her special was the fact she came to learn, to better herself. She'd taught herself to read, and now she wanted to expand her horizons in what she read. She asked me for my advice on which authors she should read. We started with popular authors, like Dickens and Eliot, and then I introduced her to poetry. The works of

John Donne became her favourite, as they were for me.

'We were happy, talking poetry. I looked forward to her visits here so much, and I was on the point of suggesting that we might meet somewhere else, go out to places together, when that vile snake, Bickerstaff, appeared.

'I'd heard rumours about him preying on young women from poor backgrounds and taking advantage of them, but I put it down to gossip. There's a lot of gossip about people, especially those in the public eye, and Bickerstaff made sure he was in the public eye because of his articles in the *Guardian*.' His mouth twisted into an angry sneer as he said, 'He claimed he was a writer, a proper one, because he got paid for writing. And he could be charming when he wanted, especially if he was after something. And he was.'

'Etta?' asked Daniel.

Hawkins nodded. 'It happened under my nose, without me noticing. When Etta and I met she started talking more and more about Bickerstaff, how clever he was, a radical writer who said he was planning to go into politics and revolutionise life for people like her, lift her out of poverty. Her face lit up when she talked about him. I tried to warn her about him, because of the gossip I'd heard, but she said people who spoke badly about him only did that because they were jealous of him, so I stopped telling her because I didn't want her to think less of me.'

He looked at them, and they could see the pain etched in his face.

'Of course, he had no real feelings for her, despite what he claimed. You can guess what happened. He used her, and then discarded her when he got tired of her. And when she discovered she was pregnant, he denied it was anything to do with him. He told her it must have been any of the other men she'd slept with, and when she told him he'd been the only one, he became hard and cruel. Said he'd have the police on her if she spread such lies about him.'

Hawkins lowered his head and was silent for a minute, before he said, 'She killed herself. She couldn't face the shame of having a baby. She'd lost everything.' He jerked his head up and said angrily: 'He'd taken everything from her. And he'd taken her from me, for ever. I wanted to kill him. But I didn't know how to do it. And I didn't want him just to die, I wanted him to suffer, as I had and Etta had. Every time he came here to do some kind of research or something, I'd look at him and rage would build up inside me so much that I thought I'd pick up the heaviest book I could find and smash it down on his head and keep hitting him until he was dead and his brains were everywhere. But I didn't.

'And then, last week when that young Irish woman came in and asked about the barracks and the army, I noticed Bickerstaff coming in. She told me she'd met him at the newspaper offices, and she felt there was something creepy about him.'

'She said that to you?' asked Abigail, surprised.

'Yes,' said Hawkins. 'I could see from the way he watched her when he was in here that he was after her, the same way he'd been after Etta. And, although she said she felt there was something creepy about him, I knew how charming he could be, how persuasive, and I felt it was only a matter of time before he used her as he'd done Etta. And I thought, and I don't know why, *I can use this. I can expose him for the vile seducer he is.* But I wasn't sure how to go about it.

'Anyway, although I didn't have a plan worked out, or even half a plan, I decided to follow the young woman, Kathleen, as it turned out to be, when she left the museum, and I tracked her to the house in Ancoats. I didn't talk to her that day; I still didn't know exactly what I was going to do. Then I decided I'd go and see her and warn her about Bickerstaff, but then I thought that might be too direct. I'd tried to warn Etta and it hadn't worked. In fact, it had done the opposite, it had pushed her towards him. I had to be cleverer.

'I thought if I left his card for her, as she'd already said he seemed creepy to her, it might put her off him, feeling he was pursuing her. I also thought I might be able to use it later in some way, but I didn't know how.

'Next day she was back at the museum again, and it was all very businesslike, no chatting. And then she was killed.'

'Why didn't you tell us you knew who the young woman was and where she was living when we first talked to you?' asked Abigail.

Hawkins hung his head. 'I was afraid,' he said. 'I could only say I knew who she was and where she came from if I said I'd followed her to her house, and that would make me a main suspect for the murders. But I didn't! I didn't kill either of them!'

'You told me that Bickerstaff was at the museum before she died, as well as afterwards. Did you say that to implicate him?' asked Abigail.

'No, that was true,' said Hawkins. 'But I admit I was pleased about it, because I hoped it might mean he'd be investigated in more depth.'

'Do you think he killed her?' asked Daniel.

Hawkins shook his head. 'No. At least, I don't think so. It seemed too brazen a thing for Bickerstaff to do, to kill her somewhere that public. He's too much of a coward. But, perhaps I'm wrong. Perhaps he did.'

The questioning finished, Hawkins left the office with Steggles's firmly delivered instruction to 'Return to your post. I shall talk to you after I've decided what action to take.'

Once the door had closed behind Hawkins, Steggles looked at Daniel and Abigail and asked, almost helplessly, 'What can we do? Do the police need to be brought in? Do you think Hawkins killed her to implicate Bickerstaff?'

'I don't believe he killed her,' said Daniel. 'I feel all he's guilty of is lying when he told Breda he was William Bickerstaff. Technically he's not guilty of any crime. However, he hampered the investigation by not being honest about going to Ancoats and pretending to be Bickerstaff, and there has to be a question mark over him because she was killed here, and Hawkins was the one who found her.

'Ordinarily, if we were in a place where I knew the local police detective division and trusted them, I'd be honour-bound to hand him in for them to question him. But from what I've heard of the local inspector, I believe he tends to carry out his interrogations very physically in order to extract a confession, and I have my doubts about that being either ethical or successful in this case, or any other.'

Steggles looked doubtful. 'I'm not convinced I can trust him,' he said. He looked at Abigail. 'What do you think, Miss Fenton?'

'I agree with Mr Wilson,' said Abigail. 'I also don't believe he killed the young woman. I share Daniel's view that the key to her death lies somewhere with the army, and I can't see Mr Hawkins being involved there in any way. My preference would be to wait a day or two and think about it before handing him over to the police, if that's what we decide. After all, we go to Ireland tomorrow, and I'm hoping what we learn there might fill in some of the gaps in our knowledge of the case: namely, the reason why she was killed.'

Steggles sat and thought their words over, then finally announced, 'Very well. I shall send him home on leave until you return from Ireland and let me know what you've discovered. Then we'll make a decision.' He lifted the internal telephone on his desk and said, 'Mrs Wedburn, could you find Mr Hawkins in the reading room and tell him to report to my office.'

As Daniel and Abigail descended the stairs towards the exit, the miserable and forlorn figure of Jonty Hawkins passed them on his way to his meeting with Steggles.

'Well, we've gained him a reprieve from the attentions of Inspector Grimley and his men,' muttered Abigail. 'But what if we're wrong about him? What if it was him, and he kills again while we're away?'

'In that case, it will show us we're not the good judges of character we think we are,' sighed Daniel unhappily.

'But if we're wrong, someone else may die,' said Abigail. 'If that were to happen, I'm not sure if I could ever forgive myself.'

CHAPTER THIRTY-SIX

When Abigail and Daniel descended the stairs of the hotel that evening to make their way to the museum for Abigail's talk, they found four tall, uniformed policemen waiting for them in the hotel lobby. The leader of the four stepped forward to greet them.

'Miss Fenton?' he asked. 'I'm Sergeant Hudson. Inspector Grimley has sent us to escort you and Mr Wilson to the museum. We have a van outside to transport you, if you wish.'

'No, thank you,' said Abigail. 'It's not far, and I'm used to walking.'

'Whichever you prefer, ma'am,' said Hudson. He snapped out an order and the three uniformed constables assembled around Abigail and Daniel, with Sergeant Hudson completing the square of four, and they marched Abigail and Daniel through the lobby, out of the hotel and towards the museum.

'This is ludicrous,' muttered Abigail crossly. 'We are presenting a ridiculous spectacle!'

'It's for your safety,' said Daniel.

'No one is going to try and kill me in the street,' said Abigail firmly.

'Why not?' asked Daniel. 'It's easier than trying to kill you inside the museum. In an enclosed space the shooter has more problems getting away.' He looked up at the buildings they passed. 'Far better to take up a position in some high building. One shot, and then disappear before anyone realises where the shot's come from.'

'Is that supposed to reassure me?' she demanded icily. She looked again at the four policemen. 'If one of these brave men gets shot instead, I shall never forgive myself for agreeing to this.'

'You didn't agree to it,' Daniel reminded her. 'You refused. It was only Inspector Grimley's insistence that he would provide an escort regardless of your objections.'

They walked on, with Abigail looking more and more irritated as people turned to stare at them.

'I'm sure people must think we're being arrested,' she said. 'If we're seen by anyone who recognises me, this will do my reputation no good at all.'

'Abigail Fenton, master criminal, finally arrested in Manchester,' chuckled Daniel.

'It's no laughing matter!' said Abigail.

'No, you're right, it isn't,' said Daniel. 'A threat has been made to kill you tonight, and Inspector Grimley is doing his best to make sure you're protected. I think we should be grateful.'

Abigail gave a sigh, then admitted, 'Yes, I am. You're right. But it all seems so . . . extravagant a procedure!'

Daniel nodded towards the entrance of the museum, whose

Gothic frontage loomed ahead of them. 'That may be, but we're here now, and you've arrived safely.'

They walked up the steps to the museum entrance and Abigail turned to the four policemen.

'Thank you,' she said with a smile. 'We are now here, so I shall be safe from now on.'

'Inspector Grimley said we've got to keep an eye on you,' said Hudson.

'And you can keep an eye on me from a distance,' said Abigail. 'I'm here to give a talk and to meet certain local dignitaries. I don't want them to be alarmed by having a close escort while we're here.'

Inspector Grimley arrived to meet them. 'Everything all right?' he asked.

'Yes, thank you, Inspector,' said Abigail. 'I appreciate your concern for my safety, and for these men escorting me here, but I was just telling them that I'm sure I will be safe now to deliver my talk.'

'Any signs of anything?' asked Daniel.

Grimley shook his head. 'Me and my men have explored every inch of the museum, and cast our eye over the crowd. Nothing and no one suspicious so far, but my men will be all over the place keeping watch.'

'I'll be keeping watch as well,' said Daniel. 'I plan to position myself to one side of the spot where Miss Fenton will be speaking from so I can watch the upper balconies.'

'I've arranged to have men up there,' said Grimley.

'Thank you,' said Daniel.

'Miss Fenton!'

They turned to see Bernard Steggles approaching them, accompanied by a couple, a tall, thin man in his early sixties and a smaller woman.

'I'll go and check things,' Grimley murmured to Daniel, and moved off.

'Miss Fenton, allow me to introduce Mr Jesse Haworth and his wife.'

'Mr Haworth, this is a great pleasure,' said Abigail shaking the man's hand.

'Nay, the pleasure is mine, Miss Fenton,' said Haworth in his soft Lancashire accent. 'I've heard so much about you from your colleagues, particularly Flinders Petrie.' He gestured towards the smaller woman by his side. 'Truth is, it was my wife here who got me into Egyptology after she read Amelia Edwards' *A Thousand Miles Up the Nile*, and then gave it to me to read. It inspired us to go there.'

'We travelled down the Nile.' His wife nodded. 'It was the experience of a lifetime.'

'Nothing to what you experienced when you were there, I'm sure,' said Haworth. 'But to have actually been there, touched the pyramids and the artefacts!'

Out of the corner of his eye, Daniel spotted Septimus Creighton and Simon Cardew hovering, obviously waiting for a chance to talk to Abigail.

He smiled. 'Excuse me. There's some people I must see.'

He left Abigail chatting to the Haworths and Steggles, and joined Creighton and Cardew.

'Good evening,' he greeted them.

'We were hoping to talk to Abigail and wish her luck,' said Creighton. 'But I can see she's tied up. That's Jesse Haworth, the rich industrialist who funds so many excavations in Egypt. I don't want to blunder in and ruin her chances of getting possible financial backing for a dig.'

'I'm sure there'll be plenty of time afterwards,' said Daniel.

'Actually, I'm glad you came, because something's happened and we could do with your help.'

'Anything,' said Creighton.

'We've had a threatening message, warning that if we don't back off from our investigation, Abigail will never leave the museum alive this evening.'

Creighton and Cardew stared at him, horrified.

'You're not serious!' exclaimed Creighton.

'I'm afraid I am. The police are taking it seriously, too, that's why there are so many officers here tonight, keeping watch. But they can't be everywhere.'

'What do you want us to do?' asked Cardew.

'Just keep a look out for anything suspicious,' said Daniel. 'If you see anything, tell one of the police officers. Don't try and deal with it yourself.'

'Right.' Creighton nodded. He shot a worried look towards where Abigail was still in conversation. 'If anything happens to her . . .'

'It won't, providing we're on our guard,' said Daniel. He added, just to try and calm the situation, 'It may also be a hoax, done to stop us looking into the case.'

'But it may not be,' said Creighton grimly. He looked at Cardew. 'Come on, Simon. Let's take a walk around.'

The two walked off. Daniel was just about to rejoin Abigail, when he found his way blocked by a large, fleshy man in an army officer's uniform adorned with many medals.

'Detective Wilson,' snapped the officer.

'Just plain Mr Wilson, sir. I'm no longer with the police.' He looked enquiringly at the much-decorated soldier. 'You have the advantage of me.'

'Brigadier Wentworth,' said the man curtly. 'You had some of my men arrested the other day.'

'I did,' agreed Daniel genially. 'They attempted to assault me. It was the second time I've had your men attack me, and after the first occasion I took precautions.'

'Poppycock!' snorted Wentworth.

'You can examine the witness statements if you like,' said Daniel. 'Given by sixteen men of good standing. They will still have them at Hulme police station.'

'High spirits!' grunted Wentworth.

'Yes, so I was told,' said Daniel. 'Your men were released, of course. I understand the military has precedence when soldiers break the law. Even though, at this time, they weren't in uniform.'

Wentworth glowered at Daniel. 'I have been told that my men were angry because you were attempting to smear the good name of the regiment.'

'Is that what RSM Bulstrode told you? In that case, you have been badly misinformed.'

'The army in Manchester has a reputation to be proud of, with a long history of successful military engagements.'

'Like Peterloo?' asked Daniel. 'Hardly one to be proud of, from what I can gather. Civilians massacred, including women and children.'

Wentworth's angry gaze hardened and he hissed, 'I might have known it. You're one of these radicals!'

'Absolutely not,' replied Daniel. 'When I was in the police force I arrested many radicals. Along with murderers. Thieves. Muggers. And people who deliberately obstructed the law in the course of its duty.'

A well-dressed man in his late fifties appeared beside them and enquired in a concerned tone, 'Everything all right, Brigadier?'

Wentworth jerked round, and forced a smile. 'Everything's fine, Percival. Just engaging Mr Wilson here in conversation.'

With that, the brigadier gave Daniel a curt nod, and walked off. The new arrival gave Daniel an apologetic smile and held out his hand. 'Robinson Percival,' he introduced himself. 'Chair of the mill owners' committee.'

'A pleasure to meet you,' said Daniel.

Percival nodded after the brigadier as he walked away. 'Don't think too hard of Wentworth,' he said. 'He's just protecting his men. We all heard what happened with you having those men of his arrested.'

'It was lucky I had support that came to my aid or I might not be here now,' said Daniel.

'Yes. That was very fortunate,' said Percival dryly, and Daniel caught the touch of mockery in his voice.

'I always make sure I'm prepared if I think I might be in danger,' said Daniel pointedly.

Percival hesitated, then he said, his voice low, 'Do you not feel it might be danger you have brought on yourself?'

'By investigating the murder of two women?'

'By implicating some very respectable people without any evidence.'

'Oh, I have evidence, Mr Percival,' said Daniel. 'And which particular respectable people are we talking about? RSM Bulstrode? The brigadier?'

'The article in the newspaper suggested the murders were linked to the mill owners,' said Percival.

'We had nothing to do with that article. That was all from Mr Bickerstaff. At no time did we ever suggest the mill owners were responsible.' He paused, then added, 'Although our investigations have led us to the matter of Peterloo, and there we understand there was involvement by the mill owners in what occurred.'

'Accusations that were never proved,' said Percival. 'The fact is, Mr Wilson, your investigations have upset many of our members the way you're stirring up old and unwanted memories. As mill owners we don't want to dwell on the past and what may or may not have happened. What happens in Manchester today will set the tone for the rest of England for the future. Nay, for the rest of the world. We don't want that . . . interfered with.'

'You would prefer that we drop the investigation?'

'Frankly, yes,' said Percival.

'Funny, that was the sentiment expressed in an anonymous letter I received recently. It urged Miss Fenton and I to drop our investigation, or else it warned us that she would not leave this place alive after she'd given her talk.' He looked blandly at Percival. 'Coincidence, or could that letter have been sent by one of your members?'

Percival glared angrily at Daniel. 'How dare you suggest such an outrageous thing!' he snapped. 'It must have been a crank! A lunatic! No one here would think of harming Miss Fenton.'

With that, Percival turned and walked briskly off.

Steggles looked at the clock.

'We shall be starting in just a minute,' he murmured to Abigail. 'Are you ready?'

'Absolutely,' replied Abigail.

Suddenly, Steggles spotted the portly figure of Hector Bleasdale about to take his seat in the audience.

'Excuse me, there's someone I must speak to,' he said to Abigail. 'One minute only, I promise you.'

He hurried over to Bleasdale with a hail of 'Hector!'

'Bernard!' responded Bleasdale with a smile.

'I was wondering if you might come,' said Steggles. 'I was

300

hoping to have a word with the brigadier, but I saw him just now as he finished talking to Mr Wilson and he looked in a bad mood. Have you managed to have a word with him about the exhibition?'

'Ah,' said Bleasdale awkwardly. 'I have, and your Mr Wilson seems to be the problem.'

'Oh?'

'Mr Wilson appears to have a bee in his bonnet about Peterloo, and I'm afraid that's upset the brigadier. The result is he'd prefer to wait until this whole business of the – ah – two women found at the museum is over and Mr Wilson has left Manchester.'

'I must say, Hector, I find that very disappointing,' said Steggles. 'We've already done a lot of work in planning for the exhibition. It's really just about finalising dates. Surely the brigadier can at least meet with us to talk about those. We have a complicated exhibition diary which needs to be scheduled.'

'I know, but I'm afraid the brigadier would prefer to wait.'

'Well, I wish he'd told me this,' said Steggles, irritated. 'I've written to him but received no answer. It's really not good enough.'

'Mr Steggles.'

Steggles turned and found Haworth beside him.

Haworth gestured at the clock on the wall. 'I really think we ought to start,' he said.

Steggles looked and saw that most of the audience had already taken their seats.

'Yes, of course,' he said. He clapped his hands loudly and in ringing tones announced that the talk was about to begin, and asked everyone to take their seats.

Abigail had moved to a lectern set up by one wall, in front of a huge map of Egypt and next to a large, ancient clay pot.

Daniel moved to a place a short distance from the podium,

within reach of Abigail, but not enough to be noticeable and draw attention away from her.

A large crowd had come to hear her talk. Every seat was filled, with more people standing at the back of the room and around the sides. Bernard Steggles introduced Abigail as one of the foremost archaeologists of the day, telling everyone what an honour and a pleasure it was to have her with them that evening, before taking his seat in the front row next to the Haworths.

There was applause from the audience as Abigail took her place at the lectern, and when she began to speak there was no trace from her of nerves or trepidation.

'Good evening, and thank you for inviting me to talk at this wonderful museum,' she began with a confident smile. 'I'm sure that many of you will have been disappointed as I am that Mr Dresser, who was originally scheduled to give his talk this evening, has had to pull out due to illness. But, like you, I look forward to hearing him when he's recovered.

'Tonight I've decided to talk about the excavations at Hawara in Egypt, mainly because the expedition was funded by Mr Jesse Haworth, one of Manchester's great philanthropists who, I'm delighted to say, is here tonight with his wife, and it is wonderful for me as an archaeologist to acknowledge his generosity.' She pointed him out and began to applaud him, and the others soon joined in, forcing the rather shy man to rise to his feet and acknowledge their appreciation. Mrs Haworth, Daniel noticed, remained resolutely in her seat. Haworth sat down again, and Abigail continued, 'Without Mr Haworth's determination, and certainly without his funding, we would not have the artefacts we see here today. Not just from Hawara, but from Kahun, Gurob, Meydum and Biahmu, to name just a few of the sites excavated by Flinders Petrie with the resources provided by Mr Haworth and Mr Henry Martyn Kennard.'

Abigail pointed to the large map on the wall behind her.

'Hawara is to the south of Medinet al-Faiyum. The first attempt at excavation of the pyramid was by the German archaeologist Karl Lepsius in 1843, but after some initial excavation he abandoned his work there after he failed to find the entrance to the pyramid. He had been searching for the entrance on the north side of the pyramid, whereas it turned out that the entrance Petrie actually discovered in 1888, after many months of work, was a narrow vertical shaft on the east end of the south side.'

As Abigail talked, Daniel sidled over to where Grimley was surveying the hall.

'Anything?' he muttered.

Grimley shook his head. 'Hopefully it's a false alarm,' the inspector whispered back. 'Or, if he was planning anything, he's backed off when he's seen the number of police here.'

Daniel turned his attention back to Abigail, who was holding the audience enthralled as she continued, sending a visible shiver through them when she said, 'By the time I joined Flinders Petrie at Hawara . . .' as they realised that they were in the presence of someone who'd actually *been* there '. . . most of the interior had been excavated, although there were still parts unexplored.

'The pyramid was the final resting place of Amenemhet III, the last king of the Twelfth Dynasty, who died in about 1797 . . . but this was 1797 *BC*, almost four thousand years ago.'

It was at this point, as he scanned the upper balcony of the room, that Daniel saw one of the curtains move slightly, and what looked like the end of a rifle barrel poke slightly through.

'Down!' he shouted as he hurled himself forward, grabbed Abigail by her arm and pulled her roughly towards him, at the same time swinging her round so that she was behind him. All this coincided with the explosion of the rifle shot, and the clay pot, on the stand next to where Abigail had been standing, erupting and shattering, the pieces falling to the floor.

'There!' yelled Daniel, pointing to the place where he'd spotted the gunman. Already Grimley and some of his constables were racing towards the stairs that led up to the balcony.

At the sound of the rifle, most of the audience had flung themselves out of their seats and to the floor. Bernard Steggles was one of the first to reach Abigail.

'My God, Miss Fenton . . . !' he gasped, shaking.

'I'm all right. Daniel saved me,' she said.

Daniel saw that she was trembling and hugged her close to him.

Jesse Haworth had joined them, his face white with shock and anger. 'I cannot believe this!' he burst out. 'He shall be hanged when we catch him!'

It was Steggles who took charge.

'Ladies and gentlemen!' he called, facing the audience and holding up his hands to them. 'Please remain in your seats. The police are already in pursuit of the criminal who did this, so I'm sure you will be quite safe, providing you remain where you are. Once we've been assured by the police that the situation is safe, that will be the time for everyone to make their departure . . .'

'No!' The ringing cry from Abigail made them all turn towards her as she stepped away from Daniel to address them. 'You came to hear a talk. I came to give that talk. The fact that my beginning displeased someone . . .' at this, one or two allowed themselves an admiring chuckle '. . . but I intend to continue. I appreciate there may be some of you who will feel inclined to leave after what has just happened, but, as Mr Steggles as just informed you, I have every reason to believe we are now quite safe.' She looked at the broken shards of pottery lying on the floor. 'My only regret is that this magnificent piece of pottery that has survived for four thousand years should fall victim. But, from experience, I have every faith in the art of the restorers that they will be able to repair it and bring it back to its glory. Now, we will have a moment for those who wish to leave to make their way out, and I promise I will not take any such departures as a personal slight. But, for those who do wish to stay . . .'

'Yes!' called Creighton standing at the back of the room, and he began to applaud, his hands clapping together loudly. Others joined him, and soon the whole audience were on their feet, clapping.

Abigail bowed. 'Thank you,' she said. 'Then, with your permission, I shall resume.'

The audience sat down, but now there was a real sense of excitement among them. They had just witnessed an assassination attempt, here, in their museum! And the target of that attempt stood there, unafraid.

'As I was saying, the pyramid was the final resting place of Amenemhet III, the last king of the Twelfth Dynasty, who died in about 1797 . . . but this was 1797 *BC*, almost four thousand years ago. Amenemhet did not survive, and sadly, today, neither did this funereal pot.

'When Flinders Petrie entered the tomb in 1888 he discovered an absolute treasure trove dating from the time of the Romans, including papyrus manuscripts, among which was a scroll containing books one and two of Homer's *Iliad*, which is now in the Bodleian Library at Oxford.'

As Abigail talked, Daniel moved to the side of the room in order to avoid distracting the audience's attention from her. Not that there was much chance of that, he reflected, judging by the looks of rapt attention on their faces.

He was aware of Grimley joining him.

'Anything?' asked Daniel.

Grimley shook his head. 'Got clear away.' He looked at Abigail. 'My God, that woman's got some guts,' he said.

'I told you,' said Daniel. 'The bravest person I've ever met.'

CHAPTER THIRTY-SEVEN

Abigail finished her talk with a final flourish, inviting the audience to come and examine the fragments of the shattered pot 'before it is taken to the restoration shop for repair'. As she stepped away from the lectern the audience rose to their feet and began to applaud. Once again, Daniel was amused to see how this overwhelming expression of appreciation brought a blush to her cheeks. He moved away to let the crowd gather around her, plying her with questions, and also with congratulations. As he did so, he saw Robinson Percival and moved to join him.

'So, Mr Percival, no one would dream of harming Miss Fenton?' he said pointedly.

'A lunatic,' snapped Percival. 'Or maybe one of these radicals!' With that he moved off in the direction of the cloakroom.

Daniel saw Septimus Creighton and Simon Cardew approaching him.

'My God!' said Creighton. 'Does this happen to you a lot in your role as detectives? People taking potshots at you?'

'Fortunately not,' said Daniel.

'That was simply incredible the way she chose to go on with her talk after it happened,' said Cardew. 'I don't think I could have done that.'

'You should go and tell her,' said Daniel. 'I'm sure she'll be pleased to know that you came.'

Cardew looked ruefully towards the crowd clustered around Abigail. 'I don't think we can get near her at the moment,' he said.

'Join the crowd and let her see you,' advised Daniel.

'Yes, good idea,' said Cardew, and he headed off to join the admirers.

'That was incredibly brave of you,' said Creighton. 'Saving her from the bullet like that.'

'Automatic reaction,' said Daniel. 'You'd have done the same if you'd been standing where I was.'

'I'm not sure about that,' said Creighton awkwardly.

'Yes, you would,' Daniel assured him. 'I know how you feel about her, and that means you'd also do something like that without thinking about it.'

Creighton hesitated, then he gave a wry smile before holding out his hand. 'You're a good man, Daniel Wilson,' he said. 'She's a very lucky woman.'

Daniel shook Creighton's hand, then Creighton moved off to join Simon Cardew among the crowd gathered around Abigail.

Daniel went in search of Grimley and found him talking to Sergeant Hudson. When Grimley saw Daniel approaching he said, 'Keep looking, Sergeant,' then turned to Daniel.

'No clues?' asked Daniel.

'None.' He shook his head. 'How did he manage to get away?'

'I've been thinking about that,' said Daniel. 'I believe he must have been wearing a police uniform.'

Grimley stared at Daniel. 'You think it was one of my men?' he demanded, angrily.

'No,' said Daniel. 'I think he managed to get hold of a police uniform in some way. What's the best place to hide a leaf? In a forest. When all the commotion started and everyone's running around searching for the assassin, the one person they're not going to stop and search is someone in a policeman's uniform.'

'Bastard!' Grimley swore half under his breath.

'I've had another thought as well,' continued Daniel. 'I don't think he was trying to kill her.'

'What do you mean? If you hadn't pulled her to one side . . .'

'The pot that the bullet struck was on the *other* side of where she was standing,' pointed out Daniel. He shuddered. 'If I'd pushed her instead of pulling her towards me, the bullet would have hit her.'

Grimley looked at him, puzzled. 'So you're saying he deliberately aimed to miss her?'

'Yes,' said Daniel. 'That's how I see it.'

'But why? Why this elaborate charade?'

'To warn us off.'

Grimley shook his head. 'He fired at her. He didn't know he was going to miss.'

'If the man was a sniper, as I suspect, he would have been good at what he does. Snipers usually hit their target.'

'So you're saying he took the risk of getting caught purely to frighten you?'

'Yes.'

The inspector shook his head. 'I don't buy it,' he said. 'It's too involved. He said he'd kill her, and he tried. That's how I see it.'

'You may be right,' said Daniel. 'But if he had killed Abigail, it would have brought a lot more attention to the situation. "Internationally renowned archaeologist assassinated." That would have brought in the big guns, and the politicians. I don't think they'd want that. Oh, by the way, we'll be going to Ireland tomorrow.'

'Ireland?'

'We've had a letter from the uncle of the young woman who was murdered, Kathleen Donlan. He's got some information for us.'

'What sort of information?'

'We won't know until we've seen him. We should be back the day after tomorrow. I just hope our sudden departure doesn't make our enemies think we've been driven out by their threats.'

'After her display at the museum tonight, I don't think that's likely,' said Grimley. 'By the way, after what you said, I had someone watching this RSM Bulstrode this evening. Just in case. I've just been told he's been in a bar all evening.'

'Thank you, Inspector,' said Daniel. 'To be honest, I never thought he'd be the sharpshooter. Although he may have arranged things, then made sure people saw him at this bar for his alibi.'

'Yes, that's my thinking as well,' said Grimley, adding vengefully, 'I'd love to have him in my office for a few words. Trouble is, the army looks after their own. At least, they do here.'

Brigadier Wentworth was heading for the exit when he found his way barred by Steggles.

'Good evening, Brigadier,' said the museum director stiffly. 'What did you think of this evening?'

'Miss Fenton's talk was excellent,' said Wentworth shortly.

'And the attempted assassination of her?' asked Steggles.

Wentworth looked uncomfortable.

'We don't know for sure that's what it was. Possibly some lunatic shooting off a gun.'

'I think that highly unlikely,' said Steggles. 'Especially as it followed a threat to kill Miss Fenton here tonight unless she and Mr Wilson left Manchester.' He glared at the brigadier. 'I understand that is your desire as well, Brigadier. That they leave Manchester.'

Again, Wentworth looked uncomfortable. 'Now look here, Steggles,' he began to bluster. 'If you're suggesting this shooting business tonight is in any way connected to the army, then that's nonsense. Absolute nonsense.'

'But the army want them both to leave the city.'

'Yes, but that's only because they're stirring up trouble, all this talk about Peterloo, and the army being responsible for this and that. Wilson even had some of my men arrested!'

'After they attacked him.'

'They didn't attack him!' snapped the brigadier. 'It was just an argument that got a bit out of hand. Nothing at all.'

'Nevertheless, the fact remains that I understand you have not responded to my letters about the exhibition because you want to wait until Mr Wilson and Miss Fenton have left Manchester. Is that true?'

'Only because of the trouble they're causing!'

'The trouble, as you put it, has been caused by the person or persons who brutally murdered and mutilated two women in this very museum,' snapped back Steggles. 'We have asked Mr Wilson and Miss Fenton to investigate, and if their investigations lead them to the army, then so be it. They will continue to pursue this investigation with the full backing of myself and the museum until the culprits are unmasked.' He paused then finished with, 'I agree with you that we should delay further discussion about the exhibition until the case is finished. When that is done, I hope we can resume in a cordial manner. But, until then, I think it important for you to know where we stand. We stand resolutely behind Mr Wilson and Miss Fenton.'

With that, Steggles gave him a half-bow, then headed back towards Abigail, who was still surrounded by an admiring crowd.

CHAPTER THIRTY-EIGHT

The early morning boat train from Manchester to Liverpool was crowded, as was the ferry to Dublin, and Daniel was glad that the night before, when they'd got back to their hotel room, he'd managed to tell Abigail his theory that the would-be assassin had only meant to frighten her and not actually kill her, because there would have been no chance to discuss such a topic on this early part of their journey without being overheard.

'So you think it was just to scare us off,' she said thoughtfully, then nodded. 'Yes, I think you're right. At the moment it's just the murder of two poor, unfortunate women who are almost anonymous. Killing me so publicly would have brought a lot more attention to bear on the case.'

'Exactly my thoughts,' said Daniel.

'If that's so, he was a good shot,' said Abigail.

'Which is why, more than ever, I'm convinced the military are involved. The man who took that shot was experienced with a rifle. Most would-be assassins use a pistol.'

There were queues of buses waiting when they docked in Dublin. They found the one headed for Kingsbridge Station, and managed to find two seats together.

'This city is as busy as London,' commented Daniel, as more and more people packed onto the bus, crushing around them.

At Kingsbridge Station they found the train to Cork, with Mallow as one of the stops, and again were fortunate to find two seats together among the crowds. Many of the other passengers started to get off soon after they'd left Dublin, and by the time the train was passing through the open, rolling countryside, they had a compartment to themselves.

'This is the emptiest countryside I've ever seen,' observed Daniel, looking out of the train window. They had been travelling for over two hours. 'Mile after mile of nothing but fields and hills and open grassland, with only the occasional hamlet, and a very small town every ten miles or so.'

'That's because you're a townie,' said Abigail. 'Born and brought up in the centre of London, and hardly ever been elsewhere.'

'I've been to Birmingham,' Daniel corrected her. 'And to Cambridge and Oxford, with you.'

'Hardly the wide open spaces.'

'They were around Cambridge,' said Daniel. 'And flat.' He gestured out at the landscape they were passing. 'Here there are hills, and mountains in the distance.'

'England has just the same vastness of empty space,' said Abigail. 'If you journeyed to the north of England along the eastern side, you'd discover a vastness of open country. And mountains. The Dales of Yorkshire. With hardly anyone living there. When

I was carrying out my excavations along Hadrian's Wall it was brought home to me just how empty of people Northumberland and Cumberland are. No person and no houses for miles in any direction. It's not until you move westward towards Carlisle that you see the industrial chimney of Carr's biscuit factory.'

'Newcastle's an industrial city,' said Daniel.

'Newcastle is,' agreed Abigail. 'But I avoided it.' Then she gave a thoughtful frown and said, 'You haven't said much about the case lately.'

'No, but I've been thinking about it,' said Daniel. 'And Inspector Grimley's suggestion that the person whose reputation everyone's protecting could have been an ordinary soldier.'

'And?'

Daniel shook his head. 'I don't think it is. I'm even more convinced that it's to do with someone who may well have been an ordinary soldier at that time, but who later rose to become an important person.'

'What makes you say that?'

'At your talk I was approached by the chairman of the industrialists' committee, who made it pretty clear that we were upsetting some very important people by making enquiries into the murder. That we were putting at risk the reputation of Manchester as a city of the industrial future. Now that doesn't suggest an ordinary anonymous foot soldier, that suggests that the reputation of someone very important is at stake.'

'One of the mill owners?'

'If so, it would have to be a major one. Someone very rich and influential.'

'Even the oldest mill owners will be too young to have been at Peterloo,' said Abigail.

'But they could well have had a father or grandfather who was,' said Daniel. 'One who later built up the business to a great degree. And a powerful family would do everything necessary to protect such a reputation.'

'With the assistance of the army,' added Abigail.

Daniel nodded. 'The person we're looking for is rich, influential and has a very strong connection to the army. I would suggest a family connection. Let's hope that this visit to Mallow will bring us nearer to the answer.'

Sergeant Merton looked at the note from Billy Scargell the small boy had handed to him at the police station. *The person you're looking for is in my backroom.*

He wondered how to play it. Tell Grimley? No, that would drop Scargell in it because the inspector would charge into the Iron Duke like a bull in a china shop, and everyone would find out that Scargell had shopped someone. He had to get hold of Adams without creating a fuss. But he couldn't take the chance of losing him. Which meant he'd need back-up. Men he could trust and depend on. The thing was, he needed to act quickly. Adams was in Scargell's backroom at the moment, but for how long? He might have already left! He wondered how long ago Scargell had written the note before sending it.

A sense of panic filled him at the thought that Adams might even at this moment be about to slip away. *I've got to get him*, he promised himself. *I have to!*

Despite their early start, by the time they stepped off the train at Mallow it was early evening and the first streaks of dark were beginning to appear in the sky.

'I'm glad we said we'd call on Mr Donlan tomorrow morning,' said Daniel. 'As you said, I'm a townie and not fond of walking through the countryside in the dark. Too many ditches and places to fall into.'

'When I was in Egypt . . .' began Abigail.

'Yes, I'm sure you spent many a night striding through the desert,' said Daniel. 'But here the trees stop any light from the moon giving a clear view of the ground.'

They found the Mallow Hotel and checked in as Mr and Mrs Wilson, without any adverse comments from Abigail.

Next morning, after a breakfast so filling that they agreed they very likely wouldn't need to eat for the rest of the day, they asked at reception where they could find the house of Sean Donlan. 'It's in the townland of Duinch,' said Daniel.

'Would you be walking or taking a carriage?' asked the receptionist.

'How far is it?' asked Daniel.

'Not far. A mile or two.'

'In that case, a walk will do us good,' said Abigail.

'Sean's house is easy to find, being beside the main road,' said the receptionist. 'Go straight along the Main Street to the edge of town. You'll find the crossroads with signposts telling you Cork is to your left and Buttevant to your right. Go straight over at the cross and carry on the main road towards Limerick. Go past the racecourse, and you'll see Sean's place on your left. It's a byre-house with the name "Donlan" on a post outside it.' She looked doubtfully down at their feet. 'Are those the only shoes you have?'

'Yes,' said Abigail. 'Why?'

'The road can be a bit uneven in parts. A few holes. And mud.'

'I'm sure we'll be fine,' said Abigail.

As they set off, Daniel said, 'A road with holes in. And mud. I'm even more glad we didn't try and walk there in the dark.'

As they walked west along the Main Street, they passed local people putting up stalls at the edge of the roadway. Some already had potatoes and cabbages set out, some had displays of crockery, teapots and cups and plates, and others had furniture for sale.

'Market day,' observed Daniel.

They continued on, past the railway station, before reaching the crossroads. Once they'd crossed the main road to Cork and were heading westward, the noise and bustle of the market and the town was left behind them and they found themselves taking in the vivid greenery of the open countryside, smelling the scents of the wild plants and fruits growing in the hedgerows.

'The hotel receptionist said Sean Donlan lived in a byre-house,' said Abigail. 'I've never seen one for real, but I read about them when I was doing my degree. It combines living quarters with a cowshed all under the one roof, the two areas separated by a corridor that runs through the middle, from front to back. On one side are the rooms where the humans live, and on the other side of the corridor is where the animals stay.'

'Yes,' said Daniel. 'The Irish families in Camden Town used to speak fondly of them. The heat from the animals kept the house warm in winter.'

'And smelly from their manure,' said Abigail doubtfully. 'I must admit, it always struck me as not very hygienic.'

'Less hygienic than a family of twelve living in a one-up, one-down terrace back-to-back in Manchester or London, with more people in the cellar, and an overflowing cesspit outside used by all and sundry?' asked Daniel wryly.

'Yes, I take your point,' said Abigail.

As they walked, they became aware that a large number of houses they passed seemed to have been abandoned and fallen into dereliction. When Abigail commented on the fact, Daniel responded with, 'The result of the famine. Or the Great Hunger, as it was called here in Ireland.'

'Your Irish roots,' said Abigail.

'No, my Irish neighbours,' Daniel corrected her. 'Remember I said to Father O'Brien, when I was growing up, Camden Town was at least half-Irish, and that was because of the famine. The potato crop failed and people fled in their hundreds of thousands. England, Australia, America.'

'But why abandon their homes?' asked Abigail. 'Surely they could have grown something else on their land. Or put animals on it.'

'That was the problem, it wasn't "their" land. Most of them were tenant farmers. When the crops failed, the tenants didn't have the money to pay their rent, so the landlords evicted them. Just put them out on the road where they had a stark choice: emigrate or die.'

'I remember you told me before about a million died and a million emigrated.'

'There were possibly more,' said Daniel. 'The authorities here weren't very good on record keeping. This area was particularly badly hit, along with the west of Ireland. The port of Queenstown on the Cork coast was one of the main points where the coffin ships departed for America.'

'The coffin ships?'

'It was what they became known as, because so many people died on the voyages. They were starving when they got on board, which resulted in many becoming ill with different diseases, and the sea journey was rough.

'I've often thought the worst thing was that while millions starved here, exports of food from Ireland were at their highest. During the famine, thousands of ships left Ireland taking meat and buttermilk and other foodstuffs to England.'

'I can understand the Irish feeling vengeful. And yet you and

I can walk along this road and I feel quite safe,' remarked Abigail.

'Not all the landlords were English,' said Daniel. 'Some were Irish. Profit doesn't have a national identity.'

At last they came to a long, single-storey building, the roof covered in straw thatch. The word 'Donlan' was painted on a board nailed to a fence.

'Here we are,' said Daniel.

They passed through the gate and were heading up the path towards the house, when the front door opened and a young woman came out.

'Would you be Mr Wilson?' she asked expectantly. 'And Miss Fenton?'

Her accent was soft, similar to the receptionist's at the hotel.

'Indeed,' replied Daniel. 'Would you be Niamh O'Keeffe?'

She smiled. 'That is me,' she said. 'My great-uncle is inside, waiting for you. I'll take you to him.'

As they entered and followed the young woman into the house and turned to the left, Abigail caught the earthy smell of cattle and horses coming from a partly open door to their right. She caught Daniel's look, and he winked and smiled at her. After what Daniel had told her about the byre-house, Abigail was expecting the living area to be little more than a stable, so she was taken aback when she entered the living room by the warmth and cleanliness of it. No, it was more than just clean, everything seemed to shine: the ornaments on display on the dresser, the crockery on the table, the wood of the furniture glowed from polishing, as did the iron of the stove and the fireplace. All the cloths, the white linen, the shawls, the coverings, also seemed to shine, giving off the welcoming scent of being recently laundered.

Has this just been done for us? Abigail wondered, awed at finding such pride in the house. But no, she realised, this place, this byre-house, was Sean Donlan's castle, and he was proud of it.

Donlan was a very small, very thin man in his sixties, and he rose from his armchair to greet them, shaking their hands and welcoming them in Irish in his soft accent.

'*Dia dhuit*,' said Daniel as he shook Donlan's hand, adding quickly as the man's eyes lit up in pleased recognition, 'but I'm afraid that's the whole extent of my Irish.'

'My uncle and I thought it might be better if I talked for him,' said Niamh. 'He has some English, but he wants to make sure that what he wants to tell you is told properly, with no mistakes.'

'We appreciate that,' said Daniel.

'It said in the paper you were wanting to know about Kathleen Donlan,' said Niamh.

'That's so,' said Abigail. 'As you now know, sadly someone killed her soon after she came to Manchester. We feel the reason for it maybe has to do with why she went there.'

Niamh spoke rapidly to Donlan, obviously translating this, but he was already nodding.

'Yes,' he said in English. Then he began to speak in Gaelic, his face serious. After every few sentences he paused and looked at Niamh for her to translate what he'd just said.

'Kathleen was very close to her grandfather, Dermot,' translated Niamh. 'Just before he died he asked her to do something – to put right a wrong his father, Michael, Kathleen's great-grandfather, had done when he was young.'

Donlan said more, and Niamh continued his story. 'Michael had been a young man in the British army in 1819 and had taken part in quelling the riot at what became known as Peterloo. Just before he died, Michael told his son, Dermot – Sean's father – on his deathbed of a terrible wrong he'd done. He'd cut down a woman and her baby at Peterloo with his sabre and killed them.

'Afterwards, he was so distraught at what he'd done that he fled England and came back here to his home townland in Ireland, where he refused to speak about it. He just told people that he'd deserted from the army because of some terrible things he'd seen and he was determined not to go back. He asked everyone locally to swear to protect him if anyone came looking for him, and everyone did. And they carried on doing that even after he died in 1830, although no one ever came looking for him.

'We didn't know all what had happened, or that Michael had told his son, Dermot, about the event on his deathbed, or that he'd asked Dermot to go to England and find the family of the woman he'd killed and ask their forgiveness so his soul could rest in peace.'

Daniel and Abigail exchanged looks of surprise at this revelation.

'And did Dermot go?' Daniel asked.

Donlan shook his head and said something in Irish, his tone full of sadness.

'No,' translated Niamh. 'Dermot said he would, but then the famine came and suddenly the most important thing was staying alive. Dermot promised himself that once things got better he'd go to England and carry out his father's wishes. But, of course, promises that are made fade as time passes: they'll be carried out next week, or next month, or next year. And when Dermot was on his deathbed, he told Kathleen about the promise he'd made, and asked her to carry out Michael's wishes.'

'Why Kathleen?' asked Daniel. 'Why not her father, or Sean? They were his sons.'

'Kathleen's father, Seamus, died three years ago,' said Niamh. She halted, awkwardly, then looked towards Sean, who nodded. 'Sean and Dermot had their differences. They hadn't spoken for a year before he died.'

'What about?' asked Abigail.

'A cow,' said Donlan suddenly.

'A cow?'

Sean Donlan nodded.

'It died and Dermot accused Sean of poisoning it,' explained Niamh. 'Sean would never poison a cow and he vowed he'd never speak to his father again unless he withdrew that accusation.'

Sean burst out with an angry speech, which Niamh translated. 'He said Dermot was a stubborn man and he refused to withdraw.' As Donlan added something in a tone that was very bitter and angry, she translated for them: 'Even when Dermot knew he was dying! He should have said something to Sean!'

'But he told Kathleen about the promise,' said Daniel.

'He did,' said Donlan, adding something in Irish, which Niamh translated: 'And now it was her promise. Sean says it wasn't fair! There was no reason to involve her! She was a lovely girl. Too good-hearted for her own good.'

'I assume she came to you and told you?' said Daniel to Donlan.

Donlan nodded, and once again Niamh translated his words. 'She didn't know what to do. How to go about it. We didn't know what part of the army Michael had been in, or who it was he'd killed. It was an impossible thing to ask of anyone. But she was determined. She swore me to secrecy until she'd carried it out, and I promised to say nothing to anyone until I saw her again and she told me it was done. Even then, I wouldn't have said anything. No one likes to think of the family being tainted with that, which is why it had remained a secret.

'I gave her the money for her fare to England, and a little bit more to keep her going at first. I gave her a letter to my cousin, Eileen, asking if she could put Kathleen up until she got herself settled. I told Kathleen she'd have to find work of some kind to support herself while she made her enquiries and found out the woman's name, and who her family were, even if any of them were still alive. Like I say, it was an impossible quest.'

Suddenly they realised tears were on the old man's face as he muttered something. Daniel and Abigail looked enquiringly towards Niamh, who said, 'He said it's his fault Kathleen's dead. If he hadn't given her the money for her fare, and Cousin Eileen's address . . .'

'No!' said Abigail firmly. She reached out and gently took the old man's hand in hers. 'You did the right thing. The person who killed her is the one who's at fault. And I promise you, we'll find them.'

Niamh and Donlan looked anxiously at Daniel and Abigail as Niamh asked, 'Does this help find out why someone did what they did to Kathleen?'

'I think it does,' said Daniel. 'I don't know exactly how, but I feel that someone didn't want her asking questions about what had happened.'

'Why? She was trying to do good,' said Niamh.

'But perhaps this person didn't know that,' said Daniel. 'But I promise you, once we find out why, we'll write and let you know.' He hesitated, then said sadly, 'We also have to let you know that your cousin, Eileen, was also a victim.'

Niamh looked at him, horrified.

'She was murdered as well?'

'I'm afraid she was,' said Daniel. 'And we're fairly sure by the same person who killed Kathleen.'

Niamh turned to Donlan and translated what Daniel had just told her, her voice shaking as she did. Donlan looked at Daniel and Abigail, aghast, then gave a low moan and buried his face in his hands.

'We're sorry to bring you further bad news,' apologised Abigail. 'But we will catch whoever did it. That we promise you.'

Donlan stood up, his face a mask of misery, and left the room.

'He'll be all right,' said Niamh. 'It's the shock. He's had time to adjust to Kathleen being killed, but this . . .' She sighed. 'I'll go and see that he's all right.'

She left the room. Abigail and Daniel looked at one another with unhappy sighs.

'I'm more than ever convinced about the army connection,' said Daniel quietly. 'A descendant of a soldier who was at Peterloo, killing them both to protect his ancestor's reputation.'

'But who?' asked Abigail.

Daniel gave a heavy sigh.

'As to that, I'm afraid we're no nearer. There's a lot more work to be done yet in Manchester.'

They sat, and after a while Niamh appeared, along with Donlan, who took his seat again. Niamh produced cups and saucers and a teapot from the dresser and proceeded to make tea from the cast-iron kettle that had been simmering on the stove. Niamh left the room, then reappeared with four plates, each with a slice of fruit cake. Over tea and cake the conversation became more relaxed, mainly with Niamh and Sean Donlan asking questions about England, and enquiring after relatives who'd moved there, with Daniel and Abigail feeling guilty that neither recognised any of the names they mentioned.

'By the way, do you know of a man called Con Gully?' asked Daniel. 'He was from Kanturk.'

The name obviously registered with both Niamh and Donlan, because Donlan let forth such an angry outburst that Abigail and Daniel didn't need Niamh to translate his despising of the man, but Niamh added the information that Daniel was looking for. 'He was arrested in Limerick about a week ago, and he's now where he ought to be, in jail, in Cork city.'

'So he didn't escape to England?' asked Abigail.

Niamh shook her head. 'As far as we heard, after he escaped from Kanturk Jail he went west to Limerick and was there until he was caught trying to rob someone.'

Donlan muttered something with great scorn, and Niamh added, 'Great-Uncle Sean says Gully's scum.'

'Yes, he is,' said Daniel.

There was the sudden sound of rain on the window, driven by a gust of wind, and as they sat there Daniel and Abigail realised that the rain seemed to be settling in, and it would be a long and wet walk back to the hotel for them. Donlan and Niamh realised this, too, because Donlan said something, and Niamh told them, 'Sean says he'll take you back to Mallow on his cart. It'll save you from getting too wet.'

Abigail turned to Donlan and said, 'Mr Donlan, that is very kind of you, and we certainly accept your offer.'

CHAPTER THIRTY-NINE

On the train from Mallow back to Dublin they discussed what they'd learnt.

'Someone connected with the army killed Kathleen to stop her looking into what had happened at Peterloo,' summed up Abigail. 'But why? Everything that happened is public knowledge. And she was no threat to anyone. She was trying to make amends for something that had happened.'

'But say the killer didn't realise that,' said Daniel. 'Kathleen arrived from Ireland intent on carrying out her grandfather's mission. But first she needed to find out who'd been killed at Peterloo so she could seek out their descendants, their relatives. She tried the barracks first, but they turned her away. But because of her asking about who the victims were at Peterloo, someone at the barracks misinterpreted what she was after. They thought she'd come to stir things up, perhaps try and extort money from someone in the army who'd been involved in the Peterloo fiasco. Possibly someone who'd killed someone during it, but kept that hidden.'

'But it was eighty years ago,' said Abigail. 'Everyone involved in it is long dead!'

'Family, then. A grandfather, possibly. Someone whose reputation his descendants are desperate to protect. Desperate enough to kill.'

'We still don't know who. It could be absolutely anyone. A high-ranking officer at the time, or an ordinary soldier.'

'Bulstrode knows,' said Daniel. 'We have to find a way to get him to talk.'

It was late when they arrived in Dublin. They booked a cabin on the night ferry.

'It may be only a short crossing, but I'd rather arrive in Liverpool tomorrow morning having had some sort of sleep, even if it's just a couple of hours,' said Abigail.

'I thought you were used to hardship when travelling,' said Daniel with a smile. 'All those tales of Egypt, and your journey down the Nile.'

'Which was on a very palatial boat,' said Abigail. 'I checked the forecast for this journey, and they believe the sea is going to be rough. I have been below decks in rough seas, and have observed it is usually awash with other people's vomit.'

'What a charming image,' said Daniel.

The sea journey was rough, and Daniel didn't get much sleep. The way the boat rolled with the strong waves meant he kept sliding off the bunk, or was crashed against the nearest wall. Abigail, for some reason, had managed to fix herself into a firm place and slept, to

Daniel's envy. The result of her years of experience of long sea journeys to foreign lands, he guessed: Egypt, Palestine, Italy, the Ottoman Empire. The only time he'd previously been on board a ship had been the ferry to the Isle of Wight, and that had been just as nausea-inducing a trip as this one. *I must get Abigail to teach me the trick of surviving long, rough sea journeys*, he decided.

The sea had been so rough that when they disembarked at Manchester, he still felt unsteady on his feet. Noticing this, Abigail asked, 'Do you want me to support you as you walk?'

'No, thank you,' said Daniel. 'I shall be all right once my brain has caught up with my feet. At the moment it seems to be going round and round, as if we're still on the boat.'

'Lots of big breaths,' advised Abigail.

Daniel was relieved when they were finally on board the train for Manchester and he began to feel almost normal again. It was mid-morning when they arrived back in the city.

'We need to tell Inspector Grimley what we've learnt,' said Abigail.

Daniel nodded. 'We do. But our first port of call should be Mr Steggles. The museum is our paymaster, after all.'

'How was your journey?' asked Steggles.

'Long,' said Daniel wearily.

'You look as if you didn't get much sleep,' said Steggles, concerned.

'We took the overnight ferry from Dublin,' explained Abigail. 'Unfortunately, the crossing wasn't really conducive to sleep.'

'How dreadful!' said Steggles. 'Do let me get you some refreshments.' He picked up the telecommunications microphone on his desk and placed an order with his secretary, then turned to Abigail and said, 'I have to let you know, the whole city is still enthusing about your talk the other evening. The *Guardian* will be running an article on it, with photographs.'

'Not of the shooting, I hope,' said Daniel.

'I still go cold when I think of it,' said Steggles with a shudder. 'How you were able to continue after that, Miss Fenton, I cannot imagine.'

'I'm still upset the pot was damaged,' said Abigail. 'I do hope your restoration people are able to repair it.'

'A small price to pay,' said Steggles. 'It could have been you!'

There was a tap at the door, then Mrs Wedburn appeared with a tray of teapots, cups, and also a plate of biscuits.

'Thank you, Mrs Wedburn.' Steggles smiled.

After tea had been poured and biscuits distributed, Steggles returned to the topic of their journey.

'Was your trip to Ireland worthwhile?' he asked.

'We believe it was,' said Abigail. 'We believe we know why Kathleen Donlan was killed. She had come to carry out atonement for a relative of hers who killed people at Peterloo. Her task was to find out their names, and then offer an apology to their descendants. Unfortunately, when she began asking questions about who'd been killed at Peterloo, her actions were misinterpreted as wanting to cause trouble for someone.'

'The fact that Peterloo happened over eighty years ago means the someone it would cause trouble for will be long gone, but their descendants are still around and we believe they killed Kathleen to stop her continuing with her search,' added Daniel.

'Who do you believe was responsible?' asked Steggles.

'Someone important, with a distinguished military ancestor who was at Peterloo,' said Daniel. 'As you know, we've met a wall of silence from the army, but our hope is that the policeman who took part in the attack on me might have been found by the police. If he has, we feel he'll be the key to identifying the culprit. We're on our way to see Inspector Grimley to find out what luck he's had in that direction.'

'What I don't understand is why she didn't say anything about her quest to Jonty Hawkins when she came to the museum,' said Steggles. 'She just asked for information about the army in Manchester. If she'd said what she was looking for, we might have been able to help her.'

'She acted the way she did because of the response she'd got at the barracks,' said Abigail. 'Her local priest, Father O'Brien, told us she'd been treated harshly when she first went to the barracks. Our guess is she'd been warned not to ask questions. So when she went to the museum, and also the offices of the *Guardian*, she didn't say exactly what she was after in case she got the same treatment.'

After leaving Mr Steggles, they made their way to Newton Street police station, where they once more related what they'd learnt in Ireland.

'So you're convinced the army were behind the killing?' said Grimley.

'Not the army as such,' said Daniel. 'Someone connected to the army. Possibly someone whose father or grandfather was in the army and was involved in the Peterloo massacre. We know RSM Bulstrode and the soldier are out of our reach; the army will protect them. But there's the police constable who took part in the attack on me; he might know who this is about.'

Grimley gave a smirk. 'He does,' he said. 'I found him. Or, rather, my sergeant did.'

'Where is he?'

'Downstairs. In the cells.'

'You've talked to him?'

Grimley nodded. 'Oh, yes.'

'I'd like to see him,' said Daniel.

'I've already got everything out of him there is to know,' said Grimley. Then he shrugged. 'But why not?'

As Daniel and Abigail began to follow Grimley, he stopped.

'Not you, miss,' said the inspector.

'Why not?' demanded Abigail.

'Because I'd rather you didn't.'

'There's nothing here that can frighten or worry me,' said Abigail. 'Whatever it is, I'm sure I've seen worse. And you saw yourself, Inspector, even having someone shoot at me doesn't put me off.'

Grimley gave a shrug. 'Very well,' he said. 'But I want your word that what you see here stays between us. I don't want you spouting off to the papers or Superintendent Mossop or the museum people, or anyone else. Agreed?'

'I give you my word, Inspector.'

Grimley looked at Daniel. 'I don't think I need yours, Mr Wilson. You were a copper. You know what's needed sometimes.'

As Grimley continued forward, Daniel took hold of Abigail's hand to hold her back.

'You may not want to come down and see this,' he muttered.

'Why?' she demanded. 'I'm part of this.'

'I don't think you're part of *this*,' he said.

'But you are?' she retorted.

She moved forward, heading after Grimley, Daniel following.

'It turns out that Adams used to be in the military, at the Hulme Barracks,' said Grimley as they walked down the stone steps to the basement. 'He left because he didn't want to go abroad any more on foreign wars. That's when he joined the police. But it seems he's remained close to his old army pals, so when they asked him to give them a hand, he said yes.'

'Who asked him?' asked Daniel.

'The regimental sergeant major, Bulstrode. Adams is his brother-in-law.'

A foul odour hung over the basement area where the cells were, a mixture of urine, vomit and sweat. Grimley led the way to where a man was lying on a hard bench behind a row of iron bars. The right side of his face was so swollen and badly bruised as to be unrecognisable as a human face, the injuries made worse by the clots of dried blood from a cut above Adams's eye. Blood also smeared his mouth and chin from his flattened broken nose. What was worse, two of the fingers of his left hand were broken, one with the bone showing through the blood.

'Injured while resisting arrest,' said Grimley with a shrug.

Daniel shot a glance at Abigail, who stood white-faced and tight-lipped as she looked through the bars at the man in the cell. She looked back at Daniel, saying nothing, but the expression of anger and revulsion on her face said what she felt. Grimley caught her disapproval and snapped, 'We needed a name. We can't get it from Bulstrode. Adams wouldn't talk. What else do you expect? It's the world we live in, among murderers, rapists, pimps, thieves, robbers. You can't reason with them by talking about ethics or appealing to their conscience. It's what they do. How they live. They set the rules. We have to play the game the same way or we lose every time.'

'The name?' asked Daniel.

Grimley gestured towards the stairs. 'Let's talk back in my office.'

The air upstairs was that of stale tobacco and sweat, but it was sweet by comparison with the smell in the basement.

'The man they're protecting is a retired general, Westerman Wainwright,' Grimley told them as they sat down in his office. 'They call him the Old Man.'

'Did Adams say that Wainwright committed the murders?'

Grimley shook his head. 'Adams says he doesn't know what it's about. Believe me, if he did he'd have coughed it up. It seems this General Wainwright is highly respected among the men; they'd do anything for him.'

'Including cover up murder?'

'I doubt if he told them why it was.'

'I doubt if he told them anything directly,' said Daniel. 'RSM Bulstrode was the conduit, passing orders on to the troops.'

'I've arranged for a warrant for the arrest of this general. We pick him up at his house at six tomorrow morning. You can come along. You've been in the thick of it so far, might as well see how it ends.' Then Grimley turned to Abigail. 'Not you, though, miss, if you don't mind.'

'Why?' demanded Abigail. 'You've seen that I can deal with things. I've just been to the cells with you and seen a man broken without flinching.'

'This is different,' said Grimley. 'From what Adams says, most of the general's servants are ex-military, and armed. I'm going to be taking a gun with me, and some of my men will be doing the same.' He looked at Daniel. 'You're a civilian, you can't.' He turned back to Abigail. 'But Mr Wilson here has experience of dealing with firearms and shootouts.'

'May I remind you, Inspector—'

'I know. You were shot at when you were at the museum. But in the situation we're going into, if there is gunfire it's more likely a stray bullet will be the one that does the damage. I won't have your death on my conscience.'

Abigail looked at Daniel challengingly. 'You support this?' she demanded.

'I do,' said Daniel. 'When this is over I'm happy to give you lessons in handling a gun. Then you'll appreciate the situation. But I can't take the chance of you being killed.'

'But you're prepared to risk being killed yourself.'

'I know what I'm going into,' said Daniel. 'I've been in this situation before. I promise you, I'm not going to be killed.'

'No?' Abigail glared at him angrily. 'So stray bullets miraculously avoid you, do they?'

'No, I avoid them,' said Daniel.

Abigail continued to glare angrily at him, then she turned to Grimley. 'If you allow him to be killed, Inspector, I shall come for you. And what you did to that man in that cell will pale by comparison with what I will do to you.'

'Bulstrode needs to be dealt with,' said Daniel. 'Once he hears what's happening, he'll vanish. And his testimony is going to be vital.'

'I'm already there, Wilson,' grunted Grimley. 'I've got a sergeant standing by with some uniformed officers and a warrant in Bulstrode's name to pick him up at the barracks at the same time as we call on the general.'

Later, as Abigail and Daniel walked back to the Mayflower Hotel, Abigail asked, 'That man in the cell. Was that how it was in London?'

'You're asking if I ever beat a prisoner. The answer's no.'

'But some of your colleagues did.'

'Not the ones I cared to have anything to do with. You've met John Feather. He never did anything like that. And my old guv'nor, Fred Abberline, would have had the hide of any of his team who did that.'

'But some did.'

'Yes.'

'And they weren't dismissed from the force? Or reprimanded in some way?'

'The people at the top want results when it comes to dealing with criminals. As do the general public. When it comes to murder, the people in power are content to turn a blind eye to some actions if it gets results.'

'Beating a man half to death?'

'Grimley got the name of the man who's been behind everything, including the murders.'

'So you approve?'

'No. I'd have tried a different approach.'

'And if your different approach didn't work?'

'Then I'd have tried different ways.' He looked Abigail firmly in the face as he told her, 'I promise you, I would never do what Grimley did. If I did, it would make me as bad as the people we're pursuing.'

CHAPTER FORTY

At 6 a.m. Sergeant Hudson stepped down from the horse-drawn police van as it pulled up outside the main gate of Hulme Barracks. Two uniformed constables also appeared from the van and together they walked towards the two soldiers on sentry duty.

'Sergeant Hudson come to see RSM Bulstrode,' he said.

'Yes, sir,' said one of the sentries. 'What shall I tell him it concerns?'

'I'll tell him that when I see him,' snapped Hudson.

'Yes, sir,' said the sentry, and he headed for the main building. He reappeared a few moments later with RSM Bulstrode striding along beside him, chest puffed out and an aggressive look on his face.

'Yes?' he barked. 'What's brought you here at this hour of the morning?'

Sergeant Hudson produced a piece of paper from his tunic

pocket. 'George Bulstrode, I have here a warrant for your arrest on a charge of accessory to murder.'

Bulstrode stared at Hudson, his mouth dropping open, then he snapped it shut.

'Like hell you have!' he shouted. He turned to the sentries and started to say, 'Private, go and tell—' before the police sergeant slammed a big hand across Bulstrode's mouth, cutting off his words. At the same time, the two constables stepped forward, each grabbing one of Bulstrode's arms, and together the three police officers hustled the angry and struggling RSM towards the police van. The rear doors opened and he was pushed inside, then hauled in by another pair of constables. Sergeant Hudson and one of the constables climbed in after him. Hudson gestured for the remaining constable to join the driver at the front, then pulled the van doors shut.

The two sentries stood staring at the van, shocked, before one said in a daze, 'The brigadier isn't in yet. Who are we gonna tell?'

Daniel and Inspector Grimley got down from the police van that had pulled up outside a grand-looking house in a road of equally expensive houses.

'This is it,' grunted Grimley. He gestured to the two uniformed officers who'd also got out of the van. 'Time to do some proper police work, lads,' he said.

Daniel and the officers followed Grimley up a hedge-lined path towards the front door, made of black oak and with two ornate Roman-style columns on either side. Grimley pulled at the brass bell-pull. When there was no immediate answer, he pulled it again, longer and louder this time. The door was opened by an angry-looking man in a valet's costume of dark trousers and striped waistcoat. His eye took in the uniformed constables, and the pugnacious look on Inspector Grimley's face, and the anger was replaced by a look of wary suspicion.

'Yes?' he snapped.

'Detective Inspector Grimley to see General Wainwright,' Grimley barked back at him.

'The general is not available,' said the valet.

'Don't give me that,' snorted Grimley derisively. 'I've had men watching this house. He's here.'

'I said he was unavailable,' snapped the valet. 'He is not seeing callers.'

'He'll see me,' Grimley snapped back. 'I've got a warrant.'

'Let me see it,' said the servant, holding out his hand.

Grimley shook his head. 'I'll show it to the organ-grinder, not his monkey,' he said. He began to move forwards, but stopped when he saw the servant had produced a pistol.

'Stupid!' growled Grimley. He chopped down hard on the man's wrist, and as the pistol fell to the carpet, he swung his boot hard into the man's groin. The man fell to the floor with a scream that brought an elderly man hurrying into the passage as Grimley led the others into the house. He looked at the fallen servant, then at Grimley and Daniel and the two uniformed officers behind them.

'What the hell is the meaning of this?' he demanded.

'General Wainwright, I presume,' said Grimley. He produced the warrant from his pocket. 'I have a warrant for your arrest on a charge of murder. Now you can come along nice and sweet, or you can resist, and get a kick in the balls like this lackey of yours.'

The general glared angrily at the inspector.

'Do you know who I am?' he thundered, furious.

'I've already told you, I'm assuming you to be General Westerman Wainwright. If you're not, I'd advise you to get the general out here sharpish.'

Wainwright stared at Grimley, momentarily speechless, then he burst out, 'This is my house! My private residence!'

'And, as I've already said, this is a warrant for your arrest.'

'This is nonsense!' stated Wainwright. 'You have no grounds for this accusation.'

'We have RSM Bulstrode,' said Daniel quietly. 'We've got enough evidence to hang him, and he'll talk when he realises that.'

'Who the hell are you?' demanded Wainwright. 'Where's your warrant card?'

'He's a private consultant,' cut in Grimley. 'He's been working with us on this case. Name of Daniel Wilson.'

Daniel saw a flicker of angry recognition in the general's eyes at the mention of his name.

'You have no right here,' he snapped.

'He has every right,' Grimley corrected him. 'He's here at the invitation of the police.'

'You still have no proof!' barked Wainwright.

'As Mr Wilson said, we have RSM Bulstrode in custody.'

'Bulstrode won't talk,' said Wainwright defiantly.

'Then he'll hang,' said Daniel.

Wainwright didn't answer at first, his eyes switching from Daniel to Grimley, then back again. Finally, he said, 'Bulstrode had nothing to do with it.'

'On the contrary, we have evidence about him organising the attack on Mr Wilson to cover up the murders. That alone makes him a conspirator to murder. He'll hang.'

'He had nothing to do with the deaths of the two women,' said Wainwright. 'He did some work afterwards to try and protect me. That was all.'

'Perhaps if we talk in your study?' suggested Daniel. 'It might be less public than you arriving at the police station in handcuffs.'

Grimley shot Daniel a look of disapproval and was about to protest, but then Wainwright nodded.

'Very well,' he said. And he walked through the doorway into his study.

'I wanted him in handcuffs,' Grimley growled at Daniel in a whisper.

'And you'll have him like that,' Daniel whispered back. 'But this way, with a confession about why he did it.'

'I get the credit?' asked Grimley.

Daniel nodded. 'You do.'

Grimley turned to the two constables. 'You two stay outside this door and make sure no one comes in. If we want you, we'll shout.'

Grimley and Daniel walked into the study and shut the door. Wainwright had already seated himself in a leather armchair by the window. Daniel lifted a wooden chair and carried it over to face the general, placed it down and sat.

'I'll stand,' said Grimley. 'This is your shout, Wilson. You ask the questions.'

Daniel nodded and turned his attention to Wainwright. 'Kathleen Donlan, stabbed to death in the back in the museum. Eileen O'Donnell killed there, her face sliced off and her body hidden in the cellar,' he said. 'Both killed by you. And all because of Peterloo.'

Wainwright said nothing, just glared at Daniel.

'Who was it you were protecting?' asked Daniel. 'Your father or your grandfather?'

'My grandfather wasn't at Peterloo,' said Wainwright.

'Father, then,' said Daniel. 'But Peterloo was almost eighty years ago. With respect, sir, if you are his son . . .'

'I was a late arrival,' said Wainwright. 'My father was in his middle fifties when I was born. He married three times. My mother was his third wife.'

Daniel nodded. 'I'm guessing it was the Irish aspect that triggered it,' he said. 'We've just returned from Ireland where we got part of the story. Enough to fill in the pieces.'

'Damned Irish!' said Wainwright venomously.

Daniel stayed silent, watching him, waiting.

Finally, Wainwright said, 'About ten years ago I received a visit from an Irishman who called himself a journalist. His name was Fergal Walsh. He said he'd been researching a story about Peterloo and he had enough information to go into print. The story, he told me, featured my father, the late General Walter Wainwright,' and here Wainwright glared defiantly at them. 'A true soldier with one of the greatest war records ever known in the modern army. He led troops in Crimea at every major battle there: Alma, Balaklava, Inkerman, Sevastopol. He survived the disaster that was the Charge of the Light Brigade, and he did it with honour. He was a hero!'

'But not at Peterloo,' murmured Daniel.

Wainwright dropped his gaze. 'The only blot on his record, and unknown to almost everyone. When he was in his early twenties he led a troop at Peterloo. Walsh had found evidence, including witness statements, that suggested my father had hacked down women and children at Peterloo, killed civilians.'

'Did he show you this evidence?'

'He did, and it seemed to bear out what he was saying. However, you must remember that Peterloo was a complete shambles from a military point of view, and my father was barely twenty and following orders.'

'He was ordered to attack civilians?' asked Daniel.

Wainwright fell silent. Then said, 'It was obvious Walsh had come to blackmail me. Pay up or my father's reputation as one of the bravest soldiers this country has ever produced would be tarnished for ever.'

'Did you pay?'

'No. One lesson I've learnt in life is that blackmailers never release their grip on you. They squeeze you till you are dry, and then, when no more money is forthcoming, they put the information out anyway.'

'You sound as if you speak from personal experience,' Daniel commented.

'But not my own,' said Wainwright. 'It happened to a great friend of mine. He paid for years, until he could pay no more, and when his secret was made public, he shot himself. That would not happen here. I would not allow my father's reputation to be ruined.'

'How did you deal with it?' asked Daniel, but he already knew the answer.

'I silenced him,' said Wainwright. 'Then got rid of the body and destroyed the evidence he'd gathered. I thought that was the end of it, until that Irish girl and that other woman turned up, asking questions at the barracks. I may be retired, but I visit the barracks to meet up with old friends, and I was there when they arrived. I heard the accent and what she was asking about, and straight away I knew she must be a relative of Walsh's.'

'What did she actually ask?'

'She said she wanted to find out who the soldiers had killed at Peterloo. I knew at once that somehow she'd got hold of what Walsh knew and had come to make trouble.'

'So you killed her. You killed both women.'

'My father's reputation was at risk!' insisted Wainwright. 'He didn't deserve that!'

'A bayonet in the back?' asked Daniel. 'How did you know she was going to be at the museum that day? Did you find out where she was staying and follow them both to the museum?'

Wainwright shook his head. 'I saw Wentworth, who told me

he was due to have a meeting at the museum, but he had to cancel at the last minute. I told him I was going into town so I offered to deliver the note for him.

'When I got to the museum I saw the young woman who'd called the day before, and I heard her asking someone there where she could find records about the army and Peterloo, so I knew she was on to things. I killed her. And as I was leaving I ran into the other woman on the stairs, the one who'd been with her when they called at the barracks. I knew I had to get rid of her as well. It was a matter of seconds. No one was around. A bash on the head and down to the cellar.'

'Why cut off her face?'

'To confuse things. Buy me time.'

'Do you always carry a weapon when you go out?'

'I've always worn a sheathed bayonet on my belt. It's part of who I am. A soldier.'

'A soldier who shoots at unarmed women,' snapped Daniel. 'That was you at the museum taking a shot at Miss Fenton, wasn't it.'

'I aimed to miss her, and I did!' barked Wainwright. 'I needed to frighten you both off.'

'And the police uniform you wore so you could get away?'

Wainwright lowered his gaze and muttered awkwardly, 'That was arranged for me.'

'By RSM Bulstrode,' said Daniel grimly. 'I understand he has connections with the local police station.'

Wainwright glared at Daniel, angrily defensive. 'I did what I did to protect my father's good name! His reputation!'

'All this was nothing to do with your father, or his reputation,' said Daniel. 'Kathleen Donlan hadn't come to blackmail you, or anyone else. She had nothing to do with Walsh. Her grandfather had been a soldier at Peterloo and he'd killed civilians too. Afterwards, he fled back to Ireland, where he kept his secret shame. But before he died he asked that his family seek out the relatives of the people he'd killed and ask their forgiveness. That was why she was here. To find out the names of the people her grandfather had killed and ask their forgiveness. The other woman, Eileen O'Donnell, only came with her to the barracks to show her the way because she was a stranger in the city.'

Wainwright stared at him, then at Grimley, before saying, his voice full of begging, 'I thought she was part of it.'

'There was nothing to be part of, except someone carrying out a promise to ask forgiveness for something dreadful that had happened. You murdered two innocent women.'

'And now you're coming to the police station to pay for it,' said Grimley. He produced a set of handcuffs.

'Are those really necessary?' demanded Wainwright.

'It's not often I get to arrest a murderer,' said Grimley.

Wainwright rose to his feet as Grimley approached him.

'It used to be accepted that a gentleman was to be left alone with a glass of whisky and a pistol to deal with things in an honourable manner,' said Wainwright.

'You're no gentleman,' snapped Grimley. 'You murdered two innocent, defenceless women and you're going to hang for it. Now hold out your hands.'

CHAPTER FORTY-ONE

Their train had left Manchester behind some hours before, and now they were passing through Staffordshire, with fewer large towns, the train had emptied enough for them to have a compartment to themselves and they felt able to reflect on their recent experience.

'A satisfactory outcome, I feel,' said Daniel. 'General Wainwright to be tried for the murders of Kathleen Donlan, Eileen O'Donnell and also Fergus Walsh. RSM Bulstrode being charged as an accessory. William Bickerstaff to be tried for attempted murder, which will go some way to getting justice for the cruel way he treated Etta Harkness. And Brigadier Wentworth sending a letter of apology to Mr Steggles once the involvement of Wainwright and Bulstrode was revealed, which means they will be resuming discussions about the army exhibition at the museum.'

'And Jonty Hawkins is to retain his position at the museum,' added Abigail.

'Thanks to your power of persuasion, speaking on his behalf,' said Daniel. 'I'm still not sure that Mr Steggles will ever trust him completely again.'

'He will,' said Abigail confidently. 'It was a moment of madness on Mr Hawkins's part, driven by his rage and grief over what Bickerstaff had done to Etta. I'm sure it won't happen again.'

'A fascinating city, Manchester,' mused Daniel. 'A clash of contradictions: the old and the new crashing together.'

'With the new rising to dominance,' added Abigail. 'And not just the technological revolutions. With social reformers pushing for change, I'm sure they will create better living conditions for the poor, the mill workers. It will be interesting to come back to Manchester in a few years' time and see what changes have been made.'

'And when we do we'll time our visit for this Christie Cup you and Creighton talked about,' said Daniel. 'See the rugby squad in action. Who knows, by then perhaps Jonty Hawkins will have abandoned poetry and returned to the pack.'

Abigail looked out of the window at the countryside, the fields and the rolling hills.

'I think someday I'd like to live in the country,' she said. 'Away from the smoke and hustle and bustle of the city.'

Daniel looked thoughtful as he considered this. 'Yes,' he said at last. 'Perhaps it's time for a change.'

Abigail looked at him in surprise. 'Daniel Wilson leave London?' she said, shocked. 'Never! It's part of you.'

'Surely life is about adapting,' said Daniel. 'Broadening our horizons. You said that's what's happening with Manchester, a city changing and adapting so it will flourish. Isn't that the same for us?'

Abigail smiled at him and took his hand in hers, squeezing it gently. 'My heavens, Daniel, you're turning into a philosopher.'

'Oh no, my love. I leave things academic to you. I'm just a copper.'

She squeezed his hand again. 'You're much more than that, Daniel Wilson.'

ACKNOWLEDGEMENTS

I would like to thank everyone at Allison & Busby, especially my wonderful editor, Kelly Smith, and Susie Dunlop, who commissioned the Museum Mystery series. It may be my name on the cover, but it has been a team effort; they have guided me gently through the creative process of producing them. My thanks also go to Jane Conway-Gordon, whose advice and guidance as I switched my career from scriptwriter and children's author to adult crime fiction has been like gold dust, worth more than I can say.

JIM ELDRIDGE was born in central London towards the end of World War II, and survived attacks by V2 rockets on the Kings Cross area where he lived. In 1971 he sold his first sitcom, starring Arthur Lowe, to the BBC and had his first book commissioned. Since then he has had more than one hundred books published, with sales of over three million copies. He lives in Kent with his wife.

jimeldridge.com